F
M18   Machlis, Joseph.
         Lisa's boy.

Temple Israel Library
Minneapolis, Minn.

Please sign your full name on the above
card.

Return books promptly to the Library or
Temple Office.

Fines will be charged for overdue books
or for damage or loss of same.

Lisa's Boy

Lisa's Boy

Joseph Machlis

W · W· Norton & Company
New York   London

Copyright © 1982 by Joseph Machlis
All rights reserved.
Published simultaneously in Canada by George J. McLeod Limited, Toronto.
Printed in the United States of America.

The text of this book is composed in Janson, with
display type set in Oakwood.
Manufacturing by the Maple-Vail Book Manufacturing Group.
Book design by Bernie Klein.

First Edition

Library of Congress Cataloging in Publication Data
Machlis, Joseph,
Lisa's boy.
I. Title.
PS3563.A31157L5 1982   813'.54   82–6293
AACR2

ISBN 0-393-01606-4

W. W. Norton & Company, Inc. 500 Fifth Avenue, New York, N.Y. 10110
W. W. Norton & Company Ltd. 37 Great Russell Street, London WC1B 3NU

1 2 3 4 5 6 7 8 9 0

In Remembrance:
The World of our Fathers

I

The Bridge

ONE

1

THE house on South Fourth Street was painted brown and had a friendly look. From the roof, David surveyed his world. He sat on a low chimney pot and gazed at the tower of Williamsburg Bridge, now floating away in a faint lavender haze. Below him, the backs of houses looked as though they had their clothes off. To the left, the spire of the church on Union Avenue sliced the sky in two. You were supposed to spit three times when you passed the church. He thought once was enough. The sound of church bells floated on the air. Shutting his eyes, David drank in the silvery music and felt a little sinful for enjoying it so.

The world below was full of surprises, but on the roof he was safe. This was his kingdom, and the rusty chimney pot was his throne. He was reading a story about a cloak that made the wearer invisible. What fun it would be to watch people when they didn't know you were there. The cloak presented only one problem: he had to find it first.

"Dovid'l, it came!" His mother was calling. He scrambled down the ladder to the landing, and ran down the stairs to the street. Neighbors had gathered around a yellow truck and were watching as three burly men slid a piano onto the sidewalk. One of the men went to the roof and attached a pulley. Then he took out the window from the front room on the second floor. The other two wrapped the piano in padded garments and tied it securely. They grasped the ropes of the pulley, and the piano went sailing up like a giant bird. All South Fourth Street was there to watch, and David felt very much like the hero of the occasion.

The piano stopped in midair, and the man at the window coaxed it toward him. When it was safely inside, his companions mopped their foreheads with crumpled handkerchiefs, and mounted the stoop. David followed. Stella Rabinowitz, who lived on the third floor, stood sucking an orange lollipop. Ever since David had told her that the piano was coming she had taunted him with her "Seein's believin'." Now he could not resist turning toward her. "See?"

Stella removed the lollipop from her mouth. "Yeah," she said dryly, and put it back.

In the little parlor, one of the movers asked in Yiddish, "Where shall we put it?"

David's mother pointed to the opposite wall. "By the window it will catch cold. Put it there." She had come from Russia only four years before and spoke no English, nor was she interested in learning any. Chekhov, she reported, said English was a language for horses.

The men pushed the piano into place and removed the padding. The mahogany box shone with a purple glow. Two ornate pillars supported the keyboard at either end. When David lifted the cover of the keyboard he could see Gothic letters in gold: "L. Perelman & Company, New York City." He pressed down the keys in the upper register. Bright tinkling sounds as beautiful as the church bells filled the parlor. The keys in the bass released rich dark tones that lasted longer than the high ones.

The piano stool was no less wonderful than the piano. It had three legs and a round seat that turned around and around as it went higher or lower. David sat down and spun until the room whirled. "Dovid'l, stop!" his mother said, "You'll get dizzy." Now he knew what a top felt like.

By the time his father came home David had thoroughly explored the keyboard. His father rumpled his hair, his mother came to the piano and pressed down a key. "Ekh, if I could have learned to play!" she said. "Who thought about such things when I was young?" She rested her hand on David's shoulder. "At least you will achieve—" she uttered the word *erreichen* with feeling "—what we never did."

2

Two families lived on each floor, with the toilet between them. There were five tiny rooms in each flat. The kitchen was at one end and the parlor—called the *frontroom*, as if it were a single Yiddish word—was at the other. Between were three cubicles that served as bedrooms. Joel and Lisa, David's parents, slept in the bedroom adjoining the parlor. The one next to it belonged to his half sister Annie. The third was reserved for various cousins who, just off the boat from Europe, needed a temporary haven.

David slept in the parlor. Through the white iron bars of his bed he could see the pattern of the wallpaper; three roses alternated with a little green bush. His mother liked the wallpaper because it gave the room a feeling of spring. On the night the piano arrived, he wondered when she would come to tuck him in. Could she have forgotten? A feeling of hurt surged up in him; it vanished when she appeared.

She put her arm around him and showered him with endearments. *"Mein faygeleh . . . mein hartsenyu . . ."* David loved to be called her little bird, her little heart. He sat up in his bed, perched on his knees, and recited the bedtime prayer with her, singing the Hebrew words like an incantation. He was not sure what each word meant, but the prayer assured God that He was the only one. God too liked to be told that he was loved.

His father joined them. Standing on the other side of the bed, he became the opposition. "Filling the boy's head with superstition," he said. "This he needs?"

"I want he should know he's a Jew," Lisa retorted, a determined look on her face.

"Don't worry, he won't forget it. Even if he should, the world will remind him."

"If I didn't have faith in God, I wouldn't be alive today."

"That doesn't prove He exists," Joel said in a superior way. "It only proves that you need Him."

From David's point of view, the arguments between his parents had one drawback; they became so absorbed in each other that they forgot about him. He put his arm around his mother to remind her that they were in the middle of the prayer.

But Lisa was not inclined to resume while her infidel husband was present. She skipped to the part David liked best, where he repeated after her the names of all the uncles, aunts, and cousins to whom God was to grant health and long life. "Uncle Baradovsky, *Tante* Faygel and their children . . ." He dawdled over the names, hoping to prolong the ritual. It came to an end. His parents kissed him, and put out the light.

Alone, he turned on his side. The pale light of a street lamp filtered into the room, and he could hear the bell of the trolley-car down below. Strange things were happening on the wall. The roses grew larger and larger until they burst open, spewing forth a host of little creatures with beady eyes and horrible claws. Now they came off the wall and began to move toward him. Slowly, ever closer. David could not stop them.

He let out a scream, and Lisa came running. "Shsh . . . my little one." The eyes and claws vanished. There was only her presence, enfolding, protecting him. She sat by his bed and in her low contralto voice sang his favorite lullaby:

> Under Dovid'l's cradle stood a little white lamb,
> The lamb went to market.
> What will be your calling?
> Raisins and almonds.
> Sleep, Dovid'l, sleep . . .

The darkness flowed over him, around him.

He awoke. Faint sounds floated from his parents' room: the creaking of a bed, then a whisper. He strained to hear what they were saying. They were telling each other secrets, as they did when they spoke to each other in Russian. If only he had the cloak that made people invisible, he would wrap himself in it and tiptoe into their room. They would never even know he was watching.

He listened carefully. There were things they did that concerned only them, from which he was forever excluded. He buried his eyes in the pillow, and a great loneliness tugged at his heart. No matter how much she said she loved him, she really loved someone else. That was how it would always be.

3

THE arrival of the piano called for a party. Lisa baked several trays of raisin cookies, and boiled the orange peels she had been saving for weeks. She prepared a platter of gefilte fish rolled into little balls that could be speared with a toothpick and dipped in horseradish. Meanwhile Annie pitted three pounds of dates and stuffed them with walnuts.

The day before the party, Lisa took David across the

bridge on an expedition to Hester Street, where the push-carts were out in full force. She stopped at one owned by a tall, thin Jew with a black beard, and selected two items. A prolonged haggling began. He demanded a dollar and a half; she offered sixty cents.

He threw up his hands in horror. "Me alone they cost more!" he yelled. "May I live to see my daughter's wedding as I'm speaking the truth."

"Don't swear by your daughter," Lisa said. "What if God hears you?" He settled for a dollar.

Lisa's purchase was wrapped in sheet upon sheet of Yid-dish newspaper and tied into a bulky package that she held pressed to her breast. When they reached home she extri-cated two white busts from their wrappings, carried them into the frontroom, and placed them on top of the piano, one at each end. Then she stepped back to survey the effect. "This is Bet-khoven," she informed David, "and that is Moh-tsart."

"Who?"

"They were great composers. Some day you'll play their music."

David studied the two busts. The one on the left, his face stern, was brooding; you wouldn't want to get into a fight with him. The one on the right, on the other hand, was gentle and dreamy.

The pushcart had held another objet d'art that attracted Lisa's attention. She went back, afraid that someone else would buy it. The peddler greeted her like an old friend; he also refrained from swearing. That night she proudly showed Joel her newest acquisition, the Three Graces in white plaster, which she placed midway between Bee-thoven and Mozart. "Doesn't it remind you of the Hermi-tage?" She called the museum of Catherine the Great *ehr-mee-tahzh*.

"All we need now," Joel said, "is a bookcase."

"That's next on my list."

The party was called for Saturday night. First to arrive

was Cousin Izzy. He was always first and always hungry. Izzy worked as a cigar maker. He was a two-hundred-pounder with enormous shoulders and tiny cold blue eyes that darted about. Proud of his physical prowess, he would lift a chair off the floor by one of its legs and balance it in mid-air. Or he would lift David, face down, on the palm of one hand and thrust him toward the ceiling. David writhed in terror as the room reeled crazily, but he was not going to spoil the party mood by letting out a yell, and suffered Izzy's gymnastics in silence.

Cousin Laibel, on the other hand, was artistic. He wore his hair long; his black silk tie, knotted in a loose bow, proclaimed him a musician even though he couldn't read a note. Laibel eked out a precarious living by singing at weddings and parties. He had a thin, sensitive face that pushed forward nervously, begging you to like him. Laibel brought a box of chocolates as a gift. "You shouldn't have done it," Lisa protested, knowing that he could not afford it, and rewarded him with a plateful of candied orange peel.

Uncle Isaac, accompanied by Aunt Sarah and Cousin Leah, arrived last; they lived on the East Side and had had to see out the Sabbath before setting out for Brooklyn. Uncle Isaac was president of the Henry Street synagogue and looked it: a dour, pompous man with a long red beard and a gold chain across his vest. One vest pocket contained a heavy gold watch, the other a little silver box from which he took a pinch of snuff. He did not offer his hand either to Lisa or Annie; God would hardly approve of his touching a woman not his wife. He did shake David's hand and came to the point. "Are you going to *cheder?*" The question was meant to put Lisa on the spot for not yet having initiated the boy's religious education.

"He'll begin this month," she answered hastily. Uncle Isaac's rigid orthodoxy was no more to her taste than Joel's atheism.

"It's time he learned God's word," Uncle Isaac said severely, and inspected the piano. He approved of the

instrument but squinted with displeasure at the Three
Graces. "Naked women you need in the house?" he inquired.

"They're not naked women, Uncle. They are statues, like
what you see in a museum."

Uncle Isaac took another look. "By you they may be statues, by me they're naked women."

Lisa stood her ground. "In Peterboorg, the Hermitage
was full of them."

"So let them stay there. The Torah says clearly, 'Thou
shalt not bow down to graven images.' "

"Uncle, may you live long, it's art." She saw she would
not convince him. "Taste my gefilte fish."

How celebrate the arrival of a piano if no one knew how
to play it? Cousin Laibel had solved the problem by bringing along his accompanist, Miss Gewirtz. He rendered the
best-known tune from *Rigoletto*. Since he knew no Italian,
he made up the words as he went along.

La donna e mobile
Senza con fobile,
  Non e si tanto,
  Con se instanto . . .

Unfortunately the key was too high. He stopped, cleared
his throat, took a mouthful of water, gargled, and with a
theatrical gesture signaled to Miss Gewirtz to begin again.
This time he made the top note and threw back his head
with a flourish. There was a burst of applause. Laibel bowed
and said, "My voice is too big for this room. You should
hear me in a hall."

Miss Gewirtz praised the piano and obliged with a solo:
The Maiden's Prayer by Tecla Baderzewska. Lisa glowed with
pleasure, nodding her head in time with the music. She was
enchanted when the melody returned in octaves in high
register. Miss Gewirtz too was highly applauded.

"Laibel tells me," Lisa said to her, "that you give piano lessons. Maybe you'll teach Dovid'l and Annie."

Miss Gewirtz signified her willigness. Lisa wanted to ask how much the lessons would cost, but this was hardly the time to discuss money. Instead she asked Joel to read aloud from Sholom Aleichem. He read *Dos Tepel*—"The Pot"— which recounted an argument between two women. The first accused her neighbor of having borrowed a pot that was returned broken. The second countered with three arguments: (1) She never borrowed the pot. (2) She returned the pot in perfect condition. (3) The pot was broken when she borrowed it. Lisa had heard the tale often enough to know it by heart. She began to laugh a split second before each joke appeared, as though signaling the others. Joel read in a clear voice, smacking his lips from time to time and reveling in the master's prose.

Before the party broke up he asked Lisa to recite something in Russian; he was proud of her command of the language. She needed a little coaxing, but in the end gave in. She recited Lenski's monologue before his duel with Eugene Onegin. A hush fell upon her guests as the doomed poet mourned his youth, resigning himself to whatever fate decreed.

Kuda, kuda, vi udalilis,
Vesni moyei zlatiye dni?
   Chto den gradushi mne gotovit?
   Yevo moi vzor naprasno lovit . . .

Pushkin's impassioned verse was meant to be declaimed, and Lisa declaimed it with total conviction. Her contralto voice imparted a dark timbre to the music of the lines, which she punctuated with a brusque forward thrust of her left hand. She stopped abruptly, visibly moved by Lenski's final avowal of his love for Olga. Her guests were moved too; all, that is, except Uncle Isaac, who drew out his gold watch, sprung open the lid, and announced that it was time to go home.

The main performance of the evening took place after the guests left. Lisa mimicked several while Joel, Annie, and David rocked with laughter. The way Aunt Esther peered at Uncle Isaac with her beady little eyes. The way Cousin Leah entered a room, as if she were apologizing for being alive. The pompous way Uncle Isaac took out his gold watch. Lisa polished off Cousin Izzy with one line: "Oy, does he love himself." Toward Cousin Louis she was kinder. "If he could only have trained his voice. How much talent goes to waste in the world!"

She removed the hairpins from the bun on top of her head, letting her hair tumble down. She stopped before the tall narrow mirror that stood between the windows; its blond oval frame rested on two legs carved into sphinxes. Studying her reflection in the glass, she brought her hands against her face and smoothed back the skin over the cheekbones. "Another day gone," she murmured. "If only time could stand still. If only we could stay as we are. Just as we are."

4

THEY were all in the kitchen when Lisa turned to Joel. "That was a stupid thing you said to Uncle Isaac."

"When?"

"When he asked you if you'd been to synagogue in the morning."

"What did I say?"

"You answered, 'If I said yes you wouldn't believe me, and if I told you no you'd be upset.' "

Joel bristled. "And why, may I ask, was that so stupid?"

Lisa never deliberately brought on a quarrel between them. But from time to time an inexplicable impulse drove her to goad him on. She turned to David. "Your father can't bear to be criticized. He has to be perfect."

"I don't have to be perfect, but—"

"But what?"

"You're saying I'm a fool."

She threw her hands into the air. "If the shoe fits."

Suddenly the air was electric between them; tempers flared, voices rose. Before either of them knew how it had happened they were shouting at each other, dredging up long-forgotten grievances. In this battle of wills, neither could give way. Pride was involved, self-esteem; to judge from the noise they were making, life itself. Thrust and counterthrust followed in a steady crescendo until Joel, face contorted with fury, shouted, "If that's how you feel, why did you marry me?"

"Because you asked me, idiot!"

"I wish I hadn't."

"So now we're at the truth!" Her eyes flashed fire. "It's not too late to change your mind."

"Oh, so you want me to leave, do you!"

"You're free to go whenever you like. This very minute, for all I care."

"Very well, you asked for it!"

He rushed to the closet, dragged out the single valise they owned, and ransacked the battered sideboard for his possessions. Into the valise went a shirt, starched collar, ready-made bow tie, comb, razor, stick of shaving cream, and toothbrush. He glanced around wildly to find what else he needed, and added the alarm clock that adorned the shelf over the sink. Coat over one arm and hat in hand, he was ready to begin his new life. From the door he hurled his final imprecation. "Good-bye. I hope you're satisfied!"

Annie, fighting back her tears, fell to cleaning the kitchen. Whenever she wasn't sure what she ought to do, she cleaned the kitchen. David looked on in horror. The wonderful day had ended in disaster. He ran to his mother, buried his head in her lap and began to cry.

Lisa, on the contrary, was jubilant. "Good riddance!" She thrust her hand through the air in a gesture of farewell. "And high time, too. Don't worry children . . ." She patted David on the head and nodded reassuringly at Annie. "We'll manage without him. I can cook and mend. You'll see, God won't forsake us."

She recited David's prayers with him and returned to the kitchen, trying to sort out her thoughts. She had married Joel against her better judgment; his departure proved her to have been right. She should have followed her instinct and remained a widow. Instead she had allowed herself to fall in love, and what had it brought her? Trouble. Some people were better off without love. She was one of them.

In fact, she had spent the greater part of her life without it. Married at eighteen to Baruch, a kind man considerably older, Lisa gave him the affection a wife owed her husband. In her world people did not concern themselves overmuch with love. They worried about making a living and bringing up their children. Love was for the story books . . .

Baruch was a printer. One day he brought home a young man who worked with him. Joel had just arrived in St. Petersburg. He was twenty when he came to live with them, she was thirty. She befriended him, treated him like one of her sons; she even tried to marry him off, but nothing came of her efforts. He helped her through the terrible time of Baruch's illness and death. Before the year was out, he asked her to marry him. At first, the idea seemed preposterous; why would a young man tie himself down to an older woman? But he persisted, and the more she thought about it the less preposterous it seemed. Before long she was madly in love. He had awakened the woman in her, and it was a disquieting experience. "What will you do with me," she asked him, "when I'm old?" "I'll carry you in my arms," he replied, and grinned in that boyish way he had. How could she resist?

Lisa poured herself a glass of tea and sat at the kitchen table, chin cupped in the palm of her hand. Love, it seemed to her, was best discovered when a person was young; she had come to it too late. She had tried to defend herself against it but did not know how. The glow occasioned by Joel's departure had faded, leaving her desolate. What madness had possessed her to send him away? Why had she destroyed the most precious thing in her life? Crossing her arms on the table, she lowered her head and fought back her tears.

At this low point a sliver of hope penetrated the darkness. Where could he go at this hour? A hotel? That cost money. Besides, where would he find a hotel? Would he travel to Manhattan? Out of the question. He had to go to work in the morning, and could not possibly spend the night on a bench in Bridge Plaza. That left him only one choice: to come home! With his ridiculous valise dangling at his side. She wiped her eyes, changed into a nightgown, and went to bed.

A silence lay upon the city. She heard the elevated train on Broadway grind to a halt at the station. Presently she thought she heard his footsteps on the stairs. Her heart skipped a beat as a key turned in the lock. She pretended to be asleep.

She followed his every movement as he lit the gas in the kitchen, opened his valise, and removed his things. Finally he turned out the light and came into the bedroom. He undressed and lay down beside her, his back to her. Then he let out a very audible sigh. This, she knew, was for her benefit.

Should she tell him how desperately she had wanted him back? No, that would only give him the victory. She pressed her lips together. A person had to have pride, no matter what happened. Especially a woman.

He sighed again, and turned around. His head was on the pillow close to hers, and his eyes shone in the darkness. Lisa forgot her scruples. Her hand came to rest upon his shoulder. "My dearest," she whispered, using the term she reserved for special occasions, "I'm sorry I offended you."

He rubbed his cheek against hers. "I don't understand women," he murmured. "I guess what they really like is to drive a man out of his mind."

She slipped into his arms. Now all was peace and affection between them. Until the next time.

5

MISS Gewirtz charged thirty-five cents a lesson, but was willing to start both David and Annie on their musical careers for half a dollar. Lisa sighed. She hated to add a weekly expense to her strained budget, yet what choice did she have?

David had been exploring the world of music on his own. Perched on the piano stool, head bent over the keyboard, he listened carefully to the sounds, comparing high with low, soft with loud. Miss Gewirtz, a thin little woman with a birdlike face, had a more practical approach. She arrived for the first lesson with Beyer's Piano Method under her arm and proceeded to initiate David into the mysteries of the staff. The lines were "Every Good Boy Does Fine," the spaces "F-A-C-E." This, he thought, was pretty dull stuff but he went along with it. Things picked up when he learned about whole, half, and quarter notes. As for eighths and sixteenths, they were positively exciting.

The high point of the lesson came when Miss Gewirtz played the opening phrase of *America* for him. David thrilled to the sound. "Do it again," he cried.

He watched her fingers carefully. "Once more."

She obliged. "Let me try," he said, and reproduced the tune.

Miss Gewirtz was astonished. "He has a fine ear," she said to Lisa.

"A health on his little head," Lisa exclaimed, filling the Yiddish idiom with unwonted fervor. Her approval set

David aglow. He sat quietly in a corner while Annie took her lesson, listening intently as the sounds floated through the room and died away. The ones high up in the treble shimmered like the bells he had heard on the roof. He liked it when Annie set them ringing, but it was much more fun to do himself.

Lisa polished the piano until the dark mahogany glowed; she did this at least twice a day. "In Russia who owned such a beautiful thing?" she asked. "Only the rich. Here people like us are able to."

Joel was surprised. "You're beginning to like America?"

Lisa nodded. "A little." She put one arm around David. "You'll play beautiful music, Dovid'l, and I'll be very proud of you. Would you like that?"

"Yes." He wanted it very much. First of all, to please her. Yet even more for himself.

TWO

1

ATURDAY morning was different from the rest of the week. There was a white tablecloth on the table, surmounted by the silver candlesticks his mother had brought from Russia. Instead of pumpernickel bread they ate challeh, which had a golden-brown crust and was soft and white inside. When David stuck his head out the window, the world had a holiday look. The street was clean, and the air smelled sweet.

He walked to the synagogue between his mother and Annie. His father stayed behind. This was Joel's free day, and he had no intention of wasting it on the Lord. He slept late and had to get his own breakfast. Since he had never learned how to boil an egg, he made do with tea and a slice of challeh covered with pot cheese. This, Lisa said, was his punishment.

The synagogue on South Fifth Street had been a church, but as Jews crowded into Brooklyn, it had been converted to the older faith. Its tall Gothic arches rose in supplication to heaven. The stained-glass windows, once luminous with likenesses of Peter and the apostles, now showed the emblems of the twelve tribes of Israel. The men wore hats or skullcaps; the women were segregated in the balcony so as not to distract them. Rabbi Silverstein preached a sermon about the sanctity of marriage. Lisa found it most edifying.

David hovered at the back of the synagogue, one of a dozen youngsters who were continually shushed by their elders. The high point of the morning came when the sacred scrolls in their white silk covers were returned to the Ark. The closing hymn, *Ain K'Elohaynu*, had a cheerful melody that reflected the pride of the text. *There is no God like our God, no Lord like our Lord.*

David waited for his mother at the foot of the stone stairs. She kissed him on the forehead as if she were blessing him; Annie kissed him too. For him the world was divided into children and grownups; his sister stood somewhere between. She was too old to be his friend, and was more like someone who took care of him when his mother was busy or tired.

As they set out for home, his mother let out a sigh, "I feel cleansed of all my sins," she said.

"What sins?" David asked.

"Is it not a sin to feel well when others are sick? To have enough to eat when others go hungry?"

"Why, Mama?"

She thought a moment. "Well, if it's not a sin it feels like one."

David understood nothing of this and suspected she was saying it for God's benefit. He scanned the sky for clouds; if it rained, he would be cheated of the Saturday afternoon walk across the bridge. There was no point in asking God to keep the rain away, as that might only remind Him to send it. The sensible way was to say to himself, just loud enough for God to hear, "It can rain for all I care."

When they returned home, his father was at the weekly game of chess with Mr. Levine. Mr. Levine was bald and had large, irregular teeth stained by tobacco. He had taken part in the Revolution of 1905—Lisa called it *revolutsye*,

which made it sound beautiful—and had been exiled to Siberia. Lisa regarded him as a martyr and treated him with
respect.

The game went from silence to passionate argument
whenever one of them tried to retract a move. The rule was
clear: once you moved your hand away from a pawn, you
could no longer change your mind. It was the application
of the rule that caused trouble. "I didn't move my hand
away," Joel shouted. "Look, it's still there."

Mr. Levine took the cigar out of his mouth. "I saw you
with my own eyes."

Joel looked aggrieved. "Would I lie to you?"

Mr. Levine appealed to an invisible bystander. "Would
he lie to me?"

Joel in turn appealed to David. "Can you imagine, we've
been friends for twenty-five years and he still doubts my
word."

Lisa, who was accustomed to these outbursts, kissed her
prayer book, returned it to its red-velvet coverlet, and prepared lunch. It consisted of plump patties of gefilte fish and
sliced tomatoes, accompanied by carrots that had been
cooked the day before and warmed over. Strictly speaking,
you were not supposed to light the gas on the Sabbath; but
cold carrots had an awful taste, and Lisa was sure that God
would overlook the transgression. She heaped a generous
helping on Mr. Levine's plate; he was unmarried and had
no one to cook for him. She liked to point out to him that
he would be happier with a wife.

"It's not good for a person to live alone." She passed the
horseradish to him, which made a red stain against the fish.
"You'd have home-cooked meals instead of eating in restaurants. You know what they serve you there? Poison."

Levine, embarrassed, tugged at his collar, which was too
large for his neck. "What if my wife couldn't cook?"

"She'd learn. If you love someone, you learn." She handed
Mr. Levine an extra large slice of challeh.

Mr. Levine blushed easily. Joel watched the pink flush

spread over his friend's cheeks and decided to take the heat off him. "It's a strange thing about your mother," he said to David. "No matter what the conversation's about, it always ends up with love."

"Why not?" The dark eyes flashed. "What's more important to a woman?" She gave them a quick summary of Rabbi Silverstein's sermon.

"All sermons are alike," Joel said. "They tell the men what their wives want them to hear: not to drink, gamble, or run around. No wonder women support religion."

Lisa made a face. "Tfui! Spoken like a man." She used the word *mansbil*, meaning male, and turned to Mr. Levine. "I won't even answer him."

For dessert they had a baked apple and the crescent-shaped cookies garnished with raisins that were Lisa's specialty, with a glass of tea. The glass, thick on bottom so as to contain the heat, rested on the palm of the left hand and was guided by thumb and forefinger of the right. They drank in the Russian style, sipping the tea through a tiny cube of sugar on the tip of the tongue. Among the possessions that Lisa had brought from Russia, none was prized more than the silver scissors with sawlike edges that cut a lump of sugar in two.

The men returned to their game; Lisa washed the dishes, Annie and David dried them. He waited for his mother to say, "We're ready for our walk." She finally did.

They made their way to Bridge Plaza and passed the trolley-cars lined up in the middle of the square. Beyond was an equestrian statue, perched on a massive stone base on which were engraved two mysterious words. David was under the impression that the horseman's name was Valley Forge.

The approach to the bridge was crowded with Jews who were not riding on the Sabbath. The first part of the walk, where the bridge sloped up, was the hardest. They passed the white building with "Williamsburg Dime Savings Bank" inscribed in large letters on the side facing the bridge. Then came the enormous tower from which the cables were suspended. Before long the bridge was higher than the nearby rooftops. Brooklyn lay behind them, and David walked on top of the world.

The walk leveled off. Trolley-cars humming pleasantly passed in either direction. The sky was blue, and the air smelled of spring. Far below, the river swirled in green-gray eddies. David gazed down through the little squares in the steel railing. He had heard of people jumping off the bridge. The thought filled him with horror.

When they reached the middle of the span, they stopped to rest. Ahead, the city looked clean and beautiful. Tall buildings reached for the sky, their outlines veiled in yellow and pink. Southward the river broadened into the bay where the Statue of Liberty stood. Lisa recalled how she had seen the bronze goddess for the first time. "It was raining, and we all gathered on deck as we came to the end of our journey. Oy, was that a ship. They should have broken her in bits and pieces before they let her sail across the ocean."

Lisa clung to her memories, especially the painful ones, which she recounted with gusto in set pieces that Joel called arias. The two and a half weeks she spent in the steerage of the S.S. *Korea* were among her most harrowing ones. The ship sputtered across a stormy Atlantic, buffeted by giant waves. "I was sick all the time and was sure I would die. God was with us."

More painful even than the stench of the steerage, the noise and filth that surrounded her, was the knowledge that she was coming to America before Joel was ready for her. He had gone on ahead in order to prepare a place for them, but there was a crisis in the land, he had no steady job, and his letters begged her to wait. "In Europe," he had written, "people call this the golden land. They think money is lying on the streets waiting to be picked up. Don't you believe it, my dearest. Have patience." But patience was one trait Lisa lacked. Her despair mounted as the days stretched into weeks and months. When they had been separated for a year and a half, she decided to wait no longer. She sold what she could, scraped together enough for the voyage, and set out.

Once on the boat, doubt assailed her. Here she was, on her way to join a husband ten years her junior, bringing him the little son he barely remembered, forcing herself upon him when her presence would only be a burden. What desperate impulse had driven her to this journey? She knew. It was her love for him, that burning, gnawing love which was like an illness. There was no logic in what she was doing, only the madness of loving Joel without ever being sure that he loved her in return. Her last night on the *Korea* brought her to the low point of her journey. The ship reeled, the old Jews donned their prayer shawls and resigned themselves to the will of the Almighty. She tied David to the bunk they shared and struggled to the foul cubicle that served as toilet. Once she was inside, the door stuck and she couldn't get out. The boat was rocking, she was thrown from side to side, she tried to scream but vomited instead. Now, gazing down at the river, she said to David, "I was afraid you'd be thrown to the ground and there would be no one to pick you up. Finally they pried open the door. I ran to you and saw you lying where I had left you. I burst into tears."

David's eyes misted over. No matter how often he heard the story, this part never failed to move him. He turned to Annie. "Were you there?"

She smiled down at him. "No, I came later."

"We couldn't all come together, it cost too much," his mother explained. "After a while I brought over your sister and brothers." Lisa leaned on the railing, stared across the bay, and resumed her monologue. "Then we landed, and I bent down and kissed the ground. This is how we came to America." Her voice was determined. "In this life you have to be stronger than iron. And you must hold your head high."

They continued their walk.

2

LISA kept the family photographs in an album with a green plush cover. Inside was a miniature music box. When you inserted a key and cranked it, the first eight measures of the *Blue Danube Waltz* tinkled delicately. The album fed Lisa's chronic need to relive her past. She used it also to take David on a guided tour of his family. As she put it, "I want he should know where he comes from."

First came a photograph of her with Joel. "This is how I looked," she informed David, "when I married your father." The photographer had posed her on a stool so that she seemed almost as tall as he. She wore a black dress with puffed sleeves and high lace collar, and her hair was piled high in an upswept coffure. Aware that her eyes were her best feature, she had opened them as wide as she could, which made her look not only intensely alive but also surprised. The lips were pressed together firmly, the chin jutted forward over her elaborate lace jabot. It was an expressive face. You could see that she thought herself a woman of decision, like most people confusing bone structure with character.

By contrast, Joel exuded an easy charm. He wore a tight-fitting jacket with high collar and bow tie. The camera captured no expression in the light-blue eyes, but the full lips and straight nose belonged to a good-looking young man who appeared to be content with his lot. Why, he seemed to be asking, did people have to be complicated when it was so much easier to be simple and enjoy life?

Lisa balanced the bulky album on her lap and turned the leaves. Her father wore a neatly trimmed Vandyck instead of the beard and earlocks of his ancestors. He had freed himself sufficiently from the confines of the ghetto to become a pharmacist. "He was kind and gentle," Lisa said. "Oh, how he loved me! My tragedy was that he died when I was ten." His successor, pictured with her mother in a faded daguerreotype on the next page, was a stocky man with a jutting jaw and no neck. "He was a wild animal," Lisa said. "Cruel, mean, and when he was drunk, he beat me." The memory always brought tears to her eyes.

"Why do you cry?" David asked. "It happened such a long time ago."

"There are wounds," she answered softly, "that never heal. You carry them inside you till the day you die."

She was proud of her family tree, which included four rabbis; her behavior, she felt, must at all times justify this noble lineage. This conviction was summed up in the phrase *es pahst nisht*—it is not fitting. Certain things were not done, and it pained her deeply when those close to her, especially her children, did them.

There followed the photographs of her three brothers. Yuri, the eldest, was an impressive bald gentleman whom the photographer had posed against a background of swans. "When he was young he was a revolutionary. He took part in the Movement and was sent to Siberia. Later he forgot all about that, gambled on the Moscow Bourse, and became rich." Lisa omitted the fact that Yuri forsook Judaism for the Greek Orthodox faith and atoned for his apostasy by being extremely generous to his relatives, whom he never saw.

Adolph, the middle brother, was shown seated, holding a book and a pair of black gloves. "Poor Adolph," Lisa sighed. She censored Adolph's story even more stringently than Yuri's. A fop and a rake, he had caught the disease that God reserved for anyone who slept with all the chambermaids in Odessa. As her sons reached adolescence, she held up Uncle Adolph's sad end as a warning. One morning, as he was strolling along the esplanade by the Black Sea, his little finger fell off. The following week it was a toe. One winter day he took out his handkerchief to blow his nose. The result was too dreadful to contemplate. Thus poor Uncle Adolph ended ignominiously strewn over the esplanade by the Black Sea.

For exhibit B in her lecture on sex Lisa drew upon Czar Nicholas's younger brother, Grand Duke Michael Alexandrovich. All St. Petersburg knew that the unfortunate grand duke went out of his mind because he played with himself. Lisa consequently did not offer her sons much choice. Either you slept with chambermaids and fell apart or you played with yourself and lost your mind.

Uncle Mischa's photograph showed him from the shoulders up, hair neatly parted in the middle and an apologetic expression on his face. Mischa owned a junk shop in Boston. He had come to Lisa's assistance, when she married Joel, by assuming responsibility for her two older sons. He brought them over from Russia and put them to work in his shop for bed, board, and three dollars a week. The boys visited Lisa every month; Uncle Mischa paid for the trip. Lisa wanted them in New York, but how could she impose them upon Joel when he already had her daughter on his hands? Her role as a wife pushed her in one direction, her duty as a mother in another, leaving her with a conflict she could not resolve. "No matter what you do," she said, "there's a price to pay." It became one of her favorite maxims.

David turned to the next leaf. "Who's this?" he inquired.

"Uncle Baruch," she equivocated. Sooner or later she would have to tell him about her first marriage; she kept putting it off. Why burden him with things he was too young to understand? In the meantime she would warn visitors not to broach the forbidden subject. Fortunately, she was able to do so in Russian, the perfect language for what she did not want the boy to know. Baruch's photograph too filled her with guilt. He had died before his time, and she had gone on to build a new life for herself. In India, she had heard tell, when a great man died, they buried his wives with him. That was one way of solving the problem. For seventeen years her every thought had revolved around Baruch and their children. Now he was a shadowy memory. Would it be the same when she died? She pictured Joel settling down with her successor in an idyllic existence from which she was forever excluded. The thought filled her with sorrow. Let him marry again if that was what he wanted, she told herself bitterly; she wished him well. And to David's question she replied, "That's another uncle."

One afternoon, after they had been leafing through the album, Annie asked her mother to put on the black dress. Lisa laughed. "What a silly notion! I don't think I could even fit into it."

When Joel endorsed the idea, she changed her mind. He took down a box from the top shelf of the closet and Lisa, tightening her corset, slipped into the most splendid gown she had ever owned. "It was a present from Uncle Yuri," she explained, "and came from the best dressmaker in Peterboorg." Ample in the bosom and tight in the waist, the dress gave Lisa the hourglass figure prized by a former era. The skirt fell in graceful folds around her and could be lifted from the floor by a black silk loop that curled around her wrist. She pressed her hands against her hips, thumb and forefinger extended. "Ekh, you should have seen me as a girl. My fingers almost touched." She held up her arms to exhibit the elaborate lace trimming on the leg-of-mutton sleeves. Then, humming one of her Russian waltzes, she whirled around the room, swaying as she danced.

To David she seemed to have stepped out of a fairy tale; she was a beautiful queen on her way to a ball. Suddenly she stopped before him. "Dovid'l, why do you look so surprised?"

"You don't look real," he murmured.

"But I am." She laughed as she bent over to kiss him. "It's only the dress that isn't."

3

THERE was much coming and going among the women of the house. They called each other *nexdorikeh*—a Yiddishized form of "next door" with a feminine ending—and were continually dropping in on each other to borrow a pinch of salt or an egg. Lisa took no part in this camaraderie. What could she possibly have in common with these peasants? They came from the shtetl whereas she came from Peterboorg, the capital of all Russia. They were illiterate whereas she had read *Anna Karenina* and *Brothers Karamazov*. They spent their days gossiping whereas she had better things to do with her time.

Especially she disliked Mrs. Rabinowitz who lived directly overhead, with whom she did have something in common: Mrs. Rabinowitz's floor was her ceiling. When little Stella went clumping from kitchen to front room and back, which she did from the moment she came home from school until she went to bed, the walls in Lisa's apartment shook and the mantel that perched precariously on the gas light in the kitchen was dislodged and smashed to bits. Lisa went up to the third floor, knocked on Mrs. Rabinowitz's door, and protested.

Mrs. Rabinowitz bridled. "What d'you expect my Stella to do, sit in a chair all day? A child has to play."

"Of course. But a child doesn't have to run wild and drive people crazy. Why can't she walk?"

"Listen, missus, maybe you should live in a house of your own where you don't have neighbors."

Lisa turned on her heel. In recounting the incident to Joel she polished it off with a quotation from Sholom Aleichem. "I should stand arguing with her? Who is she, and who am I?"

Mrs. Rabinowitz struck back. One afternoon in April, as David made his way down the ladder under the skylight, she lay in wait for him. "You were on the roof again?" she boomed.

"Yeah." He wished he had the invisible cloak. Mrs. Rabinowitz was fat and sweaty, and had a moustache. She was a widow; David was convinced she had eaten her husband.

"Someday you'll fall off and that'll be the end of you."

"I don' go near the end. I sit in the middle."

"What d'you do up there?"

"I make believe."

"And for that you have to go on the roof? A nice Jewish boy like you. . . . What your father does?"

"He's a printer."

"What he prints?"

"Books."

"And from that," she sang, "he makes a living?"

David wondered what she meant but nodded in agreement.

"H'm." Mrs. Rabinowitz glanced toward the staircase and lowered her voice. "Your mother was married before?"

David was puzzled. English was a strange language and grown-ups were strange people.

"Your sister is from the first husband, no?" Mrs. Rabinowitz persisted. "Your father's too young."

David clasped his hands before him. There was an ogre in the *Green Fairy Book* who belched smoke from her nostrils.

Mrs. Rabinowitz gave him a knowing smile. "Me you can tell. I won't tell nobody."

Any moment now the smoke would be followed by a flame that would burn away the top of his head. David backed up against the bannister and fled.

His mother was at the kitchen table arranging little crescents of dough in the baking pan when he came bursting in. "Dovid'l, *mein kind!*"

He knelt beside her and, burying his face in her lap, began to sob.

Lisa wiped one hand against her apron and brushed her fingertips over the back of his neck, while continuing to sprinkle raisins over the crescents with the other. "What did they do to my little one?"

David had no intention of sharing her attention with the baking pan; he let out a yell. She dried the other hand and stroked his hair.

He quieted. "I came down from the roof, and Mrs. Rabinowitz was there." It was good to be back in Yiddish. "She
asked me questions."

"What kind of questions?" Her voice was pitched lower
than Mrs. Rabinowitz's, and soothing.

"She said Papa wasn't my papa. Someone else was my
papa." He raised his tear-stained face. "Why did she say
that, Mama?"

She cupped his chin and looked into his eyes. "Because
there are bad people in the world who like to make trouble."

"Is Papa my real papa?"

"Of course he is. Would he love you if he weren't? Look,
I'm baking the cakes you like. Sprinkle raisins on them
before I put the pan in the oven."

The kitchen was filled with the friendly smell of dough
when Joel came home. "Well, David . . ." He had named
his son for the psalmist-king and never used the diminutive
Dovid'l as Lisa did. "Tell me what you did all day."

Lisa cut in with an impassioned account of their neighbor's treachery. Joel tried to calm her. "What do you care
what those yentas say? Why d'you let them upset you?"

They switched to Russian. David loved the rich sound of
the language. At the same time he was annoyed that they
were telling secrets. He glanced from one to the other as if
to wrest from their faces what they were hiding from him.

"Sooner or later," Joel was saying, "the boy will find out.
After all," he added with a grin, "if I had no objection, why
should he?"

"I'll tell him when the time comes." Lisa gestured
brusquely. "That cholera upstairs knew where to hurt me.
Right in my heart. And don't you defend her." Her eyes
seemed to swallow up her face. "Why don't you try to
understand what I feel? My sorrow, my pain."

"I try, but there's so much to understand." He smiled, as
he generally did when she became what he called *dramatish*.

"Talk Yiddish!" David said.

"Yes, Dovid'l." Lisa glanced up at the ceiling. "May God not punish her," she said fervently. It was her way of suggesting to Him that He just might.

4

THE cellar, David thought, was different from the roof in every possible way. The roof was open and airy, the cellar was dark and damp. The roof looked up at the sky, the cellar was buried in the ground. The roof gave you clean, healthy thoughts, the cellar filled you with dirty ones. As in the phrase "He took her down to the cellar." David was not sure what that meant, but when Stella Rabinowitz asked him to go down with her, he knew he would find out.

Stella picked a secluded spot behind a pair of wooden crates near the stairs to the back yard. Light filtered in feebly, creating a mysterious half darkness. She pulled out a tattered blanket on which they lay down, and taught him a game she called "papa and mama." She let down her drawers, pulled down his trousers, and they explored each other. David didn't mind the game but he took exception to its title. Maybe some parents played it; certainly not his. The next game she called "playing doctor," which turned out to be nothing more than a variation of the other. He thought the title inaccurate. Certainly Dr. Cohen never behaved this way.

His next visit to the cellar was in the company of Jack Kazin, a tall, skinny boy who lived on the first floor. Since Jack was older, David was flattered to be singled out in this manner. They sat next to each other on the smaller crate while Jack told an exciting story. It was about a girl he had met on the beach at Coney Island; they went into the water and swam far out. Then they took off their bathing suits and rubbed against each other. Jack's eyes glowed, and as he spoke, he drew David's hand along his thighs, up, down, and between. Then he stood David against the wall, dropped the boy's trousers, and leaned against him. Presently David asked, "Did you pee?"

"No," said Jack.

"But it's wet."

"It's wet," Jack said, "but I didn' pee."

Mystified, David pulled up his trousers. They came up the stone steps to the street just as Lisa returned from the grocery store.

Upstairs, she asked, "What were you doing in the cellar?"

"I was playing in the back yard with Jack." He lied only when it was necessary.

"What were you playing?"

"Marbles."

"I don't want you to go down to the cellar with him. Never!"

"I won't."

"Promise."

"I promise." If Jack asked him again, they would use the stairs to the back yard.

Suddenly there was bad news: an epidemic of infantile paralysis. Lisa made David wear a little bag of camphor under his shirt. The fear that always lay inside her spilled over. "I wish I could take him away," she told Joel.

Joel tried to soothe her. "Germs are everywhere."

She was especially affectionate with David these days. He was the child of her love, the last link to her youth. She clasped him to her as if she would ward off the enemy by sheer force of will, and showered him with endearments: "My little lamb . . . my little bird . . . my soul . . ."

The enemy struck close to home: Stella came down with the disease. The neighbors panicked, but took comfort in the thought that lightning never struck twice. The thought of Mrs. Rabinowitz's anguish filled Lisa with guilt. "I asked God to punish her."

"You asked God not to punish her," Joel reminded her. "Besides, what makes you think you have so much influence with Him?"

All the same, Lisa could not get it out of her head that she had in some way contributed to Mrs. Rabinowitz's tragedy. "I'd go upstairs and ask her to forgive me," she said, "but what if I bring back germs? Maybe I'll meet her in the street."

They met on the stoop one day when Lisa returned from the fruit store. She put down her bags and held out her hand. "How is the little girl?"

Mrs. Rabinowitz took Lisa's hand and burst into tears. "Such a lovely child. A cripple for the rest of her life."

With terror, Lisa realized that *she* might have been saying this about David. "Sh . . . We're all in God's hands." The two women stood weeping together. At length Lisa wiped her eyes. "What does the doctor say?"

"Can he give her a new leg?"

Lisa winced, remembering that she had objected to Stella's running around overhead. Now the child would never run again. "Give her a kiss for me," she said. "I'll come see her when—" She fell silent.

"I know, when it's over. May you never know of it."

Stella looked pale and drawn when she reappeared, her left leg encased in an iron brace. Her friends fussed over her and pretended not to notice it. She walked with a limp, and when they went to the back yard, David brought out a chair for her. The little garden was drenched in sunshine; the morning glories had come out. The epidemic was over; life resumed.

Stella met him near the stairs. "You don' like me no more," she said.

"Yes, I do." Why didn't she move off the block?

"Les' go down to the cellar."

"No!" David heard the word in his mind but was unable to utter it. Instead he said, "Sure. Follow me." He could hear her uneven steps behind him as he opened the back door, went down the wooden stairs and waited. The cellar was silent and musty. He wanted no part of it.

They reached the space between the crates. Stella found the tattered blanket and spread it on the ground, smoothing down the corners. They lay down. "Let's play house," she suggested, although David knew perfectly well what game they were going to play. She grasped him firmly by the wrist, led his hand along her right leg and, having brought it to its destination, pressed it against her as hard as she could. "Oo, it feels good," she squealed, and pushed his hand against the sick leg.

He felt a hard leather strap, and the cold smooth surface of an iron clamp. His heart raced, and he glanced over her shoulder. In the dirty gray light the plaster on the wall began to crawl around and around. Suppose someone locked you in a wooden box and you tried to get out but couldn't. His hand was locked against the iron clamp of the brace. "Les' go," he whispered. He drew his hand away, jumped up, and pulled up his pants.

"You don' like me no more," she said.

"Yes I do. But I had enough."

There was a silence. Then she said, "Help me."

David took her hand and pulled her up. If she moved off the block she would never bother him again. "I'll go first, then you."

"No. Lemme go first."

He listened as she clomped unevenly up the stairs. He had a sudden need to be alone on the roof, but decided to wait until Stella was safely in her apartment. Then he ran up to the third floor, climbed the wooden ladder, and came out into his kingdom.

The light dazzled him, the air felt clean and sweet. A breath of wind cooled his forehead. The tower of Williamsburg Bridge rose blue-gray in the distance, and on the opposite roof the pigeons were taking their afternoon stroll.

From this vantage point the cellar seemed darker and dirtier than ever. He sat down on the chimney pot that was his throne; his eyes searched the sky. Somewhere up there God was hiding, spying on people, seeing everything they did and writing it all down in His big book. God had watched Stella go down to the cellar and do bad; He had decided to punish her. David swallowed hard. A fierce anger tore through him. What right had He to make Stella a cripple for the rest of her life? It wasn't fair.

5

A LETTER arrived from Russia from Lisa's mother, that spoke of sorrow and loneliness. The old lady could not die in peace, she wrote, unless she was reunited with her only daughter.

Lisa was reluctant to lay another burden upon Joel. Yet how could she possibly enjoy life in the new world while her mother languished in the old? Joel argued with her. "We already have our hands full," he said. But Lisa was not to be deflected. She countered his objections, she pleaded, she minimized the difficulties. He finally gave in and the old lady set out on the long journey from Riga to New York.

On a rainy Monday in May they went to Ellis Island to meet her. They waited outside the cage where the immigrants were processed. Lisa looked around her with distaste. "Those ugly yellow walls. What misery they've seen. How many tears."

"Your mother is being *dramatish*," Joel said to David.

Lisa ignored the comment. "The day we arrived it rained. It always rains on Ellis Island. We had to wait in that prison there." She pointed to the fenced-off area, and addressed herself to Joel. "When I caught sight of you my heart beat so fast I thought it would burst. At last they let us through.

You picked up the child, saw that his nose was running and put him down again." This was one of the choice items in her collection of injustices, and she was not one to let him forget it.

"It's not running any more," Joel said, and drew David to him.

After a number of delays, the old lady was released. Lisa was overcome with emotion at their reunion. Hannah was a little woman who wore the wig required by tradition, and a black bonnet.

"Dovid'l," Lisa said, "you remember your grandmother?"

David was afraid he would offend his mother if he said no. He shook his head, and his grandmother kissed him. Her wrinkled brown face had a friendly look, like the house on South Fourth Street.

The grandmother always wore black. On sunny afternoons she sat in front of the stoop on a little folding chair. She spoke to David, but he rarely understood what she said. She seemed to live in another world than his, like the birds or trees. She called him *mein kind* as his mother did, but on her lips the words seemed to come from far away.

It puzzled the grandmother that she saw only Jews on South Fourth Street. "Tell me," she finally said to Joel, "are there any *goyim* in New York?"

Summer had come to Williamsburg, smiling and fragrant. The sidewalks were streaked with sunshine, the thin little trees sprouted leaves, and the tiny garden in the back yard was joyous with forget-me-nots and violets.

Joel decided that the time had come to explore Coney Island. The grandmother was afraid she might be a burden and offered to stay home, but Lisa would not hear of it. "We'll see America," she gaily informed her mother. She would have preferred not to go on the Sabbath, when such junkets were forbidden; but it was Joel's only free day, and she knew that God would understand. David too had a problem with the Almighty. Always apprehensive about the weather, he fooled Him by asking for rain.

The preparations were intense. Lisa wrapped a dozen hard-boiled eggs in wax paper and arranged them neatly across the bottom of a shoe box. Salt, pepper, mustard, tomatoes, cucumbers, pumpernickel bread, farmer cheese, and a box of Uneeda biscuits followed, plus an orange for each of them. She had made a special trip to the pushcarts on Hester Street and picked up five bathing suits at forty cents apiece. She also packed towels.

Since Coney Island was twice as far as Prospect Park, the fare was two nickels. They rode in a summer trolley that was open at the sides and had a footboard along the length of the car. David read aloud the names of the unfamiliar streets that sped past them, while Annie clutched the shoe box. When they reached Coney Island, Lisa sniffed the salty air and exclaimed, "It smells like the Baltic!"

They passed a merry-go-round with a calliope that was playing *Stars and Stripes Forever*. Farther on was another playing *The Merry Widow Waltz*. David stopped to listen where both melodies overlapped, reveling in the din. The popcorn and taffy cart boasted a steam whistle whose high, piercing sound mingled with the music yet stood out against it. A sign on the sidewalk announced ice cream in five flavors. "When I first came to America," Joel said, "I saw this sign everywhere. I read it as if it were in Russian, *Itcheh Krem*. I wondered who he was and why he was so popular." Joel burst into laughter.

They crossed Surf Avenue and the ocean lay before them, blue and beautiful. Lisa's eyes opened in wonder. "It's like in Peterboorg, when you looked across the Gulf of Finland. This is even prettier." It was not often that something in the New World struck her as more attractive than what she had left behind in the old.

They came to a grim-looking building with a huge sign in front: Municipal Baths. Joel took David with him; Lisa and Annie went to the door marked *Women*. David watched his father undress. It disturbed him that he alone, among all the men, had no hair around his *shmekeleh*. Joel assured him it was only a matter of time.

On the beach, Lisa led the way past a tangled mass of bodies. They spread their towels on the sand and made their way to the water's edge. Children shouted, jumped, and splashed each other. Little waves tumbled against the shore. Farther out, the ocean stretched to the rim of the horizon, endless and calm.

David waded in one step at a time, a shock of cold spurting up his legs. He dived in and kept jumping up and down until he felt warmer. Then, comfortably ensconced on his sister's arms, he made his first attempt at swimming. To be weightless was a new sensation, and one very much to his taste. Meanwhile his parents, holding on to the rope, bobbed up and down. Lisa was enchanted with their newly discovered sport. It was refreshing. It was healthy. It was wonderful.

Then the hard-boiled eggs, and the tomatoes that had squashed, and the taste of farmer cheese on pumpernickel bread, and a slice of orange with a Uneeda biscuit for dessert. There was something special about eating on the beach after a swim. "This is what I call living," Lisa exclaimed. Joel, echoing his Socialist friend Mr. Levine, added, "A proletarian paradise."

It was late afternoon when they reached the magic realm of Luna Park. A mirror near the entrance transformed David into someone eight feet tall and incredibly thin. Another made him out to be two feet short and incredibly fat. He faced a bewildering array of swings, slides, and rides. There was also a frightful din. "You know what Maxim Gorki said," Lisa observed, "when he was taken to Coney Island. 'How sad a people must be to find pleasure in such a place.' "

"How do you remember these things?" Joel asked. They came to the most exciting ride of all. David drove a padded car into headlong collision with six others.

But then, as they sauntered along, he somehow took a

left turn while the others went right. Before he knew it, he was among a crowd of strangers. He retraced his steps, searching wildly for his parents. Fear poured over him.

Suddenly he knew. They had left without him—they had forgotten him! A terrible suspicion raced through his brain: what if they had brought him here to get rid of him? He found himself in front of a small fountain surrounded by a low white-plaster wall. He plumped down on top of the wall and began to sob. He had always known they did not really love him. Now he had the proof!

His mother darted out of the crowd. She knelt beside him, pressed her cheek against his. "My child . . . my soul . . . did you think we would leave without you? My little bird . . ."

His sobs would not cease. Lisa wiped his eyes; the others came up. His father bent over him, lifted him by the armpits and planted him on the ground. "All you had to do," he said in a reasoning tone, "was to go to the gate. We would have found you there." He consoled his son with an extra-large strawberry ice cream cone.

David held his father's hand as he sucked the ice cream. His tears dried, but the disquiet remained. The towers of Luna Park lit up, looking like the towers in the Arabian Nights. The magic towers on the palace of the Sultan Haroun-al-Raschid. The sky was awash with pastel shades of blue, green, and orange that deepened in the west to scarlet and gold. High above, a crescent moon cut an arc of pale silver against the sky, and the first star appeared.

"Make a wish," his mother said. He wished never to be lost again.

Going home was not easy. The depot was crowded, and when a trolley appeared the holiday mood vanished. People shoved, screamed, and cursed as they fought for a seat. The same thing happened with the next trolley. "They're like wild animals," Lisa said. "Let's wait." They made their way to the wall behind the crowd. She glanced at her mother. "Are you all right?"

"A little tired," Hannah replied. "Maybe it was too much for me."

Lisa noticed a box of empty bottles against the wall. She pulled out the bottles, stood the box on end and made Hannah sit down. "There's always a price," she said. "The more you enjoy, the more you have to pay."

What now? Several trolleys left, but the crowd grew larger and more unruly. Finally Lisa had an idea. "We'll go in there," she said to Annie, pointing to the depot, "and find someone in charge. You'll explain to him that your grandmother is not feeling well. Maybe he will help us." Joel stayed behind with David and Hannah.

They found a policeman with a cheerful face. Lisa spoke to him in Yiddish and Annie translated. The appeal worked. He told them to bring the grandmother into the depot and led them to an empty trolley. Lisa thanked him profusely; in five minutes they were on their way home.

They discussed the policeman at length. Lisa summed him up in a single sentence. "He was Irish, but he had a heart."

6

MUSIC was a kind of magic. When David pressed down the keys the sounds were released even as the genie was released from the bottle if you knew the spell. Melodies floated through the air, each different from all others as faces were different, or the houses on South Fourth Street. *My Bonnie Lies over the Ocean* was gentle and sleepy, *Oh Susannah* gay and jumpy, *Battle Hymn of the Republic* strong and bright red. The melody floated over the chords that he picked out in the bass. Sometimes he played the wrong chord on purpose, just to give himself a shock. Each part of the keyboard had its own color. The bass was a rich purple, the treble soft gray, the upper register as bright as sunlight. He held down the pedal and all the sounds mingled in a kind of rainbow.

On his way home from school he passed the record shop on Broadway. Inside, a row of booths was painted to resemble little cottages where the customers could play the records and decide which they wanted to buy. He stood outside and listened. From the nearest booth came the sound of a piano. Dark sounds in the bass alternated with massive chords in the treble that clanged and throbbed like the ringing of bells. David looked up. The sky seemed to open and a golden light poured down. He mustered up his courage and entered the shop. A woman sat in the booth. "What's the name of that?" he asked.

She smiled at him. "Prelude in C-sharp minor."

"Who wrote it?"

"Rachmaninoff."

"Oh." He said it as if he had heard the name before. "That's the most beautiful piece in the world."

"I think you're right," the woman said.

The chords resumed with even greater power, sending little arrows racing along his spine. His eyes filled with tears. "Some day I'm going to play it."

The woman pressed her lips together skeptically, reminding him of Stella Rabinowitz's "Seein's believin'." "You're sure?" she said.

"Yes." His voice was resolute. "I'm sure."

His parents decided that Miss Gewirtz had taught him all she knew. The new piano teacher, Professor Capaccio, was a tall, thin Italian whose aristocratic face was framed by a mane of silver-gray hair. He came highly recommended by Cousin Laibel and looked like a professor. Like Laibel, he proclaimed his calling by wearing his hair long and knotting a black silk tie into a loose bow.

His fee was considerably higher than Miss Gewirtz's: seventy-five cents a lesson. This set off a debate as to whether Annie should continue her lessons. She felt she had gone far enough, and finished her career at the piano with a piece called *Reproches d'amour*, which was identified on the title page as being "par I. Schatz." When company came it was generally David who was called upon to play. However, if the parents of an eligible young man happened to be visiting, with or without the young man, Lisa would turn to her daughter and say, "Aniushka, my soul, play us Reprotchez dahmoor." Whereupon Annie would go to the piano and perform her war horse. David felt that she did not play with enough expression, but he said nothing about it because he loved her. In any case, the notes were there.

The professor had been a trumpeter in Abruzzi and was somewhat hazy on the bass clef, but he knew the treble. Unlike some of his more learned colleagues, he did not believe in slavish adherence to the printed page; he allowed David to add notes, omit a measure here and there, embellish a chord or change it if he felt like it—in short, to help the composer along.

The professor taught David the Miserere from *Il Trovatore*, Simplified. The cover of the piece showed a gloomy tower, with an oblong of light from a small barred window below the roof. "Manrico ee in prizon and seeng-a da song," the professor explained. The A-minor chords deep in the bass were just as beautiful, David thought, as the bell-like ones in Rachmaninoff's Prelude. When he reached Manrico's aria, which was identified as "Ah, I Have Sighed to Rest Me," the professor sang along. David decided he liked Cousin Laibel's Italian better.

Lisa, puttering about in the kitchen, listened with delight. Everything about the professor was to her liking, especially his sad eyes. He looked to her like a man whose wife beat him. She offered him a plate of raisin cookies and a glass of tea flavored with raspberry jam. She also brought out the silver scissors that cut cubes of sugar, but the professor had never seen anyone drink tea in the Russian fashion and dumped three lumps into the glass.

They had a slight problem of communication, since the few English words Lisa knew did not coincide with the few

he understood. They managed somehow. "How do you speak to each other," Joel inquired. "In Esperanto?"

"With the hands mostly," she replied. "Besides, a heart feels a heart."

7

MR. Levine was courting Cousin Leah. Joel was astonished. "What can he find to say to her?"

"You don't understand human nature," Lisa informed him. "He needs a wife, and she needs a husband."

"He reads Karl Marx, and she doesn't have an idea in her head."

"For a good marriage," Lisa announced sententiously, "you don't have to have ideas. All you need is love."

In any case, the weekly chess game was disrupted by the courtship. Saturday afternoon lost its zest for Joel. Lisa advised him to go for a walk. "It's good exercise," she said, "especially if you remember to fill your lungs."

Thus began Joel's weekly walks with David. Together they explored the unfamiliar neighborhoods—Italian, Irish, Polish—that surrounded the ghetto. Joel held David's hand as they walked and engaged him in long conversations.

Fatherhood had come to Joel before he was ready for it. When he first saw the little boy with the running nose who had just come off the boat, he had too many worries to be able to enjoy him. Only gradually had he come to love him. For Joel, love was an exuberant emotion that demanded physical expression. He hugged the boy, mussed his hair, kissed him; and on these long walks he tried to shape his mind. He never talked down to David but addressed him in the same tone he used with Mr. Levine.

When they passed the church on Union Avenue, David remembered to spit.

"Why did you do that?" Joel asked.

"You're supposed to."

"Who said so?"

"Everybody on the block."

"Nonsense!" Joel exclaimed. "Jesus was a Jew, and if they want to worship him, why do you have to spit? Promise me you will never do it again."

"I promise."

They walked along Montrose Avenue, a broad thoroughfare bathed in sunlight and lined with Italian groceries. "Of all the people in Europe," Joel explained, "the Italians are most like Jews. They talk with their hands, they have warm hearts, and they love opera."

Their Irish excursion was less successful. They followed Union Avenue to Greenpoint, where the Irish lived. Joel didn't feel at home in Greenpoint. "The Irish are Catholics like the Italians, but they are different. In America people look down on the Irish, so the Irish hate the Jews because it gives them someone to look down on."

They wandered along Meserole Street among the Poles. "Of all the *goyim*," Joel said, "the Polish are the worst. They drink up antisemitism with their mothers' milk. I know, because I grew up among them. Why do they hate us so? They themselves don't know. People like to hate because it makes them feel important."

He considered it his duty, on these walks, to prepare his son for a world that was inhospitable to Jews. Only a superior nation, he maintained, could have survived two thousand years of homelessness and persecution. What other group had produced so many outstanding individuals? He justified the Jews' right to exist with a long list of illustrious names, from Spinoza, Disraeli, and Mendelssohn to Karl Marx, Sarah Bernhardt, and Jascha Heifetz. (Some of those he included, like Bizet and Charlie Chaplin, were not even Jewish.) Or he conjured up for David the glories of the past, the psalms of the warrior-king for whom he had been named, and the magnificent temple that Solomon built in Jerusalem. He took it as a personal affront that so great a writer

as Shakespeare should have created Shylock. "They don't tell you that Jews were not allowed to own land in the Middle Ages, or to enter the professions. All they could do was to wander from one country to another and become money lenders. Shakespeare never even met a Jew. Why do they teach you Shylock in their schools when he wrote so many other plays?"

Like Lisa, Joel regretted his lack of formal education and tried to make up for the deficiency. At sixteen he had been apprenticed to a printer. He liked his work because a printer was in constant touch with "the little black dots," as he called the letters of the alphabet, and was thus in a position to pick up all kinds of knowledge. Joel had endless faith in the power of reason. Man had only to achieve a rational understanding of the universe and all his problems would vanish.

On the other side of Broadway was Bedford Avenue, the handsomest street in the ghetto. Elegant brownstones were set back from the curb; an occasional oak tree cast its shade on the sidewalk. They passed by the synagogue on Keap Street, an impressive structure of gray stone which, like the one on Marcy Avenue, had begun as a church. David gazed in awe at the twin towers.

"Papa, where does God stay?"

"Some people think," Joel replied, pointing at the synagogue, "that He lives in there."

"Does He ever get sick?"

"Not that I know of."

"Does he ever get angry?"

"According to the Old Testament, He's angry most of the time."

"Why?"

"Because His Chosen People do not obey Him."

This piece of information somehow made David feel better. "Does He write down everything we do?"

Joel temporized. "Your mother thinks so."

"Do you?"

Joel thought hard. "David, my son, suppose you stepped by chance on a pile of ants. Some would die, the others would run away and try to figure out why you had punished them, and you wouldn't even know they existed. Could they in a million years imagine what you are like? That's how we can figure out what God is like."

"Has anybody ever seen Him?"

"Of course not. But that doesn't keep people from speaking in His name."

What about the cellar and Stella Rabinowitz? David was reluctant to pose the next question but took the plunge. "Papa, does God punish us if we do bad things?"

Joel considered this carefully. "There's only one bad thing, and that is to cause pain to the people around you. As for everything else, I don't think He cares."

God didn't care? David relaxed. It was good to know.

THREE

1

LISA was astonished to find herself pregnant. At her age! A deep joy enveloped her at the prospect of presenting Joel with another son (she was sure it would be a boy). She spent the long summer afternoons beside the window in the kitchen, looking down on the garden in the back yard, waiting. The gnarled tree near the fence had put forth blossoms. That was what bearing a child was like.

Her serenity was shattered by the news that her brother Mischa, after three years in Boston, was returning to New York. This meant that her two older sons were coming back too. Where to put them? They could sleep, she decided, in the kitchen. Mischa presented her with two iron cots that could be folded during the day, and the two young men moved in. For the first time Lisa had all her children—Morris, Willie, Annie, and David—under one roof. Now she was happy.

"Do you mind?" she asked Joel, trying not to show her apprehension.

"Why should I?" Joel replied. "They're yours, so they're mine."

Lisa threw him a grateful glance. What better proof could she have that he loved her?

"Of course, it would have been better," he continued, "if they had come after the baby was born. You're working too hard, too many mouths to feed. I worry about you."

"I'll manage," Lisa said, deeply touched. He was an angel. "Life doesn't follow a plan," she generalized. "You have to take things when they come."

David liked the idea of having two big brothers around. On South Fourth Street if you ever got into a fight, it was good to have someone you could depend on. They were too far removed from him in age to become his friends, but they did things for him. Morris brought him a little sailboat that floated gracefully in the bathtub, and Willie took him to the movies on Saturday afternoons when the price was right: two for a nickel. Between the *Perils of Pauline* and a box of Cracker Jack, David's joy was complete, even though he was puzzled when he heard that Pearl White's misadventures were part of a serial. "Cereal is what you eat in the morning," he told Willie.

"It's a different kind of cereal," Willie explained.

On a Friday in September Uncle Mischa moved his family into a top-floor flat on Grand Street. Lisa took the trolley across the bridge and hurried to her brother's. She was not feeling well; the climb up four flights of stairs left her exhausted. At nightfall she began to have spasms. Mischa summoned an ambulance from Gouverneur Hospital that took her to the emergency ward. In her anguish she turned to God. "Let me bear his child," she begged; but He was not listening. At midnight she had a miscarriage. She lay breathing with difficulty, beads of sweat on her forehead, trying to erase from her mind the agonizing knowledge that but for this accident she would have given birth to a boy.

Joel brought David to visit her. The hospital was a ramshackle building, rust-colored, with enormous windows that curved on top. The ward with its long row of beds lay at the end of a corridor that had dark-green walls and smelled of carbolic acid. David decided that his mother must be very ill, otherwise why would she stay in such a smelly place? Her face was pale and her eyes, deep in their sockets, seemed larger than ever. When she caught sight of them she began to cry.

Joel sat down on the bed beside her, bent over, and kissed her. "I was afraid something would happen," he said.

"It was not destined," Lisa answered. *Beshehrt*, one of her favorite words, lifted all issues from the human level to the divine. How could a thing come to pass once He decided against it? Lisa turned on her side and put her hand on David's shoulder. "I was going to bring you a little brother," she said, "but it was not God's will."

David tried to picture what the baby brother would have looked like. He tried to imagine where the infant had gone, but all he could summon up was a dark place in the sky that was somewhere between the stars.

Lisa wiped away a tear and added, "Dovid'l, I can never have another child. You are my last-born." She took his hand. "The one from whom I expect the most."

David nodded his head as though he understood what she meant. Here too the picture was vague. He knew only that she was laying a burden upon him, and that it would not be light.

Lisa had one problem with her brother Mischa: she could not abide his wife. Aunt Bessie was a plump, willful woman who had an invaluable weapon in her struggle with the world: asthma. She would have an attack whenever it suited her. She would turn red, gasp, groan, heave, and shake until she got what she wanted. Bessie's goal in life was to be as American as possible. She had been brought to the United States as a child and regarded Lisa's European ways as ludicrous. The least flattering epithet in her vocabulary was *greenhorn*. Lisa considered her ignorant, foolish, and— the least flattering epithet in *her* vocabulary—"false."

She resented Bessie's flirtatiousness, particularly when it

was directed at Joel. Bessie followed the American custom of addressing men by their first name. "Joel, would you please hand me my shawl?" took on a seductive ring that Lisa found impossible to ignore. Nor was Bessie above stooping to innuendo, as when she inquired of Lisa with an innocent air, "Did I hear you say that David was born nine months after the wedding?" Nevertheless, Lisa was determined to be friendly when Mischa, Bessie, and their son Arthur made their first visit to South Fourth Street. She brought out a sponge cake and a plateful of dates stuffed with walnuts. Aunt Bessie looked around her and passed judgment: "How can you live in such small rooms?" To which Lisa countered, "A person doesn't need space if he's content with his lot."

For David, the most interesting thing about Cousin Arthur was the ball he had brought from Boston. It was a sponge ball colored a delicate shade of orange and it bounced with a very special grace. It was the most beautiful ball David had ever seen. His problem was how to lure it away from Arthur.

The two went downstairs with the ball, and when they returned, the atmosphere among the grownups had deteriorated. Aunt Bessie was saying, with considerable acerbity, "It's not our fault that you ran up four flights of stairs. Are we supposed to live on the ground floor to please you?" She added as an afterthought, "Maybe if your brother earned more, we could." She gave him a dirty look.

"I didn't say it's your fault" Lisa replied, struggling to conceal her anger. "I only said that if I hadn't climbed all those stairs things might have turned out differently."

"If you want to know the truth, you were too old to have the baby."

"If I wanted to know the truth," Lisa retorted, "I wouldn't ask you. Truth was never one of your strong points."

Mischa tried to intervene. "Shhh . . ."

"Don't you shush me!" Bessie was twenty years younger than her husband and felt that she had conferred an inestimable privilege upon Mischa by marrying him. "Why d'you take her part?"

"I'm not taking anyone's part," Mischa said meekly. "I'm only trying—"

"No one asked you to." Bessie turned to Joel. "I kill myself to get here, I shlepp over the bridge, and what do I get? A kick in the ass, that's what!" She used the Yiddish word *tochis*.

Lisa glared at her. "Vulgar you always were—and always will be."

"You weren't so particular," Bessie snapped, "when I was taking care of your boys while you were—"

Lisa cut off what she sensed was going to be an allusion to her marriage. "You weren't doing me such a favor! They were working for Mischa and earning their bread."

"That's right, insult me!" Bessie shouted. To Mischa, "Is this why you brought me here? For that sister of yours to wipe the floor with me?" Jumping up from her chair, she sucked in her breath, pressed her hand against her heart and fell back. "Water! I'm choking!"

Mischa ran for a glass of water, Joel fetched a towel, Cousin Arthur hurried to his mother's side, and David saw his opportunity. He slipped into his parents' bedroom, where the sponge ball lay. With a deft kick he sent it rolling into the farthest corner of the room, under the bed.

Now that she had the upper hand, Aunt Bessie went through her routine. She coughed, sputtered, gasped, and groaned, turning in what Lisa later described as a brilliant performance. Her husband and son hovered solicitously until the seizure subsided. Bessie stared about her as though trying to recall where she was. Finally she fixed her eyes on Uncle Mischa and announced, "Take me home." As an afterthought, "Unless she takes back what she said."

Lisa stood her ground. "I'm not taking back anything unless you change your attitude."

"So take me home," Bessie commanded and pulled herself to her feet.

As they were preparing to leave, Cousin Arthur demanded his ball.

"I didn' see it," David protested, "after we came upstairs."

"I wan' my ball," Arthur insisted.

"Maybe we lost it. I think we lost it in the street."

"No we didn'. Gimme back my ball."

"I ain't got your ball. How can I give you back what I ain't got?"

"Shhh . . ." Uncle Mischa said. "I'll buy you another ball."

"No, I wan' that one."

Aunt Bessie had her hat and coat on. "I'm ready," she said. Mischa took his son firmly by the hand.

Cousin Arthur began to howl, leaving a trail of lamentation as his father led him down the stairs. When they had gone, David retrieved his treasure, brought it to the front room, and hid it under his pillow. His mother came to say his prayers with him. They went through the list of uncles and aunts for whom they requested the Almighty's benevolence. To his surprise, she included Aunt Bessie.

"I thought you were mad at her."

"May God forgive her," his mother said. "I never will."

Later, David drew out the ball. He cupped it reverently in both hands, then slipped it under his nightshirt. It felt wonderfully smooth against his skin. He sighed with happiness and sank into sleep.

Lisa put away the uneaten cake and dates, turned out the light in the kitchen, and joined Joel in their cubbyhole of a bedroom. "Tfui! It was like a Tartar invasion." She fell silent. Then, "I'm sorry I lost my temper. After all, they were my guests."

"Don't worry," Joel reassured her. "By tomorrow it will all be forgotten."

"It's Mischa I'm sorry for. A man pays when he marries beneath him."

Joel grinned. "Maybe it's not as painful for him as you think."

Lisa did not appreciate his levity. "She's such a yenta. And I love the way she says, 'Joel, will you please hand me my shawl.' " Lisa mimicked Bessie's intonation.

"You're jealous!" Joel pretended astonishment. "I don't believe it."

"Why shouldn't I be when I have a handsome husband every woman in the world would want."

"Don't stop," he said. "Tell me more.'

"I shouldn't. You'll be impossible to live with."

He took her face between his hands. "How can you think I would be interested in her?"

"She's young."

"Is what? Why do you always think that's so important?"

"Men are strange animals. Who can account for their tastes?"

"It is you who are strange, my dearest. You will never believe I love you, no matter how often I tell you."

"So tell me."

He lowered her head against his chest. For once he felt older than his wife. Stronger. Wiser.

2

THE following day, when David returned from school, the ball was on the kitchen table. Lisa came to the point. "I heard you tell your cousin last night that you lost the ball in the street." She used the word *ball*, which stood out in its Yiddish surroundings as if it were in italics.

David screwed up his face as though trying to remember precisely what he had said. "I thought we left it in the street."

"So why did I find it under your pillow this morning?"

He shook his head in honest bewilderment. "When I got to the front room it was there. That's how."

"David"—he noticed that she did not call him Dovid'l—"you're telling me a lie."

"I swear," he said, hoping still to save himself.

"I know exactly what happened. You hid the ball so that you could have it after Arthur left. That is stealing. The Bible says, 'Thou shalt not steal.' My son, you must return the ball at once."

To surrender his booty? He was horrified. "Arthur lost it," he cried, "and I found it. So it's mine!"

She put her hands on his shoulders. "You come from a line of rabbis, and you want to be a thief?"

"It's my ball!"

Her eyes lit up and her voice was stern. "My son a thief?" She thrust him from her.

His defenses crumbled. He knew only that she was angry with him and no longer loved him. He ran into the front room and threw himself on his bed, pressing his lips firmly together as he so often had seen her do.

When Joel came home the case was reopened. Joel listened quietly, then said to Lisa, "Why do you make such a fuss? I'll buy him another ball and we'll return this one."

"That's not the point. It's a matter of principle." *Printsip* crackled righteously on her lips. "The boy must learn that he did wrong, otherwise what kind of person will he grow up to be?"

"Don't worry, he'll learn. Everybody learns."

"And look how everybody is." She suddenly turned to David. "My child, say you're sorry and that you'll return the ball."

He pushed his lips together and thrust his chin forward. It was no longer an issue of right or wrong but a battle of wills between them. He was not giving in.

There was a long silence. At last she spoke. "Very well, I have nothing more to say. If your father wants to spoil you, that's his affair."

That night Lisa did not come to the front room to recite his prayers with him. He failed to say them. What if God found out? David was too miserable to care. He thought of his sister Annie, who always did as she was told. She never got into trouble, nobody was ever angry with her. Why couldn't he be like her? He dug his head into the pillow and closed his eyes, shutting out the world. Stars floated up out of the pink-gray void, moving around and around in a stately dance. Behind them he could see a beautiful coffin like the one in the window of the funeral parlor on South Second Street. The box was of walnut, with silver trimmings at the corners, and the lining was a light-blue satin that shone. He lay in the coffin decked in white, hands folded across his chest, while his parents, uncles, and aunts stood wailing and wringing their hands. Now they were sorry. Oh, how they wept, but it was too late.

For three days Lisa did not speak to him, but he would not yield. He had his pride to consider. Joel kept his word and brought him a sponge ball to replace the one that had been returned to Cousin Arthur. Instead of bright orange it was an ugly brown-red, like calf's liver. Instead of bouncing up from the pavement with a graceful spring, it came up any which way. He hated it both for itself and for the sorrow it had brought into his life.

On Friday afternoon, when school let out he went to Bridge Plaza, past the statue of Valley Forge, and turned in the direction of the bridge. He walked purposefully up the ascending slope. At the middle of the span he peered down at the water and pulled the ball from his pocket. Without a moment's hesitation he flung it high over the railing. This was his sacrifice to God, and David hoped He would receive it in a friendly spirit. He followed the ball with his eyes, hoping to see it float off toward the bay. But the dark dot disappeared in a swirl of greenish-gray eddies. Besides, he was in a hurry to tell his mother what he had done.

She was in the kitchen, slicing carrots into thin round wafers. He knelt beside her, confessed all, and described how the ball had ended as an offering to God. She drew him to her, and covered his face with kisses.

David rested his head in her lap. Miraculously the heavy burden of his defiance had lifted. He felt neither shame at this total surrender nor remorse for his theft. Nothing mattered, not his pride, not even Cousin Arthur's orange-colored ball, now that she loved him again.

3

JOEL belonged to a social club that went by the grand name of Warsaw Young Men's Benevolent Protective Society. During his first year in this country it had been a great help to meet other immigrants who came from the same town as he. Once Lisa had arrived, his interest in the group waned. "The only thing we have in common," he complained to her, "is that we were all born in Warsaw. It's not enough." By this time, however, he had been elected treasurer and could not drop out.

The club held its annual concert and ball in September. This event touched Lisa closely as David was to take part in the concert: his first public appearance. From a pushcart on Hester Street came two yards of black velvet out of which she fashioned a suit trimmed with lace collar and cuffs, as befitted a musical prodigy. But she herself had no dress for the occasion. To buy one was out of the question; she had more pressing needs at the moment. It was David who suggested: "Mama, why don't you wear the black dress?"

Lisa laughed. "They don't wear such clothes in Columbus's country." On second thought the suggestion seemed reasonable. Why not? So elegant a ball gown was certainly good enough for the Pike Street Mansion.

She prepared for the party hours in advance. First she laid out the black dress and removed a few stains. Then, from the same box, she extracted a dark-green feathered boa—she called it *boo-ah*—which, she felt, would add a festive touch. She shined the high-heeled slippers that hurt her feet; two extra inches were worth the discomfort. When evening came she slipped into her corset, which Joel called a "soul-squeezer." She asked him to lace the strings in back as tightly as he could; over it went the black dress. Her hair was piled high on her head. On it floated a pancake of a hat from which rose a solitary white feather. She flung the boa over her shoulders and paused before the tall mirror in the front room to survey the effect. *"Tchudneh!"* she whispered. It was the Russian word for *marvelous.* Pressing her hands against her face, she smoothed the skin back over the cheekbones. Even on so special a night she refused to use makeup, on the ground that rouge and face powder clogged the pores, preventing the skin from breathing.

It was cool enough that evening for her to wear a cloak, so that Mrs. Rabinowitz, who watched from her third-floor window as they departed, had no opportunity to gawk at her outlandish costume. Chattering gaily, she walked ahead with Joel on their way to the Bridge Local; David and Annie brought up the rear. He was taking his music along even though he knew the two pieces by heart. Just in case. Annie held his hand when they crossed the street; she always treated him like a little boy. "Are you scared to play before all those people?" she asked. David replied with an emphatic No! The trolley across the bridge was crowded. "Are they all going to the ball?" Lisa inquired. Joel laughed.

Pike Street Mansion lived up to its name. A grand staircase led to the ballroom. Lisa slipped the black satin loop over her wrist, lifting her skirt off the red carpet, and adjusted the boa around her shoulders. At the head of the stairs stood the president of the society, Abraham Katz, a short wiry man in a tuxedo that had been rented for the evening and was too large. The ballroom was decorated with festoons of red, white, and blue—a gesture, amidst all the nostalgia for the old country, of allegiance to the new. The waxed yellow floor shone under the lights. David went slid-

ing across it hand in hand with a girl named Estelle. She
had blond curls, wore a pink dress, and was going to do a
toe dance to a piece called *Glow Worm*.

"Can you play it?" she asked.

"Sure." What luck, he thought, to be able to enter her
life so easily. He inspected the piano, which stood on a
narrow stage at one end of the ballroom. The ivories were
yellow, three were missing from the keys. He felt sorry for
the old box.

Uncle Mischa and Aunt Bessie arrived with Cousin
Arthur. Bessie was still not speaking to Lisa. This did not
prevent her from turning to Mischa and saying in a loud
voice, "Where did she get that dress?"

Uncle Isaac came late as usual, Aunt Esther and Cousin
Leah in tow. His heavy gold chain gleamed across his vest.
Even on this special night he would not touch a woman's
hand and addressed Lisa with the formal *ihr* instead of the
intimate *du*. To Joel he said dourly, "Your wife looks like
an actress."

Joel beamed. "She is one."

The guests sat on slender gilt chairs lined against the wall.
The president of the club made a speech, and the concert
began. David came out, clapped his left hand across his
middle and bowed low. It was a wonderful sensation to
stand in the center of the stage, to feel everybody's eyes
upon him and hear the applause. He wasn't nervous, and
his first number, the Miserere from *Il Trovatore*, Simplified,
came off without a hitch. True, the G above middle C didn't
work, but he kept the loud pedal down so that a bright halo
of sound covered the gap in Manrico's melody. He was
playing it for the whole world to hear and the world was
listening.

Without a pause he launched into *A Trip to Niagara*,
March and Two-Step. This was a snappy number that made
a fine contrast with the Miserere. Also, it didn't use the G
very often, so that the gap in the tune was scarcely notice-
able. When he reached the end of the piece there was a

burst of applause; Cousin Izzy shouted Bravo! as they did at the opera. David stood up, took a bow, and walked off. The applause persisted. What a pleasant sound it made! He came out and announced his encore in a clear voice: Für Elise by Ludwig van Beethoven. The brooding face on top of the piano at home would be pleased, he thought, at this tribute. He fumbled slightly as his right hand shaped the broken chord on page 3, but no one seemed to notice, for the applause at the end was as enthusiastic as it had been before.

Afterward, his mother kissed him and said, "Dovid'l, I'm so proud of you." His father hugged him and rumpled his hair. Cousin Izzy slapped him on the shoulder but made no attempt to lift him off the floor on the palm of one hand. Cousin Laibel, as one artist to another, asked, "Were you nervous?" David assured him that he wasn't. And to cap it all Aunt Bessie said in a loud voice, "Mark my words, he'll play in Carnegie Hall yet."

The program continued. Cousin Laibel obliged with "La Donne e mobile." David, who accompanied him, noticed that Laibel was not singing the Italian words printed on the page and assumed that he was on another stanza. The protracted high G at the end was widely admired; David noticed that it was a trifle flat. Laibel's encore was a Yiddish folk song about a rabbi who commanded his disciples to dance and make merry.

Estelle had changed into a white tutu and ballet slippers. David, as he played *Glow Worm*, watched her out of the corner of his eye. It seemed miraculous to him that she was able to stand on her toes; she appeared to be floating on air. She was the most beautiful creature he had ever seen, and he was happy that she received almost as much applause as he had. Estelle took several bows, but as this was the only dance she knew, there was no encore.

The ball followed. Three musicians—violin, piano, and drum—struck up the arduous Russian two-step known as *kazatskah*. The younger men performed it in Cossack fashion, arms akimbo, trunks erect, and legs flying out from under them, while those not dancing formed a circle and clapped the rhythm. The musicians then broke into the soulful Russian tune that came to be known as the *Anniversary Waltz;* the violinist played the melody with much expresson. Lisa danced with Cousin Izzy. She waltzed in Russian fashion, with a little hop on the third beat and swaying from side to side as she looked over each shoulder in turn. She danced with abandon, almost defiantly, as if she were saying to Aunt Bessie, "See, I still can!"

Joel sat by the wall, watching Lisa whirl around the room. "How is it," Cousin Laibel asked him, "that you never learned?"

"Who had time for dancing? I had bigger worries on my mind."

Estelle had changed out of her ballet costume and was wearing shoes again. She joined David in sliding across the floor. By the end of the evening he was madly in love with her. Unfortunately she lived in the Bronx and he never saw her again.

It was almost midnight when they returned to Brooklyn. A stillness hung over Bridge Plaza; Valley Forge was deep in shadow. They made their way to South Fourth Street. "Ekh, it's good to have a little excitement," Lisa said. "The trouble is, there's not enough of it."

Later, she came into the front room. Bending over, she chucked David under his chin. "You gave me real pleasure tonight, Dovid'l." She thought a moment. Then, "You are the child of my love," she murmured. He wondered what she meant. Was this why she expected so much from him?

In the middle of the night Lisa awoke Joel.

"What is it?" he asked sleepily.

"My heart. It's beating fast. I danced too much."

Joel sat up. "Shall I—?"

"Take a piece of ice and wrap it in a towel. That'll help."

He brought her the compress and rested it against her

heart. Beads of sweat appeared on her forehead. Joel pan-icked. "You need a doctor."

He dispatched Annie to fetch Dr. Cohen, who lived around the corner on Union Avenue. Lisa rested her head on the pillow; Joel wiped her brow. Her hand found his. "I want so much to live."

"Sh . . . do not speak."

Her eyes were wide with sorrow. "When the time comes, I will have to leave you."

"My dearest, do not even think such things."

She pressed the ice against her breast. By the time the doctor arrived the spasm had subsided. He prescribed sed-ative and told her to stay in bed for three days. Joel sat by the bed and held her hand.

"It was an evil eye," she whispered.

"How can you believe such nonsense?"

"Yes it was. Bessie . . . Tante Esther . . . they will never forgive me for marrying you."

"Don't upset yourself."

She stared into the dark. "It was a lovely evening and I had a wonderful time. But there is always a price to pay." She fell silent.

After a time, "What are you thinking?" he asked.

She smiled ruefully. "I'm saying good-bye to my youth."

She never wore the black dress again.

4

LISA was happy that Joel treated her children as his own. Of the three, he knew Annie best. She was a shy girl with gray-green eyes and a tiny snub nose, who had inherited neither Lisa's temperament nor looks. Annie's one spurt of originality came in her work. When she finished business school, she combined her knowledge of Yiddish with ste-nography and typing. This specialized skill brought her the munificent salary of fourteen dollars a week—almost as much as Joel earned—at a time when most typists received eight. Since she gave most of her earnings to her mother, the finances of the household took a dramatic turn for the better.

Annie was a dutiful daughter. On Sunday, her free day, she would wrap a towel around her head and proceed to sweep and dust every cranny of the flat. Lisa urged her to go out with young men, as Cousin Minnie of the Bronx was doing. To no avail. Annie's idea of a good time was to sit home and be entertained by her mother. Or she took her kid brother across the bridge to the theater on Grand Street. There was something about that balcony which made Annie hungry; she came armed with a brown paper bag filled with goodies. David and she sat in the dark quietly munching raisins, almonds, and honey cake, while two floors below the great Jacob Adler suffered as the Yiddish King Lear. David enjoyed being with Annie. She listened to everything he said, she never contradicted or argued with him, and she was always buying him presents.

Annie was convinced that if she let a man kiss her she would become pregnant. She knew this wasn't so but believed it nonetheless. Lisa tried to talk her out of this notion but couldn't. She dispatched Annie to a sociable at Cousin Minnie's; Annie came home scandalized. The girls had thought nothing of sitting on the young men's laps, and they had played spin the bottle. Lisa sighed when she contemplated her daughter's future; a girl wasn't getting any younger. Annie would make someone a perfect wife, but where was she to find him?

Lisa had no such worries with Morris, her eldest son. He was continually bringing girls home for her to meet. Her reaction was the same to all of them: they weren't good enough. Otherwise she could not complain of Morris. He worked hard in Uncle Mischa's junk shop, which had been transferred from Boston to Allen Street near Brooklyn Bridge. Rain or shine he got up at six in the morning to open the shop, and contributed to the household half of the nine dollars a week that Mischa paid him.

It was his younger brother Velvel who was the problem. Velvel, who became Willie in English, had a talent for attracting trouble. One night he and an older boy stole into the grocery store on the corner and made off with a carton. In the excitement of getting away he left his cap behind; the grocer was thus able to trace the culprits. Lisa had to pay six dollars to hush up the matter. She was crushed. "Four rabbis in the family," she lectured Willie, "and you do a thing like this? Can I hold my head high with such a son? What evil spirit made you want twelve jars of coffee? Tfui! You should be ashamed of yourself."

How, she asked herself, could such a disgrace befall her when she had tried so hard to instill moral principles in her children? To Joel she said, "I know what's eating him. He's paying me back."

"For what?"

"For falling in love with you instead of devoting myself to him. First he lost his father, then he lost his mother."

"I didn't take you away from him."

"He thinks you did, and that's what counts."

Willie's next peccadillo took place at school. In a fit of temper the descendant of four rabbis threw an eraser and chalk at the teacher. Lisa was summoned to a conference with the teacher. She had no intention of venturing into the goy world, and sent Joel instead. He returned from the interview exhausted.

"*Nu?*" Lisa asked. "What did the teacher say?"

Joel shrugged. "She talked and talked, I didn't understand a word."

"Why didn't you tell her? She would have asked someone to say it in Yiddish."

"I didn't think she wanted to be interrupted."

"What do you think she said?"

"What do you suppose? That he should be a good boy and not throw things at her."

"I feel so ashamed." Lisa sighed. " 'Small children press the knee, big ones press the heart!' " It was to become her favorite adage.

She tried to reason with Willie. "Your father is ready to give you an education. Do you realize what a golden opportunity that is?"

Willie stared at her with darkly intense eyes. "He's not my father."

"He would be if you let him. My stepfather hated me. You have one who wants to help you, and you throw the chance away." Her anger overflowed. "What right have you to embarrass me so?"

She faced his sullen gaze and knew the answer. He had every right in the world.

Lisa had made every effort to conceal Willie's behavior from David; the discussion of that episode had been mostly in Russian. All the same, David had a hunch that something was wrong. He broached the subject as Willie and he were coming home from the movie theater on Broadway. "Mama's mad at you," he ventured. "What for?"

"I got into trouble."

"What kind?"

Willie was evasive. "Just trouble."

"Mama was mad at me too," David said, and launched into an account of his involvement with Cousin Arthur's sponge ball. Partly he was demonstrating to his brother that he too had problems, partly he was trying to show that he understood Willie's predicament. His tale had a moral, that it was better to be in their mother's good graces than to quarrel with her, but he got so bogged down in details that he never reached it. Besides, Willie lost interest in the story. "That's kid stuff," he said. Willie took his hand as they crossed Broadway. An elevated train rumbled overhead. "You're lucky," Willie said out of the blue. "For you everything's easy."

David didn't ask him what he meant. Talking to grownups was like shouting to someone far away. You could never be sure they heard you.

5

THE grandmother was failing. She would forget what she had said and would say it again. And she was constantly ill. Lisa's life revolved around the tiny bedroom where Hannah lay. Dr. Cohen was not optimistic. "If I could give her a new body," he said, "she would be fine."

"If I could give her mine" Lisa replied, "I would."

She felt guiltier than ever. Toward Hannah, for not being able to keep her well. Toward Joel, for saddling him—in addition to all his other burdens—with a sick mother-in-law. Toward her children, for neglecting them in favor of her mother. Finally Joel took a stand. Uncle Mischa was her son; let him take care of her. He presented his proposal to Mischa and Tante Bessie; they wouldn't hear of it. Joel came home angry. If Hannah's own son refused to help, why was he supposed to put up with this impossible situation? There was only one sensible solution. His boss knew the director of the Pride of Judaea Home for the Aged near Prospect Park, where they had nurses around the clock. Hannah would be under constant medical supervision and would have everything she needed.

"Except love," Lisa said. She was horrified at the suggestion, but as the old lady's condition worsened, she knew she was waging a losing battle. Each visit of the doctor took two dollars from her budget; the constant outlay for medicine was a further drain. In addition, she was up half the night tending to Hannah's needs. Joel insisted that things could not continue this way; he finally wore her down. She sat down beside the bed and told her mother what Joel had in mind.

The old lady lay very still, gazing at her gnarled hands

on the coverlet. Then she said, "Lisotchka, would I want to be a burden to you? A wife should listen to her husband."

Lisa let out a sigh. "I brought you to America so that we could be together. And now I'm sending you away."

"You're not sending me away," Hannah said. "I'm going."

"I feel so ashamed," Lisa said. She took Hannah's hand in hers and stared at the coverlet. If she had never married Joel she would be in control of her life, for better or worse; her decisions would belong to her alone. As it was, she was sacrificing her mother because of him. How many sacrifices did love demand of its victims? She hated her love for Joel because she was helpless against it, and because she was helpless she dropped her head in her mother's lap and wept.

Hannah stroked her hair. "Do not weep, my daughter. God will help and I will get better. I already had my life. It is not right that I should spoil yours."

A few days later, on a Saturday morning, Lisa brought out her *reisetasch*—a huge duffel bag of brown denim on which she had embroidered her initials in red—and packed Hannah's things. The grandmother wore the same clothes as on the day she had arrived from Europe: a black dress, black cloak, and black bonnet over her wig. She was escorted on her melancholy journey by Lisa, Joel, and her grandchilden. They took the Tompkins Avenue trolley to Prospect Park; there was only a short ride beyond to the Pride of Judaea Home, a sprawling red-brick structure surrounded by a garden. The corridors were spotless and smelled of antiseptic. "Like Gouverneur Hospital," Lisa said, and remembered her miscarriage. Hannah surveyed her new surroundings with equanimity, but Lisa could not fight back her tears.

Thereafter, Saturday was sacred to her visits with her mother. Sometimes Joel came with her, sometimes she took along one of her children. Uncle Mischa and Tante Bessie joined her occasionally, with or without Cousin Arthur. But Lisa never missed a week. She would bring Hannah packages filled with cookies, candied orange peel, a jar of gefilte fish, or stewed peaches. Hannah was not supposed to eat these; but Lisa continued to ply her with goodies, and no amount of arguing could stop her.

Now that the old lady was kept on a diet, her health took a turn for the better. She pretended to like the Home, and Lisa pretended to believe her. Only once did Hannah complain. It was depressing, she said, to be surrounded by old age all the time. Lisa pointed to three elderly gentlemen who were sunning themselves on a bench in the garden. "Why don't you flirt with them, Mama?" she suggested. "It would cheer you up."

Hannah looked them over. "Oh, Lisotchka," she said quietly, "I could better flirt with the Angel of Death." She called him by his Hebrew name, *Moloch hamovess.*

Lisa returned from the Home toward nightfall, utterly spent. "What do you talk about all day?" Joel would ask.

"I read the newspaper to her. Then we chat. You'd be surprised how much we have to say to each other. More than when she was living with us." Sometimes she would say, "I betrayed her. And she has forgiven me."

"You had no choice."

"I know." She raised her hand to her breast and her voice was low. "My sorrow presses like a stone on my heart. And it will stay there till the day I die."

6

THE war in Europe bewildered Lisa. "French Jews shooting at German Jews, Russian Jews at Austrian Jews. Killing each other because of the Kaiser. Why?" Her answer was positively Marxist. "Only the rich need wars. And for this, poor people have to die. Does it make sense?"

The war reached Brooklyn. Joel and Morris had to register for the draft. Joel was deferred because of wife and child; Morris was taken. Lisa had not been close to her first-born since her marriage to Joel; suddenly all her thoughts revolved around him. Morris came home on a furlough in an ill-fitting uniform; he was short and bony, and reminded her of his father. He showed her how he wound his puttees around his legs. "Oy, my hero," she said, and insisted that he take back with him two jars of chicken soup. He tried to tell her that there was no place in Camp Upton to heat chicken soup, but she refused to listen. He took the two jars and left them on the train.

When Morris was shipped to France, the war became a daily part of her life. She tried to imagine what he was going through. Her inability to do so somehow made the war more frightening. She had seen a movie called *Civilization:* bombs bursting in air, great chunks torn out of the earth, bodies huddled in trenches surrounded by severed arms and legs. Now it was actually happening, and her son, her flesh and blood, was in the midst of it: young, helpless, doomed. At times she felt it was somehow her fault. Perhaps if she had not come to America he would now be safe. She knew this was an irrational feeling, yet could not shake it off.

Her anxieties reached their peak on the Day of Atonement. She fasted and prayed all day, as was her custom. This time, however, she had something to pray for. The service in the synagogue on Marcy Avenue was long and tiring. What with the heat in the women's gallery, the lack of air and her hunger, she felt light in the head and in direct communication with God. He began vaguely to resemble the photograph in the green plush album of the loving father she had lost when she was ten. She had never before asked Him for special favors, but this time she addressed herself to the Almighty as to a friend. He saw what was in her heart, He knew what she needed from him. *Sweet Father in heaven, protect my Morris from harm.*

A golden light filtered in through the stained-glass windows. The cantor's voice sank to a tremulous pianissimo, followed by the blast of the shofar. Like a trumpet summoning the dead to judgment, the ram's horn sounded its call, ushering in the awesome moment when the Merciful Father (who was also God of Vengeance) balanced His accounts and meted out His sentence: ". . . who shall be lifted up and who shall be cast down, who shall live and who shall die." The faithful wept, the sinners repented; Lisa swayed back and forth, throat parched, stomach empty, her soul in torment. She smote her breast with clenched fist in the traditional gesture that accompanied the solemn prayer *For the sin that I have committed.* A vision floated before her eyes of an enormous goblet near the throne of God into which were gathered the tears of all the mothers in the world. Millions of mothers who prayed to Him while their sons murdered one another. Jewish and Russian tears, German, French, and Italian tears, all flowing together. When the goblet overflowed, God would finally listen and bring peace . . .

The ram's horn repeated its call. Lisa's heart contracted with fear. When David came to the women's gallery, she fixed him with a somber gaze. "I prayed to God to bring Morris back alive. I have a feeling He won't."

"Why?" David asked. The war was far away, and in school the boys looked up to him because his big brother was in the army. "God has so many to choose from, why would He pick on Morris?"

It was a good question.

7

THE time had come for Joel to join the union. He passed the examination with flying colors and looked for a job with one of the Yiddish newspapers. Circulation was booming and they needed more printers. *The Morning Journal* was conservative and religious in its outlook. Joel never read it.

The Forward was the socialist paper, but it catered to the ignorant Jews from the *shtetl*. Both Joel and Lisa considered it a vulgar sheet. Their newspaper was *The Day*, which had a liberal point of view along with cultural pretensions. It printed short stories, poems, and literary essays that Joel read aloud to Lisa with gusto. He was delighted when he was taken on at *The Day*.

Suddenly he was earning sixty dollars a week, not counting overtime. This new-found prosperity called for a better apartment, which they found in one of the new buildings on on the other side of Broadway. It had all the latest improvements: electric lighting instead of gas, and a bathroom off the kitchen instead of a toilet in the hall. The neighborhood was better too. Lisa insisted that they move to their new home on a Thursday, as that was a lucky day. "How," Joel asked severely, "can you be so superstitious? You're living in the twentieth century!" Lisa nodded in agreement, but Thursday it was.

She did most of the packing, and was ready long before the movers arrived. They were bewildered by her cries of *astarozhne!*—the Russian for *careful*—as they carried the tall mirror with the sphinxlike legs down the stairs. The piano followed through the window. Lisa had no intention of allowing Beethoven, Mozart, and the Three Graces to be smashed to bits in the moving van. Wrapped in thick towels, they were deposited in two pails for Joel to carry.

The little parlor looked strange, denuded of its furniture. When only the chairs were left, Lisa made Joel and David sit down beside her. "Just for a minute. It's an old Russian custom. So that we won't miss what we're leaving." She looked around at the empty flat. "It wasn't so bad here. Now a new chapter begins. May it be no worse." She jumped up and armed herself with the package she had prepared, containing bread and salt so that life would be bountiful in their new home, and a jar of honey so that it would be sweet.

They went upstairs to say good-bye to Mrs. Rabinowitz.

Stella sat on a low bench, her sick leg resting on the other. "You movin' today?" she asked.

Now that he would not have to see her any more, David had only kind feelings toward her. She had given him, he felt, a lot of trouble.

Mrs. Rabinowitz turned to Lisa and said, "It should be in a good hour."

"With *mazel* may you live," Lisa responded.

"Oy, my *mazel!* On my worst enemies I wouldn't wish it." Mrs. Rabinowitz looked as if she was going to cry.

"We are in God's hand," Lisa answered quietly.

When they reached the street the movers were loading the piano onto a truck. David stopped for a last look at the house. The wrought-iron gate that opened on the stone stairs to the cellar. The tiny stoop. The light-brown front with its friendly look. The windows of the front room on the second floor. The roof where he had sat on his throne and surveyed the world.

II

The
Budding
Grove

ONE

1

Ross Street was wider, cleaner, quieter than South
Fourth; no trolley car rattled past at all hours of
the day. To Lisa's delight, two young trees grew
in front of their apartment house, brightening the scene.
The gentiles had fled, leaving the neighborhood to the Jews.

You entered the apartment by the kitchen; the bathroom
was to one side. The dining room was decorated in the latest fashion, its walls papered with a thick dark-brown card-
board that gave the illusion of oak paneling. Most elegant
was the low-hanging chandelier, a dome of multicolored
glass that filtered the light of three electric bulbs into a soft
radiance. This, Lisa declared, was the kind of light a woman
needed.

One wall accommodated the piano, with its busts of Beethoven and Mozart, and the Three Graces between; another
was taken by the bookcase, an imposing mahogany chest
with glass doors to keep out the dust. Sets of Tolstoi, Chekhov and Pushkin were on the left, the complete works of
Sholom Aleichem on the right. Also one work in English—
Graetz's *History of the Jews*, in six volumes, that Joel had
picked up at an auction for David to read some day. The

bookcase looked bare until Lisa imported a new group of divinities from her favorite pushcart on Hester Street: Venus, Europa on the bull, and Apollo. She had some qualms about Apollo, but he did wear a fig leaf. "Wait till Uncle Isaac sees these," she exclaimed, anticipating the patriarch's displeasure.

After dinner, which in Williamsburg was referred to as supper, David went downstairs to meet his friends. He was one of six boys who had gone together from P.S. 16 into high school. They generally met in front of Hymie Gershon's house on Lee Avenue. Hymie was the politician of the group. He accompanied his father twice a week to the local Democratic Club and had the kind of smile that promised you whatever you wished. More important, his house had a basement room that served the group as a gathering place.

Bill Cooperman, plump and pimply, was the comedian of the group. Whenever two girls went by he could be depended upon to say in a loud voice, "I like the one in the middle," whereupon his comrades would be convulsed. No less mirth-provoking, if someone brushed up against his jacket or sleeve, was the warning: "Leggo the Hilton." Unlike comics who are constantly looking for new material, Bill didn't have to. His public was more than content with his two witticisms.

Hymie generally awaited them in front of his house, where they were joined by Solly Cohen, the only blond member of the group. Everything about Solly was big—his head, his ears, his nose, his feet; also, he proudly confessed, his cock. Since his older brother was going to be a doctor, Solly was slated to become an accountant. With girls he cultivated an air of bored indifference, the effectiveness of which was spoiled by the fact that he blushed easily. Given his fair complexion, it showed.

Last to arrive were Abe Rosen and Carl Lipkowitz. Abe, like David, was short for his age. Behind his thick glasses lurked the darkly beseeching eyes of a cocker spaniel.

Although no one in the group had yet begun to shave, Abe came closest to needing it. He had a dark fuzz on his upper lip and black curly hair in his armpits. He was continually straightening up, as if by sheer will power he could make himself as tall as his friends. Painfully shy, he mumbled in a deep unfocused voice, and kept feeling his Adam's apple as though to make sure it was still there.

Carl was the good-looking one. He was tall, broad-shouldered, and resembled Wallace Reid. When he could think of nothing else to do he drew a comb out of his pocket and passed it through his hair. He had been the first of the group to get into long pants. Carl wanted to be an actor, belonged to the Dramatic Society, and was taking part in the Semi-Annual, an evening of declamation at the end of which the best speaker was awarded a prize. Unfortunately, he kept forgetting his lines. "Do your stuff," Solly said. "We'll listen."

The boys sat on a rusty bed that had no mattress, Carl took up an orator's stance and launched into Kipling's poem:

> If you can keep your head when all about you
> Are losing theirs and blaming it on you,
> If you can trust yourself when all men doubt you,
> But make allowance for their doubting too . . .

Falling silent, he passed his hand across his forehead, and stared blankly. David, who had heard Carl rehearse many times, prompted him with "If you can wait and not be tired by waiting."

"I'll start again," Carl said.

"You have to listen to the sound," David advised. "It's the same as memorizing music. The end of each line has to remind you of the next, then you won't get stuck."

Carl pondered this. "Let me do it my way." He began again and got through the poem. "But what if it happens when I'm on the stage?"

"It won't," David assured him. "You'll be too scared to forget."

It was almost nine: time for a hot chocolate in the ice cream parlor on Lee Avenue. They always sat at the same table where they could see what was going on outside. Then they walked each other home, chatting, arguing, jumping, shouting, laughing, and swaggering as if the street belonged to them. Abe lived a block away from David, on Rodney Street. After they had left the others David walked him home, then he walked David back. Abe was an avid reader and introduced David to the stories of Henty, Rider Haggard, Kipling, Dickens. When they were alone he threw off his shyness. He had an uncanny knack of making the world of books come alive. He had just finished Haggard's *She* and talked about Alan Quatermain and Ayesha as if they were friends of his, until it seemed to David that at any moment the two would alight from the Lee Avenue trolley.

"Imagine, she's nine hundred years old but she's beautiful as long as she stays in her cave."

David stopped in his tracks. "Then what?"

"She's in love with Alan, so she comes out. Once the air hits her, She-Who-Must-Be-Obeyed is finished." Abe's near-sighted eyes glowed. "I wish I'd been there to see it."

"What happened to her?"

"She dissolved."

"Wow!"

The two boys parted in front of a gnarled oak on the corner of Lee and Rodney, midway between their homes. As he walked the block to Ross Street, David reviewed the wonders Abe had told him about. He found them mind-boggling.

His parents were in the kitchen drinking tea. David knew that his mother did not quite approve of his friends. To her they represented "the street"—the America she neither knew nor liked. "You're growing away from us, Dovid'l," she said sadly. "Sooner or later you will leave us."

His father took a broader view. "He needs his own friends. Us he will always have."

"Not always!" she answered in the tragic tone she reserved for anything connected with her death. "Some day he will look for us and it will be too late."

"Stop being *dramatish*," his father said.

David saw no conflict of loyalty between his family and his friends. They were a kind of family too, whom he needed almost as much as he needed his own. In some ways they were even closer. They surrounded him, protected him, gave him a feeling of belonging. In return he loved them almost as much as he loved his real family. Especially Abe.

2

EASTERN District High School, on Marcy Avenue, was a fine example of pseudo-Gothic. David, who was reading *Kenilworth*, thought the building with its mullioned windows and crenelated towers came straight out of Walter Scott's novel. There was a lower-level courtyard that, if filled with water, could serve as a moat. In the main hallway were murals with allegorical figures clad in brightly colored mantles, whose significance David never discovered. They resembled the beautiful maidens in Rossetti's illustrations for *Idylls of the King* that hung in the library.

David's teachers belonged to the *goy* world that was so far removed from his own. Miss Davenport, a gray-haired, motherly woman, was his grade adviser. He never could think of anything to ask her advice about. Miss Sullivan taught him geometry. He was fascinated by Euclid's puzzles, but her thin blue lips put him off. His English teacher, Mr. Hartwell, was a pixyish little man who peppered David's compositions with semicolons in red ink. Señora Escobar was a plump, pretty woman with a mean look who called him Señor and had him write his name on the blackboard preceded by *Me llamo*. David was sorry he hadn't picked French.

Best of all he liked the music class. Miss Ennis encouraged her pupils to sing at the top of their lungs; the bigger the sound, the happier she was. David followed the curve of the melody as it soared above the chords, but the real power, he realized, lay in the harmony. In songs like *My Bonnie Lies over the Ocean*, *Annie Laurie*, or *Battle Hymn of the Republic*, the same chords followed each other in practically the same order. He could almost see the change in color as one chord melted into the next.

The orchestra rehearsed in the auditorium. It was here that Mary Gwendolyn Ennis revealed her talent. She was a tall, thin Irishwoman with red hair, a fiery temper, and a determined downbeat. Her baton sliced the air as she bullied her ragged group of players into something resembling an ensemble. She gave them special arrangements in which the piano substituted for whatever instruments were missing. David enjoyed his importance.

Miss Ennis was teaching them the *Peer Gynt Suite*. She described how dawn broke over the Norwegian fjords, crystal-clear and cool. This was the tone she wanted from the flutes and clarinets in the opening piece, *Morning*. David loved the gentle flow of six-eight time and the broad curve of the melody, to which one of the violinists sang, "Morning is dawning and Peer Gynt is yawning in front of the statue of Grieg." Miss Ennis shushed him and proceeded to the second piece of the suite. The opening chords of *Ase's Death* were dark and brooding. To David they suggested bodies bent and twisted as they pulled a heavy coffin up the side of a hill, only to be lost to view as the chords in the second half of the piece began to descend. *Anitra's Dance*, in three-four time, was light and graceful. "I want a fluffy upbeat," Miss Ennis shouted. David looked at the violinists in bewilderment. What was a fluffy upbeat? Nobody knew, but they tried to give it to her. The most exciting number of the suite was the last, *In the Hall of the Mountain King*. The piece began in low register, dark, soft, and slow; it grew steadily louder, higher, faster. David crouched forward, his fingers kneading the keys. When the final crescendo began he had the sensation of being lifted off his seat. The Mountain King was flying through the air, and so was he. Miss Ennis's long thin arms were waving wildly. Cymbals crashed, trumpets blared, woodwinds tootled, and the walls seemed to shake as the piece ended in a blaze of excitement. Miss Ennis mopped her brow in triumph. "*That*," she exclaimed, "was a climax!"

The only Jew among David's teachers was Mr. Lederman, in phys ed, whose avowed purpose in life was to transform boyish boys into manly men. Mr. Lederman was something of a sadist. He would make the boys climb the ropes for the sheer pleasure of seeing them dangle two feet below the ceiling of the gym. David looked down from his perch, and felt he was about to throw up. He clambered down before Mr. Lederman gave the word.

Mr. Lederman went up to him, his round face creased with the special smile he reserved for his victims. "Whatsa matter? Scared?"

David was breathing heavily from his exertions. He found no answer.

"Go on up again," Mr. Lederman commanded.

David took a step toward the rope. Then he stopped. "I can't."

" 'I can't,' " Mr. Lederman mimicked. "And why can't you?" He waved one hand as a signal that the other boys could descend.

David felt his face go hot. "I—I just can't," he stammered.

"Sissy!" Mr. Lederman spat out the word. "Wouldja like a glass of milk?" He glanced toward the boys at the ropes, as if to invite their appreciation of his wit. They obliged by bursting into laughter.

David swallowed hard, paralyzed by his embarrassment.

"Go on up!" Mr. Lederman barked. David did not stir. At that moment, luckily, the bell rang. Mr. Lederman, having had enough sport for one day, called "Class dismissed"; the boys broke ranks. Just before David passed through the doorway to the locker room he turned his head and muttered, "Drop dead!" Unfortunately, only the two boys behind him heard his parting shot.

It was Abe, that night, who plotted revenge. "The Emperor of Morocco," he informed David, "kept a collection of sand bugs. If he didn't like someone, he had him put in a glass cage together with the bugs. In half an hour the guy was picked clean. The Emperor sat watching in front of the cage until only the bones were left. Eating a sandwich."

"What kind?"

"Salami on rye, of course."

"With mustard?"

Abe nodded. "And a pickle. Guess who we're putting in."

David pretended not to know. Finally, "Lederman?" he suggested.

Abe nodded gleefully. "Will we start the bugs on his head or feet?"

David was suddenly decisive. "Feet."

"Why?"

"So he'll stay alive longer."

"What'll we do with the skeleton?"

"We'll stand it in Hymie's basement."

"If we put a pillow in the middle, where the stomach used to be, we can throw darts at it."

David thought carefully. "What if the down comes loose and messes up the floor?"

"So what?" Abe asked. "Look at the fun we'll have."

David smiled. Magically the hurt had disappeared.

3

THE high point of Professor Capaccio's year was the Concert and Ball at which all his pupils performed. This took place on the first Saturday night in February at Palm Garden in Manhattan, no less. The professor, despite his dreamy Italian eyes, was not altogether devoid of a business sense. The tickets were fifty cents apiece and he unloaded ten on each pupil, to be sold to relatives and friends. Joel thought it ungracious to dun the family, and paid for the ten. David's contingent at the concert was to include—besides his parents, sister and brothers—Cousin Izzy, Cousin Laibel, Uncle Mischa, Aunt Bessie, and Cousin Arthur.

Lisa always had a horror of being late—according to Joel it sprang from her fear of missing anything. On the great day they set out betimes, across Williamsburg Bridge to Manhattan and one stop beyond Times Square. Palm Garden, so named because of three anemic palms in the lobby, turned out to be a grander version of Pike Street Mansion. The professor stood at the top of a wide marble staircase that rose gracefully to the ballroom. A red satin ribbon ran diagonally across his chest, as if he were an ambassador. He held a pair of white gloves in his left hand and greeted his customers with the right. "He looks like in the movies," David whispered to his mother as they ascended the stairs.

The ballroom, square and festive, was lined with mirrors, like the Hall of Mirrors, he decided, where the Treaty of Versailles was signed. There was a stage at one end with a grand piano in the center. David examined it carefully and decided it was a great improvement over the one on Pike Street.

The professor had rented the sandwich concession outside the ballroom. Here the relatives, while awaiting their prodigy's turn, could refresh themselves with corned beef on rye and huge mugs of root beer. Lisa would not touch the corned beef—it was not kosher—but she enjoyed the root beer. In the hall there was much coming and going. As each performer finished his stint, his contingent made for the food. The professor encouraged his pupils to play with music, for he knew that as long as they had the notes in front of them they would muddle through somehow. Besides, his role as page turner gave him an excuse for remaining on stage. He stood by the piano, his aristocratic face etched in the glow of the footlights, conducting the music with graceful movements of his hands and hovering over each pupil as though, like Svengali, he were conjuring up the sounds.

When it was David's turn, he walked to the center of the stage, thwacked his arm against his middle and bowed low, to the vociferous applause of his backers. He remembered the evening at Pike Street Mansion, the feeling of standing on top of the world with everyone looking up at him, admiring him, loving him. This was even better because the hall was larger.

At that moment a girl came through the doorway; she wore a brace and walked with a limp like Stella Rabinowitz. David's good humor dissipated. He took her appearance as an unlucky omen. His eyes followed her as she hobbled to a chair. Shaken, he sat down at the piano and attacked the *Poet and Peasant Overture*. The majestic opening chords led into a lyric section that represented the Poet. David kept his mind on the music, forcing the girl out of his mind. Out of the corner of his eye he followed the curve of the professor's hand, meanwhile singing along very softly with the melody. That helped. Pretty soon he had the situation under control.

The music changed abruptly with the entrance of the Peasant. This section was ushered in by a two-measure trill in the bass. David heightened the suspense by extending it to four measures; the Professor beamed at him. Next came the part that everybody knew because it was played in the movies whenever cowboys chased Indians. The waltz section provided a light interlude, after which the chase resumed. Climax followed climax with steadily mounting tension. In the exciting finale David clamped down the pedal until all the sounds swam together in a glorious blur. He finished fortissimo, Cousin Izzy shouted his usual Bravo! and everybody applauded. The professor congratulated him, he bowed again and walked off stage, elated.

At the sandwich counter, his admirers made a big fuss over him. His mother kissed him and said, "I'm so proud of you, Dovid'l," the same words she had used on the occasion of his debut at Pike Street Mansion. His sister embraced him. Cousin Laibel, his eager face thrust forward, also repeated the question he had put on the earlier occasion: "Were you nervous?" David assured him that he wasn't. His father asked him if he would like a corned-beef sandwich. This touched off a debate with his mother as to whether he should eat the nonkosher meat. "What kind of example are you setting him?" she asked, but reluctantly gave in.

Aunt Bessie too repeated herself. "Mark my words," she announced in shrill tones, "he'll play in Carnegie Hall yet." David looked at her and smiled. This was more than prophecy. It was a promise.

4

THE door to the waiting room opened, Morris shuffled in. He wore a light-blue cotton robe over his pajamas and terry-cloth slippers. He looked thinner, bonier than ever; Lisa embraced him and began to cry. "You came back," she exclaimed, "and in one piece. God be praised."

He had been wounded in the Battle of the Argonne. A bullet passed through his shoulder, and infection had set in. The wound had healed, but he hadn't. As he put it, he was nervous. The doctors were giving him sedatives along with a course of exercises to help him regain the use of his arm.

They sat down. Lisa fixed her eyes on him. Like his brother and sister—the three children of her first marriage all resembled their father—Morris had what she called a Kalmuk face. The high cheekbones made the nose and mouth seem slightly flattened. It was a kind, honest face. These two qualities, in her estimation, more than made up for his lack of conventional good looks.

"Tell me . . . what was it like?" She knew it was a foolish question. How could he ever describe to her what he had been through?

Morris smiled wanly. "What do you want to know, Mama?"

"Everything."

He frowned. "It was terrible. What more can I tell you?" He fell silent.

She felt she ought to get him to talk, but did not know how. "Were you afraid?" she finally asked.

"Wouldn't you be afraid if they tied you to railroad tracks and a train was rushing toward you? I was so afraid I couldn't think of anything else." He seemed relieved at being able to reveal his secret at last. "The fear is still here"—he pointed to his chest—"inside me."

The belt of his bathrobe was tied in a bow. He flicked at it nervously until the knot came undone. His gray eyes had a startled look that she had never seen before. "You're all skin and bones," she said. "Do they give you enough to eat?"

"Sure. I don't feel like eating."

"I brought you this." She undid the box of chocolates in her lap. "Take one."

He helped himself to a candy. Lisa put the box on the chair beside her. Another silence flowed between them. Lisa felt a desperate desire to cross over to his side of it. "Did you ever"—she could not bring herself to say *kill*, so she changed it to "shoot someone?"

"How should I know? You shoot into the dark, the noise never stops, you don't know where you are. I had nightmares all the time."

Lisa put her hand over his. "They take a good Jewish boy like you and teach you to be a murderer."

"That's what war is about," Morris said.

"Here there was no war," Lisa said. "People made money. It made me sick to watch."

"It's a matter of luck," Morris continued his thought. "Who dies, who lives."

"All the same it puzzled me. I read what was happening over there, yet here life went on. People went to the movies as if nothing was wrong."

"Mama, you have to understand. When it's day here, it's night over there. If it's day for you, why should you think of all the others for whom it's night?"

"I did think of you," she said defensively, and felt the guilt from which she never wholly freed herself. "All the time."

"I'm glad you did," he said in a flat tone.

She glanced around. "It's so clean here, so unpleasant. How much longer will you have to stay?"

"Until they say I can go."

The Jewish doctor had explained to Lisa that Morris was emotionally disturbed. She saw no sign of this, but knew it was better not to ask for details. "You look fine to me," she lied.

"I'm not yet—" He looked for the right word, and came up with "in one piece."

"What will you do when you get out?"

"I haven't thought about it."

"When you leave here, you'll come home with us. I'll take care of you."

"Thanks, Mama, but I don't like Brooklyn."

Was he saying this, she wondered, to make things easier for her? "We'll decide when the time comes," she replied. Something more had to be said, and it wasn't easy. "I haven't been a good mother to you," she said softly. "Not as good as I should have been. Believe me, I had my hands full."

"I believe you, Mama."

"I did the best I could."

"I know you did."

"It was not enough."

"You tried. What more can a person do?" He stood up. "I'm tired, Mama. I want to go now."

She rose and handed him the box of candy. "Would you like me to come again?"

"Sure. How's David?"

"He's a good boy."

"I brought these for him." Morris drew two five-franc pieces from the pocket of his robe.

Lisa took the coins. "When you were in France I would pass a window that had a little flag with a gold star. I prayed it shouldn't happen to me. God heard my prayer and brought you back alive."

They embraced. "He shouldn't have let them start it in the first place," Morris said.

At her next visit Lisa met Faigel, whose head was a trifle large for her short body. Faigel was a determined young woman in her mid-twenties. Her first exchange with her future mother-in-law left something to be desired. Faigel asked Lisa how she felt. Lisa responded that she was a little tired, whereupon Faigel remarked, "Younger ones than you also feel tired." Lisa did not strike back until later, when she reported the conversation to Joel. Punning upon Faigel's name, which was the Yiddish equivalent of Birdie, she evened the score with "Oy, is she a bird!"

As with all the girls whom Morris had brought home to meet his mother, Lisa felt that Faigel was not good enough for him. For once she soft-pedaled her objection. She sensed that Morris at this point needed a firm hand to guide him, and in Faigel recognized a will as strong as her own. She found some consolation in the fact that the girl was Jewish. "What would we have done if he had picked a *shiksa*?"

"I thought," Joel said with a smile, "you considered all people equal."

"I do, I do. Still, he's better off with his own kind. What he needs right now," she added irrelevantly, "is to forget the war. She'll help him."

"You still think love cures all?"

Her eyes flashed, challenging him. "Doesn't it?"

5

FOR Lisa time was the enemy; the minutes never ceased ticking away. She studied her face in the mirror, taking stock of the telltale lines. Gently she pulled the skin back over her cheekbones, smoothing away the two furrows that ran from her nostrils to the corners of her mouth. Her life was slipping by, and she couldn't hold it back.

This awareness translated itself into a need to taste each experience to the full. She threw herself into each day, trying to extract from it as much as she could; but the high points alternated with the low in a mysterious rhythm that sent her plummeting from joy to despair. When she was on the upswing, she tackled each task with inexhaustible energy. On her way down she surrendered to a lethargy made up of discontents and regrets. Joel compared her emotions to the giant roller coaster in Coney Island. "Either your mother is flying high," he told David, "or she's plunging deep down." How could a reasonable person expect to understand such complexity?

In her moments of depression, Lisa became an angry woman. She resented the inferior position of women. "The world respects the man. Without him the home would fall apart. But the woman cooks, cleans, markets, bakes, sews,

yet no one thinks anything of it." Her eyes flashed with the
old fire.

Joel tried to humor her. "You have your job and I have
mine. Why is one more important than the other?"

She was not to be placated. "At the end of the week they
pay you for your work. No one pays the woman. No one
even thanks her."

"Thanks," Joel said and grinned.

"I'm serious and you make jokes." She turned to David.
"You don't know how lucky you are, my son, to be able to
study with a clear head. I had to work from the time I was
sixteen, I tried to educate myself, I grabbed a little here and
there, but it had no foundation, no outcome."

David looked up from his book. "What would you have
wanted to be?"

"To be educated, to go to the university. In my day, few
women went. It was a man's world then, and it's still a
man's world. I wasted my life on a thousand little things."

Joel looked at her, puzzled. "It's not enough for a woman
to be a wife and mother?"

"For many women, yes. For some, no." She pressed her
hand to her heart. "Here lie so many dreams that'll never
come true."

When her inner tensions had built up beyond the point
of comfort, she found relief in a movie. She had a childlike
capacity to believe what she saw, no matter how improba-
ble the story. She threw herself into the action and, after
an hour and a half of make-believe, returned to reality
refreshed and reconciled. Much as she enjoyed going out
with Joel, he was too critical to make a good movie companion. She preferred David, whose capacity for make-believe
was as great as her own. She would wait for him after school
in Bridge Plaza, seated on a bench in front of Valley Forge.
In her lap was a brown paper bag containing a napoleon
bulging with goo, and an apple. "Eat, my child," she said,
and watched him lick the custard from the flaky layers of
the napoleon. When he had done, she wet a handkerchief

in the water fountain nearby; he wiped his hands and lips, and they were ready for adventure.

She crunched the paper bag into a ball and deposited it at the first trash can. Neatness was as important, in her pantheon of virtues, as punctuality and honesty. She chattered gaily as they walked toward the movie house on Roebling Street. It was dark and cool inside, at that hour of the day almost empty. Lisa preferred to sit toward the back. She was fascinated by historical spectacles that combined entertainment with information about important events such as the burning of Rome or the French Revolution, of which she had only a hazy idea. Her loyalties in this never-never land bore no relation to what she felt in real life. The Czar, for example, represented everything that was terrible in the Russia she had left behind—oppression and antisemitism. But in the movies she became a staunch royalist and wept when Marie Antoinette walked heroically to the guillotine, her powdered head held high, while Mme. Lefarge leered over her knitting needles and the leaders of the revolution, as unsightly a bunch of thugs as ever destroyed a beautiful queen, sat in the gallery feasting and laughing, their faces smeared with chicken fat. The English titles posed no problem. Although she was still reluctant to speak the language, she read it well enough to understand. What she didn't, David explained.

They came out into the twilight. The tower of Williamsburg Bridge was etched black against the April sky; a solitary star hung high above the elevated train on Broadway. It was early evening, when a stillness settled on the city. This was Lisa's favorite hour. The movie had left her in an expansive mood; she stopped and slipped her arm through David's. "Look around you, my son. Remember what you see. Someday you will change, everything will be different between us. This is how I want you to remember me. This street, this moment, the way we were." Her eyes were luminous and her voice was low. "And I want you to remember that your mother loved you very much."

6

SEX crept up on you so gradually you hardly noticed. One day it was there, nagging away at you like a toothache, only more fun. A mysterious force pushing out from the inside of your body, that could not be described in words. David thought of the sensation simply as It, with a capital *I*.

For the last time his mother trotted out the unfortunate grand duke and poor Uncle Adolph. David consoled himself with the thought that, since he didn't know any chambermaids, he faced little danger in that direction. As for the alternative, he promised himself before he went to bed that he would not even allow It to enter his mind. He would concentrate instead on the subterranean garden that he seemed to remember from very long ago. His parents had taken him there when he was little, and he had been wanting to return ever since. It was an enchanted garden where the trees shone with a golden light and soft music filled the air. The memory filled him with contentment.

It spite of himself his thoughts drifted to It. At first he fought It off, then a feeling of peace came over him: he knew he was going to yield. Now that the conflict was over he lay still, savoring the pleasure of anticipation. Nor was he disappointed. There was something astonishing about the violence with which pleasure came pouring out of his body. The violence had a shape, like the finale of the *Peer Gynt Suite*: it began soft and slow exactly as *In the Hall of the Mountain King* did, and worked its way up ever faster and louder to the climax where the cymbals crashed and the drums banged. Then came a wonderful sense of relief, until he remembered the grand duke and shook his head from side to side to see if anything had come loose. His friend Solly Cohen kept a handkerchief handy so as to avoid telltale stains on the sheets. David thought this a fine idea. His mother sometimes looked into the bedroom to make sure he was asleep. Luckily she never caught him at It. Bill Cooperman said he waited until he had a wet dream. David intended to wait too, but somewhere along the way lost patience.

God saw everything. Wasn't it embarrassing for Him to look into millions of bedrooms and watch people playing with themselves or each other? Yet why should He be embarrassed? Hadn't He planted It in His creatures in the first place? Surely He couldn't object if they enjoyed doing what He meant them to do. The Bible did say that He smote Onan dead for scattering his seed. David promised himself never to give in again, and held out for three days; then he fell from grace. God, he felt, should have invented a simpler method for preserving the human race. Perhaps something on the order of the amoebas he learned about in biology, who divided in two whenever they felt like it.

Danny Friedman sat next to him in Spanish class. Danny suffered from sex as other people suffered from measles; it was on his mind all the time. He told jokes that began, "There was a Frenchman, an Englishman, and a Chinaman . . ." The Chinaman always won. In the assembly they sang a marching song to the words, "We come, we come, we come/To the sound of the fife and drum." Danny sang, "We scum, we scum, we scum": the boys around him took up the improvement with delight. One morning Danny arrived with a set of French picture cards that he passed around under the desk while Señora Escobar was explaining the difference between *ser* and *estar*. There was much excitement under the desks. Señora Escobar sensed it, for she spoke louder and faster. Fortunately, she was nearsighted.

David was astonished by what he saw. Luscious women, their legs wide apart, ministered to tall gentlemen in heat. Accustomed to think of sex as a dark secret hidden deep inside him, he was invariably astonished to discover it was something the whole world knew about. As when he looked up words like *vagina* and *penis* in the dictionary and found them printed there for everyone to see. Beneath the visible world was another, hidden and mysterious. If you could look beneath the surface you would see what people were like when they took their clothes off. Then you'd know what they were really like.

The following week Danny arrived with a new batch of pictures. He passed several to David, who examined them breathlessly and slipped one into his back pocket before returning the rest to Danny. Señora Escobar was explaining the conjugation of intransitive verbs. She suddenly realized that another kind of conjugation was going on beneath the desks and pounced upon Danny just as he was passing the cards to the boy on his left. The señora let out a soft *Dio mio!*, put one of her favorites in charge of the class, and hauled Danny off to the principal's office. With the cards.

Dr. Vlyman was a bald, pompous gentleman given to weighty pronouncements such as "Do each day's work each day." He examined the naughty pictures, ordered Danny to leave them on his desk, considered the case for two days, and meted out a punishment to fit the crime: expulsion.

David was aghast. "How can he expel you for a thing like that? I don't believe it."

Danny took the sentence stoically. "Whatja expect from that scumbag? I bet he's peeping at the pictures right now."

"But it'll change your whole life," David said.

"No it won't. I don' have to go to school. I'll go to work. It's what I shoulda done in the first place."

"To take away your education! It's unfair." Indignation swept through David, directed against the whole structure of law and order that Dr. Vlyman represented.

"He can shove it up his ass," Danny said. "I had all I need, b'lieve me. Don' worry, I'll make my way."

There was a silence. Then David confessed. "I kept one of the cards. You want it back?"

"Keep it," Danny said, and grinned. "Somethin' to remember me by."

In the next weeks the empty desk next to David seemed like a warning to him what "they"—meaning Dr. Vlyman and his ilk—could do to you if they felt like it. He realized that if the señora had swung into action ten seconds sooner he would have been caught with the cards instead of Danny. What would his parents have said if he were thrown out of school? He shuddered.

The postcard he had slipped into his pocket remained a treasured memento. David exhibited it to his friends in the basement of Hymie Gershon's house. The card stimulated Hymie to propose a contest. Which of them could make himself come the fastest. The winner would receive a prize of one dollar, to be contributed by the five who lost.

Bill had an important objection. "How will I know you came?"

Hymie brushed it aside. "Dope, you smell my hand."

The contest proceeded smoothly until it was David's turn; he went into the bathroom with the precious card. Although he had been in the cubicle repeatedly, he seemed to be seeing it for the first time. The tiles on the floor were discolored, the plaster on the wall was cracked. This was clearly the basement bathroom that was hardly ever used. He lowered the toilet seat and sat down. In the middle of the day, with his friends waiting outside, he was supposed to feel like It? What a crazy notion. After a few half-hearted attempts he came out. "I lose, I couldn't even get it up."

"You conk out?" Carl asked in surprise.

"Look," David remonstrated. "I got to be comfortable. I'm not an animal."

"That's what you think," Carl said. "We're all animals. The only thing sets us apart is that we have a brain."

"Well, it's the brain that counts," David said. It seemed to him that he had won the argument, even though no one else thought so.

Solly won the contest by twelve seconds. His friends forked over twenty-five cents apiece for his prize. Solly enjoyed his victory so much that he paid for the hot chocolates that night. It was past ten when they left the ice cream parlor on Lee Avenue. Two girls went by; Bill seized the opportunity. "I like the one in the middle," he said appraisingly, sending his comrades into the usual explosion of laughter. On this note the boys parted; David and Abe walked off toward Rodney Street.

A change came over them when they were alone. It was as if they entered a world of their own from which the horseplay of their friends was excluded. David was suddenly aware of the bond that united them. He wondered if Abe was thinking of this too, but was reluctant to ask. It was Abe who took the initiative. They were standing in front of the oak tree on the corner. He peered up at the sky through his thick glasses. "That might be Castor and Pollux," he said, pointing.

David looked up. The stars glimmered faintly over Brooklyn. "Who are they?" he asked.

"Two Greek heroes. They were twin brothers, and they wanted never to be separated. When they died their father Zeus changed them into two stars, so they'd always be together." He turned toward David, his voice suddenly soft and fuzzy. "That's how I feel about us, Davey. You and me—it's special. I hope it never ends."

"Why should it?"

"I don't know. Could happen."

"I won't let it."

"You promise?"

"I promise."

Abe put his hands on David's shoulders and leaned forward until their cheeks touched. He held him close for a moment, then let go.

David studied Abe's face—the dark myopic eyes, the flat nose, the dark fuzz over Abe's upper lip. He loved Abe more than anyone he had ever known. Beyond him he loved the whole world, the sky, the stars, the houses, the oak tree. It seemed to him that if Abe were ever in danger he would do all he could to save him. Even if—the thought brought a lump to his throat—he had to die for him.

"Now," Abe said, "you know how I feel about you."

"I feel the same about you," David replied, and in a burst of politeness added, "Only more."

As he lay falling asleep that night he tried to hold on to the glow that Abe had left with him. His thoughts turned to the subterranean garden. Suddenly the naked women who had eluded him during the contest in Hymie's basement came crowding into his mind. He wanted desperately to return to the enchanted garden with its golden light and mysterious music, but its time was over. He had left the garden far behind, and there was no returning.

7

SATURDAYS Lisa spent with her mother. No matter how inclement the weather, she rode out to the Pride of Judaea Home on Dumont Avenue. During the trip on the Nostrand Avenue trolley, which took almost an hour, she punished herself: she should never have allowed Joel to persuade her to put her mother in the Home. By the time she reached her destination she was overwhelmed with remorse. The jar of cookies she had baked for Hannah seemed a totally inadequate expiation.

They sat in the visitors' room, or, when it was pleasant outside, in the garden. Lisa read to her mother from the Jewish newspaper. Then she spoke to the nurse who took care of Hannah and slipped her a dollar. The Home was depressing, she realized, because it lacked love; Lisa tried to leave enough with Hannah to last her for the rest of the week. She came home drained. "We don't die suddenly," she told Joel, "but a little at a time. First we don't hear so well, then we don't see so well, or move around so quickly. When the day finally comes, we're ready."

She had only two weapons against the Angel of Death: love and chicken soup. In any case, time was on his side. The old lady was bedridden; Lisa no longer read to her as it confused her. She sat by the bed, holding Hannah's hand in her own as if she would prolong her mother's life by sheer force of will. When the five o'clock bell rang, Lisa bent over the pillow and kissed the wrinkled brown face. She was swept by emotion. "Mama, forgive me."

"What is there to forgive?" Hannah's face was serene and loving.

Lisa fought back her tears. "God willing," she said, "we'll see each other next Saturday," and wondered if she would.

Hannah died in her sleep on a Friday evening. Lisa wept all night. "Only one day more," she said over and over, "and I would have been with her." She could not rid herself of the notion that if only she had been at Hannah's bedside, she'd have driven the *Moloch hamovess* away.

Joel had no patience with such irrational thinking. "Her time was up," he said. "What difference would it have made if you were there or not?"

"At least I would have shut her eyes. She would not have died among strangers."

"Do you know how it is among primitive tribes? The older people fall behind and lie down to die, the younger ones keep going without even looking back."

"Don't bother me with your primitive tribes." Lisa wiped her eyes. "It's a strange thing. As long as your mother is still alive, no matter how old you are, you're still a child. Once she dies, you're finally grown-up, you're alone in the world."

The funeral took place on a cold rainy Sunday. Joel, Lisa, and her children rode in one car, Uncle Mischa with Aunt Bessie and Cousin Arthur in another. They gathered round the open grave. An old Jew attached to the cemetery recited the prayer for the dead; David noticed that he mispronounced several of the Hebrew words. The coffin was lowered, and Uncle Mischa threw upon it the first shovelful of earth. Huddling under their umbrellas, they returned to the automobiles that took them to Williamsburg.

From then on, everything went downhill. No one remembered how Lisa's final quarrel with Tante Bessie developed. They were sitting around the table in the dining room, eating herring and potatoes; Annie went to the kitchen to bring the next course—pot cheese and sour cream. Aunt Bessie, with a thick slice of pumpernickel in her hand, turned to Lisa. "It was not up to me to keep her," she said in her high-pitched voice. "After all, you were her daughter."

"You're forgetting," Lisa said defensively, "I kept her with me for three years."

"Not for nothing," Tante Bessie goaded Lisa. "I know she had some money when she came here. Mischa didn't get any of it, that's for sure."

For an instant Lisa was torn between the courtesy due a guest and her rage. Rage won. She threw down her fork. "How dare you speak to me like that!"

"It's the truth. I believe in calling things by their right name." Bessie turned to Joel for confirmation. "Am I right?"

This was the last straw. Lisa jumped up, eyes ablaze. She faced Uncle Mischa. "Do you allow her to talk to me like this on the day of our mother's funeral?" Back to Bessie, "This is my house and I want you out of here. You're a mean, vulgar woman, and I never want to see you again. Never!" She strode to the bedroom and slammed the door.

The red flush that spread over Tante Bessie's round face heralded an asthma attack. She coughed, sputtered, heaved, and gasped. Uncle Mischa held her hand, Cousin Arthur fished a pill out of her bag, Joel pushed a cold compress against her forehead. Finally she came to.

Uncle Mischa fetched his wife's coat; the good-byes were subdued. Presently Lisa opened the bedroom door. "They're gone," Joel said.

"And good riddance. For years I put up with that woman. For Mischa's sake. Today I reached the end." She returned to the table, but not before referring the dispute to the Supreme Arbiter. "May God not punish her," she said significantly, and sat down before what was left of the herring.

The meal over, she took down the family album. She

cranked the miniature brass key in the green plush cover and listened to the first eight bars of the *Blue Danube Waltz*. Then she opened to Hannah's picture. It showed her mother in the black bonnet and dress she had worn when she came to America. Lisa studied the photograph. "I was not worthy of her," she said. "And I will never forgive myself for it."

8

STELLA Rabinowitz turned up in David's history class. He was not particularly pleased, but tried to be friendly. One day she waited for him after the orchestra rehearsal. "Where you going?"

"Nowhere."

"Why dontcha walk me home."

Not knowing how to extricate himself, he agreed.

They walked along Harrison Avenue, her body jerking to the right each time she put down her withered leg. He carried her books. "You don' like me no more," she whined. "You never come to see me."

"I been busy."

"Yeah. But if you really wanted to . . ."

There was no gainsaying her logic. He said nothing.

They crossed Broadway and reached the streets he knew so well. He seemed to be seeing them from a new vantage point; they were narrower and less attractive than he remembered them. Only the people hadn't changed.

They turned the corner. There was the old house, brown and friendly, and the candy store next to it with the bench in front. They stopped in front of the little stoop. She turned to him. "Le's go down to the cellar, like we used to." Her voice was suddenly tense, both commanding and pleading.

He could not bear to turn her down. "People will see us," he temporized.

"No they won'. We'll go through the back yard." She hobbled up the stoop and into the hallway.

What if he walked away? She couldn't force him. Yet in a strange way she *was* forcing him. He glanced around to make sure no one was looking, and followed her into the dark corridor.

He came out in the back yard. The little garden looked exactly as he remembered it; already the morning glories were out. He went down into the cellar and joined her in the space behind the storeroom. What if someone came by and caught them? He half wished they would.

He lay down beside her. She put her hand against his midriff. "I don' think you want me," she whispered.

"Sure I do," he lied. He tried to respond by passing his hand along her thigh down to her leg, and remembered the iron brace awaiting him. Her hand was still against his middle. He could sense it getting ready to descend; this was one test he knew he would fail. He shut his eyes and tried to summon up the seductive image of the naked lady on Danny Friedman's picture card. He turned Stella on her back, and, simulating desire, tried to get by with what his friend Solly called a dry fuck. To no avail. The naked lady vanished and left him pushing and shoving in vain, as far away from desire as he had been during the contest in Hymie's basement.

"I toldja y'didn't want me," Stella said finally, her face taut with reproach.

"I got other things on my mind. Besides, I'm not comfortable here. Anyway," he added, forgetting that three reasons are weaker than one, "what if someone caught us."

She sat up, smoothed down her dress and patted her hair. "You're a funny boy." Her expressionless tone made it sound like an accusation.

"Dogs can do it anywhere," he retorted, "but people can't." This was the best defense he could muster.

She was not yet ready to release him. "Come upstairs and say hello to my mother."

"Okay." He got up, helped her to her feet, and gathered their books. They went through the back yard to the hallway and up the stairs. Mrs. Rabinowitz greeted him warmly. "How you like it over there?"

"I liked it here," he said diplomatically, "and I like it there."

Mrs. Rabinowitz buttered a thick slice of rye bread and covered it with pot cheese. "Eat something," she said and held out the bread.

He took it. She let out a sigh. "Where you live is near the school, and my poor little one has to walk so far. It tears my heart." She poured him a glass of milk. "How much you pay there?"

"Twenty-three dollars a month."

"Oy, if I could only afford to get out of this tenement." She shook her head. "If my poor Jake were alive." Her curiosity about Lisa's marital situation got the better of her. "Your brothers live there with you?"

"No, it's not big enough. They live in Manhattan."

"How come?"

"They work there. Besides, my big brother's getting married." David decided to head off further questioning. "I'd like to see the roof again."

"Why not? If only my Stellenyu could climb the ladder." She wiped her eyes. "It was her luck . . ."

"Don' talk like that, Mama," Stella said sternly.

David climbed up to the roof. The tower of Williamsburg Bridge floated in a lavender haze as it always had; the spire of the church on Union Avenue cut the sky. Four bells struck the hour. He sat down on the chimney pot that had served as his throne and reflected on his situation. It was wrong of him to take Stella to the cellar just because he felt sorry for her. It was wrong to do anything for anybody just because you didn't know how to get out of it.

The shadows lengthened and the sky grew pale. David drew a deep breath. He was glad he would never see the cellar again.

TWO

1

THE time had come to try Rockaway Beach. Joel considered this a step up from Coney Island. "No more eating on the beach like gypsies, sandwiches mixed with sand, and fighting to get on the street car. We'll live like people." When warm weather arrived Lisa and he went off to Rockaway and rented two rooms in the Ocean View House, an establishment in which each family occupied its own sleeping quarters but cooked in a communal kitchen. You brought your own bedding and dishes. The season began when school closed at the end of June. Lisa packed two pails full of cups and saucers, Annie carried mop and broom, David took charge of towels and sheets, and Joel lugged the pillows. No one who saw the caravan could doubt that they were going to spend the summer by the sea.

The Ocean View House turned out to be a squat two-story structure that was not accurately named; the only view it commanded was of the grocery store on Rockaway Beach Boulevard. But it was only a block from the water, which was all that mattered. On your way to the beach you passed a row of summer cottages surrounded by bright green, neatly clipped hedges that had a holiday look. As Joel put it, on this street every day was Sunday.

The communal kitchen led into a huge dining room where each family had its own table. This proximity with her neighbors—she still thought of them as peasants—was hardly to Lisa's taste. However, since most of the day was spent at the beach, she put up with them. She avenged herself by mimicking their peculiarities while Joel, David, and Annie howled with laughter. Mrs. Flamm, for example, was too lazy to cook and fed her husband sausages night after night. Lisa worked up a comedy routine in which Mrs. Flamm took the sausages out of their package and threw them into a pot of boiling water; the climax came when Mr. Flamm thrust his fork into a sausage and found it too tough to eat.

Because of the incessant din in the dining-room area, no one minded or even heard when David practiced on the old upright piano in the corner. He began every morning with the major and minor scales, followed by all the exercises in the first book of Hanon. The second hour was devoted to what was unquestionably Professor Capaccio's most important contribution to his musical growth—the *Red Circle Book of Overtures*. From *Poet and Peasant*, David broadened his repertory to include *Light Cavalry, Morning Noon and Night in Vienna*, and *The Caliph of Bagdad*. He performed the cavalry attack in von Suppé's overture at a great clip, holding down the pedal until the chords in the bass sounded like the booming of cannon.

David discovered that he loved the sea, its smell, its sound, its changing colors and moods. Its smooth blue surface under a cloudless sky, with a thousand sunbeams dancing upon it. Or the waves breaking with a roar on a cloudy day, gray-green and trimmed with foamy white. The jetties on their rickety stilts encased in thick green moss, with the water sliding in underneath. The shock of cold as he waded in, and the wonderful feeling of weighing nothing as he coasted in with the waves. Best of all he enjoyed swimming out beyond the ropes where it was quiet, slashing his way through the water or floating on his back and looking up at the sky. He became part of the sea, there was no telling where he ended and the sea began.

He was part of a group that met on the beach every afternoon. They played games or went exploring; there was much to explore. To one side lay Far Rockaway, to the other Rockaway Park. Between stretched an expanse of sand whiter and more powdery than any they would ever find again. The group revolved around Henny Jershow, who wore her blonde curls tied with a light-blue ribbon. Her dimples showed when she laughed, which was most of the time. Henny had a way of making each boy she smiled at feel that he was the one. It became overwhelmingly important for David to find himself in her company; even more important, to conceal his eagerness from her. She lived in a cottage down the street, and would be sitting on the porch as he made his way to the beach.

She looked up from the magazine in her lap—she was an avid reader of *Film Confessions*—and smiled. "Hi."

"What you doing?" he inquired in his most casual manner.

"Nothing much. Silly story about Gloria Swanson."

"Why don't you come to the beach?" He asked this as if the thought had just occurred to him.

She shook her head. "I've a lot of things to do."

She was giving him the business, but he was helpless against her wiles. "Aw, c'mon," he pleaded.

She thought a moment. "Okay. I'll meet you there."

His position in regard to Henny was the direct opposite of what it had been with Stella Rabinowitz. Here he was the eager one while she sat back relaxed. Was it always like this, he wondered, when two people met: a kind of hidden struggle as to who would have the upper hand? For the first time he realized how much courage it had taken Stella to ask him to come down to the cellar with her. Now it was his turn to do the asking, to grow tense inside as he waited for Henny's answer, fearing a "No" and hoping for a "Maybe."

In his nightly fantasies about her he lingered boldly on each feature: her golden hair, her laughing blue eyes, her dimples. The way her shoulders sloped down from her neck. The way her little round breasts promised at any moment to pop out of her bathing suit. Her sunburnt legs. Her thin ankles. But when all these came together in the living girl his boldness left him. He waited to be alone with her, yet when it finally happened he couldn't think of a thing to say. He would try to tell her a joke and forgot the punch line. He would begin a sentence and break off in the middle. And the more embarrassed he, the more relaxed was she.

Teaching Henny to swim was a major sport on Beach Seventy-fifth Street. David eagerly awaited his turn. She floated on his outstretched arms as he reminded her to kick and breathe, his eyes meanwhile wandering inside her suit. His left hand, supporting her pelvis, timidly strayed a little lower, his right, under her midriff, probed a little higher. The resultant excitement caused a stiffening between his legs. Fortunately the water covered this disturbance. Henny pretended to have only one thing on her mind: how to master the crawl. "Lift your arm over your head," he told her, "and don't splash when you strike the water. Just pull. Like this."

"Ooh, I'm getting it," she gurgled, and smiled up at him. The water made her eyelashes stick together like the lashes of a kewpie doll. Her smile slowly spread across her face and crinkled the corners of her eyes. He loved to watch it, feeling hopelessly in her power.

He wanted to impress Henny, but how? The boys on the beach were taller, more athletic than he. He studied his face in the mirror. It was a nice enough face, what with his mother's dark eyes and his father's straight nose and full lips; but it didn't add up to much. His rivals, he felt, were better-looking. The only thing special about him was his piano playing. It was his one weapon, and he used it whenever he could. There was a square grand in the ballroom of the Seacrest Inn, where his new friends gathered after supper. He went through his repertoire for Henny, who listened carefully while the others told jokes on the huge verandah overlooking the ocean. She liked *Poet and Peasant Overture* and the exciting section in *Light Cavalry*. She also liked *Dardanella*, with its rumbling bass, and *The Sheik of Araby*, both of which he played with bravado.

Before the Jews took it over, the Seacrest Inn had been an elegant hotel. Now it was on the seedy side, although not without traces of its former splendor. On weekends a jazz combo played in the ballroom: piano, violin, saxophone, and drums. Henny distributed her dances evenly among her admirers; David was lucky if he had two. She taught him all kinds of intricate steps, the main purpose of which, as far as he could see, was to keep his body from touching hers. Dancing with her was like chasing a shadow: wonderful yet maddening.

He walked Henny home as a full moon trailed its golden light across the waves. They stopped before the neatly trimmed hedge that surrounded the cottage where she lived. She had been talkative, but now that it was time to part, an awkward silence fell between them. "Well?" Her lips curved into a challenge.

He screwed up his courage. "There's something I been meaning to ask you."

"So ask."

"Do you like me?" He bent forward, as if his life depended on her answer.

"What kind of a question is that? Of course I like you. Would I spend time with you if I didn't?"

"I mean—" He stopped short, and forced himself to go on. "Do you like me more than the others?"

She pouted. "I'd have to know how much I like the others. Besides," she led him on, "who are they?"

"You know who I mean." He cursed himself for being so timid with her. "Am I someone special?"

"I'll have to think about that."

Her coquetry emboldened him. "D'you like me enough to kiss me good night?"

"Sure." She leaned forward and pecked him on the cheek.

"I didn't mean like that." Suddenly he was brave. He put his arms around her, pulled her to him, and planted his lips on hers.

She allowed them to stay there for an instant. Then she pulled away and gave him a little push. "Fresh, aren't you," she said and laughed.

He let her go, hurt. "So you don't really care for me."

She put her hand on his shoulder. "Of course I do. A little."

"So kiss me good night."

"All right." She pressed her lips against his and lingered.

"Now I feel better," David said. It occurred to him that they were like two figures on a dance floor. When she drew back he followed forward; when he retreated, she advanced.

Henny ran up the steps to the porch and turned. "You're different from the other boys, Davey. But you're nice." She waved to him and went inside.

David smiled. She was what his friend Solly Cohen would call a cockteaser. She really was.

2

"LET's sit where it's quiet," Lisa said as she led David to a secluded part of the beach. "I've something to tell you."

They settled themselves near the jetty. She ran her hand through the sand. "I don't know how to begin, but it's time I told you something about my life."

"Like what?"

She played with the sand a little longer. Then, "I was married to someone else before I married your father," she said quietly.

David stared at her, uncomprehending. "What's that?" he blurted out.

She raised her eyes to his. "You heard me."

"Wow! You mean—?" His voice expressed disbelief. "Why didn't you tell me?"

"I am telling you."

"Why didn't you tell me before?"

She patted the sand into a little mound. "There were reasons. You were too young to understand such things. And I wanted us to be one family, not two. Besides," she added defensively, "parents don't have to tell their children everything."

"Yes they do." He was suddenly belligerent. How could she have done such a thing? And how could she possibly defend it? He struck back. "Especially if they go around saying how important it is to tell the truth."

"Stop making me feel I did something terrible. I didn't lie to you. I just didn't tell you the whole truth."

"It's the same thing." Someone had left a toy shovel on the beach. He grabbed the wooden handle and jabbed the blade into the sand. A host of details about his family that had always puzzled him began to fall into place. "Who was he?" he demanded.

"He was a kind, gentle man. I was very young when I married him."

"Did you love him?"

"Of course." She thought awhile. "Not the way I love your father." A faint smile crossed her lips. "There are different ways of loving."

David struggled to contain his anger. It was a violent anger that poured through him swiftly and made his head ache. They had been such good friends, his mother and he; suddenly they were strangers. "What happened to him?" he asked.

"He died. Then your father and I fell in love."

He hated to think of her in the arms of a man he didn't even know about. "Is his picture in the album?"

"Of course."

"Which one?"

"Baruch. On the same page as your grandfather."

"Oh, the one you called Uncle Baruch," he said, giving the *Uncle* a sarcastic ring. Her duplicity aroused a fresh wave of resentment. "How did you manage to hide this from me?"

"It wasn't easy, but I managed." Her lips pressed together in that firm line he knew so well.

"That's why you talked so much Russian when I was there."

"Not only. Parents have lots of secrets from their children . . . just as children have from their parents. Surely you know that."

"How many years were you married to him?"

She was suddenly coquettish. "That's a question you must never ask a woman."

He seemed to be seeing her in a new light. Strangely, everything around him—the beach, the sky, the water—looked different. "How would you feel," he threw at her, "if it turned out there was a whole part of my life you knew nothing about?"

"I would realize you must have had a reason for keeping it from me, and I'd understand."

He was not to be won over that easily. "Still, you should have told me."

She leaned forward. "Dovid'l, you're not angry with me, are you?"

He thought. "Angry's not the word," he said slowly. "Maybe I'm . . . disappointed."

"Well, you shouldn't be." Suddenly she was firm.

A thought occurred to him. "So that's what Mrs. Rabinowitz was after," he said. "And that's why you were so mad at her."

"Poor woman. God punished her."

His resentment was giving way to a dull uneasiness. How much more was there that she hadn't told him about?

"Didn't you suspect anything?" she said.

He shrugged. "Kids believe anything you tell them. Especially the kind of kid I was. Half the time I couldn't tell the difference between what was real and what was make-believe." He reflected. "Maybe I noticed a few things without even knowing I did. Besides, Morris and Willie were away a lot and you explained why. Then the war came and Morris left."

"I wanted you to think of them as your real brothers. I thought you would feel closer to them that way." She hesitated. "Do you?"

He sensed how much she wanted him to say yes. "Sure. But don't forget, when I was ten they were almost twenty. That's a big difference."

She sighed. "I suppose so. And Annie?"

"That's different. She was home all the time. Besides, she kept taking me to the Yiddish theater."

Lisa smiled. "When I met your father," she said, "I was already a wife and mother. He taught me what it meant to be a woman. It was like being awakened from a deep sleep."

The shadows fell slantwise across the beach, taking on a bluish tinge. She bent forward. "It wasn't easy for me to tell you this."

His anger had receded; he decided to make things easier for her. "Look, Ma, it's all right. If you'd have told me years ago, I wouldn't have known what you were talking about."

She put her hand on his arm. "I knew you'd understand." She glanced up. The sun had moved westward and threw a path of gold across the waves. "It's time for supper," she said. She kissed him, got up, and brushed the sand from her bathing suit.

David watched her go up the stairs. He loved her very much, yet how could he ever trust her again? Out of the dark corners of his mind floated up the sense of betrayal that had haunted his childhood. No matter how much she said she loved him, she really loved another. Now, it turned out, there had even been someone else.

At last he understood why he was the child of her love. That was why she expected so much of him. He wished she'd stop telling him this. What if he disappointed her?

3

THE weekend brought company. Morris and Willie needed a breath of sea air after a week in Uncle Mischa's junk shop; Faigel came with them, along with Cousin Laibel. He still sang Italian arias to his own texts, but he had aged; the demand for his services as an entertainer had fallen off. David saw him weaving along Rockaway Beach Boulevard one night. "I think Laibel was drunk," he commented to his parents.

"Jews don't drink," Lisa countered sternly, in the tone she reserved for matters that admitted of no argument.

Abe came out the last weekend in July. He had spent a month in a hotel in the Catskills working as a bellhop. David had written him about Henny, and had told Henny about his best friend. He could not wait for them to meet.

Things went wrong from the start. Confronted with Henny and her satellites, Abe fell into a moody silence from which nothing could rouse him. As for Henny, who was prepared to make another conquest, she quickly decided he was not worth the effort. To make matters worse, Abe neither swam nor wished to learn. He had not brought a bathing suit, the one he borrowed from David hung loosely on him, and he sat alone on the beach while the others frolicked in the water.

An uncomfortable silence fell between David and his guest as they walked toward the Ocean View House. Finally David said, "You weren't very nice to my friends."

"Am I supposed to be?" Abe growled. "I don't know them and they don't know me."

"Big deal. So you get to know them."

Abe stopped. "Look, Davey, I came out to be with you. Instead you drag me along to meet a whole new crew. I've nothing in common with them, I don't even know what to say to them. I should be the one who's angry, not you."

"I'm not angry. I just wanted you to like my new friends."

"They're not friends, they're just summer acquaintances. You'll see, the day after Labor Day you'll forget all about them."

"I won't forget Henny."

Abe did not answer. Instead he slipped his fingers through David's; they resumed walking. "Did you miss me?" he asked.

"What kind of a question is that?" David replied, and realized that he was answering Abe exactly as Henny had answered him the night before. "Of course I did."

"But not as much," Abe said slowly, "as I missed you."

"Do we have to measure," David smiled, suddenly realizing his power over his friend.

"No, let's not," Abe said, "because if we did I'd come out ahead."

David had looked forward to the Saturday night dance at the Seacrest Inn, but decided to forgo it for Abe's sake. "I'll show you the boardwalk after supper," he said. It annoyed him to make the sacrifice, especially since he decided not to tell Abe he was making it.

The conversation was animated at supper, although not without its problems. Lisa and Joel spoke Yiddish to Abe, with a few English words thrown in. He replied in English, with David acting as go-between. Abe told them about the Catskills. Lisa listened carefully but was not tempted. "I'm sure the mountains are beautiful," she said, "but I love the water. Nothing in the world is as beautiful as the sea."

The sun had set by the time the two boys reached the boardwalk. A sliver of pale moon hung in the aquamarine sky. The waves broke near shore, dappling the twilight with their white crests. Abe spoke in his deep fuzzy voice, telling David of the books he had read while he was in the country.

"Heathcliff is some character. He's like Cain in the Bible—his hand is against everyone. You know he's doomed from the first time you meet him." Abe thought a moment. "Imagine, a girl living far away on the moors creating a character like that. It's hard to believe."

They sat on a bench facing the water. As he listened to Abe's voice, David surrendered to a drowsy contentment. Always, when they were together, Abe led the way into a world of their own. David no longer regretted that he was not dancing with Henny. The Inn seemed strangely remote and unreal. Real was the sound of Abe's voice, the dark beauty of *Wuthering Heights*, the loneliness of Heathcliff, the genius of Emily Brontë. He admired Abe's intellect, his love of literature, his capacity for abstract thought. When he was with Abe he seemed to breathe a purer air, he caught a glimpse of the realm of ideas—the only realm, according to Abe, that really mattered. Henny and her friends might not see anything special about Abe, but what did they know?

It was almost eleven when they came home. Lisa gave them each a glass of milk and an apple, and they went to David's room. He was in a confiding mood. "There was a dance tonight at the Inn. I knew you wouldn't want to go."

"You were right," Abe said. He laid his glasses on the rickety sideboard near the bed, took off his clothes, and lay down. "Are you sorry you didn't?"

David lay down beside him. "I had a much better time with you."

"You sure?"

"Sure."

A pale light filtered in from the street lamp outside their window. The noises on Rockaway Beach Boulevard flowed together in a steady hum. Abe slipped his fingers through David's. His eyes glowed in the half darkness and his voice was husky with emotion. "I love you, Davey," he said, moving his head sideward on the pillow until their cheeks touched. "Even as David loved Jonathan."

David felt himself enveloped in a tenderness that would always protect him from sorrow and loneliness. An image floated out of the dark, of Henny's golden curls with the light-blue ribbon tied in a bow, and the smile that spread slowly from her lips to the corners of her eyes. He brushed the vision out of his mind. "It's nice," he said, "just the two of us. I wish it would always be like this." Suddenly he grinned. "Gosh, I sound like my mother."

They fell asleep with their arms around each other.

4

THE beach had a holiday look on Sunday morning. David decided to sidestep another confrontation between Abe and his summer friends by taking him on the trek to Rockaway Park. Abe was too introspective to make a good sightseer; his gaze was fixed within rather than on his surroundings. Yet even he worked up some excitement as they made their way from one beach to the next, outwitting the obstacles—jetties, piers, breakwaters—that stood in their way.

They didn't turn back until late afternoon. In a deserted area between two bathhouses they came upon the kind of dinghy lifeguards used to patrol the beach. It consisted of a flimsy seat supported by two pontoons.

David stepped on one and lifted an oar. "How about taking it out?"

"Think we could?"

David looked around. "There's no one to stop us. Anyway, you don't like swimming, and you do like rowing."

The sea was a calm expanse of blue except where it caught the shimmer of the sun. They pushed the boat across the sand and into the water where it floated lightly, bobbing up and down. The boys rowed until well beyond where the waves broke, and let themselves drift with the tide.

"This is fun!" David said. Bending over, he scooped up

some water to cool his face. The sea, he thought, was like a friendly bosom. He decided not to repeat the image to Abe. Abe, after all, was the literary one.

Abe was holding forth on his latest discovery, *Vanity Fair*. As he spoke, there rose before David the perfumed world of Becky Sharp and Lord Steyn. "Imagine," Abe said, "you turn the page and read, 'And George Osborne lay on the field of Waterloo with a bullet in his heart.' " He thought awhile. "One morning Thackeray ran out of his room with tears rolling down his face and cried, 'I just killed Rawdon Crawley.' It was that real to him. Like in a movie, you know the guy you're watching is not starving. Comes the end of the day he'll take off his greasepaint and go home to his Beverly Hills mansion with three swimming pools. All the same, you believe he's starving and feel sorry for him. That's the magic of story telling. You believe!"

David listened, spellbound. He did not notice that a light breeze had sprung up which sent the dinghy skidding across the water. Nor did he see the gray-black cloud that moved into the sky like a probing finger. Suddenly the scene changed. The sun disappeared, the sea was gray-green instead of blue, the wind gathered momentum. "It's going to rain," David said. "How'd we get so far out? We better step on it."

The boys began to row as hard as they could. But the dinghy was too light to make headway against the waves. In spite of the wind, David felt drops of sweat coming out on his forehead. He glanced sidewise at Abe, who bent forward with the oar and pulled. "You're doing fine," he called and glanced around, hoping to catch sight of one of the motor boats that usually patrolled the beach. None was in sight.

The clouds were now a grayish black, and the wind came in sharp gusts that churned the water. David felt the spray on his back. He was panting as he pulled the oar. The ocean had suddenly become a powerful enemy against whom he felt helpless; he realized that he must not reveal his fear to

Abe. "Keep it up, we're doing great," he cried. Abe turned to him, and David saw the terror in his eyes.

The dinghy kept sliding down the back of one wave, only to be caught up on the crest of the next. It reached the top of a huge wave, rode down at a crazy angle and capsized, throwing both boys into the water. David remembered that Abe couldn't swim, grabbed the shoulder strap of his bathing suit with one hand and, seizing the narrow beam between the two pontoons, pulled him toward it. "Hold on here!" he cried, and saw that Abe's glasses were gone. He pushed Abe's hand to the beam.

They bobbed up and down with the dinghy. It was dark now. A flash of lightning streaked the sky, followed by thunder and a downpour. "Hold on!" David screamed. At that moment the dinghy soared high up and flew out of Abe's grasp.

David let go the beam and dived after his friend. He grabbed the top of his bathing suit and with his other hand kept flailing the water, pulling Abe after him. His mind was clear, he was thinking fast, he knew what he had to do. At the same time he had an eerie feeling that all this was happening to someone else, someone he had read about or seen long ago in a movie. He struck at the water with his free arm, dragging Abe after him and kicking hard to stay afloat. Suddenly the dinghy came down on top of him. One of the pontoons struck his head. A dozen stars exploded before his eyes and sent a terrible pain stabbing through his brain. When it subsided, he realized that his hand no longer held Abe's bathing suit. He had lost Abe forever. A wall of water crashed over him. Then a black abyss opened up before him and he went sliding down to the bottom of it.

He awoke and found himself lying on a blanket. He felt drowsy. Two men were looking down at him. He remembered. "Abe! Where's my friend?"

"Take it easy," one of the men said. "Coast Guard" was printed across his shirt in large black letters. "You're a lucky kid," the man said. "If we hadn't come along you'da been dead."

David turned on his side. Abe lay a few paces away, face down. A life guard straddled the small of his back and was massaging his ribs. David rolled over on his stomach and buried his face in the blanket, afraid to look. He was the one who had suggested that they take out the boat. If Abe died, he would be the one who had killed him. Even as Cain killed his brother Abel. For the rest of his life he would bear the mark of Cain on his forehead, he would never be able to wipe it away. *Please, God, don't let him die.* His vision blurred, he beat his clenched fists up and down against the blanket. *Please, God . . .*

"Okay, he's breathing," the life guard said.

A bell tore through the air. It clanged closer and closer, making a joyous sound. Abe was alive! David looked up and saw the ambulance. Two orderlies dressed in white came down the steps to the beach. They lifted Abe and laid him on a stretcher. Tears streamed down David's face, he was laughing and crying at the same time. He wanted to tell the orderlies why he was so happy but couldn't shape the words. He lay back and let himself be carried from the beach, while the word sang in his brain: Alive!

5

"WOE is me!" Lisa bent over the bed, clasping her hands against her breast. "When I think what could have happened." Her joy turned to anger. "How many times have I told you not to swim beyond the ropes?"

Joel threw up his hands in his habitual gesture of puzzlement. "I don't understand you. Instead of being happy that they were saved, you're angry."

"Of course I'm angry. What the boy needs in discipline"—*dis-tzi-plin*, with a hiss—"and you tell him everything he does is right. This is the result." Her left hand indicated the bed.

"There were no ropes," David said. He felt better now that his parents were there, but his head was still spinning.

Lisa turned to the other bed, where Abe lay, and smoothed his hair back from his forehead. "Can you imagine . . . your parents entrust you to me for three days, and I'd have had to tell them—" She stopped short. "I wouldn't have lived through it. God was with us." She sat down on David's bed and sighed. "Small children press the knee, big ones press the heart." She took out her handkerchief, wiped her eyes, and grew stern. "If you ever again swim out that far, we'll pack our bags and go right back to the city. Just remember this, my son."

David was about to answer, but thought better of it. "Where are we?" he asked.

"Rockaway Beach Hospital."

"I want to go home."

"The doctor said tomorrow."

At that moment the door opened and Henny stood in the doorway. David's heart leaped. She looked around, caught sight of his parents, and walked past the row of empty beds toward his. The light-blue silk bow floated jauntily above her golden curls, and the slow smile crinkled the corners of her eyes.

For an instant he couldn't find his voice. Then, "Henny!" he cried. "Gee I'm glad to see you."

"Ditto." She greeted Joel and Lisa, and turned to David, "That was a close shave."

Lisa by now understood a few English idioms, but this was not one of them. "What did she say?" she demanded in Yiddish.

David realized that a correct translation would only release a new flood of reproaches. "She said the same as you," he temporized, and went back to English. "Howja find out?"

"News travels fast," Henny said. "Specially bad news."

He gazed at her, reveling in her beauty. "You always look as if you're on your way to a party."

At once she was the coquette. "Maybe I am." She glanced at the adjoining bed. Abe had curled up on his side and pretended to be asleep. "Davey, what did it feel like?"

"It didn't seem real. I had a strange feeling it was happening to someone else."

"Did your whole life pass in front of you? They say that's what happens when people are drowning."

"I was too busy staying afloat to see anything. I couldn't even see him." He pointed toward Abe.

Lisa rose and kissed David. "We've stayed too long. We'll come for you in the morning."

"What shall I tell them on the beach?" Henny asked.

David grinned. "Say I'll be back tomorrow. And thanks for coming."

"Anything else?"

He would have liked to tell her that her visit had made him feel much better, but this was too personal to be said in front of his parents. "I'll tell you later," he said.

"You mean, tomorrow." She waved two fingers. "So long."

His eyes followed her. At the door, she looked back and smiled. David, completely happy, turned on his side and realized that Abe was watching him. "You weren't asleep," he said. "You pretended."

"That's right," Abe confessed pleasantly.

"What have you got against Henny?"

"Do we have to talk about her?"

"No." There was a silence. Then David said, "Were you afraid?"

Abe thought awhile. "I couldn't see anything. I was swallowing water, I knew I couldn't make it, so I gave up."

"Didn't you want to fight back?" David asked. Abe looked curiously helpless without his glasses.

"What was the use?"

"Weren't you afraid of dying?"

"No. It had been such a perfect day, being alone with you. What more could there be?"

"You mean, you wouldn't have minded?" David was astonished.

"Not really."

"But there's so much more."

"There is?"

"We're just starting out. Everything's ahead of us."

"Like what?"

"Doing things. Becoming somebody."

"Who?"

"I don't know yet. But I want to be somebody."

"You mean, somebody important."

"Yes. Somebody the world'll know about and look up to."

"I don't worry about the world," Abe said. "I just care about what's happening in here." He tapped his forefinger against his chest.

"We're different, you and I."

"Yes, Davey. We're different."

"One thing upset me," David said.

"What?"

"The ocean was so friendly. Suddenly it turned against us, it was ready to do us in. Y'know what I'm thinking?"

"What?"

"People are like that. They can be friendly, then they turn against you."

"Not always."

"You'll never do it?"

"Do what?"

"Turn."

"No, Davey, I'll never turn against you."

"Promise?"

"I promise."

A bell rang, the lights went out. Abe held out his hand in the narrow space between their beds. David took it.

6

SUDDENLY it was Labor Day and everybody went home.
A sunny stillness descended on Rockaway Beach Boulevard.

As soon as he was back in Brooklyn, David telephoned
Henny, who said he could come to see her that Saturday
night. Then he went to Rodney Street and rang Abe's bell.

"Glad to be back?" Abe asked.

"Yeah." He fell silent.

"You're remembering."

David nodded.

Abe put his arm around him. "Don't think about it any
more. Let's take a walk."

Lee Avenue was as noisy as ever. The same houses, the
same stores, yet everything looked different to David. "As
if it had been freshly painted," he said.

They had a hot chocolate at the ice-cream parlor, then
David walked Abe home and Abe walked David home.
"Let's see a movie Saturday night," Abe said.

"Gee, I can't."

"Why not?"

"Because—" He was not going to let Abe think that he
preferred Henny. "Because an aunt of mine is coming to
visit, and I got to be home."

"That's a lie," Abe said quietly. "You're going to see
Henny."

"What's so impossible about my aunt coming to visit?"

"It's not impossible. It just isn't so."

David shrugged. "I won't convince you, so have it your
way."

He wished afterward that he had confessed to lying. At
the same time he felt vaguely resentful. What right had Abe
to doubt his word? Or, for that matter, to pry into his
affairs?

On Saturday night he put on his blue serge suit and best

tie, and took the Marcy Avenue trolley to Putnam Avenue. It turned out to be a tree-lined street that was broader and quieter than his own. Henny and her parents lived on the second floor of a brownstone. The parlor had a bay window. Its parquet floor reminded David of the polished floor in the ballroom of Palm Garden. There was a different atmosphere here than in his home. Henny's parents had come from Romania as children, and prided themselves on having become as American as possible.

They retired early, and David was delighted to find himself alone with her. She sat beside him on the sofa, with an open box of chocolates next to her. She offered him one and took one herself. A pale light flowed from the floor lamp next to the sofa, touching her hair with gold. To his adoring eyes she looked completely lovely and completely unattainable.

He put one arm around her and tried to kiss her. "Don't get fresh," she admonished him, obviously enjoying the opportunity to do so.

"I'm not fresh," he said, "only curious."

She offered him another chocolate and her most winning smile. "Look, Davey, I'll be honest with you. There are two kinds of girls. The tramps let you mess around and there are plenty of them, so you have no problem. I happen to be the other kind. Sure, I'll go to bed with the man I marry. I'll even go to bed with him before the wedding night. But I'll have to be pretty sure of him, believe me."

She said all this with a virtuous look that removed her far beyond his reach. "So where does that leave me?" he asked.

"It leaves plenty of room for you. I like you and you're very nice. You can come around and we'll be friends. But that's how it's going to be." Whereupon Henny leaned forward, drew him to her, and kissed him fervently on the lips, as though to wipe out the severity of her admonition.

David could not but admire how she managed to remain on top of every situation—while forcing him to the bottom.

"Does what I say make sense?" She tilted her head coquettishly.

"Sure it does. But I wonder—"

"What?"

"Whether you would talk this way if you really wanted me."

"That's a big 'if,' " she said, and waggled a forefinger at him.

She kissed him again when they said good night, which sent him on his way in high spirits. His elation dissipated, however, as the Marcy Avenue trolley carried him back to Ross Street. She was a flirt, she was a tease, she had him in her power—and she knew it!

A pallid yellow light enveloped the trolley; the motorman clanged his bell and picked up speed. David pressed his cheek against the window and watched the empty Brooklyn streets slip by. With Stella he was top dog and it meant nothing to him. With Henny he was the underdog and it meant so much. Would it always be this way?

7

PROFESSOR Capaccio vanished. No one heard from him or knew where he was. Lisa telephoned, but the number had been disconnected. He had either died, she decided, or returned to Italy. A pity, she said. Such a sensitive man.

His successor was Boris Lomashkin, who was tall and so thin that his bony face with its sunken cheeks outlined the shape of a skull. His cavernous dark-gray eyes gazed at you with the visionary look of a fanatic, from under bushy eyebrows that were jet-black although his hair was graying. Mr. Lomashkin was very Russian. He called Lisa by her patronymic, Lisa Natanovna, as if they were back in Peterboorg. He drank tea as she and Joel did, using the silver scissors to cut off a morsel of sugar which he placed on the tip of his tongue. He had to be a better teacher than Professor Capaccio since he charged two dollars a lesson. The lesson ended at around six, and Lisa often asked Mr. Lomashkin to stay for the evening meal.

Their friendship took off when she discovered that he came from Odessa. "Then you must have known my brother. He sold pianos."

"What was his name?"

"Adolph. Adolph Eichisky."

Mr. Lomashkin threw back his head for emphasis. "Did I know him! I bought three pianos from him." Mr. Lomashkin was given to exaggeration.

Lisa had no intention of revealing how Adolph's unfortunate predilection for chambermaids had brought about his dismemberment on the esplanade beside the Black Sea. She contented herself with "Poor Adolph" and a sigh.

Mr. Lomashkin responded with "Ah, yes," to hide the fact that he hadn't the faintest notion what she was sighing about. "Your brother was a fine man," he declared. "When Boris Lomashkin says so"—he frequently referred to himself in the third person—"you can believe."

Mr. Lomashkin was an animated dinner guest. He talked steadily as he devoured great hunks of food. Surprisingly, he looked as hungry at the end of the meal as he had at the beginning. "Eats like a horse," Lisa commented, "yet is all skin and bones." His conversation concerned the famous and the great, especially in relation to himself. "Only the other day Josef Hofmann said to me, 'Lomashkin,' he said . . ." Or: "Yesterday I happened to run into Rachmaninoff. 'Sergei Vassilievich,' I said to him, 'when will you give us another symphony?' " These fantasies derived their charm from the fact that Mr. Lomashkin wholly believed as he invented them. Occasionally his imagination overreached itself, whereupon Lisa would say, after he had gone, "Oy, does he bake!" Her favorite euphemism for lying made it seem less reprehensible.

"Is what?" Joel countered. "If his stories aren't true, at least they're interesting."

"It's a matter of principle," Lisa said. "A person should speak the truth."

"Who knows, maybe some of it is true. Then he adds a little here and there for the fun of it."

Mr. Lomashkin's taste in piano music was strictly Russian. His repertoire centered about the twelve salon pieces, each named for another month, that Tchaikovsky wrote under the title of *The Seasons*. He was enchanted, as was Lisa, by the soulful melody of *Barcarolle* (June), and the suggestion of sleighbells in *Troika* (November). Equally favored was Anton Rubinstein with *Kamennoy Ostrov*—any piece named for an island outside Peterboorg was bound to have a nostalgic appeal for Lisa—and the *Romance in G*; also, of course, the *Melody in F*. Mr. Lomashkin's basic text was a collection called *Piano Pieces the Whole World Loves*. From the Russian items it was but a step to the easier mazurkas of Chopin, *Angel's Serenade* of Braga, *Rustle of Spring* by Sinding, and Cecile Chaminade's *Scarf Dance*. German music he considered too deep for comfort, except for Beethoven's *Minuet in G* and *Country Dance in E Flat*, which he followed with Brahms's *Hungarian Dance No. 5* and the *Lullaby*. Despite these limitations of taste and training, Mr. Lomashkin did have one constructive idea. He insisted that David play the exercises in Hanon's book in all the major keys.

In order to bolster his tales of friendship with the great pianists of the day, Mr. Lomashkin collected their autographs. He spent his Saturday afternoons at Carnegie Hall; after the concert he waited his turn in the line outside the green room and presented his program for the coveted signature. If the artist was gracious, he included Lomashkin's name along with his own. This tangible proof of friendship could be exhibited, on one pretext or another, at the next lesson.

If Mr. Lomashkin was weak on technique, he was strong on expression. He believed that *tekh-neek*, as he called it, with a horrendous guttural in the middle of the word, must never exist as an end in itself. On the rare occasions when he sat down at the piano to illustrate a passage—it had to be fairly simple—he would raise his shoulders, shut his eyes as if in a trance, snort, and clamp down the pedal. The notes might not always be there, but the rapture was. "You mahst feel," he told David, "you mahst say sahm-teeng. Of what good is tekh-neek," he asked rhetorically, "eef you say nah-teeng?"

Their great adventure together came with Rachmaninoff's Prelude in C-Sharp Minor. This was the music David had listened to outside the record shop on Broadway, when the heavens opened and a great light came pouring down. He had decided then that this was the most beautiful piece ever written, and saw no reason to change his opinion now. Mr. Lomashkin was not strict when it came to rhythm. Indeed, he considered strict rhythm incompatible with expression. David took every possible liberty as he thwacked the magnificent chords of the climax, pressing down from his shoulders and sinking deep into the keys. On the cover of the piece were the colorful onion-shaped towers of a Russian cathedral. Would its great bells be swinging in strict rhythm? Or course not.

Mr. Lomashkin was reticent about his private life. He believed, it seemed, in free love and was living with a lady whom he rarely mentioned. All this wreathed him in an air of mystery that went well with his romantic eyes. "A good cook she can't be," Lisa conjectured. When November came, Mr. Lomashkin appeared in the greatcoat he had brought from Russia. It reached almost to his ankles and had a luxurious collar of gray karakul; he wore a round Cossack hat to match. "When he was young," Lisa commented, "he must have looked like Evgen Onyegin. You know what?" she added. "He still does."

All in all, Mr. Lomashkin took himself seriously. He never appreciated the humor of his remark to Cousin Izzy when they were introduced: "Hah you know I am Rahssian?"

THREE

1

D AVID, on the sofa, turned sideways to Henny. "It'd be so much easier if you and Abe liked each other. The three of us could do things together."

"But we *don't* like each other," she pouted.

"I'm caught in the middle. If I see you, I can't see him, and if I see him . . ."

"Lucky you. Always in the middle."

Her tone put David on the defensive. "He's the best friend I ever had."

"That's why he hates me. He thinks I'll take you away from him."

"Would you?"

"Why should I?" She tossed her head. "Maybe he's afraid of losing you. I'm not."

It was her way of reminding David that she could do without him. When he was with her, he seemed to be playing a game at which he was not quite good enough. He tried constantly to impress her, to prove himself. Was this, he wondered, why he found her so exciting?

"My friend Selma was telling me"—Henny spoke quietly, almost as if to herself—"that she wants to get engaged. I told her it was too soon. We have to find out what it's all about before we tie ourselves down. Right?" She smiled at him.

Tongue-tied, he agreed. Henny indulged herself in a little yawn, delicately covering her mouth with the tips of her fingers. "It's getting late, Davey, and I'm tired."

She got up and went with him to the door. "My senior prom's coming up this month, and if you behave"—she tapped him on his chest—"I'll let you take me."

She sounded like an empress conferring a special honor. He responded with a properly enthusiastic "Gee, that's great!" She let him kiss her, first on the cheek, then on the lips. "But you have to behave," she reminded him.

"When will I see you?" he asked. The question made him tense up.

She furrowed her brow. "I'm kind of busy the next few days. Call me after the weekend."

He had the feeling—by now familiar—that he was an outsider looking in. "I'll call you Monday," he said, trying not to show her how much he hated to be kept dangling.

It was different when he was with Abe the following evening. No tension, no contest of wills; only a sense of belonging, of being accepted as he was. Abe and he were on an equal footing; neither of them sought the upper hand. They stopped at the oak tree on Lee Avenue. "I got a present for you, Davey," Abe said.

"What."

"It's a surprise."

"C'mon, tell me."

"I bought two tickets for us for Rachmaninoff's concert." He put his hand in his pocket and pulled them out.

"Wow!" David threw his arms around his friend and hugged him.

"They're in the dress circle."

"Beautiful!" David was touched, knowing that Abe would

have preferred to see a play but had chosen the concert because of him.

"When will I see you?" Abe asked. David realized this was the same question he had put to Henny the night before. "I want to practice tomorrow night. Let's make it Wednesday."

As he walked home he reflected that there was a big difference between his treatment of Abe and Henny's treatment of him. He never kept Abe dangling the way she did him. He never made Abe feel that he didn't care whether he saw him again or not. He was a true friend to Abe, whereas Henny didn't begin to know what friendship was.

She finally confirmed her promise that he could take her to the prom. Because Abe had the tickets for the concert, several weeks passed before David realized that both events were scheduled for the same night. In a panic, he consulted his parents.

Joel's solution was simple. "You can't do both, so decide on what you'd rather do and stick to that."

Lisa assumed a moral tone. "It's not a question of what he'd rather do. It's a matter of principle. If Henny can get someone else to take her to the dance, he can go with Abe. If Abe can get someone else to go to the concert, he can go with Henny. Either way, he must do what will give his friends the least trouble."

David pictured Henny's reaction if he phoned to tell her that he couldn't escort her to the prom. And what about Abe's reaction when he called to say that he could not go to the concert? He seesawed back and forth between the two alternatives; each seemed worse than the other. Finally he took Lisa's advice and decided the matter on moral grounds. Abe had saved up the money for the tickets, and no one in their group was interested in hearing Rachmaninoff. Henny, on the other hand, would have had to buy tickets for the prom in any case, and knew a number of fellows who would be delighted to take her. It was clear to David where his obligation lay. All he had to do was muster the courage to tell her.

It took some time for him to pick up the receiver. He finally did.

"Davey!" Her voice was friendly. "I wasn't expecting to hear from you today."

"Something came up, Henny, and I—" His voice sank to his toes. He pulled it back. "I won't be able to make the prom."

"What's that?" She obviously hadn't heard him.

"I said, I'm afraid I won't be able to make the prom."

"You must be joking. It's three days before. This is a nice time to tell me."

He broke into a sweat. "It's all my fault, but I didn't realize . . . Something came up."

"What?"

"I can't tell you."

"Seems to me that's the least you can do."

She listened while he told her. Then, addressing herself to an imaginary bystander, she exploded: "He must be out of his mind! He promises to take me to the prom, he says he wants to go, and just because Abe buys two tickets for some silly concert everything changes!" She switched back to the second person. "You can't be serious," she screamed. "You can't!"

He tried to reason with her, but she talked louder and faster. Finally, "Listen to me, Davey," she cried. "If you stand me up it's all over between us. I'll never see you again. Make your mind up right now. Just say yes or no."

His answer, when it came out, was barely audible. "Yes." He imagined her face at the other end of the wire: the slight pursing of the lips, the slow smile. She had won.

There was another call to make. He sat staring at the telephone. At length, with a deep sigh, he picked up the receiver.

"Abe, there's something I got to tell you. Something came up, and I won't be able to—"

"Oh." Silence; then Abe said quietly, "I figured you would do this."

"Whaddya mean?"

"My cousin goes to Erasmus High, so I knew about the prom being on the same night. I figured Henny'd want you to take her."

"Gee, Abe, I . . . I'm really sorry about this. I'll be glad to pay for the tickets. My parents can go."

"Don't worry about it, Davey." There was a click. Abe had hung up.

David remembered Abe's favorite term of contempt: *skunk.* So-and-so was a skunk, or had dome something skunky. Now he himself had. He winced.

2

HENNY'S dress at the prom was light-blue and gauzy, with a wide skirt that billowed gracefully round her ankles. Her high heels made her slightly taller than David; he kept pulling himself up as straight as he could. The ballroom of the Hotel St. George was larger and more splendid than any he had ever been in. He remembered Pike Street Mansion and Palm Garden. There was no comparison.

Henny was light on her feet, and her sense of rhythm was as good as his own. The band played *Bye Bye Blackbird* and *Charleston* while they hopped up and down. They also did the Ritz: three sliding steps across the floor, then he flung her sideways and for one exciting moment she lay snugly in his arms. "Dancing," David theorized, "must've begun because people felt good and had to express their feelings by jumping around. But it also works the other way. Once you jump up and down you begin to feel good." The music ended with *It's Three o'Clock in the Morning.* It was.

"Aren't you glad you came?" she asked.

"It was great."

"This is one date I sure had to work for."

He was not going to let the evening end on a sour note. "Let's not talk about it," he urged.

She gave him that slow smile of hers. "I don't want you to upset me ever again."

He put his arm around her and kissed her. That, he decided, was the best answer.

The next day he telephoned Abe. There was a sharp click in his ear as his friend hung up. He put on his coat, hurried over to Abe's house, and rang the bell.

"I'm sorry about last night," David said when Abe came out.

Abe kept his eyes on the ground. When he finally raised them to David's, they had a hostile look. "You let me down, Davey. What can I tell you?"

"Henny had me up against the wall. Honest, I couldn't help myself."

"You've been hurting me ever since the summer," Abe said, as if he had not heard David's reply. "Ever since she came along. I don't want to be hurt any more. So let's forget the whole thing."

"Abe!"

"You betrayed what we had," Abe said coldly, "so we don't have it any more."

Abe seemed to be moving further and further away. A chasm had opened between them, and David felt helpless to bridge it. That terrible moment in the water when he had thought he had lost Abe forever . . . *Please Abe, come back. Don't do this to me!* He heard the words in his mind, but knew he could never say them. Instead he found his voice, brought out coolly, "If that's how you feel, it's okay with me," and walked away.

At the corner he stopped by the oak tree. *As David loved Jonathan.* Suddenly, without knowing how it happened, his left fist shot out and slammed against the tree. The shock brought tears to his eyes. Stunned, he pulled back his hand

and rubbed his knuckles against the palm of his right hand. His throat felt dry. He had betrayed Abe? Oh, no. It was Abe who had betrayed him. It was Abe who had turned, even as the sea had turned that summer day.

3

BACK in St. Petersburg Joel had been friendly with a Hebrew teacher named Mr. Elman. Mr. Elman's little son Mischa played the violin, and Joel was frequently invited to hear him. He considered these evenings extremely cultural, and during the next two years acquired a passing acquaintance with most of the violin literature. Then Mr. Elman took Mischa out of the Conservatory, and off they went to Germany and world fame.

Whenever Mischa played in Carnegie Hall Lisa, Joel, and David climbed up the long narrow staircase leading to the family circle. Five stories below stood Mischa, his bow drawing forth the luscious tone for which he was famous. When the concert was over, Lisa said to Joel, "I think you ought to go backstage and say hello to Mr. Elman. After all, you were such good friends in Peterboorg."

"What for? To tell Mr. Elman that I exist? Like in Gogol's play *Revizor* Dobchinsky and Bobchinsky live in the province of Tchk . . . on the banks of the River Pssssss. So they write a letter to an official in Peterboorg he should know they exist. Mr. Elman lives in his world and I live in mine."

"I guess you're right," Lisa said, and down the stairs they went.

At the close of Mischa's next concert Lisa said to Joel, "I think you ought to go backstage and say hello to Mr. Elman. After all, you were such good friends in Peterboorg."

With a grin, Joel trotted out Gogol's *Revizor*, Dobchinsky and Bobchinsky, the province of Tchk . . . and the River Psssss. Lisa conceded that he was right, and down

the stairs they went. Then, one day in December, Joel came
home from work in high excitement. It seemed that Mr.
Elman had appeared at the newspaper to place an ad for
Mischa's next concert. "Just then I came out of the printing
room. Mr. Elman recognized me, he came over and threw
his arms around me. We talked about the old days. He
promised to come and see us—of course, he won't—but we
parted like old friends."

A few days later Mr. Elman telephoned. He was in the
neighborhood, could he come up? Lisa frantically tidied the
living room and fell to in the kitchen. By the time Mr. Elman
arrived she had the situation in hand. He turned out to be
a plump, bald gentleman, extremely nearsighted and vivacious. The evening meal was a success. Borscht with sliced
cucumbers under a blanket of sour cream. *Gefilte* fish.
Cheese blintzes and sour cream. Mr. Elman regaled his hosts
with wonderful tales: what the king of England said when
Mischa played for him, and what the queen of Spain said.
Into the dining room filed a procession of the mighty ones
of the earth. Mr. Elman was in the vein, and his audience
listened raptly.

After he left, Joel said, "His stories are as interesting as
Mr. Lomashkin's. There's one big difference: they really
happened."

"Which means," Lisa corrected him, "they're more interesting."

This was the first of a series of visits, all of which followed the same pattern. Mr. Elman called to say he was in
the neighborhood; Lisa busied herself in the kitchen. From
then on events followed in their appointed order: borscht,
sour cream, gefilte fish, blinchiki, sour cream, the king of
England and the queen of Spain, with whom David by now
was on a familiar footing. There was only one moment that
marred these otherwise idyllic gatherings. This came at the
end of the evening when Joel and Lisa accompanied their
guest to the door. They knew, and he knew they knew, that
by all the laws of hospitality he should invite them back.

Mr. Elman cleared his throat, giggled nervously, and said, "Well, if you are ever in the neighborhood, I hope you'll drop in."

"We certainly will," Joel would reply. "Give our regards to Mrs. Elman."

When Mr. Elman had gone Joel added, "He doesn't have to say that. He lives in his world and I live in mine." He thought a moment. "Besides, his wife blows." He used the Yiddish idiom for a snob.

One night Mr. Elman found a way out of his dilemma. Turning to David, "We're having string quartets this Saturday night," he said. "You're interested in music, why don't you come?"

David looked at his parents, who thought this was a splendid idea. Mr. Elman gave him the address and told him to present himself at eight o'clock.

Lisa bought him a new tie for the occasion and dusted off his blue serge suit. On the appointed night David was inspected, approved, and sent forth into the world. He took the train across Williamsburg Bridge to the West Side, and arrived at a huge apartment house near Riverside Drive. The apartment too was huge, and in the drawing room people conversed in Russian, French, English; there was no trace of Yiddish. Mr. Elman introduced David to Mischa, plump and bald like his father, who was holding forth about his most recent concert. David had never been in a room with a Steinway grand. It was covered with a Spanish shawl, on which stood a crystal vase filled with white chrysanthemums. He imagined himself seated at the piano ripping off *Kamennoy Ostrov* before this elegant gathering. Unfortunately, nobody asked him.

The guests took their seats; the music began. Mischa and three young men played a quartet of Haydn. David, accustomed to the fuzzy sound of the piano at home, was charmed by the pure intonation of the strings. He followed avidly as the theme was tossed from one player to the next. It was as if the four instruments were having a pleasant conversation.

Everyone applauded at the end; the players repeated the Scherzo.

After the music, supper was served. The pianist Pierre Luboshutz arrived and was greeted by his friends with "Pieritchki, comment ça va?" David listened spellbound. On Ross Street the boys were called Abe or Joey or, like himself, Davey. But Pierre . . .? He was reading *War and Peace* at the time—it was one of the books to which Abe had introduced him—and was fascinated by the character of Pierre Bezukhov. Suddenly the thin line between the real and the unreal—between Ross Street and literature—snapped, the unwonted scene before him seemed to merge into the larger canvas of Tolstoi's novel. For a moment he was not quite sure where the one ended and the other began.

At midnight he thanked Mr. Elman, left the party, and made his way to the subway train that took him back to Brooklyn. His parents were waiting up. "Nu . . .?" Joel asked.

David described the room, the people, the music. He searched for something that would bring home to them how extraordinary the evening had been. "Imagine, there was someone in the room actually named Pierre," he finally said, pausing to let this momentous detail sink in. "It's a big world out there, and it seems so far away."

"Why?" Lisa asked. "It's only across the bridge."

"It's another world."

Lisa smiled. "Some day it will be yours, my son."

"I guess so," David said. He was not sure.

4

LISA thought it would be interesting to bring together Mr. Lomashkin and Mr. Elman. However, since Mr. Elman always visited on the spur of the moment, the encounter had to wait until he turned up on the day of the lesson. This occurred on a Wednesday in February and proved to be different from what she had expected.

The lesson centered about Tchaikovsky's *Romance in F Minor*. When Mr. Elman arrived, Lisa asked David to repeat the piece for him. Mr. Elman chose his words carefully, in the manner of a connoisseur. "Not bad," he said, "not bad at all." He made it sound like extravagant praise. "Do you play Bach?" he inquired.

"Bach?" David said. "Who's he?"

"In Odessa," Mr. Lomashkin interposed hastily, "we didn't play Bach until the last year." He didn't specify what last year.

"How can you become a musician," Mr. Elman asked in astonishment, "if you don't play Bach?"

Lisa came to Mr. Lomashkin's rescue. "But he plays *Kamennoy Ostrov*. Dovid'l, why don't you play it for Mr. Elman."

David obliged. Mr. Elman was not to be bought off so easily. "And Beethoven?" Like Lisa, he called him Betkhoven.

"Of course," Mr. Lomashkin said brightly. "We just finished the *Moonlight Sonata*." It was not true. He had taught David only the first movement, as he was somewhat hazy about the other two.

There was a silence. Mr. Elman was obviously preparing the next assault. Lisa bailed out Mr. Lomashkin with "Let's have a bite."

The borscht had just arrived when Lomashkin encountered his next defeat. "I ran into Josef Hofman the other day, and he was telling me—"

Mr. Elman looked at the piano teacher with a pitying smile and lunged. "How could you? He's in Vienna."

Mr. Lomashkin was caught off guard. "In Vienna?" He recovered quickly enough to say, "I know he was, but he came back."

Mr. Elman was relentless. "Really? I just received a letter from Mischa saying they met in Vienna. A person can't fly across the Atlantic."

Lisa felt sorry for Lomashkin, who was beginning to turn green. "If Mischa's letter arrived," she said reasonably, "so could a person."

For once Mr. Lomashkin lost his appetite. Lisa filled his plate with two blinchiki smothered in sour cream. He ate only one, announced that he had another lesson to give, and fled. Mr. Elman enjoyed his victory. "A nice man," he summed up, "but music he doesn't know."

Now that Mr. Lomashkin's authority had been irretrievably shaken, Joel took the only sensible course. Where, he asked Mr. Elman, should David study? Mr. Elman explained that there was nothing in this country to compare with the conservatories of Moscow and Peterboorg. However, there was a school that offered young musicians a thorough education. Since he knew the director, he would have no problem in arranging an audition.

It was Lisa who had the problem: how to tell Mr. Lomashkin. She could say, Joel suggested, that they were moving away from New York. Lisa considered this carefully, but decided against it. "The truth is always best," she said, and wrote Mr. Lomashkin a long, loving letter in Russian.

On the appointed day David presented himself at the music school. He was ushered into the director's office and found himself in the presence of a distinguished-looking gentleman with piercing eyes and a white goatee. Dr. Damrosch spoke with great precision, emphasizing each word as if he had rehearsed it. "Do you love music?" he inquired.

"Very much." The question seemed strange. "Doesn't everybody?"

The director smiled. "No. And you wish to be a musician?"

This was asked in so kindly a manner that David found it easy to confide in the stranger. "I'd like to."

· "The Romans," Dr. Damrosch continued, "had a saying, 'Ars longa, vita brevis.' That means, 'Art is long but life is short.' It takes a lot of work to become a musician. There is so much to learn. Are you prepared to do all that?"

"Oh, yes." David remembered reading somewhere that the Knights Templar took a vow when they entered the Order. The director was making him feel a little like that.

"What will you play for me?"

David sat down and launched into *Rustle of Spring.* Dr. Damrosch listened to the end. "Anything else?"

Thinking to impress the director with the improvements he had added, David attacked *Poet and Peasant Overture.* Dr. Damrosch listened to the introductory section, then stopped him. "This music was written for orchestra. Why would you play it on the piano?"

Taken aback, David looked for a reason. "Because it sounds good." He was disappointed at the director's reaction.

"Try something else."

David swung into the belllike broken chords of *Kamennoy Ostrov.* The director listened to the end, then said, "You're musical, but you've been badly taught."

David was about to defend Mr. Lomashkin but thought better of it.

"Very well, then," the director said. "I'll assign you to Miss Parissot." He instructed David to go upstairs to Studio M, on the second floor, where he would meet his teacher.

David bounded up the stairs, opened the double door of Studio M, and entered a large room that contained two grand pianos. Two windows faced the Hudson and the dome on Grant's tomb. Between them stood a tall woman with enormous dark-brown eyes and a coiffure of coal-black hair piled high. Three rows of coral beads rode on her bosom. She had a double chin and was heavily rouged. Holding out her hand, she said, "I'm Elena Parissot," in a deep husky voice that sounded like a man's. David noticed that she wore several rings.

"I'm David Gordin," he said. They shook hands.

She motioned him to the piano. "Will you play something?"

He went through Rachmaninoff's Prelude in C-sharp minor, churning up a storm with the massive chords at the climax. Miss Parissot nodded and said, "Anything by Chopin?"

"C-sharp minor Waltz, but I don't remember it."

"Bach?"

He knew better than to ask who Bach was. "No."

"What did you play for Dr. Damrosch?" she asked.

"*Poet and Peasant Overture*. He said I was not supposed to, because it's for orchestra."

For the first time Miss Parissot evinced interest. "Play it for me." She listened to the entire overture. At the end she said, "Amazing!" and broke into a soft laugh.

"What's so funny?" He did not mind her laughter because it was friendly.

"Some day you'll understand." She took a pad, wrote quickly, tore off the sheet and handed it to him. "Bring these to your lesson."

David read what she had written: Bach, Invention in C. Beethoven, Rondo in G. Chopin, Prelude in D-flat. He stopped at the music store in the basement of the school to buy the three pieces. He felt exhilarated. At last he was going to play Bach.

5

DAVID looked forward to his lessons with Elena Parissot. He had never met anyone remotely like her.

She had strong opinions about everything, especially music, and presented them as if they were the ultimate truth. "Piano playing," she told him, "combines two elements as different as body and soul. On the one hand, the pianist has to have full control over his muscles. He must train them as carefully as if he were trying to master tennis or skiing." But the technical aspect of an art was valid only as a means to an end. In this sense Parissot echoed Mr. Lomashkin's strictures against *tekh-neek.* "Some people gallop across the keys without understanding what they're doing. The keyboard is not a typewriter." The real purpose of technique was to make possible the presenting of musical thought and feeling. "You have to unlock what the composer put into the music," she said, fixing upon David her lustrous, heavily made-up eyes. "You have to discover his secret. And that, my boy, takes doing."

On the first Sunday of the month Miss Parissot received her pupils at home. She lived in an old house on West Fifty-second Street near Broadway, in the heart of the theater district. David had seen the Great White Way only at night, when it was ablaze with lights. It looked strangely prosaic at four in the afternoon, even shabby. Miss Parissot's drawing room was cluttered with mementos of the various trips to Europe she had taken with Maman. Maman was a frail old lady who spoke English with a French accent and sat in an armchair, her feet resting on a little stool, a blanket over her lap. Miss Parissot was extremely devoted to mamman, but she must have inherited her aquiline good looks from her father, as she bore not the slightest resemblance to the little old lady in the armchair.

Dark-green velvet drapes covered the windows, shutting out light and air. The furniture consisted of overstuffed chairs, a hideous sofa, and a Steinway grand covered with a batik shawl. On it rested several photographs of musicians. The collection, small but distinguished, included Fritz Kreisler, Josef Hofmann, and Leopold Godowsky, all of whom had inscribed their photos with appropriate expressions of regard. Miss Parissot's pupils took turns playing before the class. She analyzed each performance, praising some details, criticizing others. The atmosphere was informal and friendly. Nonetheless, David was nervous when it was his turn. For the first time in his life he was playing before an audience that knew more about music than he did. He had just memorized the Bach Invention. Unaccustomed to music in which several lines unfolded contrapuntally, he was afraid of a memory lapse, but he came through without mishap. The Beethoven Rondo offered no problem. He did best with the *Raindrop Prelude*; the middle section built up to the kind of rich sonorities that sent little arrows racing along his spine.

His fellow students applauded when he finished. Miss Parissot pointed out that he had overpedaled, blurring some of the harmonies, and when he grew excited at the climax of the Prelude he had rushed the tempo. But his playing was musical, and musicality stood first on her list of virtues.

Tea followed. The maid brought in several plates of cucumber sandwiches from which the crusts had been removed. Also a trayful of French pastries. Miss Parissot, leaning back against the curve of the piano, summed up the lesson for the day. "Some of you get carried away and bang. Remember, please, the piano is not a box of wires that you hit. It is a living creature; you must treat it with love." She flung her arm over the top of the instrument in a protective gesture. "Sometimes I think it has a soul!" Her throaty voice dropped to a whisper on the final word.

With that mound of blue-black hair rising above her head, her lustrous eyes and theatrical gestures, she seemed to David like some fascinating creature from another world. In a way she was like his mother: she too was dramatic, she too was always on stage. Of course, her material was better.

He corrected himself. Not better. Just different.

6

So many things were happening that David did not have much time to think about Abe. When he did, he felt sad.

And angry. It was his fault, he knew, that the friendship had come to an end. All the same, Abe shouldn't have ended it.

The break had left him with a sense of his own unworthiness; he had failed to live up to what was expected of him. Abe had proven to be the loyal friend while he had turned out to be the one who couldn't be trusted. David refused to accept this conclusion, yet it nagged at him. For years he had had someone to share his thoughts and do things with. Suddenly he didn't, and there was an emptiness around him he had never known before. He tried to ignore it by throwing himself into his work; yet it persisted, like an ache that refused to go away.

Out of the blue, Lisa said, "What happened to Abe? I haven't seen him in weeks."

David's first impulse was to pretend that nothing was wrong. He decided instead to be truthful. "We're not friends any more."

"Why?"

He told her.

"I'm sorry to hear it," she said. "You two really loved each other. Are you upset?"

"Sure I am." David had thought it would be too painful for him to admit that he was hurt. Yet here he was, talking about it as though it had happened to someone else, and to his surprise feeling better for doing so.

"A person has to learn," Lisa said, "from each experience. What did you learn from this one?"

He thought. "That you can't ever trust anybody, not even your best friend."

"Oh, no." Lisa was horrified. "That's not what you should have learned."

"What then?"

It was her turn to think. "That for every happiness in life there's a price to pay. You enjoyed going to the dance with Henny. So you had to pay."

It occurred to him that he and Lisa were talking as if they

were equals. Better still, as if they were friends. "You've enjoyed being with Papa," he said. "Was there a price?"

"Of course there was."

"Would you do it again?"

She considered the question carefully. "Yes. I'd be a fool to do it, but I would."

Her frankness put him in a confiding mood. "Trouble is, I don't think I'll ever find a friend like Abe again."

"Sure you will. We meet many people in a lifetime, my son, and some of them get to like us."

He appreciated her trying to make him feel better, even if he didn't believe her. That night, after he finished practicing, he went for a walk. The stars were out in multitudes, the air was crisp. Although it was only ten o'clock, Lee Avenue was deserted. He passed the old oak at the corner of Rodney Street. On an impulse he turned, walked to Abe's house, and stopped in front of the cast-iron gate. The familiar feeling of emptiness gnawed at him; he grasped the railing with both hands and bent over it. For an instant he felt a longing so intense it was like physical pain. He wanted at all costs to be Abe's friend again. All he had to do was ring the bell, call him out, explain. He pushed the rail away and straightened up. What was the use? He turned and walked back to the corner.

He remembered smashing his fist against the tree. What a stupid thing to do; he could have hurt his hand. What *had* he learned from the experience? Well, he had learned that the world was constantly changing. Around us, inside us. The earth seemed to be standing still, but it was hurtling through space at a terrific speed. The oak seemed to be standing still but it was all movement inside, on its way from winter to spring. Time could not stop, as his mother kept wishing it would. Change could not stop, as *he* kept wishing it would. For a while Abe and he had traveled together; now each of them had to go his own way. If Henny hadn't come between them, something else would have.

A gust of wind blew across Lee Avenue and cooled his

face. The air smelled of spring. He looked up at the sky. The stars were flung across it like so many shiny pebbles. Where were Castor and Pollux? He couldn't find them.

David touched the bark of the old oak with his forefinger, for good luck, and proceeded on his way.

7

HENNY kicked off her shoes. Pulling her legs under, she curled up in a corner of the sofa. "And what d'you suppose she said to him?" The lamp wreathed her hair in golden light.

"What?" David asked mechanically, having lost the thread of her narrative. *She* referred to some friend of hers whom he didn't know, and *him* to a friend of the friend whom he didn't care about. The trouble with Henny was, she chattered.

" 'You can go fly a kite!' Just like that."

Now that he knew her better, he was able to cope with her sudden changes of mood. She was willful, she was spoiled, but she was not unpredictable. In fact, most of the time he was able to figure out what she was going to say next. Half the battle, in dealing with her, was to make her feel that he was no longer tied up in knots over her. The minute he did this she came off her high horse.

"I was glad she told him off. Good riddance!" Henny said with conviction.

David looked at her. All her stories had the girl and boy playing a game that only one of them could win. For her there was only one issue: who would come out on top. She was fascinated by each detail of the contest: how they met, how they clashed, how they parted. Why did he have to listen to this nonsense? Because she was the prettiest girl he knew and he hoped to make her. The prospect excited him as much as ever, even if it did not wipe out the fact that they had almost nothing in common. They were still engaged in that strange dance: when he moved forward, she withdrew; when he withdrew, she moved forward.

He had withdrawn somewhat in the past few months, ever since he had come to know the girls in Miss Parissot's class. With them he shared a common interest. As a result, his awareness of them as girls was part of something bigger, something that had to do with the kind of people they were and the kind of things they hoped to do in life. But with Henny there was nothing apart from the sex angle. Of course, that was pretty absorbing.

For the first time they were alone in the apartment; her parents had gone to a wedding in Manhattan. The next step was to move over to her side of the sofa. He did.

To his surprise, she offered no resistance. On the contrary, she met him more than halfway. She curled up in his arms, kissed him, and slipped her tongue through his lips as people did in the movies. He felt the warmth of her body, the softness, the yielding. The moment he had so often dreamed about was finally at hand.

He ran his lips lightly over her cheek. Yet, now that he was about to realize his dream, part of him seemed to split off, to be looking on from the outside. Inexplicably his desire ebbed away, replaced by a strange fear that he would fail to live up to her expectations. He pictured her cool, mocking smile; it seemed to him that she felt nothing, she had no real wish to share anything with him. All she wanted was to assert her power over him. Her kisses were fake, her desire was fake; she was pretending. Underneath the soft white skin and the golden curls she was hard as nails, cold as ice.

Henny moved against him, her fingers clutching his shoulder. Then her hand descended slowly. Terror poured over him. Soon his limpness would be revealed and he would be forever disgraced in her eyes. Wildly he sought refuge in the trick he had used with Stella Rabinowitz: he tried to conjure up the sexy images on Danny Friedman's French pictures. It hadn't worked then, and it didn't work now. Henny's hand reached his crotch. There was absolutely no way he could fool her.

She thrust him from her. "What's the matter, I'm not pretty enough?" She addressed her invisible confidante: "Here I am, ready to go all the way with him, and he don't even want me. Can you beat it?"

The breath went out of his body. All he wanted was to get off the couch and out of the room as fast as possible. He got up. "Maybe—" He knew it would be useless to try to explain his failure but could not keep from trying, "Maybe I'm not in the mood." He felt like an insect that she was examining between her fingers before crushing. "Sometimes," he continued in spite of himself, "you want a thing so badly that when you finally get it—"

"You're scared," she broke in triumphantly. "That's what you are!"

"You don't care a thing about me," he countered. "You don't care about anybody but yourself. All you want is to throw me a bone so I'll know who's master."

"If that isn't the craziest thing I ever heard!" Her smile became vindictive. "Maybe you'd rather be with your friend Abe. Maybe *he's* the one you want."

His hand shot out against her cheek. "Shut your dirty mouth!" he shouted, and realized in horror that he had struck her.

With her hand to her face she stared at him in unbelief. Then her foot shot out and caught him above the knee. "You sonofabitch," she snarled, "get the hell out of here. And don't you ever come back."

He strode to the door and clenched the knob. "Abe was the best friend I ever had. To think I broke up with him because of you. I could laugh."

"You could drop dead for all I care!"

"Don't worry, I won't." Pleased with himself for having had the last word, he slammed the door behind him.

By the time the Marcy Avenue trolley arrived, his victory no longer seemed as brilliant. Why had he screwed up his chances just as he was on the verge of getting what he wanted? He dropped a nickel into the coin box and sat down at the back of the empty car. Folding his hands on top of the seat in front, he lowered his head on them. His forehead felt uncomfortably hot. The trolley picked up speed, its wheels rumbling against the tracks in a clickety-clack. He began to breathe in time with the rhythm. She was a fuckin' cunt, that's what she was. Still, a wave of regret broke over him as he realized she would never see him again.

First he had lost Abe, now he had lost Henny. A neat trick if ever there was one. How had he managed it? The question hammered at his brain; he sought the answer in the smooth hum of the wheels. To lose them both you had to have talent. You had to be a loser.

8

APRIL was important. Graduation was approaching and decisions had to be made. Bill was going into his father's clothing factory and would study business administration at night. Hymie picked law, Solly would be an accountant, Carl was entering pre-med at NYU. And David?

He wasn't sure. When he thought about his future, he saw himself doing remarkable things for which the whole world admired him. He had a daydream in which he stood on top of a mountain while a lot of people looked up at him from the valley below. But how had he made it to this high point? He hadn't the slightest idea.

His parents and relatives already saw him on the stage at Carnegie Hall, acknowledging the plaudits of a crowded house. His teacher, without promising anything definite, encouraged him to believe that if he worked hard he might become a concert pianist. Attractive though such a career seemed, it was not as sure a thing as what his friends were going after. In order to become a doctor, lawyer, or accountant all you had to do was to take the required courses and pass the exams. But to become an artist was not so simple. It depended on talent, luck, and a number of circumstances you couldn't possibly figure out in advance. He thought of the pianists whose concerts he went to hear—Godowsky, de Pachmann, Hofmann, Rosenthal, Rachmaninoff. Did he have it in him to become one of them? Certainly he was going to continue his musical studies; he couldn't conceive of not doing so. But no one could tell him if he was going to get there, wherever *there* was. He would have to take his chances.

His high-school graduation was a memorable affair. The seniors marched into the auditorium to the strains of the *Triumphal March* from *Aïda*, which he played with the orchestra. Miss Ennis conducted with sweeping gestures; she was in a jovial mood. Then Dr. Vlyman made a long speech to his mostly Jewish audience on what it meant to be an American. David had never forgiven him for expelling Danny Friedman, and let his mind wander during the speech. He listened carefully when his friend Carl gave the valedictory address. Carl had practiced it for the past two months; this time he remembered his lines.

The high point for David was his piano solo. Miss Parissot thought he should play the Beethoven rondo, but he wanted something more dramatic and trotted out Rachmaninoff's Prelude in C-sharp minor. He no longer thought it the most beautiful piece ever written, but he thrilled as much as ever to the massive chords of the climax. David wished the piano were on stage, where everyone could see him. Unfortunately, it stood next to the orchestra and could not be moved. He threw himself into the music and ended with a bang. When he stood up and bowed, he wanted to see his mother's face but did not know where she was sitting. The audience applauded enthusiastically, so he took another bow. Alas, Dr. Vlyman had not allowed time for an encore.

After the ceremonies, Joel celebrated by taking Lisa and David to the Capitol Theatre on Broadway. The majestic marble staircase, flanked by bronze candelabras, reminded her of the imperial opera house in Peterboorg, the Marinsky. "That was smaller," she said, "and more beautiful." There was an elaborate stage show followed by *The Passion Flower* with Norma Talmadge, Lisa's favorite movie star.

That night David met his friends at the ice cream parlor on Lee Avenue. It was Carl who expressed what the others were thinking. "Hey, fellers, this may be our last hot chocolate together."

"So we better make it last," Bill said.

Solly took a more sanguine view. "Just because we're going to different schools don't mean we won't see each other."

"But it won't be the same," Hymie said. "It'll be different."

"Dope, if it's not the same, it's got to be different," Abe pointed out.

David felt awkward in Abe's presence, but put on a casual air. Just as the two of them had concealed the special nature of their friendship from the others, they had—as if by agreement—revealed nothing of what had happened between them. As far as their friends were concerned, the group was still intact.

Two girls passed by. Bill swung into action. "I like the one in the middle," he announced, and the others laughed with gusto.

"Now that you're going to college," David suggested, "how about a new joke?" The suggestion was greeted with noisy approval.

The boys went inside and sat down at their usual table. "I wonder where we'll be ten years from now," Carl said.

"I know what," Solly exclaimed. "Let's make a date to meet." They solemnly agreed.

"Who'll be the first to make a million bucks," Hymie wondered.

"You're gonna be the accountant," Bill said. "You should know."

"I'll settle for a hundred thousand," Carl said.

"What about you, Davey?" Hymie asked. "How much d'you expect?"

David had never thought of himself in relation to money. "I'm not the kind of guy who makes it," he said. "All I expect is—" What did he expect? Compared to the other boys, his goals were so indecisive, his plans so vague.

"What?" Hymie wanted to know.

David grinned. "I'll be satisfied if I get by."

"Trouble with you is," Hymie said, "you're not ambitious."

"I'm ambitious all right," David countered. "But in my own way."

"What way is that?"

David thought a moment. "There's two ways to get to where you want to go. You can follow a straight line, that's the one you guys are taking. Or you can kind of go in a circle, so it takes longer, but you cover more ground."

"Looka him," Hymie said. "A philosopher yet."

David glanced around. What if Carl was right and this was the last time he'd be sitting here with his friends? He certainly wouldn't come back by himself. He took in the old-fashioned fixtures, the jars with syrups of different flavors lined up against the looking glass behind the counter, the dark wood paneling with carved ornaments like those on the tall mirror in his bedroom. They didn't make ice-cream parlors like this any more, and he was saying good-bye to it.

It was after ten when they left. First they walked Hymie home, then Carl. Next it was Bill's turn, and Solly's. Finally

only Abe and David were left. They walked in silence along
Lee Avenue, David thinking of all the things he would have
liked to say to Abe but wasn't going to. They reached the
corner of Ross Street, and David wished Abe would say, as
he so often had in the past, "C'mon, walk me home." Instead
Abe waved his hand casually and said, "So long."

"So long," David replied. He watched Abe walk off
toward Rodney Street. It seemed that an invisible thread
stretched between them. It grew longer and longer the farther his friend walked away, reaching beyond Abe to encir-
cle the world they had shared, the people they had known
and the places they had been in. Suddenly David wished
he were a magician so he could use the thread like a lasso to
bring Abe back. If Abe crossed the avenue, he decided, and
turned the corner of Rodney without looking back, the
thread would snap. Forever.

From an open window came the sound of a Caruso record.
The drugstore on the corner opposite the grocery was dark.
On Lee Avenue a trolley approached and buzzed past at
high speed. Abe crossed the avenue with that loping gait of
his and reached the oak tree. David watched as his former
friend turned the corner and disappeared. The thread
snapped.

Lisa had insisted that he go to college. That he was able
to do so was one of the things she liked best about Columbus's country. The morning after graduation David took
the subway to Manhattan to register at City College. If he
had thought his high school resembled Kenilworth, it now
seemed to him that he was seeing the real thing. The Gothic
towers floated in medieval majesty atop Morningside
Heights; the arched gateway on Convent Avenue seemed
to beckon him into a new world. Most impressive of all was
the great hall with its stained-glass windows, massive pillars,
and soaring arches. This was as close as he had ever come
to being in a cathedral.

He described it all to his parents. "How I envy you!"

Lisa exclaimed. "You have the opportunity your father and I never had. A person who finishes college," she stated with conviction, "can never be unhappy."

"C'mon, Ma, you don't really believe that."

"Of course I do." She pressed her lips together firmly, her eyes serious yet vivacious, their dark depths aglow.

David shook his head. "No matter how well I know you, you still surprise me."

She smiled. "Is good!"

III

The
Dream

ONE

1

Now that David was going to City College, there was nothing to keep them in Brooklyn, especially since, according to Joel, everybody was moving to the Bronx. By *everybody*, he meant three of the printers who worked with him. In any case, the Bronx was definitely a cut above.

Lisa at first vetoed the idea; for her any change was a threat. But Joel talked her into an exploratory visit, and she was enchanted. It turned out that the Bronx was situated on hills, hence the air was purer. They found a four-room apartment that looked out on Crotona Park.

Joel viewed their successive apartments as so many steps forward. The one on South Fourth Street had the toilet in the hall and was lit by gas. The one on Ross Street had a bathroom and electricity, but was heated by a coal stove. The new one had steam heat. They were unquestionably on the way up.

The apartment on Crotona Park North was on the second floor of a red-brick house whose pointed gables suggested the Tudor style. From the dining room you saw an expanse of trees, tennis courts, and a lake. "We're living in a palace," declared Lisa. A narrow molding ran along the wall of the dining room. Here she arranged her Greek divinities: on one side Venus and Apollo, on the other the Three Graces and Europa on her bull. David had obviously outgrown the upright piano from J. Perelman & Sons. Its successor was a rebuilt Steinway grand that Joel, because of his connection with *The Day*, was able to buy on reasonable terms. The instrument was carried up the winding stairway by three husky men, and very grand it was. Lisa polished the mahogany box until it shone, and kept it free of encumbrances. Mozart and Bethoven were shifted to the bookcase.

Once the new apartment was in order, Lisa was ready to receive. She cooked and baked in anticipation of the weekend, when a constant stream of visitors supplied the excitement on which she thrived. She fed them innumerable balls of gefilte fish dipped in red horseradish, and her golden-brown cookies flavored with cinnamon and raisins. Imperceptibly the guest list was changing. Uncles, aunts, and cousins were less in evidence, replaced by Joel's cronies and their wives. Lisa regretted the change, for she saw it as a weakening of family ties, but Joel regarded it as inevitable. As usual, he found a rational explanation. "When you come to a strange country you have only your relatives to depend on. You had the same grandmother as they, so you feel close to them. After a while you begin to make your own friends and forget the grandmother."

Joel divided people into two categories: the money grubbers who thought only of themselves, and the *idayishe menschen*—people of ideas, more accurately, people of ideology, whether socialist, Zionist, or anarchist—who related to something larger. These were the only kind worth knowing. His own beliefs led him to the labor grouping within the Zionist movement that envisaged a Jewish homeland in Palestine based on socialist principles. However, he was not doctrinaire in his beliefs, with the result that diverse points of view mingled at Lisa's parties.

Mr. Yankelovich, who worked with Joel in the printing room of *The Day*, represented anarchism. He was a corpulent, pompous gentleman whose fluffy mustache and goatee gave him a literary look. He worked for six years on a Yiddish translation of Kropotkin that brought him wide admiration among his friends even though it was never published. The Zionist point of view was eloquently expounded by another printer from *The Day*, Meyer Feinstein, a man in his early forties whose hair was prematurely gray. Feinstein belonged to a group that was losing faith in England's intentions regarding the Balfour Declaration. He put his hope in bombs and assassinations. "That will make them listen," he maintained, "where nothing else will."

Yuri Katz, the communist in the group, was sustained by a childlike faith in the party line. A tall, soft-spoken gentleman who wore starched collars and was immaculately neat, he rarely smiled. Rumor had it that he had read all ten volumes of Lenin's *Materialism and Empiro-Criticism*, in Russian. Lisa called him Stalin behind his back.

Of all his fellow printers Joel felt closest to his chess partner, Mr. Levine; but the old friendship was undergoing a strain. Mr. Levine had been converted to Mr. Katz's philosophy and followed the communist party's view that Zionism was a form of imperialism. Increasingly the Saturday afternoon chess games exploded into fierce arguments that Lisa strove in vain to mediate. "You'll both get heart attacks if you don't stop shouting," she hectored them. "Why can't you keep your minds on the game?"

They tried. But the delicate balance between knight, pawn, and bishop no longer sufficed to keep out the tensions of the world. Sooner or later the uneasy truce had to collapse. It happened the Saturday after an Arab gang massacred a group of Jewish boys in a school near Hebron.

"They shouldn't have been there in the first place," Mr. Levine insisted.

Joel glared at him. "Are you saying the Arabs had a right to kill them?"

Levine gestured impatiently. "Why do you put silly words in my mouth? I'm only saying that the land belongs to the Arabs, who've lived there for hundreds of years. If the Jews insist on taking it away from them, there will be trouble."

"But the land was Jewish in the first place," Joel shouted. "Haven't you read the Bible?"

"I read it in the same *cheder* as you, in case you forgot. So why don't you stop talking nonsense. Zionism is a bourgeois movement," he said, "and it will only create more problems than it can solve."

The muscles in Joel's face twitched as though he were undergoing a severe inner struggle. When he found his voice it was strangely quiet. "Levine, we've been friends since we were boys, but I cannot allow you to say such things in my house. I must ask you to leave."

Levine pulled at his collar, which was still a size too large for his neck. Abruptly he rose and swept one hand across the chess board, scattering king, queen, knights, and pawns across the floor. He found his hat and coat and without another word flung out of the room, slamming the door behind him. Lisa ran in from the kitchen. "How can you behave like this?" she cried, beside herself. "Wait till he gets home, then you'll call him and say you're sorry."

Joel shook his head. "I'm not sorry, and I won't call him."

"But you loved playing chess with him."

Joel was thoughtful. "Could be the time for chess is over."

"My dear, he's your closest friend. You'll miss him."

"Of course I will. That doesn't change anything."

"What's the world coming to," Lisa asked, "if friends break off because of politics?"

"We're living in a hard time," Joel said. "Maybe friendship has become a luxury we can't afford."

Lisa was right: Joel missed his oldest friend. But he did not telephone him, nor did he play chess any more.

2

To get to City College David took the train down to 135th Street, walked two long blocks through the heart of Harlem to the foot of Morningside Park, and began the climb to the Heights. By this time it was ten to nine and he had to take the stairs at a clip if he was going to make Professor Burke's Latin class. Professor Burke played a cruel game with his students. As the nine o'clock bell rang he stuck his nose through the doorway, glanced at three or four breathless youths who were running down the hall towards his classroom, slammed the door in their faces and turned the lock. He thought he was building character. Instead he gave you an enlarged heart for the rest of your life.

Professor Burke had the red nose of a Tammany politician. He led his students on a tough journey through Caesar's *Commentaries*, Cicero's orations, and the *Aeneid*. Every so often he remembered that Virgil's epic was more than a collection of verbs to be conjugated. He glared at the class and bellowed, "This is high-class poetry, boys. High-class poetry!" Having done his duty by culture, he was free to return to the ablative absolute and dative of reference.

Professor Burroughs taught phys ed and hygiene. He was full of tales about young men who did not keep themselves clean. The peak of his efforts in this direction was a film on the dangers of venereal disease. It unfolded a succession of horrors that made Uncle Adolph and Grand Duke Michael look like a couple of boy scouts. Having allowed a moment for the moral to sink in, Professor Burroughs faced his victims and demanded rhetorically, "Would you risk your health for ten minutes of pleasure?" There was a dramatic pause. "Any questions?"

A hand shot up. "How d'you make it last ten minutes?"

Everybody laughed except the professor. The questioner was Sidney Weintraub, a skinny fellow whose angular features were surmounted by a shock of unruly red hair. Later,

when he and David were in the locker room drying themselves after their shower, Sidney looked down at himself,
twirled his penis and exclaimed, "Just think, a Beethoven
could come out of here."

"Why not a Mozart?" David asked.

"No, Beethoven's my boy. That's where the power is.
Pah-pah-pah-*pah!*"

Sidney played the violin. As a result, David and he were
soon friends. They talked about music or gossiped about
their professors, who seemed very old and remote. David
had the impression they would much rather be teaching at
Harvard, Princeton, or Yale and resented the fate that had
set them down among the sons of Jewish, Italian, and Irish
immigrants from Brooklyn and the Bronx. "There's a certain look on their faces when they come into class," he told
Sidney. "Their noses curl up, as though they were sniffing
the unwashed."

"They're a bunch of assholes," Sidney said philosophi-
cally.

One figure in this august pantheon differed from the rest;
the English professor, Donald Sheldon. Every two weeks
David had a fifteen-minute conference with him in his little
cubicle in Lincoln Corridor. Sheldon would go over David's composition, changing semicolons to commas and
exclamation points to periods. The professor was a wiry
little man who radiated good will. His eyes were like two
black raisins stuck into a cake. He spoke in a low voice and
made his corrections almost apologetically. David turned in
a composition on Isaiah that the professor liked very much.
He sprinkled it liberally with comments in red ink.

David's next composition was about a piece of music.
Professor Sheldon was delighted to discover he was a pianist. "When I was young," he told him, "I wanted very much
to study the piano, but my parents felt it would be a waste
of money. Will you come play for me?" David said yes, and
the professor invited him for the following Friday night.

To visit a professor, Lisa felt, was a high honor. She herself, since laundries were not to be trusted, washed and ironed his shirt. On Friday evening he put on his blue serge suit, was inspected, passed muster, and set forth on his first visit to a non-Jewish home.

Professor Sheldon lived in a roomy apartment on Riverside Drive. The sun had just set behind the Palisades when David arrived; through the windows that overlooked the Hudson, the afterglow splashed orange and gold across the sky. The Sheldon living room was filled with heavy pieces of furniture that looked like heirlooms, as did the ebony square piano that rested on fat round legs. The professor greeted him with a warm, "My, don't we look handsome!" and introduced him to a tall woman who seemed to be the lady of the house. The professor referred to her as Miss Pratt; David assumed that she must be a Lucy Stoner and had retained her maiden name. Also present was the professor's daughter, a doctor. David felt constrained. It seemed to him that if he wasn't careful he would knock something over—something fragile and irreplaceable. The professor must have sensed this, for he drew him out in the friendliest manner. "Are you enjoying the college?"

"It's a little too big, too impersonal." Had he said the wrong thing? He forced himself to go on. "Maybe if there were more contact between the professors and students . . ." It didn't seem necessary to finish the thought.

Presently, the professor asked him to play. The piano had a deep, mellow sound, although it was not quite in tune. David began with a Chopin nocturne, and followed it with the Beethoven sonata he was working on, the Opus 10 No. 3. In the middle of the slow movement, which was marked "slow and sad," someone in the next apartment flushed the toilet, and for a few moments the sound of a waterfall mingled with Bethoven's *Largo e mesto*. His listeners applauded with verve at the end of the sonata, and by the time he launched into the final piece—Debussy's *Soiréedans Grenade*—he felt he was playing for old friends.

When he finished, the professor shook his hand. "That

was lovely!" he exclaimed. "I cannot thank you enough. I don't know anything about music," he added, "except that I love it."

"That's the best way of knowing it," David replied, whereupon the professor glanced at him as if he had said something clever.

Coffee was served; Miss Pratt plied him with honey cake. The professor asked questions about playing the piano; David told him about Elena Parissot. "She has all sorts of exercises for strengthening the fingers, especially the fourth and fifth, which are the weakest. At the same time she warns you against being fascinated by technique. The technique has to serve the music, not the other way around."

"It's the same in writing," the professor observed. "The *how* is never as important as the *what*."

At ten thirty the professor escorted him to the door. "You've given me great pleasure, David," he said. It was exhilarating to have the professor call him by his first name; in class he addressed his students by their last names, with or without the "Mr." As David boarded the train for the Bronx, he felt as though he had taken a test and passed with a high mark.

As usual, his parents were waiting up for him. "Nu?" Joel asked. David described the room, the furniture, the professor, Miss Pratt.

"How are they different from us?" Lisa asked.

"They never raise their voices, they don't talk with their hands. And they're not as lively."

Lisa smiled as if vindicated. "What do you expect from Anglo-Saxons?"

"They have better manners than we do," David ventured.

"Why not? They're educated. But are they like us at all?"

"Yes. They're friendly, and they tried hard to make me feel at home."

Lisa reflected. David's comments put her in an international frame of mind. "Jew or goy," she announced grandly, "there's not as much difference as we think. If you dig down deep enough, all people are alike."

3

THERE was a passage in Cicero's *De Senectute* that aroused Professor Burke's admiration. It came when the great Roman enumerated the advantages of old age. First and foremost among these was the fact that a man was finally freed from the bonds of passion. Much as he hated to agree with his Latin professor, David felt that Cicero had a point. Sex was a blind, irrational force, an itch that grabbed you without a by-your-leave, kicking, pushing, thrusting its way through your middle until it shot out of you and left you in peace—until the next onset.

Women, where he was concerned, fell into two categories. There were the girls he had come to know in Elena Parissot's class. Like Henny Jershow, they didn't sleep with a man unless they were going to marry him, or at least were in love with him. He thought of them as fellow students and friends rather than as potential bedmates. Then there were the mysterious creatures he encountered in the subway or on the street, who seemed like the women on Danny Friedman's French picture cards. Knowing nothing about them, he was free to concentrate on their sexual attributes as he mentally undressed them and reveled in their arms, legs, thighs, tits, behinds.

One morning, on the way to school, a tall, rather plump girl was squeezed against him on the crowded subway, her buttocks directly against his middle. He looked around guiltily to make sure no one noticed the bulge inside his trousers. No one did, so he pressed forward slightly. Either the girl didn't notice, or could not move; or—a possibility—she didn't mind. In any case, what with the gentle movement of the car, the pushing and the shoving, he ejaculated

as the train pulled into 135th Street. Did she suspect how
well she had serviced him? He never found out. He never
even saw what she looked like, nor did he want to. For him
she was a pair of buttocks—literally a piece of ass—and
altogether satisfying in that guise.

He described the incident to Sidney, who felt it was high
time David lost his virginity. "If we were living in a French
novel," he said, "some older woman—probably a friend of
your mother's—would initiate you."

"Yukh!" David said, thoroughly repelled.

Sidney volunteered to take David to a brothel he went to
as often as his meager funds permitted. The visit was set
for a Wednesday night. David's imagination was inflamed
all that day. The experience, he told himself, would have
to be pretty good to live up to his expectations. A faint
apprehension unfurled at the back of his mind: what if he
didn't know how to go about it? He told himself that if the
birds, bees, and butterflies knew, why wouldn't he? The
thought was reassuring. He remembered his defeat with
Henny Jershow, but in that instance other factors had
intervened: pride, ego, hostility. There was one advantage
in paying for sex: he didn't have to prove himself. This time
it would be up to the woman to arouse him.

He met Sidney at nine; they took the subway downtown.
The house of pleasure was lodged in a dilapidated brownstone on West Fourteenth Street. A basement door led into
an oblong room shrouded in half darkness. Several girls sat
at the bar; one of them, named Tessie, greeted Sidney. She
was a plump blonde in a very short, low-cut red dress dotted with spangles. Her companion, a brunette with blue
eyes and narrow shoulders, concentrated on David.

"What's your name?" she asked, her lips shaping an eager
smile.

When he told her, she said, "That's a nice name, I like
it." This was clearly routine patter with her, but she tried
to sound as if she meant it. "Mine's Barbara."

"Hi."

The four of them sat down at a table; Sidney ordered drinks. Barbara struck David as very pretty in a quiet way. Her skin was lovely, her little breasts were clearly outlined under her dress. Unlike Tessie, who chattered, she had very little to say.

Alcohol depressed him, but he was afraid the others would laugh if he asked for a soft drink. When Sidney ordered a Scotch on the rocks, he said, "Make mine the same."

The drinks arrived. "Down the hatch," Tessie said cheerfully and drained hers. David took a sip of his and put it down.

"You're not drinking?" Barbara asked.

He made a grimace. "I don't like the taste of liquor."

"Why didn't you order a Coke?"

She was really very nice, he decided. "I will if you'll finish my drink."

"Tessie will," Barbara said, and pushed the drink toward her friend.

By the time David finished his Coke, Sidney and Tessie were in a heavy embrace. Barbara turned to David, suddenly businesslike. "Why don't we go upstairs?"

He found himself in a small room, most of it occupied by the bed. The yellow bedspread was trimmed with little balls of brown wool. She flipped it off, revealing a rumpled sheet. "Make yourself at home," she said.

He took off his jacket and lay down. With a practiced gesture Barbara slipped off her blouse and skirt, bra and panties. Naked except for the black stockings that reached above her knees, she faced him. "You like?" she asked, and smiled.

"Yeah."

Between her thighs, her pubic hair made a dark triangle that looked lovely. She lay down beside him. "How do you like it?" she asked.

He shrugged his shoulders, at a loss for words.

A thought struck her. "Am I getting your cherry?" she asked.

He grinned. "Kind of."

"Ooh, that's nice." She unbuttoned his fly, drew out his penis and squeezed the tip appraisingly. "Circumcised," she said.

"Yeah."

"Jewish?"

He nodded.

Without further ado she bent over, placed its head between her lips and sucked it in. The moist, tickling sensation caught him by surprise; he almost cried out with pleasure. Then, as his member responded to her ministrations, he lay back and put his hand on her shoulder, guiding her movements. He wanted above all to prolong the sensation; this was much too good to have it over with quickly. He felt himself approaching orgasm but had the presence of mind to stop her. "Let's do it the other way," he said in a whisper.

Barbara lay back, resting her head on a not altogether clean pillow. David threw off his clothes and mounted her. Her thighs enfolded him as she guided him in, all the while making little noises of counterfeit desire. He had spoken none too soon. A few thrusts and his passion poured out of him. He pushed into her again and again, gasping with pleasure. For a moment he remained perfectly still; then, slowly, he withdrew and dropped flat on the bed, cheek pressed against the mattress. He could hear the rapid beat of his heart. A feeling of well-being spread through him, an aliveness he had never known before.

"Did you enjoy it?" Barbara asked, resting her hand on his shoulder.

"Wow!" he muttered.

She trailed her fingers across his back. "I'm glad you're not disappointed."

His ear was still against the mattress; it seemed to him that he could hear the blood surging through his veins. She glanced at her wristwatch and, businesslike again, said, "Honey, I gotta get going." She said it gently, as though reluctant to hurry him.

Slowly he lifted himself off the bed and began to put on his clothes. He watched Barbara slip into her dress; unlike Tessie's, it was dark and had no spangles. A discolored mirror was nailed to the back of the door. She paused before it to pat her hair into place. She lifted a bottle of cologne from the chest of drawers beside the bed, inserted her forefinger, shook the bottle and dabbed the scented water behind each ear. Then she faced him, waiting.

He buttoned up his trousers and pulled out his wallet. The price, Sidney had told him, was twenty. He handed her two ten-dollar bills.

"Thanks," she said.

"Thank *you*," he answered, as politely as if he were at one of Miss Parissot's tea parties.

"And that'll be five dollars for the drinks," Barbara added.

He handed her another bill. She raised her skirt and tucked the money inside her stocking. "I hope you'll come again," she said and opened the door.

"You bet," he answered with feeling.

Once they were downstairs, Barbara became curiously impersonal. There were two new customers at the bar, one of whom engaged her in conversation. David moved tactfully to the end of the bar, where he sat waiting for Sidney. Barbara took no further notice of him. He stepped into the men's room; when he returned, the bartender asked him what he was drinking. This time he ordered a Coca-Cola without embarrassment.

The air was cool and damp when Sidney and he came out on the street. A brisk wind blew from the river. Sidney stopped in front of a cafeteria on Sixth Avenue. "I need a glass of milk," he said. "To replace lost tissue."

The milk called for cheese cake. They found an empty table near the window. "How did you make out?" Sidney asked.

David grinned. "It was great."

"Today you are a man."

"And liking it."

"My first time, I thought, 'Heck, is this what all the shooting's about?' Didn't seem like much."

"You were wrong. It's everything it's cracked up to be."

"I found that out later," Sidney said.

The cheese cake floated on a layer of pineapple. David relished the fresh foamy taste. He was thoughtful. "I feel sorry for the girls."

"Why?"

"They've got to take every comer."

"We're not so bad."

"Yeah, but what if a guy is fat and sweaty."

"Maybe they're oversexed."

David shook his head. "I'd say the opposite. They don't care enough about sex."

"They could get a job at Woolworth's if they were unhappy at what they're doing."

"It's not as simple as that."

Sidney laughed. "You remind me of some character in a Russian novel. He sleeps with a prostitute, then he feels guilty, so he gets down on his knees and weeps, and prays with her. And forgets to pay her, of course."

"I don't feel guilty. I feel fine."

"Good." Sidney washed down a mouthful of cheese cake with milk. "Did you take a leak after you were through?"

"Yes."

"Wash it well when you get home, and use this." From his pocket he drew a little tube that ended in a point.

"What's that?"

"Prophylactic . . . and say a prayer."

"Which one?" David thought of his poor Uncle Adolph.

"Any one, as long as it's in Hebrew."
David finished his milk and smiled happily.

4

SIDNEY decided to form a jazz band that would be available
for a summer job in the Catskills. He planned the usual
group for small hotels in the borscht circuit—piano, violin,
saxophone, and drums. David was cool to the idea, mainly
because he did not play jazz as well as he thought he should,
but Sidney kept after him. "We don't have to sound like
Ben Bernie's band. Besides, we play for dancing only at
night. At mealtime they want classical, and that's up your
alley. You'll see, we'll have a great time." David let himself
be persuaded.

Lou Jaffe, the saxophone player, was expert at the wah-
wah sound of the blues. Herbie Dichter beat up a storm on
bass drum and cymbal. When Herbie wasn't banging his
drum, he was polishing an old Ford he called Elsie. The
four boys rehearsed in Herbie's living room and Sidney
found a job at the Mountain Flower House in Ferndale.
They would each earn fifteen dollars a week plus room and
board, July 4th to Labor Day.

Lisa was of two minds about David's going away. On the
one hand, it would do him good to breathe mountain air for
nine weeks. On the other, this was the first time he would
be away from her. She viewed the separation as part of the
inevitable process that was robbing her of her baby. Nor
was she reassured by her conviction that all hotels and restaurants served poison. "What d'you think, they're in it for
your health? They should live so long." Joel was more sanguine. "The place is kosher, so how bad can the food be?"
For once he approved of religion.

The day of leave-taking arrived. "Be a good boy," Lisa

said, "so that I don't have to be ashamed of you." David
wasn't quite sure what she meant but shook his head in
assent. Joel put forth only one condition, that David write
home once a week. He promised. His parents accompanied
him downstairs where Elsie was waiting, loaded with
valises, drums, and sheet music. They kissed him; Elsie
sputtered off as Lisa, brushing away a tear, muttered the
proper incantation: "May it be in a good hour."

Elsie bore up under the rigors of the trip like the old pro
that she was. David was disappointed by his first view of
the Catskills; they looked more like tall hills than mountains. Dotted with Jewish boarding houses, the region had
certainly changed since the days of Rip Van Winkle. The
Mountain Flower House turned out to be a sprawling yellow wooden structure that boasted three verandahs and a
lake. A sign on the front lawn announced its name in tall
black letters against a pale-yellow background, above the
legend "Famous for It's Table. Jake Schulman, Prop." David
pointed out to Mr. Schulman that the apostrophe was
superfluous. Mr. Schulman, a stocky, bald man who kept
mopping his forehead and puffing at his cigar, didn't take
to the idea. "I'd have to pay a man to repaint the sign," he
said. "Besides, I don't like college boys who are too smart."
He looked appraisingly at the sign. "You know what? It
looks better this way."

The duties of the musicians were not onerous. Their main
chore was to play for dancing every night in the casino, a
gaily decorated one-room building adjacent to the main
house. The dance floor was surrounded by little tables that
invited the guests to pinochle and poker. Sidney had brought
with him a limited repertory that centered about such sure-
fire hits as *Bye Bye Blackbird*, *St. Louis Blues*, and *You're the
Cream in My Coffee*. The Charleston was performed with
passionate abandon by thin and fat alike. After several fox-
trots a waltz was called for, something smooth and dreamy
like *All Alone* or *What'll I Do?* There was always the danger
that one of the guests, carried away by the charm of Irving

Berlin's melody, would step up to the microphone and massacre a chorus.

David had no problem in furnishing a solid background for the violin and saxophone solos. Where he fell short was in bringing the printed copy to life with improvisations of his own. He didn't have the right touch for jazz, and was always slightly embarrassed when Sidney signaled to him to take a chorus by himself. The best that could be said for it was that the beat was steady and could be danced to if you felt like dancing.

The boys also played in the dining room during meals. Lunch and dinner were announced to the hungry horde by a waiter ringing a bell, whereupon the band would break into what Sidney called the "Cannibals' Entrance March." It might be Sousa's *Stars and Stripes Forever* or a medley of Stephen Foster songs taken at a snappy tempo. The rest of the meal was enlivened by piano and violin music. Sidney had brought along an anthology out of which he and David pulled an endless stream of "gems"—Kreisler's *Caprice Viennois*, Liszt's *Liebestraum*, Drdla's *Souvenir*, Raff's *Cavatina*, Elgar's *Salut d'Amour* and—most precious gem of all—Schubert's *Serenade*. These were received by the diners with warm applause.

During weekends the music could hardly be heard over the din at mealtime. Sidney had the bright idea of trotting out the overtures David had learned years before—*Poet and Peasant, Light Cavalry, Caliph of Bagdad, Barber of Seville*—that took up ten minutes and ended with a bang. He also served more serious fare, such as single movements from the piano-and-violin sonatas of Mozart and Beethoven. Mr. Schulman had an ear for music and felt that the classics lent tone to his establishment.

The food, despite Lisa's prophecies, was delicious. Mr. Schulman assumed that his guests had starved all year and had come to the Catskills to regain their strength. Eating, consequently, was the principal diversion of the day, to which all other activities—swimming, rowing, hiking, tennis, dancing—were subsidiary. The enormous breakfast went from orange juice, cereal, and eggs to hot bagels, cream cheese, herring, lox and whitefish. It was assumed that by midmorning you would be famished. A hot broth was served at ten thirty to enable you to last till one, when the main meal appeared. An assortment of soups and meats, buttressed by stuffed derma, chopped liver, and similar delicacies, was topped with elaborate cakes, pies, and fruit. Since ice cream was forbidden after meat, ices were served instead. There was another snack at four thirty to help you get through to dinner, which was a huge dairy meal built around sour cream, vegetables, cheeses, and fruits. No one expected you to go hungry to bed; a collation was served a little before midnight. Even with the mountain air and exercise, this was a diet for horses. No wonder Mrs. Mermelstein, a beefy matron from the Bronx, was heard to complain daily to her brood, "Eat, eat, it's costing me plenty."

One woman stood out among the guests: Mrs. Kelenyi. It was known that she came from Budapest, which was sufficient to give her an exotic aura. She was slender and beautiful, with dark hair, violet eyes, and chiseled features; she dressed with exquisite taste, generally in pastel shades; and at night she wore a diaphanous lilac scarf round her neck which she tied in a bow. She held herself aloof from the other women, her only companion being an attractive young man whose bedroom on the third floor adjoined hers. It was known that her husband, an elderly merchant in New York's diamond center, was traveling in Europe on business. Mrs. Kelenyi managed to unite the ladies of the Mountain Flower House against her. Were they furious because she had a lover or because she ignored them? David could not decide.

He was thrilled when she approached the musicians with a request for a particular number, such as the *Merry Widow Waltz* or *Deep in My Heart* from *The Student Prince*. One afternoon she asked him for Chopin's Nocturne in E-flat. By this time Mrs. Kelenyi had taken on a romantic allure for him; he could not bear to hear her maligned. The maligners were led by Mrs. Mermelstein, whose only exercise consisted of waddling from the dining room to the card tables in the casino and back. "What right," she demanded rhetorically, "has a *bummerkeh* like that"—the epithet consisted of *bum* with a Yiddish feminine ending—"to come among decent people."

David, as an employee, was supposed to avoid arguing with the guests. For once he refused to remain silent. "She has every right, Mrs. Mermelstein," he declared firmly. "She isn't harming you or anybody else."

Mrs. Mermelstein looked at him in astonishment. "So you're sticking up for her? A nice boy like you. What would your mother say?"

David was not to be stopped that easily. "All I'm saying is that people have a right to live their own life, as long as they don't hurt other people."

"And supposing she was a fat old lady, would you stick up for her?" Mrs. Mermelstein looked at the other women and shook her head to show that she had won the argument hands down.

"What has that got to do with it?" David asked weakly, knowing that she was right.

Mrs. Mermelstein waved her hand. "You men make me sick, you're all alike." As far as she was concerned, the discussion was over. That evening Mrs. Kelenyi asked David to play Schuman's *Träumerei*. He was glad he had defended her.

His first impression of the Catskills had given way to a more accurate assessment. After the music was finished at night, Herbie would take Elsie for a spin to Monticello or Liberty. The road unwound before them like a silk ribbon; the air was cool and crystalline. A silence hung over the mountains. In the distance the tall crags rose like black shapes crouching in the night, unearthly and remote.

He sometimes went walking in the woods around the hotel, but he was too citified to feel comfortable there. What if an animal suddenly appeared? He preferred nature as he had come to know it in Prospect Park, held in check by paved alleys, iron railings, and signs that told you where you were: nature corseted, manicured, and safe. He kept his promise to Joel about writing home. The weekly letter, he realized, was intended by his father as an exercise in writing Yiddish. When he wrote from right to left instead of the other way, the lines kept slanting down the page. English was easier too, because the letters ran into each other; here each one had to be fashioned by itself. Nonetheless he managed to cover both sides of a sheet. The first letter was the hardest; the others came more easily. He ended his third with what he felt was a clear statement on how he felt about the Catskills. "People love either the mountains or the ocean. The mountains hang over you and make you feel unimportant. The ocean takes you in so that you become part of it. I remember that you both prefer the ocean. I feel the same way."

5

THE chambermaid who cleaned their room had the same name as Herbie's car. Elsie was around thirty and not bad looking. She had watery blue eyes and a weak smile. Wisps of light-brown hair kept tumbling over her forehead, which she pushed back with a vague movement of her hand. Sidney came to the conclusion that she could be had.

David decided to give it a try; he had, he told himself, nothing to lose. One morning, when she came to tidy up the room, he was still in bed. Propped on two pillows, he pretended to be reading. He looked up when she entered. "I'll get out of your way," he said brightly.

"You're not in my way, Elsie replied, and began to make Sidney's bed.

David got up. He wore only his shorts. Elsie, who had

her back to him, could see his reflection in the sideboard mirror. "You better put some clothes on," she said, "or you'll catch cold." She gave him that weak smile of hers.

He wanted to guide the conversation into erotic channels but didn't know how. "If I caught cold—" he began tentatively, and stopped.

"Yes?" Elsie asked of the mirror.

He took this as an encouragement. "—would you help me get well?"

She sucked in her lower lip, as though considering his offer. "Depends on what I'd have to do."

Things were moving at a faster pace than he had thought possible. "I know what I'd like you to do," he said, amazed at his courage.

She became coy. "For instance."

It was too late for caution. He stepped behind her, put his hands on her hips and spun her around. "Guess," he said, and rested his hands on her shoulders.

She threw back her head and laughed. "I can't imagine."

He narrowed his eyes as he had seen Ronald Colman do when in the grip of desire. Ronald Colman was famous for narrowing his eyes. "Try."

She pretended to be thinking hard. David decided it was time to come to the point. He drew her to him and pressed his lips against hers.

When he drew back for air, "You got nerve!" she cried. He took this, correctly, as an invitation and kissed her again. Only the brave deserved the fair. That, he remembered, was from the "Ode to St. Cecilia's Day," but he couldn't recall who wrote it. Milton? Dryden? Pope? "Could I see you sometime?" he blurted out.

She considered the question, pursing her lips. Without lipstick, which she didn't apply until the evening, they were thin and bloodless. "I don't see why not," she drawled.

He breathed a sigh of relief. "When?"

"Oh, I don't know."

His anxiety returned. "How about tonight?"

She looked as if she were mentally consulting her date-book. "Could be."

"Where?"

"I'm in Room 5. At the back of the house."

"We get through playing around eleven thirty. How about midnight?"

"Okay."

Bells rang inside his brain. He had pulled it off! "Tonight, then." Wait till Sid heard about this. He went in search of his friend.

Sid let out a low whistle. "What d'you know! I didn't think you had the nerve."

"Well, I did," David reported proudly, and added in a more humble tone, "But now that it's settled I'm a little—"

"Scared?"

"Kind of."

"Why? She's just another lay, like the girls on Fourteenth Street."

"It's different. We paid them, but she's doing it for fun."

"So?"

"So it's different."

"Shut your eyes and pretend she's them." David looked unconvinced, whereupon Sidney added, "Tell you what! I'll come along. Up to the door, that is, just to make sure you get there."

The afternoon dragged. Sidney suggested that they read through the D-minor Sonata of Brahms. He was always suggesting that they read through works he knew, which gave him the advantage. After a particularly thorny passage, David gave up. "Hey, this is not music to sightread. Let me learn it first." They switched to Mozart's Sonata in E-flat, which went better. Then David took a swim in the lake. Country lakes had fish in them, and he was obsessed by the notion that one of them would touch him. He kicked hard to let them know they should keep their distance.

After the swim he went to his room for a nap. The thought of Elsie drove sleep away. He knew he should save himself for the assignation, but his imagination was over-heated. There was only one way to overcome temptation: to yield to it. A vision of Elsie nude brought him swiftly to the climax. He drew a deep breath. The rehearsal had gone well enough; what about the performance? He grinned and fell asleep.

That night the dancing continued until a little after eleven thirty. The boys played *Goodnight Ladies* as a hint to the guests. When they finished, Herbie sorted out the sheet music and arranged each number in its folder. At five to twelve, David, flanked by Sidney, stole down the long corridor that led to the back of the house. The hallway ended in a small quadrangle beneath a skylight, through which streamed the light of a waning moon. David's shadow fell, foreshortened, against a greenish-white wall. Sidney withdrew to the opposite wall, where Elsie would not see him when she opened the door. David knocked twice, softly.

Sounds of a bed creaking floated down the hall. He could not tell whether they came from Elsie's room or the one next to it. The transom showed a dim yellow light, which meant that she was inside, but the door did not open. David looked uncertainly at Sidney, who motioned to him to knock again. He did.

Silence, punctuated by the creaking sounds. Sidney indicated the doorknob, which David turned. It did not give. Puzzled, he was uncertain of his next move. "Knock again," Sidney whispered. "Louder. Maybe she didn't hear you."

David rapped the door sharply with his knuckles. He was tense now, and afraid he might awaken the occupants of the adjacent rooms. Suddenly the door flew open. In the doorway loomed the hulking figure of the chef, a beefy man in his forties, who muttered, "If you fuckin' kids don't get away from here I'll kick your balls in!" and slammed the door.

As if on cue, doors 4 and 6 opened. David flew down the corridor followed by Sidney. Neither stopped until they were safe in their room at the opposite end of the hallway.

"That no-good cunt!" Sidney exclaimed with venom. "She got her signals mixed."

David flung himself on his bed and buried his face in the pillow. The disappointment that overwhelmed him seemed to stretch beyond Elsie to include every defeat he had ever known. "God damn her!" he cried, on the verge of tears.

Sidney sat down beside him. "Look, Davey, it's not the end of the world. She's only a piece of ass. There'll be plenty of others."

"It's such a slap in the face."

"From a slut like that? Forget it!" He put his hand on David's shoulder. "But there's something else you shouldn't forget. If you think you're gonna get the things you want out of life just because you want them, you have another guess coming."

"You trying to cheer me up or make me feel worse?"

"I'm just trying to tell you the way it is. In this world you got to fight for things."

David gazed at the patch of moonlight on the wall opposite his bed. "Maybe if it's going to be such a struggle, I won't want to fight."

"That's up to you. Just so you learn how to handle it."

"What if I don't?"

"Then you'll have a rough time. You better believe it."

David thought awhile. "Let's turn in," he said. "We've had enough excitement for one night."

They brushed their teeth and changed into their pajamas. " 'Night, Sid," David said as he got into bed. "Thanks for everything."

"Just remember what I told you."

David listened to the ticking of Sidney's alarm clock. Already the initial pain of his disappointment had lost its sting. Elsie could drop dead for all he cared.

There remained a larger question. Was this what it was going to be like?

6

THE following morning Mrs. Mermelstein lay in wait for him. Without preliminaries, "Nice things I been hearing about you," she said.

There was no point in replying, "I don't know what you mean." But how had she got wind of the affair? For an instant David had a vivid image of secret wires leading from all parts of the house to her room, enabling her to hear all, know all, judge all.

"No wonder," Mrs. Mermelstein continued her offensive, "you stuck up for that *bummerkeh* Mrs. Kelenyi. Now you found yourself another just like her. What would your mother say?"

David put up a front. "Ask her, so she'll tell you."

"Look at him! He has the nerve to answer me back yet." She returned to the second person. "If I knew your mother"—she shook her head from side to side—"oy, would I ask her."

The bare prospect destroyed what remained of David's composure. "Mrs. Mermelstein, what d'you want from me?"

"I want you should behave."

"That's a big order," he managed to bring out before he retreated ignominiously in the direction of his room.

"And your friend the violin player," Mrs. Mermelstein called after him, "is no better than you. In fact, he's worse, because he put you up to it."

David repeated the conversation to Sidney. "Gee, I feel so naked."

"Come off it," Sidney said. "It's Elsie who should feel embarrassed, not you."

"How d'you suppose Mrs. Mermelstein found out?"

"I didn't tell her, you didn't tell her. Must've been someone who saw us run."

"Don't those yentas have anything else to talk about?"

"Don't worry, Davey, by supper time it'll all be forgotten."

Sidney was right. Life at the Mountain Flower House was so eventful that by nightfall the incident was hardly remembered. Except for one outcome. As David returned from the lake he encountered Val, who worked in the kitchen. She was a plump, cheerful blonde in her mid-thirties. "I hear you had a rough time last night." She gave him an understanding smile.

David was sheepish. "I guess you could call it that."

"I felt sorry for you."

"You did?" He looked at her with new interest.

"Yeah. It's tough being young and"—she stopped, hunting for the right word—"stood up."

David basked in her sympathy. "It sure is," he said, hoping for more. Her breasts, shapely under her flimsy summer blouse, seemed to be reaching for him.

"Tell you what," Val said very deliberately. "Tonight, after you get through, knock on my door. I'm in number 2."

"Sure. But I'm not knocking on any doors," he added as deliberately as she.

"Okay. I'll leave it open. When?"

"Midnight." He didn't narrow his eyes like Ronald Colman, or breathe heavily. He didn't need to.

"Seeya." Val made off as casually as if she had been discussing the weather.

David's first impulse was to tell Sidney; he decided against it. This time there would be neither consultation nor buildup. Not even a rehearsal. He would simply open Val's door and let nature take its course.

When they finished playing that night, his comrades decided on a ride to Monticello. David begged off. Promptly at midnight he made his way down the corridor to the help's quarters, opened the door marked 2, and slipped in. Val lay on the bed. The lamp on the night table beside her was not lit, but the room was flooded with moonlight. "Lock the door," she whispered. David slipped the bolt.

"Come here," she said without stirring. He undressed, leaving shirt and trousers on the floor in a heap. She opened her robe and held out one hand. "Lie down." He obeyed. She turned on her side and moved over so that her body touched his. "Relax," she whispered. "Tonight'll be easier for you." She ran her hand lightly over his body, from his shoulder to his thigh.

"It's easier already." Her skin, it seemed to him, was smoother than anything he had ever touched. It was soft and smooth the way velvet was. White velvet. He told her so.

She was amused. "It don't feel like that to me. I rub it with olive oil."

She made everything so easy. She accepted the fact that he was younger, and less adept at making love. To her this meant simply that she had to teach him how to give her pleasure. She reminded David of the sleek Angora cats who kept preening and licking their bodies, except that she expected him to do the licking. He was happy to oblige. She played with him tenderly, her fingertips gently stroking his penis, scattering delicious little arrows of pleasure in their wake. Yet hers was an impersonal tenderness. She would have done the same, David realized, for any male she liked.

His eagerness sprang from anxiety as much as from ardor; it was an anxiety that made him want to reach the end of the journey as soon as possible. Val, on the other hand, liked to prolong the trip, to savor it, and explore bypaths on the way. She took long to be aroused. For this reason the foreplay was as important to her as the act itself. When David was finally inside her she guided and encouraged him through the pressure of her fingers on his back. He abandoned himself to the sheer pleasure of being, to a sensuality unmarred by thought. He felt intensely alive and bursting with energy. He no longer had to do the pushing because it was he who was being pushed, by a force stronger than his will, a force that propelled him irresistibly to the climax. A final thrust, and the life fluid poured out of him. Val's fingers dug into his back, she gasped, and he realized that she had come at the same moment as he.

David withdrew and lay back, his head next to hers on the pillow. A deep contentment spread through him. He took Val's hand and slipped his fingers through hers. "There was a Roman poet who said, 'Post coitum triste.' That means, after fucking it's sad."

"Is it?" Val asked and smiled.

"I've got news for the old geezer. He was wrong."

"What was his name?"

"Horace, I think."

"I once knew a fellow named Horace. He was great in bed." She must have thought that David might feel slighted, for she added, "So are you."

"Thanks."

She lit a cigarette. "You smoke?"

"No. I don't like the taste." He had news for Sidney. This was better than being with the girls on Fourteenth Street. Here you were doing it with someone who had picked you, and that made a difference.

She inhaled slowly and let out little smoke rings. "Did you enjoy it?" she asked.

"It was terrific."

"Good. We'll do it again."

He felt too completely at peace to want to do it again. She must have read his thought, for she added, "I mean, some other night."

"Great." He was in a mood for confidences. "Y'know, when things go right between two people, it's beautiful."

"I told you it would be," Val said. "I don't believe in giving anyone a hard time. I put myself in their place." She glanced at the clock. "It's getting late, lover boy," she said, "and I've a long day tomorrow."

He got off the bed, pulled on his shorts and trousers. "May I come again?"

"Sure." She slipped into her robe and sat up, letting her legs dangle over the side of the bed.

"When?" David noticed that he felt no anxiety in putting the question.

"How about Thursday night?"

"Same time?"

She nodded. "Same place."

He buttoned his shirt, bent over, and kissed her. "Same people."

She smiled.

" 'Night, Val. And thanks." He moved toward the door.

She placed a forefinger against her lips. "Sh . . ." David shut the door noiselessly behind him and tiptoed down the corridor. Impatient to tell Sidney the news, he burst into their room. It was empty. By the time the boys returned from Monticello he had decided not to let Sidney in on the secret. At any rate, not for the time being. Sidney might want to take over, and what he didn't know wouldn't hurt him.

He did not reveal his good fortune until a week before Labor Day; by then he had been with Val more than half a dozen times. Sidney let out a whistle. "I don't believe it!"

"Sure, you do."

"It just goes to show—"

"What?"

"Still waters run deep."

"What's that supposed to mean?"

"Here we're all trying to get laid, and you, the quiet one, make out while we're beating our brains out."

David decided to be modest. "Sid, it wasn't because of anything I did. She decided."

"Only because you happened to be in the right place at the right time." Sidney thought a moment. "Maybe that's what luck is."

"So I was lucky."

"You gonna see her in the city?"

"That's up to her."

"How come you kept it from me?"

"Could be I was afraid you'd spoil it for me."

"Why should I?"

"You might have wanted her yourself."

"Damn right I would." Sidney laughed. "Afraid of competition?"

"No, just being careful."

"As a matter of fact, you're wrong," Sidney said. "It meant so much to you, I wouldn't have had the heart to spoil it, assuming I could."

"We'll never know."

"Besides, that much of a bargain she ain't."

"Sour grapes."

"Anyway, I'm glad you had it."

Always in the past, when the subject of women came up, Sidney had talked down to him. David noticed a deference in Sidney's tone that had never been there before. Nothing, he reflected, succeeded like success.

7

LISA looked him over carefully. "You've changed," she said.

"How?"

"You're a man now."

"Is that bad, Ma? You wouldn't want me to stay a child, would you?"

She smiled. "Of course I would. But time changes everything."

The sun had set. The trees in Crotona Park were etched against the fading light, their branches tracing intricate patterns like the filaments on anatomical charts. It was the hour that induced Lisa's favorite brand of melancholy. "Another day gone," she said with a sigh. "Did you behave?"

"Depends on what you mean by behaving."

"Behaving means to have principles," she said. As always, *printzipen* crackled righteously on her lips. "Without principles a man has no character, and without character he's a nothing."

"I've been away for two months, I just got back, and already you're lecturing me." David put his arms around her and waltzed her around the room. "Did you miss me?"

She put her hand against his cheek, and her eyes were lustrous. "You know I did, my son. When I lecture you, I'm only trying to make you into a better person."

"The trouble is," David said, "you expect too much from yourself, so you expect too much from others. You don't make allowances."

"For what? For all kinds of *schweinerei?* Not me!"

"Deep down," he teased her, "you belong to the old school. You believe praise is dangerous for a person. You think it'll do him more good if you pick out his faults."

"And the new school is better?" she inquired. "No matter what you did, your father approved. Had I left it to him you'd have grown up a wild animal."

Joel lowered his newspaper. "Leave me out of this," he said. "It's my day off."

Now that he was back with them, David realized how much he had missed his parents. Yet there was an element of tension between him and his mother that he never felt with his father. He remembered how, whenever he came into Henny Jershow's presence, he would straighten up to show her that he was a little taller than he was. There was the same need in him to prove himself to Lisa, to impress her, and at the same time to convince her that he wasn't as bad as she made him out to be. Thus they led each other a kind of dance, his need of her praise all the greater because of her need to withhold it.

"Did you meet anyone interesting?" she asked.

"Not really." Val was interesting, but hardly in a way that his mother would appreciate. "There was a Mrs.

Kelenyi, very beautiful, who loved music. The other women resented her because she was with her lover while her husband was away on business."

"I would resent her, too," Lisa said.

"I'm surprised to hear that," Joel said. "I thought you were all for love."

"I am, but not that kind. It's not right to do this to a husband, especially if he's an older man."

"You're too *moralish*, my dear," Joel said with a smile.

"If you don't mind my saying so," she shot back, "you're not *moralish* enough."

Now they had each other to fence with, they didn't need him. David went into the kitchen, poured himself a glass of milk, and sat down at the kitchen table. His mother's lecture had deflated him. The trouble was that when she harangued him about his shortcomings he was more than inclined to agree with her. It amazed him how successfully he resisted her efforts to improve him. There was a whole catalogue of virtues that she strove to implant in him. She wanted him to be decisive, self-reliant, sincere, truthful, punctual, responsible. Yet he never could make up his mind about anything, he needed someone to lean on, he never told people what he thought of them so as not to hurt them, he was not above lying when it suited his purpose, he had so little sense of time that he was constantly late, and as for taking responsibility, he was always putting off the things he was supposed to do or forgetting to do them altogether. Except where his music was concerned. She managed to pick off his vulnerable points with unerring aim, but instead of freeing him from them, she only succeeded in making him feel guilty about them.

She had enjoyed him as long as he was her little boy, to shape and mold as she saw fit. Now that he was someone apart from her, she felt disappointed. Whose fault was it that he had not become the person she had expected him to be? Hers, for trying to make him into someone he wasn't, or his, for refusing to be anybody but himself? The conflict between them went much deeper than the trifles that served to bring it to the surface. He simply wasn't her kind of guy and he never would be!

They had started out as such good friends, they had had such good times together, but time had come between them. The years had pushed them apart until they could no longer reach each other.

TWO

1

IT was time for Annie to find a husband. Lisa found him. His name was Nathan, he was a distant relative of Joel's, and had recently emigrated from Russia. He came from a village near Białystok that had been devastated during the civil war between the Bolsheviks and Petlura's Cossacks. During a savage pogrom, Nathan had survived by hiding among the barrels in a wine cellar. From his hiding place he heard the shouting of the Cossacks and the screams of their victims. The memory still haunted him.

The courtship proceeded smoothly. Lisa invited Nathan to dinner and had him listen to Annie play *Reproches d'amour*. She asked him again and served her most dependable dishes. Nathan was overwhelmed by the honor. Truth to tell, he stood more than a little in awe of his future mother-in-law. In his shtetl he had never met anyone like her.

Once the bird was caught, Lisa's interest waned. According to her, Nathan had never left the shtetl. On the rare occasions when he stood up to her, she called him a Polovetzkian, the name of the barbaric tribe who captured Prince Igor. Also, to Joel's amusement, she looked down on Nathan's extreme orthodoxy, compared to which her own religious practices were quite progressive. He spent most of his waking hours in observing a ritual so complicated that it hardly left him time to think of anything else. The one liberty he permitted himself was to shave his beard, for which he used a powder in order to circumvent the Biblical injunction against the cutting of hair. He was persuaded that he had been saved from the Cossacks by the direct intervention of the Deity, a point that Lisa was not prepared to dispute. The match had one thing going for it. Annie's eyes lit up whenever she caught sight of him.

The wedding took place in Crotona Manor. Joel was generous with his stepdaughter; for fifty dollars extra, live roses flanked the wedding canopy. Annie, who had followed her mother's lead in never using make-up, felt that the occasion called for it. Her lips blossomed into a bright red and her broad Kalmuk face took on color. In her white satin gown she looked prettier than she ever had. The ceremony unfolded in strictly Orthodox fashion. Lisa had a good cry when Nathan put the ring on Annie's finger, and the groom completed the ceremony by crushing a glass under his foot. David suspected that the ancient custom had a sexual connotation, but the rabbi insisted that the glass was broken to commemorate the destruction of the Temple. Everybody shouted mazel tov!, there was much kissing and merrymaking, and the couple departed for a brief honeymoon in Atlantic City.

Lisa was aware that she had not sufficiently indoctrinated the bride into the basics of marriage. Outspoken as she was in regard to the sex education of her sons, a curious shyness kept her from discussing such matters with her daughter. She hoped for the best, but her fears were realized when, upon the couple's return, she learned that the marriage had not been consummated. Annie loved her husband, but the prospect of allowing that thing of his to enter had frightened her out of her wits. The very thought made her want to vomit.

For Nathan the sex act had religious significance, as it

fulfilled God's command to His chosen people to be fruitful and multiply. How would they multiply if a husband did not cohabit with his wife? Lisa advised him to be patient. Annie, she told him, was a sensitive girl. Time was on his side, and love would find a way.

She knew she had to have a heart-to-heart talk with her daughter, but put if off as long as she could. Finally, "Aniushka, my soul," she said.

"Yes, Mama," Annie replied and burst into tears.

This provided Lisa with the opening she needed. "Nathan loves you and you love Nathan. So why are you crying?"

"I don't know why," Annie replied between sobs. "I'm afraid."

"There's nothing to be afraid of," Lisa said firmly despite her embarrassment. "Babies have been born for thousands of years. Which means that what you're afraid of has been happening since the world began." She suddenly knew why she was embarrassed. She was admitting—not that this was anything Annie didn't suspect—that she herself had indulged in what Annie was afraid of, first with Annie's father, now with Joel. True, this was nothing to be ashamed of, but it was nothing to talk about either. "Dry your tears, my darling. You are a woman now, and loving a man is part of a woman's life"—Lisa thought a moment and added, "the most important part."

Annie, always obedient where her mother was concerned, dried her tears. Time helped; according to Nathan, so did God. Annie accepted her wifely duties to such good effect that the Lord's will was done and she became pregnant. Lisa thrilled to the news. She could see herself cradling the baby in her arms, crooning a lullaby, her heart swelling with tenderness and pride.

At the same time, she was aware of a faint dissatisfaction that she would never confess to anyone. Deep down she was not yet ready to become a grandmother.

2

V<small>AL</small> was working as a waitress in Child's on Fourteenth Street. David waited for her when she finished at night. Sometimes he came a little early, and ordered something in the restaurant. Val made out his check for less than he owed. She enjoyed screwing the company, she said.

They walked through Union Square to her apartment. The little park, with its threadbare trees and rickety benches, had a forlorn air. Small groups gathered around the statue of Washington. Socialists confronted communists, anarchists raised hell with Trotzkyites, each speaker persuaded that he alone held the cure for society's ills. David liked to stop at one group before proceeding to the next, but all the arguments blurred together in his mind. Val made no effort to follow the discussion; she was too tired after a day of waiting on tables.

Her apartment consisted of a square studio with kitchenette and bath. Always, as she unlocked the door, she would say, "You'll see, it'll look real cute when I get a chance to fix it up." The bed was disguised as a couch on which sat a large doll in a red-and-black Spanish costume. A dilapidated sideboard held a photograph of her parents and a picture of Val at sixteen proudly displaying her junior high school diploma. Also her most prized possession, a mandolin she didn't know how to play.

David saw her every Wednesday night. "What d'you do the rest of the week?" he would ask, to which she replied with a coquettish "Wouldn't you like to know?" This accorded with her desire to keep their friendship on as casual a basis as possible. They came together for what his friend Sidney called pure fuckery, and that goal seemed best served by their not becoming too deeply involved with each other. It was a new experience for David to have sex regularly. He found it quite wonderful. All through the week he anticipated the approaching rendezvous. Suddenly sex was no longer a problem; it had become an expectation that was sure to be fulfilled. This alternation of tension and appeasement gave his life a shape, a rhythm it had never had before. He felt extremely lucky to have found Val. Sidney agreed.

What he liked, too, was that she made no demands upon him. Her sole concern, where he was concerned, was that he contribute to her pleasure. He had never asked himself how women felt about sex; he had assumed that for them it was inextricably bound up with love. Hence he was astonished that Val's sexuality functioned on so primitive a level. She was not interested in his mind or soul. For her he existed primarily as a healthy young male whose desire leaped forward to meet her own. The best thing she could do for him was to show him how to enjoy his body, to find pleasure in its rhythms and needs. He had grown up in a home where love was talked about constantly but sex was hardly ever mentioned, and when it was mentioned his mother managed to make it sound sinful. Val's easy attitude was nothing short of a revelation.

She took the same pains to teach him how to make love as Elena Parissot did to teach him the piano. Under her tutelage he became aware of a woman's body as a finely tuned instrument that could be played upon as sensitively as any Steinway. The sex act for her was the climax of an elaborate ritual of excitation whose subtleties she devised with endless ingenuity. Such inventiveness, David decided, could come only from someone who had nothing more important on her mind. He would suddenly find his head where he would expect his toes to be; Val constantly created variations on what was a fairly simple theme. For the first time in his life David had come up against a thoroughgoing pagan.

Nor did familiarity dull her appetite; she transformed each encounter into a fresh adventure. As she put it, laughing, "I love cock." She enjoyed stroking his penis, pulling up the tightly stretched skin ever so gently as her fingertips moved toward the head. "It looks like that thing on top of the Chrysler Building," she said; to which David replied, "Thanks, but it's not that big." Her earliest experience with men had been clouded by her fear of pregnancy. Using her lips not only eliminated that danger but with practice she grew to like this as much as the real thing. She expected total reciprocity. "Eat me, honey," she would say as she stretched out lazily on her back and guided him, fingers lightly on her head or shoulders, to her most sensitive spots. This kind of love-making was like the play of two young animals, but it also had an element of body worship. By going down on him, she made David feel more desirable in his own eyes. Here, too, a ritual was involved. She invariably made him promise not to come in her mouth. He duly gave his word but in the heat of the moment failed to keep it, whereupon she would smile and say, "Shucks, I swallowed your kid." To which he would answer, "Well, it's protein."

At seventeen she had given birth to an illegitimate baby, which she gave for adoption. She dismissed the experience with a laconic "I'm not the motherly type. When I think of all the kids I might have had . . ." The thought made her sigh. Sometimes, after a particularly pleasurable climax, she would murmur, "That could have been twins."

David learned that she came from a mining town in Pennsylvania, was of Polish background, and had been married twice. She had lost contact with both men; according to her they were drifters. David asked how she acquired the mandolin. "That's a long story," she replied. "Someday I'll tell you about it." She never did.

Suddenly, one night toward the end of November, Val exploded a momentous piece of news. She was getting married.

David looked at her in disbelief. "What's that?"

She smiled happily. "It's all settled."

"Just like that you tell me?"

"How else?"

"I—I don't understand."

"What's there to understand? I lived with the guy some years ago. I told him to make his mind up but he wasn't ready, so we broke up. Now he's back."

"Where does that leave me?"

"It doesn't, Davey. This is it."

"You mean, I won't see you anymore?"

"I don't think he'd like that."

"Wow!" He was silent awhile. Then, "Seems to me," he protested, "you should've thought of me, too."

"Thought what? Would you like to marry me?" She smiled at the idea.

"You know I can't. I'm not settled or anything."

"Well, you think I want to wait on tables all my life?"

"What does he do?"

"Auto mechanic. He makes a living, he's a nice guy, and"—she paused a moment, to soften the blow—"he's my age. I'll not be robbing the cradle."

He made a grimace. "As if age is important."

"Okay, it's not important. But he's my kind, and that is. You aren't, and never could be."

"I tried."

"Davey, y'have to understand. A person has to think of their future." She chucked him under the chin. "Let's go to bed."

She was tender with him and giving, to no avail. He would not let himself be distracted from his unhappiness. "Davey, think of all the fun we've had together," she said. "And all the fun you'd have missed if you hadn't met me."

"That's exactly what I'm thinking of," he replied. "And now that I'm gonna lose it, you expect me to enjoy myself?"

"Don't be a spoilsport. Nothing is forever."

"Look, Val, I can kiss you good-bye, I can cry you good-bye," he said ruefully, "but I can't screw you good-bye."

"Try," she said, and continued to play with him. It was no use.

When the time came for him to leave, Val said, "Stop moping."

"I feel like I was used," he said glumly.

"And I wasn't? That's what people are for—to use and be used."

He kissed her again and again, tears in his eyes. Val stroked his cheeks. "You're like a little boy," she brought out tenderly.

His last glimpse of her was from the stairs. She stood in the doorway and smiled, one hand pressed against her dressing gown while with the other she blew him a kiss. "Thanks for everything, Val." It seemed like such a foolish thing to say. "And all the best."

The next morning he poured his heart out to Sidney, who stopped him short. "What are you bellyaching about? You had a good thing and you enjoyed it. And it didn't cost you anything."

"Except a heartache. I feel—" David groped for the right word and came out with "betrayed."

"Betrayed my ass. She taught you a lot, she made a man out of you. Be grateful."

"You sound like you were glad I lost her."

Sidney grinned. "Of course I am. Just because I'm your friend doesn't mean I didn't envy you."

David tried to fight off his bitterness. "I guess she was right," he said. "Nothing is forever."

3

THE music school was an enclave apart, with its own rules and interests. Each of the students had been the only kid on the block who showed musical talent. Now all the prodigies were herded together under one roof where their egos could rub against each other like beans in a bag.

Studios and classrooms resounded with the strains of

Mozart and Beethoven, Paganini and Verdi, as the faculty
worked to initiate their charges into the higher reaches of
professionalism. The emphasis was upon performance,
achievement, success. Although art was supposed to be free
from the kind of competition that went on in the business
world, in its own way the school atmosphere was fiercely
competitive. The students competed for the best positions
in the orchestra, for the leading roles in the opera produc-
tions, or for the privilege of performing a concerto with the
orchestra. Life was a race, and the prize went to the swift
of foot and bold of heart.

Elena Parissot fit well into this hermetic little world. She
fought for her students and intrigued shamelessly so that
they would receive their share of honors and awards. "Many
are called but few are chosen" was one of her basic maxims,
but she said it so sweetly that her pupils never suspected
the statement might apply to them. She sent them to hear
the great pianists of the day and encouraged them to hope
that if they worked hard and followed her precepts, they
too might find themselves in that illustrious company.
Obviously not every one of them could become a famous
virtuoso. However, there was nothing to keep them from
dreaming, and Miss Parissot felt it was good for them to
dream.

She had studied with the great Leschetitsky in Vienna
and with Emil Sauer in Berlin. In her youth, she had possessed all the attributes of a concert pianist save one—the
courage to face an audience. After serveral painful attempts
she abandoned the career for which she had so carefully
prepared, developed a nervous heart as an alibi, and found
an outlet for her ambition in teaching. She brought to it an
intensely personal attitude: she lived vicariously through her
students, enjoyed their victories, suffered their defeats, and
never forgave them if they left her for another teacher.

She often gave David an extra lossion, usually in the evening. He enjoyed going to her apartment. She received him
in a blue velvet housecoat that clung to her ample figure.

When she smiled, she seemed extremely feminine, even feline, yet there was something masculine about her. With her mound of blue-black hair piled high on her head, her boldly aquiline features, heavily rouged cheeks, and double chin she looked—especially in profile—like a Roman emperor of the decadence. If she had had a few drinks during dinner, she was in a good humor. "How is my young man tonight?" she would ask in her husky baritone, making it sound as if she really wanted to know.

The lesson lasted for two hours, sometimes more. Miss Parissot analyzed what he was doing and what he should do. Sometimes she nudged him off the piano stool and sat down to play the passage in question. She was enveloped in a cloud of perfume that he thought of as musk. Though he didn't know what the word meant, it seemed to fit the heavy, sweetish scent she gave off, like a fruit or flower that was a bit too ripe. Although she had not practiced in years, she had retained her technical facility. Her hands moved freely over the keyboard, fingers close to the keys, arms relaxed. He liked her novel way of putting things. Of the beginning of the fugue in Beethoven's Sonata Opus 110: "It must sound as if the heavens were opening." And of the melody in the middle part of Chopin's *Polonaise militaire:* "That's a trumpet solo if there ever was one."

"I've no wish," she told him, "to impose my interpretation on my pupils. All I want is to get them to understand the music, then they can create their own interpretation." This sounded extremely enlightened and enabled her to think of herself as a progressive teacher. In fact, however, she recognized only one way to play a passage—the correct way: in other words, her way. Since David had a good ear and a gift for mimicry, he quickly caught her intention and gave it back to her. As a result, she considered him one of her most talented pupils, certainly the most intelligent, and the one most worthy to receive what she had to offer.

The lessons ended at ten thirty so as not to disturb the

neighbors. Miss Parissot generally invited him to stay for a cup of coffee. She talked incessantly, going from one subject to the next as her fancy led her, holding him spellbound by the vivacity of her mind and tongue. She had been educated in France and knew well the staple works of French literature: *Manon Lescaut, Les Misérables, Madame Bovary, Père Goriot, Thaïs.* She liked especially to read the letters of great composers—Mozart's, Chopin's, and the two-volume correspondence of Liszt and Wagner. "You took your life in your hands." she informed David, "if you had an affair with George Sand. She was sure to put you in her next novel. Read *Lucrezia Floriani.* Prince Karol is a take-off on Chopin. Most amusing."

Although she gave her opinions freely about the people she had known, the places she had visited, and the books she had read, she never talked about herself. David knew as little about her now as when he had first met her. Had she ever married? Had she ever been in love? Her whole life could not have been dedicated to mamman. He disapproved of his curiosity; there was no reason why she should reveal anything about herself. All the same, he would have liked to know more. One day, when she called him to change the hour of the lesson—on the telephone her voice sounded like a man's—she said, "It's a strange thing, David. When I phone people I find myself wondering about the room they're in, what it looks like, how it's furnished. Someday you must describe it all to me." He felt relieved to learn that she was as curious about him as he was about her.

It was almost midnight when he left. He walked down Broadway. The theater crowds had gone home, the lights looked pale and tired. A quiet hung over Times Square, tinged with restlessness. Solitary figures moved along the street. Whatever it was they were looking for, they had not found it. On the Times Building the latest headlines flowed across an electric signboard. David stopped to read. "RUTH SNYDER AND GRAY DIE IN THE ELECTRIC CHAIR . . . TROTZKY DEPARTS FOR EXILE . . .

STOCK MARKET HAS ITS DULLEST DAY IN YEARS; TICKER STAYS IDLE FOR MINUTES AT A TIME . . ." He made his way toward the subway station on Forty-second Street. A street vendor exhibited little dancing dolls that shimmied with a rubbery motion. Farther on, a man performing card tricks on a wooden box shouted to attract passers-by.

The evening with Miss Parissot had left David exhilarated. He had the feeling that he was sharing a rare camaraderie; even more, that she was leading him toward a distant but rather splendid goal. She promised nothing, but she hinted at much. What more could he expect? Meanwhile it was great to be studying with her. To learn. To understand. To know.

4

On Mondays and Thursdays Sidney worked as an usher in Carnegie Hall, which meant that on those nights David could attend the concert free. He generally sat in the dress circle, but Sidney was sometimes able to smuggle him into a box near the stage. He could watch as the various instruments entered into or dropped out of the orchestral interplay; in effect, he was able to see what he was hearing.

Or he followed with a score, which gave him an even clearer picture of how the masters mixed their colors, flutes with violins, oboes with violas, trumpets with horns. At certain passages he would shut his eyes and abandon himself to the sheer beauty of the sound. When he listened at his best, he listened as he had long ago outside the record shop on Broadway, when the heavens had opened and a great light had poured out of the sky. There was no name for the emotion that music released in him, even though it bore only a faint resemblance to real sorrow or joy. Rather,

it was the essence of emotion, the pure thing that didn't
need a label. You felt happy or sad without knowing what
you were happy or sad about.

The feeling was even more special when he sat at the
piano. Now it was he who created the sounds, shaping them
into patterns that floated through the air and added up to
all kinds of meaning. Yet the meaning could not be put into
words. It lay hidden behind the notes, as Miss Parissot put
it, and each time he played, he had to discover it for himself. A hundred details demanded attention. The shaping
of the phrase so as to reveal its inner structure. The rise of
tension to the climax of the melodic curve. The bringing
out of the inner voices that made harmony and counterpoint come alive. The proper emphasis on the accents that
gave the music its forward drive. The right amount of
pedaling that sustained the harmonies without blurring
them. The different kinds of weight and attack—from the
wrist, arm, shoulder—that controlled the sound and the
mood. And the understanding of style that made you play
Bach differently from Beethoven and Beethoven differently
from Chopin. David loved to work out the delicate balance
among all these. The world dropped away from him, he
gave himself completely to the music. When, after hours of
practicing, he achieved a level of interpretation that pleased
him, he felt a satisfaction, a joy unlike any other.

But to become a musician, he was beginning to realize,
involved issues that had nothing to do with music: the question of career, of getting ahead, and the mystery of how far
you were going to go. You couldn't go on playing if you
didn't make a living at it, and you couldn't make a living at
it if people didn't come to hear you. Sidney was increasingly preoccupied with this problem. "For the time and
effort I'm putting into music," he told David, "I could
become a doctor or lawyer."

"But you don't want to," David pointed out.

"I'm not so sure. Davey, think hard for a minute. Where
are we headed for?"

"Meaning—?"

"Meaning that we don't know. We're preparing for the concert stage. Of the hundreds who try, how many make it? What if we don't?"

"Stop, you're depressing me!"

"That's a good sign. Ask yourself, what are our chances? Suppose I don't turn out to be be a Heifetz? Where will I end up? Sawing away in the second-violin section of some orchestra. Bitter. Frustrated. And you? Teaching little girls their scales? The trouble is, it's all or nothing in our field. There's no room in the middle. And we're in for a terrific letdown if the cards don't fall our way."

"How will we know if we don't take a chance?"

"By the time we find out it'll be too late to turn elsewhere."

"What are you getting at?"

"Simply this. I could go to law school. I have to decide."

"What about the violin?"

"There are plenty of doctors and lawyers who play chamber music one night a week. Believe me, they're having a lot more fun than if they tried to earn their living as musicians."

"You mean you would chuck the whole thing at this point?"

"Better now than later. You keep saying I'm the practical one. Well, I'm being practical."

David was silent. Presently, "What about you?" Sidney asked.

"I don't know. You see, I don't want to be a doctor or lawyer. Or even a dentist. You have a choice. I don't."

Sidney shook his head. "That's too bad," he said. "I hope you don't live to regret it."

The conversation stirred up all kinds of doubts in David. Actually, when he thought of his future he was of two minds. At times it seemed to him there were no limits to what he could achieve. He was intelligent, he was serious about his work, he had the benefit of good teaching, and he was growing musically in every way. Why shouldn't he be able to win success as a pianist? Then there were moments—especially when he sat in Carnegie Hall listening to the great pianists of the day—when it seemed to him utterly inconceivable that he would one day be numbered among them. Strangely, both views coexisted in his mind. Whichever prevailed, depending upon the mood of the moment, he believed in that one to the exclusion of the other. When he was tossed too violently between the two, he came to rest upon a simple solution. This was not something he had to decide now. The future would do that.

5

PROFESSOR Sheldon sat on his desk in his favorite position, left leg horizontal above his right knee, nursing his ankle in both hands as he held forth on *In Memoriam*. His wrinkled brown face lit up as he recited, in a gravelly voice, the famous lines from Tennyson's elegy for his friend:

> I hold it true, whate'er befall;
> I feel it when I sorrow most;
> 'Tis better to have loved and lost
> Than never to have loved at all.

The professor belonged to the last generation that had been taught to declaim poetry; he practically sang the lines. What David enjoyed about him was his enthusiasm for the works he was teaching. The recitation was followed by an eloquent account of Tennyson's noble conception of friendship. At the next class the professor got his notes mixed up and repeated his account of Tennyson's noble conception word for word. David hoped he would change his tune. He didn't.

After class Sidney was triumphant. "What'd I tell you. He's a fake."

"Why?" David said. "Just because he repeated himself?"

"Because he pretended to be making it up as he went along. All he did was repeat his lecture by rote."

"Don't you do the same when you play a Beethoven sonata? You pretend to be feeling the music while you're playing, yet you're repeating the same notes you practiced for months."

"That's different. I'm playing what somebody else wrote, he's supposed to be giving us his own ideas."

"Look, Sid, he's been teaching for God knows how long. The first time he said it, it was all new and fresh. He liked it so much he said it again the next semester. Bit by bit he got to know the thing by heart, same as you memorize a sonata. By now it's a performance."

Sidney shrugged. "If I have to hear a performance, let it be Heifetz."

David took the professor's course because he wanted to learn about English literature. Sidney took it so that he would have something to argue about with David. There was one good thing about the course: it made David read the books the professor talked about—or most of them. Long ago it was Abe who had revealed to him the pleasure of being carried away by a fanciful tale. Now it was the professor who disclosed to him the vast panorama of the Victorian novel—abandoned orphans who turned out to be of noble birth; unwed mothers, betrayed wives, rebellious daughters ordered out of the house in a snowstorm; repentant criminals more noble than the villains who sat in judgment upon them; disputed inheritances and lost wills discovered in the nick of time. From Adam Bede to Jude the Obscure, from Maggie Tulliver to Tess of the D'Urbervilles, from Pip, Micawber, and Heathcliff to Richard Feverel and his Lucy—what a gallery of characters to be loved, agonized over, and remembered.

The professor confided to David that he was fond of

chamber music, whereupon David suggested that Sidney and he come one evening to play for him. The professor was delighted; Sidney wasn't. The familiar sneer curled his pale lips. "Why d'we have to waste an evening?"

"We don't have to. I'll tell him you can't make it."

That didn't suit Sidney either. "No, I'll do it. Should be good for an A."

On a Tuesday evening in January they presented themselves at the professor's apartment. Miss Pratt seemed taller to David and thinner than he remembered her. She wore a wine-colored silk dress that didn't fit whether she pulled it up or down. She was dean of a girls' high school and clearly had more important things on her mind than clothes. David looked around for the professor's daughter, the doctor, but she wasn't there. He remembered how awkward he had felt on his first visit. This time he was at ease.

The evening began pleasantly enough. Sidney and he opened with the *Kreutzer Sonata*, which the professor knew about from Tolstoy's novel. Now that he had heard the music, he said, he would make it a point to re-read the book. Then the boys played the César Franck sonata, which they had learned during the summer at the Mountain Flower House. David loved the impassioned theme of the piano in the first movement. His fingers sank deep into the keys, and the old square grand—the professor had had it tuned for the occasion—sang out.

Miss Pratt sat in one of the overstuffed armchairs opposite the piano, a ball of gray wool in her lap; she was knitting a muffler for the professor. David glanced at her out of the corner of his eye as he played. Her knitting needles moved in a rhythm of their own that bore no relation to the four-four time of the music. He wondered what she heard.

The last movement came off especially well. The professor smiled happily and applauded. Miss Pratt rested the incipient muffler in her lap and said in her ladylike voice, "That was lovely."

She then asked David if he would play the Chopin pieces she remembered from his first visit. David glanced at his friend, afraid that Sidney might misinterpret her request as a reflection on his violin playing. Sure enough, Sidney's thin face took on the tense expression he knew so well; the marble-blue eyes glittered beneath their pink lids. David plunged into the *Fantaisie-Impromptu*, hoping for the best, and Miss Pratt resumed her knitting.

The professor's daughter arrived and excused herself for being late. David continued with the C-sharp minor Waltz, which he followed with the *Raindrop Prelude* and the Polonaise in A. Miss Pratt thanked him profusely, and Sidney glowered at her.

The maid came in to say that tea was ready; they went into the dining room. David remembered the heavy pieces of furniture—the sideboard, bookcase, and chest filled with knicknacks. On the sideboard stood two Chinese figures in ivory: a lord and lady in elaborate court costumes that the carver had reproduced in minute detail. They looked wonderfully out of place in their austere surroundings. David had a momentary vision of Sidney, in pique, thrusting his hand forward and sending one of the figurines crashing to the floor. He turned to the professor. "You like Chinese things."

"Oh, yes," Professor Sheldon replied, his dark little eyes radiating good will. The table was covered with a lace cloth on which rested porcelain-thin cups and saucers. A large plate in the center was decorated with little geishas in bright kimonos. Miss Pratt asked David and Sidney to sit on either side of her. She turned to Sidney, "Lemon or cream?"

Sidney asked for lemon and three lumps of sugar, without a *please*. David wondered if he meant to sound as surly as he did.

The maid brought out a round cheese cake. Miss Pratt cut five portions and proceeded, with the help of a silver spatula, to deposit one on each of the five plates.

"I cannot tell you," the professor said, "how much pleasure both of you have given me." To Sidney, "How do you like the college?"

"I don't," Sidney answered curtly, stirring the sugar in his tea.

"And why not?" the professor asked pleasantly.

"For many reasons," Sidney replied in a why-do-you-ask-such-silly-questions tone.

"Such as?"

"Our profs should be teaching us how to think. Instead they just repeat the facts they once learned. Facts instead of ideas."

David grew tense. What if Sidney brought up the lecture on Tennyson's noble conception of friendship? It had been a mistake to bring him. Definitely.

The professor tapped his hands together in his favorite gesture: fingers curved and touching to form a little chapel. "We do our best," he said with a wistful smile.

"It's not enough," Sidney said decisively.

Miss Pratt sat bolt upright, staring into her tea. The professor's daughter lifted a piece of cake on her fork. David felt hot under the collar. He had to shut Sidney up, but how? Leaning forward, eyes fixed on the professor, "You said in class that you were in England last summer," he remarked brightly. "Did you go to Stratford?"

"No, the three of us stayed in the Lake country. It's Wordsworth's country, you know. His cottage is still there. We followed the walks he took with his sister." He smiled at Miss Pratt. " 'I wandered lonely as a cloud,' " he declaimed in his decrepit voice, " 'that floats on high o'er vales and hills . . .' "

"It must be very beautiful," David said, looking straight at the professor so as not to catch Sidney's eye.

"That it is," Miss Pratt said, and buried her fork in the cheese cake.

"Didn't Coleridge live there too?" David went on.

"Indeed he did," the professor said. "The two poets saw each other constantly."

The cheese cake, it turned out, had a cherry base. David tasted a piece and said, "It's delicious."

Sidney was not to be bought off with cheese cake. "And that damn fool president of ours," he said, as if he had never heard about the Lake country, "is no help either."

"He's in a difficult position," the professor replied.

"What's so difficult about it?" Sidney was referring to the stand the president had taken against a student demonstration on behalf of Sacco and Vanzetti. "He's an idiot. What's even worse, he's a reactionary."

The professor shaped his fingers into the little chapel. "There's always been a conflict between young and old, it's only the issues that change. We represent authority and you young people rebel against it. That's to be expected. But at this moment the gap between generations is greater than it ever was before." The professor tapped his fingers together. "Therefore the conflict is sharper."

"I understand that," Sidney said, the little muscles in his jaw twitching, "but that doesn't excuse our president from being an ass." He waved his fork at the professor like a weapon. "He doesn't realize we're on to his tricks."

The argument continued, with the professor defending the status quo while Sidney attacked it. "Shut up already," David felt like telling his friend. Instead he finished his cake.

Promptly at ten the professor glanced at his watch and said, "We'll continue this another time. I've an early class tomorrow."

The ladies thanked the young men for the music, and the professor saw them to the door. As they walked down Riverside Drive, David said, "Gosh, you were a pain in the neck." He looked across the Hudson at the lights glimmering on the Jersey shore.

"Why? Because I told the truth?"

"You sound like my mother," David said. "Whenever

she's unpleasant to someone, she claims she had to tell the truth."

"Look, Davey, I don't see why we have to kiss his ass."

"It's not a question of kissing his ass. We're young, he's old. We're his students, he's our teacher. We owe him something—I don't know what you'd call it—respect."

"Respect?" Sidney sneered. "You must be out of your mind."

"Let's say consideration."

"Bullshit. We owe him nothing. And you forgot to mention one thing."

"What?"

"That in his eyes we're just a couple of Jew boys."

"So we have to kick him in the teeth?"

Sidney made a scornful grimace. "People like you make me sick. You go around being afraid of your shadow."

"What did you accomplish? You made everyone in the room uncomfortable."

"I gave him something to think about."

"I've news for you. You didn't give him anything because he wasn't ready to accept it. All you did was let off steam. Big deal!"

Under the light of a street lamp Sidney's red hair turned gold. "Okay, next time you go there, don't ask me."

"Don't worry," David snapped. "I won't."

It turned out that there was no next time. He was not asked again.

6

OF the girls in Miss Parissot's class, David liked Deborah Bornstein best. Miss Parissot addressed her as *ma petite.* There was, indeed, something diminutive and fragile about her: small hands, narrow waist and shoulders, delicate features, and a lovely olive complexion. Her eyes, a soft gray, looked out on the world with a perpetual expression of wonder. She wore her hair loose over her shoulders; it was dark and silky, and reached almost to the small of her back. Whenever David saw her he had an impulse to put his arm around her.

She took her lesson just after his; he waited for her in the students' room. They walked past Grant's Tomb, its white dome thrust against the winter sky, and continued to Riverside Drive. The Hudson was a pale silver, the Jersey shore rose above it tinged with lavender. "How did it go?" David asked.

"She was in a *vile* mood." Deborah had a way of pronoucing certain words as if they were in italics.

"What was wrong?"

"I brought Schumann's *Carnaval,* and she didn't like *anything* I did." Deborah never tired of discussing Miss Parissot's whims and moods. "How about you?"

"We worked on the *Appassionata*—she really knows that piece."

"Besides, she likes you." Deborah smiled, and added, "Doesn't everybody?"

"No." It pleased him that she did not indulge in the sparring, the coquettish advances and retreats that had marred his dealings with Henny. And she was not afraid to show how fond she was of him.

She held up two tickets. "Hofmann's at Carnegie Hall tonight. I got two passes. Will you come?"

He made a face. "I was planning to stay home and practice. Don't tempt me."

"He's playing the *Appassionata,* so it'll do you good to hear him."

"I don't like his Beethoven," David said. "It's cold. He should stick to Chopin."

"He's playing that too. The first and fourth Ballades."

David grinned. "You knew all along I'd give in."

"If you go home right now you can work *all* afternoon. Then you'll be ready for a concert."

Deborah had a class in music history at two. "We're still on Gregorian chant," she said. "I can't stay awake."

He was suddenly the big brother. "You have to have some history."

"Why?"

"Because you understand a thing better," he explained, "if you know how it got started."

"To play Chopin I have to know what happened a thousand years ago?"

"Yes. It'll give you—" What would it give her? "—perspective."

"I don't need perspective. I need fingers."

He walked her to her class. "Eight fifteen in the lobby," she said. "Don't be late."

"Stop sounding like my mother." He made off.

Hofmann was in good form that night. David listened carefully to the *Appassionata*. "Did you watch his foot?" he asked during intermission. "He barely touches the pedal, so there's never any blur."

"I was watching his hands," Deborah answered. "He plays from the wrist, never from the arms. It's all so light and clear."

"Lacks feeling, don't you think?"

"But it's so elegant," she said, repeating an expression she had picked up from Miss Parissot. They ran into three schoolmates, each of whom held a different opinion about the performance. There was much arguing; no one convinced anybody else. David liked the second half of the program much better. Once Hofmann got to Chopin he was in his element—by turn lyrical, fiery, capricious. "Only a Polish pianist," he told Deborah after the second encore, "could play a mazurka like that."

They took the subway train home. She lived near Bronx Park, which was several stops beyond his. Her house was not far from the station. They walked through deserted streets; the Bronx was asleep. The stars shone crystal clear in the cold air, and there was no wind. "What must it feel like to be a great artist?" David asked.

"I wouldn't know." She gave a little laugh.

"Does he get up in the morning and think, I'm Josef Hofmann?"

"He probably takes a shower and eats scrambled eggs."

"Will we ever stand on that stage, bowing to a full house, and playing six encores? I wonder."

"Is that what you want?"

David pondered the question. "Who wouldn't? To have something to say and get the world to listen . . . it should be a great feeling. How about you?"

She made a face. "I'd be scared to *death*. All I want is to be a pretty good pianist. Maybe teach others how to become one."

They reached her house. "I'm so *glad* you came," she said, and leaned a little forward. Resting one hand on his shoulder, she kissed him on the cheek.

People in the music world were always kissing each other. Their kiss, David knew, meant little more than a handshake. But Deborah's was not like that. It was warm and friendly; yet it somehow forestalled the kind of kiss he wanted to receive from her. As though she were saying to him, "I like you fine and we're great friends, but please keep it that way." Throughout the evening everything had been clear and aboveboard between them. Now, strangely, she puzzled him.

He went to Deborah's house every Sunday for an afternoon of duets. It was a pleasant way to improve his sight reading. She was not as good a pianist as he, but a better sight reader. They covered a wide range, from the symphonies of Mozart and Beethoven arranged for four hands to the *Spanish Dances* of Moszkowski and *Hungarian Dances* of Brahms. The jewel of their repertoire was Schubert's

Fantasy in F minor. They went through the first page with flying colors; after that there were problems.

David enjoyed making music with Debbie for the same reason that, long ago, he had enjoyed dancing with Henny Jershow: her sense of rhythm was akin to his own, and they felt a phrase in the same way. They would sail through a difficult passage in a state of mutual admiration and repeat the section for the sheer joy of it. Miss Parissot used to say that playing duets resembled tennis in one respect: it was fun only if both players were evenly matched. From this point of view Debbie and he were a perfect team.

The small living room was cluttered with lamps and knicknacks; six little cushions of different colors enlivened the sofa. The view of the park was spectacular; trees, lawns, and winding paths extended as far as the eye could reach. The piano, a Knabe upright, took up one wall of the room. Its deep fuzzy sound reminded David of the piano he had had in Brooklyn.

Deborah's parents occasionally came into the parlor to listen. Her father, a watchmaker, had a small store on East Tremont Avenue, where, in addition to watches and clocks, he sold cheap jewelry. He considered music a waste of time and money, yet it had a soothing effect on him: a few bars of Beethoven or Mozart and he was snoring gently. He was short and fat. Little black hairs issued from his nostrils and ears, formed a link between his eyebrows, and, when he opened his collar, were visible up to his neck. The only place where he was not hairy was the top of his head. Deborah resembled him just a little; she was the delicate, lovely version of what in him was gross and palpable. He felt that she should be studying something practical instead of music. "What kind of a profession is it," he would ask, "where you have to have talent in order to make a living?"

It was her mother who insisted that Deborah study music. She was a pale, emaciated woman who referred to her poor health in such vague terms that David never found out what ailed her. According to Debbie, her illnesses were mainly in her head. She would sit on the sofa, propped up on her little cushions, listening to Brahms's *Hungarian Dance No. 1* and waving her hand in time with the beat. She especially liked the part where David's hands descended across the keyboard in brilliant arpeggios above the haunting melody that Deborah sounded in the bass.

When the weather was fine, they went walking in Bronx Park. Nature was freer and wilder here than in Prospect Park; you forgot that you were in the city. One Sunday afternoon in February they discovered a lovely spot. A little stream flowed past, so limpid that they could see the stones at the bottom. Although the wind was sharp, there was a fragrance in the air that said winter was almost over. A rustic bridge led to a bank of moss-covered rocks that hung over the path. Affixed to one was a bronze tablet that carried a poem. David read the stanza aloud:

> Yet I will look upon thy face again,
>   My own romantic Bronx, and it will be
> A face more pleasant than the face of men . . .

"Sounds like Longfellow," Debbie said.

"It's by Joseph Rodman Drake."

"Stop showing off."

David pointed to the tablet. "That's what it says."

"Who is he?"

"A native son, I guess. I bet it's the only poem in captivity with the word *Bronx* in it."

"Well, it's good to know," Debbie announced, "that the Bronx is a romantic place. I'd never have suspected it."

Her fragile look went well with her gentleness. Most of the girls he knew wore some kind of armor to cover what they really were like. Deborah had no such shell. Her way of coping with her timidity was not to try to hide it; she was always herself. David could not imagine himself ever doing anything to hurt her.

"I'll always be grateful to you," he once told her.

"For what?"

"When I'm with you I'm the best I can be. I mean every-thing I say and say what I mean. And I feel like protecting you."

"From what?"

"I don't know. From the world, I guess. It's a nice feel-ing."

She smiled.

"And I don't make up stories," he continued, "to hide what I'm like inside. It's because you take me the way I am."

"You mean, because I like you, you like yourself."

He nodded. "I should only be with people who do; I need the encouragement. Last summer I got to know a woman named Val. She encouraged me too, but only in one direction. Sex. You encourage me in every direction—except that one, of course."

"Why do you say that?"

"I can tell. You don't like physical contact. Not really."

Debbie blushed. She slipped her arm through his. "See, it's not *true*."

He knew he was right, but let the matter drop. It occurred to him that Debbie had all the qualities his mother valued—honesty, sincerity, and the rest—but without making a fuss about them. She was not even aware of them as virtues; they were part of what she was. When he thought of the things he liked about her, those were high on the list. But he also liked her because she made him feel taller. Stronger. Better.

THREE

Miss Parissot decided that David was ready to enter the concerto competition. The winner was to play the Schumann Concerto with the school orchestra at the end of the year. It was a prize worth trying for.

Debbie played the accompaniment on the second piano in Miss Parissot's room so that David would get to know the orchestral part. He had not played much of Schumann's music and was enchanted by its exuberance and drive. The first movement was a fantasy on the romantic opening theme, which returned in various shapes and moods until it became a joyous Allegro at the end.

Also participating in the competition was Myron Green (formerly Greenberg). Myron was bright, eager, and ambitious. David thought his face was ferretlike even though he wasn't sure what a ferret looked like. Myron and he were a study in contrasts. Myron's tweed suits came from Rogers Peet; David, in his baggy trousers and rumpled jacket, managed to look as if he had been thrown into his clothes. Myron wore striped silk ties; David's shirt, open at the collar, yielded to a tie only on special occasions. Myron was always neatly groomed, while David's curly brown hair defied every effort to brush it down. They sat in the cafeteria across the street from the school. "There's too many pianists around," Myron complained and bit into his ham sandwich.

David, out of deference to his mother, chose tuna fish salad. "Most of them'll drop out, so it's not as bad as it looks."

Myron shook his head. "There just aren't enough careers to go around."

David was reminded of Sidney's doubts about a musical career. "Friend of mine," he said, "got to be a pretty good violinist, but he's giving it up and going into law. Figures he won't make it as a soloist, and he doesn't want to end up in an orchestra."

"A pianist can't even fall back on that," Myron answered. "There's no place for him to go, except teach." He made a grimace.

"Shaw said"—David had recently come across the statement and was eager to show it off—"those who can do, those who can't teach."

The quotation made Myron even gloomier. "I know I can make it," he brought out slowly, "and nothing's going to stop me." His lips came together in a thin line.

David repeated the conversation to Deborah. "I feel sorry for him," she said. "He's so ambitious, and he doesn't have a shred of talent."

"How do you know?"

"He asked me to play the second piano in the Schumann. He's a cold fish."

David trotted out another quotation he had recently picked up. " 'There is nothing so tragic as the pursuit of art by those who lack talent,' " he brought out sententiously. "I don't know who said it but it's true."

"At any rate Mike doesn't have to worry," Deborah said. "His father has money."

"Yeah, but he has that Pikes-Peak-or-bust attitude."

"Don't you?"

"It's hard to escape, especially when there's a competition. We're like race horses training for the big event, each horse wishing the others would break a leg."

"That's what it's all about," Deborah said.

David was thoughtful. "I remember when I was a kid, I went to a birthday party. We were all playing games and having a good time. Then the ice cream arrived, and there wasn't enough to go around. Suddenly we were enemies, each one shouting Me, Me, Me! It wasn't pretty."

"Nothing you can do about it."

David grinned. "Maybe there should be more ice cream."

"There'll never be enough," Debbie replied. "That's what makes it so delicious."

2

HE stood by the window of Deborah's room. It had snowed all evening—in March!—and the park was covered with a white blanket that glistened under the lamps. The snowflakes drifted down slowly, forming an ever-changing lattice against the sky.

Instantly the world was a fairyland. He returned to the couch and sat down beside Deborah. "It's beautiful out there," he said.

They had shut the door and spoke softly; her parents had gone to bed. "How about a walk in the park, Davey. We could wear galoshes."

"No, it's cozy here." He put his arm around her and sensed her withdrawal. It baffled him that she put a distance between them whenever he came too close. "You're beautiful," he whispered.

"Like the snow?"

He looked surprised. "As a matter of fact, yes. Beautiful and cold."

"Why do you say that? I have only the warmest feelings toward you, Davey."

"I know. But there's something missing."

"What?"

"You know as well as I." She looked so fragile, she seemed to be begging him not to hurt her. "You have a knack of making me feel like your big brother. But you're not my little sister. You're a lovely girl"—he bent his head and ran his lips lightly over her cheek—"whom I happen to love."

Deborah wriggled out of his embrace. "Do we have to—?" She made a face. "Why can't we just be friends?"

He pulled her to him. "I don't understand you, Debbie. Why be friends if we could be much more?"

She looked down at the floor. "There's a reason."

"What is it?"

"I can't tell you."

He chucked her under the chin, turning her face toward him. "Don't you think you ought to?"

A look of pain tightened her features. "Please, Davey, can't we drop this?"

"No," he said curtly.

She sat quite still. David held her firmly against him. "Look, you can tell me anything. Is there someone else?"

"As a matter of fact, there is," she said softly.

He moved away as if he had been stung. The old feeling of betrayal poured through him. "Debbie!" he cried, "what the hell have you been doing? Leading me on? Who is it?"

She stared at the floor.

Seizing her by the wrist, he said, "Tell me, who is he?"

She drew in her breath. "It's not a he." David looked at her, bewildered. "It's a woman."

"Debbie!"

She faced him. "You wanted to know? Now you know."

"That's ridiculous! That kind of thing happens in Paris or London, not in the Bronx."

Despite her troubled expression she broke into a smile.

She put her hand on his shoulder. "Silly! It happens wherever there are people. Even in the Bronx."

"I don't believe it," he said firmly.

"Davey, you asked me to tell you the truth and I did. I like you too much to lie to you."

"Who is she?"

"What's the difference? That's how it is."

"But . . . what about me?"

"I love seeing you and being your friend. But I just don't—how should I put it—I just don't care about men that way."

"But you're so feminine."

"I know." Deborah smiled again. "She isn't."

David stared before him as her disclosure sank in. "Do your parents know?"

"Of course not. They'd be terribly upset."

"Who knows?"

"Well, I know. And she knows. And now you."

"You don't want to tell me who she is."

"You wouldn't know her anyway."

"Damn it, you're such a lovely girl. How in the world did you ever—" He stopped, not knowing how to complete the sentence, and wound up feebly with "get mixed up in that?"

Deborah passed the palm of her hand across her forehead, as if trying to remember. "You wake up one morning and you know *something* about yourself that you never knew before. Then someone comes along and . . ." She turned her hands up in a gesture of acceptance. "It's as simple as that."

David moved back beside her. He put his arm around her and held her to him. "Did you ever try it with a man?"

"No."

"Why don't you give yourself a chance? Maybe . . . ?"

She looked at him pleadingly. "Davey, you're very dear to me, believe me. But don't suggest that. Please."

"What'd you want me to do—just accept this and let you go?" His face was grave. "I love you. I want you. Enough to put up a fight."

"There's nothing to fight about," she said. "I am the way I am."

"People change. Look at what's at stake. Us!"

"I already told you, I don't like men that way. The very thought"—she made a grimace.

"All I'm asking you is to give it a try. Then, if you still feel the way you do, I'll understand." He pulled her to him. "Put your arm around me."

She obeyed. He kissed her again and again, cupping one hand over her breast. He could feel her stiffen, but she did not resist him. She let him unfasten the gray wool dress she was wearing. She removed her bra and undergarment, and kicked off her shoes. Naked except for her stockings, she leaned back on the couch, propped on a cushion, hands folded in her lap and a resigned look on her face.

David had thrown off his clothes and faced her. She looked utterly helpless, pure and seductive at the same time. The nipples of her little breasts were a bit larger than he would have supposed. The sight aroused him in a most powerful way. "Well, do I look so terrible?" he asked.

Her eyes, traveling down over his body, came to rest on his erection. "It's pretty," she said in a tone of appraisal, as if she were judging an object from another planet.

He stepped forward, close to her. Stooping, he lifted her hand and brought it forward. She pulled it back. "Please, I don't mind looking at it, but don't make me touch it."

He bent over her. Slipping one hand under her knees and the other behind her back, he eased her down on the couch. He lay down beside her and kissed her breast. Remembering what Val had taught him, he let the tip of his tongue play with her nipple as he slid his fingertips over her body. Her olive skin was smooth and unblemished. "You're lovely," he murmured, and leaned up against her. She made as if to move away but didn't.

He turned her on her back and pulled himself over her. She stared up at him with a look of sheer horror. Passion drained from him, replaced by pity. "Debbie, I didn't mean to hurt you. I only—" He sank back on the couch and took her in his arms.

His penis, now limp, brushed against her. She pulled violently away. "Please, Davey, I can't. I wish I could, but I can't. If we don't stop, I'll throw up."

She saw the distress he felt. "I'm sorry, Davey. You mean so much to me. But I know—"

"What?"

"That it's not for me and never will be. You're asking me to go against my nature. I can't."

"Okay," he said softly. "At least you tried." He got off the couch. Looking down at his penis, he said, "See, it knew. I was dumb enough to think you'd want it, but it knew better." His shorts and trousers lay where he had dropped them. He pulled them on.

Once Deborah had dressed, she was herself again. "At least I now know what you look like," she said, "so the evening wasn't a total loss."

He smiled wanly. "There should be one day a year when people go around naked. Then we'd know what everybody looks like."

"It's not a good idea. You'd see too many fat ones."

"When did you first find out?" he asked.

"What?"

"About yourself?"

"I don't remember. Seems to me I always knew, without really knowing."

"Didn't you try to . . . talk to someone about it?"

"What for?"

"To get cured."

She gave him a quizzical look. "Davey, darling, let's not talk about it. You see it from your angle, like some terrible sickness—"

"No I don't."

"Yes you do. And I see it from another angle. Which means that if we keep talking about it we'll only upset each other. I accept the way you are, and you must do the same for me."

"All right. But it seems to me," he persisted, "that if you really wanted to, you could change."

"Well, then, I don't want to. Does that satisfy you?"

"No."

"By the way—"

David pricked up his ears. He had noticed that when people said "By the way" something important was about to happen. He was not mistaken, for he heard Deborah say, "Miss Parissot is, too."

"What do you mean?"

"You heard me."

"Don't tell me she's the woman in your life!"

"Of course not."

"Then how do you know?"

"I know."

"You mean, she tried to—"

"Don't be silly."

"Then what makes you think so?"

"I just know. The vibrations . . ."

He remembered Miss Parissot's husky baritone voice, the masculine profile that was so at variance with her coquettish smile, the attachment to maman that had kept her from marrying; above all the forcefulness and drive that was so close to what the world considered manly. David let out a sigh. People were so much more complicated than he suspected. "Not that it makes any difference," he said lamely.

"Of course not."

"Why did you tell me?"

"I thought you'd like to know." Deborah looked at him. "No, that's not it. I am a little ashamed of the real reason. I was afraid you'd think badly of me because of what I told you, and I know how much you admire her. So I figured—"

"Then it's not true."

"Of course it is. I'd never say anything like that unless it were."

"Two bombshells in one night," David said. "Wow! I better go before you explode a third."

They parted as affectionately as ever. To his astonishment, his feelings toward her had not changed. It was as if Debbie's disclosure had never taken place. When he came into the open, the city was in ermine. His were the first footsteps in the snow; he hated to break up the dazzling white surface. He walked briskly, swinging his arms. The air was clean and moist; a light wind blew in his face. A strange quiet hung over the housetops, broken by the crunchy sound of his galoshes against the snow. He remembered the summer day on the beach when his mother had told him about her first marriage. You thought you knew everything about someone close to you, then it turned out there was more. For an instant he had a vivid image of Miss Parissot and Deborah lying naked in each other's arms. He brushed it from his mind.

It was past midnight when he reached his street. Crotona Park looked unreal, a scene on a picture postcard. The trees were clothed in white, their branches glistening under the lamps like arms outstretched to the light. He stamped his feet to shake off the snow and climbed the stairs.

There were some macaroons in the kitchen. He washed them down with a glass of milk, turned in, and fell into a deep sleep. When he awoke the next morning, it was raining. The beautiful white snow had turned into slush.

3

Miss Parissot stopped him as he played the opening passage of the concerto. "The dotted notes a little shorter.

Tighter." Resting one hand on his shoulder, she illustrated what she wanted with the other.

He nodded and repeated the passage. What if Debbie had lied to him? What if Miss Parissot really was her lover?

"I'd like a firmer tone," she said, "Remember, this is the opening. Schumann wants to capture our attention right away."

He began again, incorporating her suggestions. What difference did it make if she was or wasn't? It wouldn't change anything.

He came to the lyric theme in the bass. "Sing it out," Miss Parissot said, "like a cello." She brought her fingertips down on his shoulder to indicate the kind of touch she wanted him to use. He pressed the fingers of his left hand deep into the keys, playing the accompaniment in the right hand with a lighter touch. There was that eager look on Debbie's face whenever Miss Parissot greeted her. The look he had hoped to see when he took her in his arms. Why did he keep upsetting himself when there was nothing he could do about it? Why didn't he keep his mind on the music?

The second theme appeared, a pleading melody in the upper register. "Be careful of the pedal," Miss Parissot said, "and bring out the left hand." David nodded. If they were lovers, how did they do it? He could see Miss Parissot leaning over Debbie, her lips descending across the soft olive skin. Her head moved lower over Debbie's body, and Debbie pushed up to meet her. David forced his thoughts back to the music. He reached the part where Schumann transformed the theme into a romantic episode; langorous phrases in the piano were echoed by oboe and clarinet. Miss Parissot hummed the woodwind melody in a husky voice, her cigarette dangling from her lips. David finally cleared his mind of extraneous matters. The principal themes were repeated, and the movement surged forward with mounting urgency to the coda. Miss Parissot stopped him and flicked the ashes of her cigarette into a brass tray on the piano. "David, the accelerando has to be gradual. Schu-

mann makes it clear—*poco a poco.*" Seizing a pencil, she traced
two bold lines under the words printed in the score. "Try
it again."

He made a more subtle transition into the final Allegro
and ripped off the final measures with the brilliance they
needed. "Not bad," Miss Parissot said. "Not bad at all."
This was high praise from her. "You really feel the music.
I think you'll do well tomorrow."

David made a face at this reminder of the contest; he was
scheduled to play before the jury at ten in the morning.
Miss Parissot drew on her cigarette, inhaled, and blew out
the smoke. "It's not enough to know a piece one hundred
percent. You have to know it a hundred and fifty, as you
lose fifty in performance." The bell rang; it was time for the
next lesson. The door opened and Deborah walked in. Miss
Parissot greeted her with a kiss, as was her custom with girl
students. David gathered his music, said good-bye, and left.
They were not lovers, he decided. And if they were,
it was none of his business.

He went down to the students' room on the first floor.
Myron was waiting for him. "How'd it go?"

David shrugged. "Not bad. At least that's what she said."

"All set for tomorrow?"

David sensed the apprehension in the question. "I guess
so," he replied as casually as he could. The trouble with
competitions, he reflected, was that they made people competitive. Myron studied with Hans Toeffler, one of the best
teachers in the school, whom Elena Parissot detested. The
rivalry, therefore, was not only between him and Myron
but also between their teachers. "How are you coming
along?" he asked, more out of politeness than because he
wanted to know.

"Great!"

It was typical of Myron to puff himself up. "There's three
others besides us," David said, to remind Myron that he
had several rivals.

"I know. You're pretty calm about it, Dave."

"It's only a contest."

"Everything's a contest," Myron answered, "so this prepares us for what we'll face later."

"I'm not so sure. All those prize winners in high school and college—how many of them, ten years later, are doing what they thought they would?"

"I know I will," Myron said firmly.

"If you're lucky."

He waited for Deborah. "How was your lesson?"

"Good. She's really *something.*"

They left the school together and walked past Grant's Tomb to Riverside Drive. David carried Deborah's music with his own. The park beside the Hudson was beginning to come alive after its winter sleep. The river, under its silvery surface, seemed hardly to flow. On the Jersey shore nothing stirred. "What were you working on?"

"Two Brahms intermezzi. She has some marvelous ideas."

"Yeah." Much as he admired Miss Parissot, he did not like Debbie's worshipful tone.

She took his arm. "I hope you win tomorrow."

"Why?" He wanted her to say, "Because I love you."

"Because I don't like Myron."

"That's no reason for wanting me to win."

She smiled. "With me it is."

"Why didn't you enter the competition?"

"Me?" She made a face. "You and Myron think you're going to burn up the world. I don't see myself that way."

"He's all steamed up about tomorrow. I tried to sound casual about it, but I wasn't being honest. I do want to win."

"I should hope so."

"Still . . ." He stopped, groping to shape his thought. "Loving music is one thing, wanting to win is another. One has nothing to do with the other."

"It does and it doesn't."

"There's a part of me," David continued, "that resents

being in a race like this. Yet there's another part that wants to come out first." He felt genuinely puzzled. "It's a damn nuisance to be split down the middle."

"Where is it written that we have to be consistent?"

They stopped to watch the river. David lifted her up so that she could sit on the embankment. "You're so light," he said, "and pretty." He faced her, leaning lightly against her knees, his arms encircling her. "I've been thinking about us."

She held up her hand. "Davey, let's not start that again. What's the point? I told you what you need to know. To chew it around some more won't change anything."

"If you really wanted to," he said doggedly, "you could change."

"You're repeating yourself. And you're talking about things you know nothing about. Why don't you accept what I can give you and stop worrying about what I can't?"

He remembered the look of terror in her eyes when he tried to make love to her. Their amber depths were calm and loving now. "How about a kiss?"

She pointed a forefinger at her cheek. "Here. Like a friend."

He pulled her to him and rubbed his face against hers.

4

WHEN David won the competition, Miss Parissot considered it a personal victory over Myron's teacher. Deborah was delighted, as were Lisa and Joel. Only Myron was unhappy. "I almost wish he had won," David told Deborah, "just to get him off my back. He has such a hang-dog look." But Myron soon found a suitable alibi. The piano had a stiffer action than he was accustomed to, which had prevented him from playing his best.

The concert was three weeks off, which gave David ample

time to put the finishing touches to the concerto. Miss Parissot prepared a student for a performance in a rather special way. There was always the possibility, according to
her, that you might pass out with nerves. Your fingers,
therefore, had to be drilled so thoroughly that, if you did
go to pieces, they would continue playing by themselves.
By the time the rehearsal with orchestra rolled around,
David knew the concerto inside out. It gave him a fine sense
of power to be sitting on stage, enveloped in the rich sound
of strings and woodwinds; he was keyed up and alert as he
followed the conductor. At the same time a part of him
seemed to be standing to one side, a shade incredulous that
all this was actually taking place.

As the day of the concert approached, he grew increasingly apprehensive. Of what? He hardly knew. He had a
recurring dream that as he came out on stage, his trousers
fell down. He had forgotten to wear his shorts and stood
stark naked in front of a crowded hall. The fantasy alternated with one hardly more reassuring. As he played, the
audience began to walk out; by the time he reached the final
movement the hall was deserted. Finally, the members of
the orchestra put away their instruments and he was left
alone on an empty stage. He walked off, disconsolate.

"The fuss we're making," he told Deborah, "you'd think
I was making my debut in Carnegie Hall with the New
York Philharmonic."

"Then why are you so nervous?"

"Because everyone around me is. It's catching."

It rained on the day of the concert. David's anxiety
increased steadily throughout the afternoon. He gave the
piece a final runthrough; it went easily enough. The rain let
up toward evening. He felt better once he put on the tuxedo
he had rented for the occasion. His parents inspected him
and found nothing amiss. The three of them set out betimes;
Lisa, in her usual mood of anticipation, chattered gaily. She
remembered the night he had played at the annual ball of
the Warsaw Society. "That palace on Pike Street. You wore

a black velvet suit with a lace collar, I sewed it myself. Ekh, those were the days," she sighed. "We were young."

The program opened with the *Egmont Overture;* then it was his turn. Little butterflies raced up and down the pit of his stomach as he came on stage. He bowed, sat down, adjusted the piano stool to his taste, nodded to the conductor, and tossed off the precipitous chords of the opening passage. Now his left knee took over. It began to shake up and down despite all his efforts to make it stop. He pretended that he was at home playing for himself, but his left knee knew better. He tried to concentrate on the orchestral sound, but the butterflies intruded. Miss Parissot's drilling stood him in good stead: when he was not able to concentrate on what he was doing, his fingers went on by themselves. He wondered what he would do if his mind suddenly went blank and he forgot. Luckily, it didn't.

He felt more comfortable in the second movement, where no technical problems intervened. Also, now that he had come through the first movement without disaster, he was a bit more confident about averting it in the next. The tricky cross rhythms of the Finale reawakened his fears; he raced through the movement as if it were an obstacle course. When the obstacles had been overcome and the final cadence rang out, he heaved a sigh of relief. A burst of applause rewarded his efforts. David shook the conductor's hand, bowed, and walked off. When the applause persisted he took another bow, thankful that the ordeal was behind him.

During intermission his friends came backstage to congratulate him. Miss Parissot hugged and kissed him, as did his parents and Debbie. Later that night, alone with her, he relaxed. "Well, let's have it."

"You were fine."

"No malarky. Tell me what you thought."

"It was not as good as the rehearsal, you were too tense for that. But it was very good."

"I discovered something about myself."

"What?"

"I thought I'd enjoy being up there. Instead I got awfully nervous."

"Everybody does."

"Depends on how much. Great artists get nervous too, I suppose, but their kind of nervousness makes them play better. They belong on stage; that's where they come alive. I really don't enjoy having a hall full of strangers looking at me. You know what?" he exclaimed, as if struck by a new thought. "To have a public career you have to be a public person. Maybe I'm strictly private."

"But this is the career you chose."

"It was fun when I was a kid. I enjoyed playing and having everyone make a fuss over me. Now I'm beginning to realize what's involved. You know the definition of *wunderkind?* The *wunder* goes and the *kind* remains."

When he came home he found Lisa radiant and full of praise. "It was wonderful, my son. You looked so handsome on stage. I thought to myself, 'Is this the little one I once bathed and scrubbed?' When you put your hands on the piano, my heart melted. Everything I always wanted for you suddenly came true." Her eyes sparkled. "When you finished and they all applauded, I was so proud I thought I'd burst. And I said to myself, 'What a lucky woman you are.' " She stopped. "Why do you smile?"

"For once you approve of me, Mama. It's good to hear."

The following morning Miss Parissot phoned with good news: he had been awarded a scholarship for a summer of study in France. David let out a wow! At last he had something to be excited about. He could not wait to let Debbie know. "Here I was all set for another summer in the Catskills," he told her. "Instead I'll get to see Paris. You'll laugh at me if I tell you how I feel."

"So tell me."

"When I was a kid my mother would describe how we sailed across the ocean to America. I seemed to remember a garden I had left behind, a magic garden below the ground where the trees shone and the air was full of music. It kept haunting me all through my childhood. I now have the feeling I'm going back to it."

"That's the garden we all left behind," Debbie answered. "The garden of Eden. Paris won't be that way at all."

"It doesn't matter," he said, "as long as I think it is."

His mother decided that Joel's battered valise was not good enough for so momentous a journey. She bought David a shiny black valise with brass trimmings. Her excitement was contagious. "To be young and going to Paris!" She pronounced it *Pah-reezh*, with the accent on the second syllable. "Dovid'l, how I envy you . . ."

On a bright Monday morning in June Joel and she went to see David off. Deborah was at the pier waiting for them. Lisa's words at parting were on the cryptic side. "Be careful, my son. Don't do anything foolish." She kissed him, as did his father and Deborah. He walked across the gangplank, glancing down for one fearful moment at the dirty green eddies in the river ten stories below. A bell rang, a whistle tooted, a plume of white smoke burst from one of the funnels on the top deck. David leaned over the railing of the second class, waving at the three dear faces on shore that receded as the S.S. *France* nosed her way into the Hudson. He was off to see the world.

5

HE sat on a bench on the Champs Élysées and let the life of the city wash around him. In the distance, to his right, he could see the Arc de Triomphe. Wherever he turned history loomed—Nôtre Dame, the palaces of Bourbon kings, the obelisk that Napoleon brought back from Egypt. He seemed to have stepped back into one of the novels of Dumas or Victor Hugo that Abe had made him read years before. He remembered how Jean Valjean sat with little Fantine in the Luxembourg garden with its neatly laid out flower beds.

Here he was, walking through the same garden. He found it hard to believe.

Time moved differently in Paris, which added to his sense of unreality. In New York he was always in a hurry, rushing to class, rushing home to practice or downtown to a concert at Carnegie Hall. Having allowed himself two weeks for sightseeing, he now had all the time in the world. It was a unique experience for him to wander through crowded streets, looking at buildings, visiting museums, watching people and wondering about them. He did all the things tourists did, from trundling up to the top of the Eiffel Tower to spending a day at the Louvre. The peak of his stay in Paris, it seemed to him, came when he stood in front of the *Mona Lisa*. No less exciting was his first glimpse of *Venus de Milo* posed against a background of dark velvet. He promised himself to read up on Greek art and da Vinci.

Suddenly he was aware of language. He had studied Racine and Corneille at college, which gave him a one-sided knowledge of French. He did not know how to order string beans in a restaurant or ask a chambermaid for towels, but he could quote several lines from Athalie's dream or the soliloquy of *Le Cid*. French fell on his ears with a sharper music, a more accentuated rhythm than that of English. It delighted him to utter homely phrases like *Que-ce que c'est que ça* or *Permettez moi, s'il vous plaît*. He had a real setback one afternoon when in his best seventeenth-century French he asked a passer-by to direct him to the Boulevard St. Michel. The man looked at him in surprise and answered, 'Sorree, I no speek ze eenglish."

He had found a room on the left Bank, on the Rue de l'Ancienne Comédie. Anything, he was persuaded, could happen on a street named after the ancient comedy. June in Paris was hot. He went swimming in the Seine; the river looked bright green by day, dark and mysterious at night. He loved the bridges, each curving gracefully on arches that made a perfect circle with their reflection in the water. His favorite was the one named in honor of Napoleon's victory at Jéna. He bought a dozen postcards showing various sights of Paris. His mailing list was small: his parents, Miss Parissot, Debbie, Sidney, Myron Green. He thought of sending one to Val, but decided not to; her husband might ask questions. Henny? Stella Rabinowitz? His high school buddies? It was hardly worth the trouble. As the French said, *cela ne vaut pas la peine.* He would have liked Abe to know he was in Paris, but thought better of it. He kept the unused cards as souvenirs.

He had never before been in a city where he knew no one. It made him feel curiously detached from the life around him, the perpetual onlooker. He seemed finally to have realized his childhood dream of possessing the cloak of invisibility: he could see without being seen. He discovered several things about himself. First, that he didn't mind being alone. Solitude was restful, even nourishing. Second, he was shyer than he thought. He didn't find it easy to speak to strangers and never took the initiative. Paris had its usual complement of American tourists. Several times a day, especially in the office of the American Express, someone turned to him with a "Where'ya from?" These desultory conversations, it seemed to him, led nowhere. Sooner or later he withdrew into his solitude, enjoying the flow of his thoughts even if he had no one to share them with.

"Paris," he wrote his parents, "is more beautiful than New York, and noisier. Automobiles drive faster, and their horns honk louder. The men have florid complexions from drinking too much wine. They always look as if they're late for an appointment, and they have women on their minds. The women dress more elegantly than in New York"—he was about to add, "even streetwalkers," but decided not to. "The city is all dressed up for the tourists, but the gaiety is on the surface. I still haven't gotten used to the thought that I am actually here.

In the evening he listened to music. Tickets were cheap enough that he could go every night. *Carmen* at the Opéra Comique sounded more French than at the Met. The voices were not great, but the spirit was there. *La Bohème*, in spite of Puccini, became a French work. What fun it was to hear the chorus in Act II sing in praise of the Latin Quarter and to realize that he was living there. He fell under the spell of *Pelléas and Mélisande;* he had never heard the opera and listened to it as in a dream. On one of the quais he picked up a volume of Debussy's essays, and came across a passage that seemed to him to capture the essence of the French spirit in music:

"The French forget too easily the qualities of clarity and elegance peculiar to themselves and allow themselves to be influenced by the tedious, ponderous Teuton. Couperin and Rameau—these are true Frenchmen. French music aims above all to please."

On his last night in Paris he went to the Opéra, which was larger and more beautiful than the Opéra Comique. With its majestic façade, magnificent marble staircase, and spacious promenades, the building seemed to sum up the nineteenth-century notion of what a grand opera house should look like. They were giving *Marouf, Cobbler of Cairo* by Henry Rabaud; David had never heard of either the composer or the work. The opera received a lavish Arabian Nights production. Of the entire evening David remembered only the moment when the soprano, gazing soulfully at the hero, launched into an extended aria on the words "O Marouf . . ."

The applause at the final curtain was no more than polite. David made his way to the marble staircase. Halfway down, the man beside him suddenly said, "Did you like the opera?"

David glanced sidewise. The stranger was a tall, rather large man in his forties with a white fleshy face; the skin hung in folds around his neck. His eyes were dark-bright and keen; a pince-nez perched on the bridge of his prominent nose. "It was all right, I guess," David answered. "Nothing special."

"You are American?"

"Yes."

"Where from?"

"New York."

"Ah . . . that's what I thought," the man said, evidently pleased that his hunch had been correct.

They passed through the foyer into the street, and crossed to the other side of l'Avenue de l'Opéra.

"Why didn't you like *Marouf?*" the man wanted to know.

"The music had no . . . no guts. It was wallpaper music—the kind that covers space." David stopped, and, mimicking the soprano's stilted gesture, sang "O Marouf . . ."

The stranger laughed in a high-pitched voice. "Charming. As a matter of fact Mme. Honfleur was in good form tonight. She's usually flat."

"I didn't notice," David said. "I listened mainly to the orchestra." Now that he felt more at ease, he didn't mind questioning the stranger. "Are you English?"

"No, Hungarian, but I was educated in England." Turning toward David, he held out his hand. "Serge Apponyi," he said, and bowed slightly.

David held out his. "David Gordin." The stranger had a firm grip.

They were outside the Café de la Paix. "How about a drink?" Apponyi asked.

"Sure."

"I've a better idea." Apponyi's face brightened. "Why not have supper at my hotel? It's not far." He pointed in the direction in which they were walking.

"If you like. I've been alone for two weeks. It'll be fun eating with someone."

"You weren't lonely?"

"Not really. There was so much to see."

"Are you staying long?"

"No. I'll be studying at the American school in Fontainebleau. This is my last night in Paris." Smiling, he added politely, "And it couldn't be nicer."

"You are a musician?"

"Yes. Pianist."

They reached the St. Moritz. Apponyi led the way through the lobby of the hotel into the restaurant. Potted palms stood at intervals along the walls, and cream-colored silk curtains were draped in curves over the windows. The head waiter greeted Apponyi and guided him to a table by the window. David followed.

Supper was a lively affair. Apponyi suggested *côtelettes à la polonaise*, which reminded David of Chopin. "He wrote polonaises and dreamed of Poland all his life, but he stayed in Paris. This way he didn't have to spoil his dream."

Apponyi drew David out and seemed to enjoy everything he said. He told David that he never attended concerts. Opera, on the other hand, he could listen to every night, and often did. His profession, he informed David, was living. As he lacked the talent to create works of art, he tried to transform his life into one—to live as fully and beautifully as possible. Apponyi thrust his face forward. "You know what Oscar Wilde said? 'I put my genius into my life, and only my talent into my art.' He was a great writer, and he is still misunderstood."

As far as David could gather from Apponyi's description, the good life consisted of good food, good clothes, good music, and good company. "It's a fine way to live," he observed, "especially if you took care to pick a father with money." He was afraid he had said the wrong thing, but Apponyi did not take it amiss.

"Fortunately, I did." He smiled good-humoredly. "You're a darling boy," he said and, putting his white manicured hand on David's, pressed it lightly.

"I'm not a boy any more. I'm twenty-one."

"In my eyes," Apponyi replied, "you're still a boy."

It was well past midnight when they finished. Apponyi led the way back into the lobby. He picked up his key at the desk and, pointing toward the elevator, said, "This way."

David glanced at his wrist watch. "I have to make an early train in the morning."

Apponyi's pasty white face expressed astonishment. "You're not coming with me?"

"At this hour? What for?"

They stared at each other across a widening gulf. David suddenly understood. "Oh—!" The exclamation broke from his lips.

The white face had turned sullen. "You mean to say I wasted an evening? And supper?"

David fixed his eyes on the older man. How could he ever have thought this spoiled prima donna intelligent and charming? "I'll be glad to pay you for my supper," he said quietly, hoping Apponyi would not accept the offer. The St. Moritz looked expensive.

"Pouf!"

"What's that supposed to mean?"

"I don't want your money. I want you."

"I thought you were interested in my mind," David said. "What you're after, any young fellow can give you."

"Don't be vulgar. Besides, it's not true. Of course I was interested in your mind. That didn't prevent me from wanting your body."

"If you'd have said so right away, I'd have told you not to waste your time."

"You didn't suspect?"

"Not in the least."

"How could you be so naïve?"

"I'm Jewish," David answered. He suddenly remembered his mother's remark about Cousin Laibel: 'Jews don't drink.' "And I come from the Bronx."

"That, I suppose, explains everything."

David ignored the sarcasm. Wasn't he right when he told Debbie that such things happened in Paris or London but not in the Bronx? It occurred to him that this situation was the exact reverse of what he faced with her. He wanted Debbie but she said no, Apponyi wanted him but he said no. Didn't anyone ever find what they were looking for? "I didn't mean to lead you on," he said. "I'm sorry if I did."

Apponyi had recovered his equanimity. "And I didn't mean to be unpleasant. Believe me, I thoroughly enjoyed the evening. You're a delightful young man. Why don't you let me visit you next weekend?"

"No."

" 'And why so great a no?' as Cyrano said."

David did not catch the allusion. "Because I've enough problems as it is, and you would only add more."

"Very well." Apponyi resigned himself with a shrug. "I collect memories. You'll make a lovely one."

"Thanks. Tell me, how do I get to where I live?"

"The buses don't run this late. Take the Metro."

"I'm just across the river. I'll walk."

Apponyi accompanied David to the street and pointed the way. David held out his hand. Apponyi clasped it in both of his. "Good luck, dear boy."

"Good-bye. And thanks for supper."

Apponyi suddenly pulled David to him and, holding him close, kissed him on both cheeks. Then he let him go.

David walked to the Pont St. Michel, which was deserted. The Seine gleamed darkly underneath. Out of the shadows in the middle of the river rose the dark gray mass of Nôtre Dame, its towers silvered by moonlight. He leaned against the iron rail of the bridge and gazed up at the cathedral. It seemed to him the most beautiful sight he had ever seen.

He drew a deep breath and continued on his way to the Street of the Ancient Comedy.

6

THE Conservatoire Américain, along with an École des Beaux Arts, was housed in the palace of Fontainebleau. The students were billeted on the town but took their lessons and meals in the palace; it had originally been a hunting lodge of the Bourbon kings and later became the favorite residence of Napoleon, whose imperial eagles were inscribed on its gates and walls. David described it all in a letter to his parents: "They show you the bathtub in which Napoleon's little boy was washed. It's like any other bathtub, of course, but dressed up. Also the bed in which Marie Antoinette slept. I don't think it was easy to live in a palace. To tell you the truth, the place isn't homey. The carp in the pond are of great ancestry." He used the word *yichos* which figured so prominently in his mother's talk. "Napoleon himself threw hunks of bread to their grandparents. If you put your hand in the water they look down their noses at you, as if they were doing you a favor. Snobs."

The piano faculty was headed by Isidore Philipp, who had been a celebrated pianist in his youth. Now he was a little old man with a white walrus mustache, who reminded David of Clemenceau. The resemblance was more than skin deep, as Philipp too was a diplomat. He never told an American student to his face that he lacked talent, but always found something pleasant to say. With his gifted students, on the other hand—they were the only ones who mattered to him—he was severe and honest. When he was pleased his face brightened, and he murmured into his mustache "Pas mal"—the exact equivalent of Miss Parissot's "Not bad."

His approach to the piano differed markedly from hers. Where her soulfulness stemmed from the Middle European tradition, he emphasized the French virtues of elegance and restraint. She mobilized the strength of the arm and the shoulder; he preferred the suppleness of wrist and fingers. She sank deep into the keys; he rippled over the surface of the keyboard and achieved astonishing sonority with a minimum of effort. "It must be clear and light," he told David. *Clair* and *léger* were his favorite adjectives. "And you must never force the piano beyond its capacity." *Jamais!*

Philipp's assistant, Camille Decreuse, prepared you for the lesson with the master. He was witty, fun-loving, and very French. When he heard that David was a pupil of

Elena Parissot he became effusive. "When you write to 'er you must geev 'er my warmest greetings." They had been students together in Paris. 'Eet was a deeferent world zen," he reminisced. "A better world." He spoke English to David only at their first meeting. After that, the lessons were in French.

The practice rooms were in a sprawling wooden structure that had been the original hunting lodge. It was built by Francis I or Henry IV, David didn't remember which. He wondered if Catherine de Medici ever came there. The studios were not soundproof, so that when he stopped playing, a jumble of piano sounds came at him from all sides. After practice he joined a group of students who bicycled to Samois or Valvin for a swim in the Seine. The river at this point was wide and silver-gray, like the Hudson; the countryside reminded David of the Catskills. What was different was the transparent quality of the air, a kind of honey-golden softness that floated through the late afternoon; the deep-blue sky of northern France; and the fact that he rode a bicycle.

The French people around them looked upon the American students as a homogeneous group, unaware of the divisions among them. The Southerners formed one clique, the Midwesterners another. David felt more at home with students from the New York area. The Jews had their own table, even as the Negroes did in the alcoves at City College. David had spent his life in Jewish communities. For the first time he was part of a group in which Jews were in the minority. Antisemitism raised its head. One of the girls in the Jewish group, Sylvia Lefkowitz, went out with an art student from Georgia. "He was after one thing only," she reported to David. "And when I refused, he called me a dirty kike."

"It makes me sad," David said. "We're all here to be exposed to French culture. But what's the use if it leaves us as bigoted as ever?" There was a big world outside Brook-

lyn and the Bronx, he reflected, and it seemed to be full of
people who hated.

Yet boundaries could be crossed. He became friendly with
Jennifer McBain, a pianist from Indiana. They read four-
hand and two-piano music together—French, naturally:
Bizet's *Pour les enfants*, Saint-Saëns's *Carnival of the Animals*,
Debussy's *En blanc et noir*. Jennifer had a perky little nose
and lively blue eyes that looked out incongruously from her
large-boned face. She was tall and heavy, and painfully
aware of her unwieldy body. Also, she loved being with
David. He enjoyed her adulation without being attracted to
her physically; she was simply too big for him. Why, he
wondered, couldn't she have been petite and cute like Debbie?

They went walking through the forest that skirted the
town. The elms and hemlocks stood with branches inter-
locked, their leaves dappled with sunlight. A thousand war-
blings mingled in a tapestry of silence. This was the forest
of the Barbizon painters; it was they who had revealed its
beauty. David followed the winding paths with Jennifer;
there was much laughter between them. She threw her head
back when she laughed, her voice deep and resonant. He
told her about the elderly couple who owned the house he
lived in.

"Madame Gazagnaire is fat and stingy, she loves American dollars. Monsieur Gazagnaire is thin and stingy, he loves
American dollars. They follow us around at night, putting
out lights. Monsieur has a cousin who's a pastry chef at
Longchamps on Fifth Avenue. The first thing he asked me
was whether I knew him. Was he disappointed when it
turned out I didn't! I think he holds it against me. Madame
believes that night air is bad for the lungs. She reminds me
to close my windows tight when I go to bed. She's puzzled
by my City College French, but she understands it, sort of.
My prof made us memorize three fables of La Fontaine.
The other day I knocked her out by reeling off *La Cigale et*

La Fourmi. She listened to the end, then called out, "Gaston, viens ici. Écoutes çà, c'est extraordinaire!"

They reached his favorite spot, a clearing in the woods surrounded by majestic oaks whose branches were weighed down with age. Slanting shafts of sunlight pierced the shadows between the gnarled trunks. "It's the perfect setting for *Pelléas,*" David said. "We'd begin in the late afternoon, so the final scene would be played in twilight. The French call it *le crépuscule.* A lovely word. The lovers would stand there"—he pointed to the tallest oak. "Pelléas knows Golaud is going to kill him, but he kisses Mélisande all the same. What a moment."

"Where would you put the orchestra?" Jennifer inquired.

He looked around, as if seeking the right spot, and gave up. "You're too practical," he said.

She laughed, and took his hand. He let it rest a moment in hers, but when he began to speak, casually withdrew it. Long ago he had given in to Stella Rabinowitz's need; he had no intention of playing that game again. "Instead of going from one great climax to the next, as Wagner does, Debussy keeps it down to a whisper. Yet when the great moment comes it's as powerful as anything in *Tristan.* Shows what understatement can do."

August was devoted to preparing for the *concours.* Competitions, it turned out, were the same everywhere. He spent hours learning the dreary contest piece, Paderewski's Theme and Variations in A minor. Fortunately David knew the other two pieces—Beethoven's Sonata Op. 110 and the Chopin Ballade in G minor; he could therefore concentrate on the Paderewski, for which he conceived a violent dislike.

The competition was scheduled for the last Sunday in August. A week before, as if by clockwork, all his anxieties returned. The dream about his coming out on stage only to discover that his trousers had fallen down. The dream about the audience walking out of the hall as soon as he began to play. The fear of forgetting. And underneath these a general apprehension, the sense of being confronted with a nameless danger from which there was no escaping.

Sunday finally arrived. The moment he launched into the sonata his left knee began to shake. He plunged ahead, trying to keep his mind on the music and wishing he were somewhere else—anywhere!—rather than in this exposed position. He felt more comfortable during the ballade, although that damn leg of his was still jumping up and down. By the time he reached the Paderewski he had almost conquered his stage fright. He whipped through the final fugue at a great clip, which heightened its brilliancy, and was so keyed up that he forgot all about the danger of forgetting. After he finished, he sat at the back of the hall and listened to the other contestants. They played, he felt, much better than he. The judges thought otherwise, for they awarded him the first prize—two hundred and fifty dollars, which seemed much more in francs. At the reception after the concert, people kept coming up to congratulate him. All the same, a grave doubt settled at the back of his mind. His left knee was obviously trying to tell him something.

The reception took place in a formal salon whose skyblue wallpaper was ornamented with white figurines in the severely classical style of the Empire. "Just think," he told Jennifer, "the Empress Josephine received her guests in this room."

"The curtains need cleaning," was her comment.

"I've always felt sorry for her."

"Why?"

"She had it all and lost it."

They stopped before a table laden with sweets. "What d'you know," David said, "we're eating napoleons in Napoleon's palace." He picked up a little cake filled with custard. "My mother used to buy me a napoleon after school. I ate it in front of a statue marked Valley Forge—I thought that was his name. Then we went to the movies."

"They were larger and creamier then," Jennifer said.

Monsieur Decreuse called David aside and engaged him in a short conversation. When he rejoined Jennifer, he said, "Guess what!"

"What?"

"They're offering me a scholarship for a year's study with Philipp."

"Marvelous! What did you tell him?"

"I said I'd have to think it over."

"Well?"

He reflected. "I'm flattered, but I won't take it."

"Why?"

"It would pay for my lessons but not my keep. At home I can earn some money by teaching or playing. If I stayed here my parents would have to support me."

"Why don't you tell them? They might be willing."

"I know what they'll say: 'Do whatever seems best to you.' I have to make up my own mind."

"It's a difficult decision," Jennifer said.

"Not really. Decisions are difficult if you're not sure of what you want."

"You mean you want to go home?" Jennifer's voice expressed disbelief.

David nodded. "I've had a wonderful time here, but I'm homesick all the same. Like a peasant for his village."

"New York is hardly a village."

David smiled. "The Bronx is. I've seen enough of the world for the time being. Now I want to go back where I belong."

"Are you sure?"

"Quite. There's another reason. The great pianists today, the ones I really admire, come out of the Russian or German school. Hoffman, Rachmaninoff, de Pachmann, Paderewski, Rosenthal, Friedman, Godowsky, Bauer—there isn't a Frenchman among them. The French have a beautiful style, but it's strictly for them. And it works best with French music. I learned a lot, and I think it's great for any musician to come here, but another year of it would be too much of a good thing."

On the last day of the session both his teachers signed their photographs for him. M. Philipp wrote in florid French that David could become a brilliant pianist if he worked with care and patience. Decreuse was even more effusive. David decided that as soon as the pictures were framed he would display them on his piano as Miss Parissot did, in the manner of trophies. There was a final reception in Empress Josephine's salon, with much exchanging of addresses and telephone numbers, and the session was over. David had one more chore to perform. He had promised his parents to visit his grandmother in Poland before he sailed for home. On the first of September he made his way to the Gard du Nord to catch the Paris-Warsaw express. Jennifer saw him off.

The train came puffing into the station. She held out her hand. "You've been a lot of fun."

"So have you."

"I don't get to New York much, so it may be a long time before . . ." Her voice trailed off.

He didn't contradict her.

"I had a real crush on you," she said.

"Why?"

"Who can say? It's always a mystery, what one person sees in another. When the chemistry is right, that's all you need. I loved the way you talked, the way you made me laugh, the way you made my heart beat whenever I caught sight of you. Too bad you didn't feel the same way."

There was no gainsaying that. "I enjoyed you too," he brought out kindly. This wasn't enough, he knew, but at least it was honest.

"Good-bye, David. All the best."

He wanted to kiss her on the cheek, but she gave him her lips. A bell clanged, a whistle blew. He grabbed his valise and boarded the train.

7

ALL grandmothers, he decided, looked alike. His had a brown, wrinkled face and wore the wig required by tradition. Her sight was failing, and she wept when she kissed him. "It's as if my Joel had come back to me. For twenty years I haven't seen him. You look exactly like him."

This was not so, but David knew better than to contradict her.

"And your mother, may she live long. Tell me about her."

David understood why his father had wanted him to go to Warsaw. He suddenly realized why his mother did too. She had sent him to his father's family to justify the marriage they had once opposed; she was showing them what she had produced. "She sends her regards," he replied, "and wishes she could have come too."

There followed a round of visits to various aunts, uncles, and cousins. The menu, always the same, was like what he was accustomed to at home: gefilte fish with horseradish, chicken soup with matzoh balls, roast chicken or pot roast with the carrots-and-prunes pudding known as tsimmes, for dessert a baked apple, sponge cake, and tea. Except for his grandmother, the family was not religious. Milk or cream was served after meat, and no one thought anything of it.

After four days of this he sent off a long letter to his parents. "Our family lives in the heart of the Warsaw ghetto, in huge, old apartment houses built around courtyards. I spent my afternoons wandering through crowded streets that are called Muranowska, Mila, Leszno. They remind me of the East Side when I was little. Everybody speaks Yiddish with bits of Polish thrown in. Yiddish is really an international language. Without it I'd be lost here.

"My aunts and uncles are very much like the aunts and uncles in New York except that they're much more involved with the family. Especially quarrels, some of which seem to have been going on for years. Each one takes me aside to gossip about the others. Yesterday Uncle Naftali asked me, 'You're going to visit your Aunt Faigel?' I said yes. 'Don't tell her,' Naftali said, 'that you saw me.' 'Why not,' I asked. 'It's a long story,' he answered. 'When we have time I'll tell you.' Aunt Faigel's first question, after she kissed me, was 'Did you meet your Uncle Naftali?' 'Not yet, Tante Faigel,' I said. 'When you do,' she went on, 'don't tell him you saw me.' 'Why?' 'Don't ask. Someday I'll tell you all about him.' As you can see, I'm having a lovely time."

To most of David's remarks his relatives answered "Dob-zheh," the Polish equivalent of "okay." Most of them had an upright piano in the parlor and asked David to play, but their interest in music was minimal.

There was much talk about the attitude of Marshal Pil-sudski's government toward the Jews. They also plied David with questions about his mother, whom they knew only through her letters. "She keeps writing us," Naftali said, "that we ought to emigrate to Palestine or America. How can we leave Poland? We were born here, we grew up here, our homes and friends are here. Why should we leave our country?"

"But there's so much antisemitism," David said. "Even I feel it."

"Ekh," Uncle Naftali said with a wave of his hand. "wherever you live there are problems."

He took David sightseeing through the non-Jewish part of the city. The tour ended in the main park, which was called the Saxon garden.

"What's a Saxon garden doing in the middle of Warsaw?" David asked.

"What kind of a question is that?" Naftali replied. "It's always been there."

David thought hard. "I know," he said. "Bach wrote the B-minor Mass for a king of Saxony who was also king of Poland." He was delighted with himself for having made the connection. His music-history course, which so often had lulled him to sleep, had turned out to be of some use after all.

Uncle Naftali gave a party for David on his last night in Warsaw. His cousin Janna, whose blond curls and snub nose made her look like a typical Polish girl, regretted that she could not attend. She had to see Garbo and Zhan Geelbehr in *Love*. David assured her that the film was not to be missed. His other relatives came. There was much food and wine; one of his cousins played the accordion for dancing. They waltzed, as his mother used to, with a little hop on the third beat. The festivities went on long past midnight. Why not? They were having a good time.

The S.S. *France* nosed her way into the harbor. David stood on the forward deck. On his right lay Long Island; he was sailing past the Rockaways. To the left he could see Sandy Hook and the Jersey coast. The ocean lay calm beneath a cloudless sky; the boat pursued its course past the Statue of Liberty. Brooklyn Bridge came into view, with its intricate web of cables. Farther upstream was his bridge, the Williamsburg. Long ago he used to see its tower from the chimney pot on top of the house on South Fourth Street. The boat sailed into the Hudson, past the metallic skyline of Manhattan. The slender towers shone in the sunlight, thrusting upward like so many fingers reaching for the sky. It was good to come home. Europe had been exciting, certainly; but what could compare with the excitement of seeing New York again?

The *France* floated gently into her berth. A flock of seagulls wheeled across the sky. The September sun was warm, the ship's whistle blew loud and clear, and the air was filled with promise.

IV

The Awakening

ONE

1

NEW houses were going up in Brighton Beach that offered Joel and Lisa an irresistible inducement: they would have the ocean at their doorstep all year round. On the top floor of a six-story house on Brightwater Court they found an apartment that commanded a view of the boardwalk and the sea. Joel saw the move as another step up. "On Crotona Park we got steam heat, here we have an elevator. Is bad?"

Lisa found Brighton Beach much livelier than the Bronx; the boardwalk served as promenade and communal living room. Here, when the weather was pleasant, Joel and she could listen to all the groups in the political spectrum, from socialists, Zionists, anarchists, and communists to New Deal Democrats and an occasional Republican, not to mention vegetarians, sun worshipers, and the self-styled Polar Bears who insisted on taking a dip in the ocean even in winter. Discussion was fierce and nonstop. After half an hour Lisa had had enough, and suggested to Joel that they go for a walk. "Fill your lungs," she told him. "Such air we never had in the Bronx."

After twenty years in America, they had only the haziest

notion of what the country was like. Their image of it, shaped during the Twenties, was one of boundless optimism and progress, qualities the very opposite of those they associated with Russia. Hence they were totally unprepared for the Depression. How could such a rich country move so rapidly from prosperity to crisis? They found it hard to believe that the National Guard had been called out to shoot at veterans in Washington. The incident reminded them of the massacre in front of the Winter Palace on the Bloody Sunday that had launched the Revolution of 1905. Could such things happen here? Later, the voice of Roosevelt reassured them. Him they loved and trusted. How could anyone in his right mind vote for anyone else?

The Yiddish newspapers were not affected by the hard times; on the contrary, they prospered. Jews were only too eager to lay out two cents to read the bad news. "Thank God you're with the paper," Lisa repeatedly said to Joel as unemployment spread around them like an epidemic. Yet they were not untouched by the stock-market crash. Joel, along with his fellow printers, had organized a loan society that had zoomed throughout the years of prosperity. There were theater parties to mark its progress, with supper afterward and gifts for the ladies. Suddenly the bubble burst. Before anyone knew how it happened, the corporation went bankrupt. Joel was mystified by the debacle. Not Lisa. "My financier!" she brought out disdainfully. "From the beginning I considered you all a pack of dreamers."

Joel, always an optimist, resigned himself to the loss of their life savings. "We're alive and healthy, and it's only money. What if we had never had it in the first place?"

"Workingmen," Lisa pontificated, "shouldn't try to become millionaires. You wanted to make money? So God showed you that you don't know how."

They walked past Ocean Parkway to Coney Island. Now that the summer was over, its gaudy roller coasters and ferris wheels looked sadly deserted. "Like toys," Lisa remarked, "that someone forgot to put back in the closet." She gazed at the towers of Luna Park. "You remember the first time we came here?"

"The trolley cars were packed," Joel said, "and people fought to get on. Like animals."

Lisa thought a moment. "It was all so beautiful."

"It only seemed beautiful."

"We were young," Lisa said.

Joel put his arm around her, bent over, and kissed her. "Women are romantic," he generalized, giving *romantish* a condescending ring. "But men see things as they are."

Lisa pondered that. "Strange," she finally said, "I thought it was the other way around."

2

DAVID sat in front of the small table by the window that served him as a desk. He liked the room, even if most of the space was taken up by the piano. The view of the ocean was even more spectacular than the view of Bronx Park from Debbie's window.

His eyes returned to the sheet of paper before him. *Dear Miss Parissot . . .* He played with the pen wondering how to begin. This was not an easy letter to write. How could he tell her that he wanted to go to another teacher? It was like writing a note to a woman to inform her that you loved someone else.

He was not even sure that he wanted to change. True, he had been with her for five years and there was not much more she could teach him. It would be exciting to work with another musician, and now that he was in the graduate course, he had the opportunity to study with Carl Friedberg, an artist of international reputation. On the other hand, he owed her a lot and hated to seem ungrateful for all she had done for him. "I hope we will still be friends." The phrase took shape in his mind. This was what people told each other when they parted, knowing quite well that they were kidding each other. Not only would she not remain his friend; she would hate his guts.

He crumpled the sheet in his hand and threw it into the wastebasket. There had to be a way of telling her. Or was there? He decided to go speak to her.

She listened carefully. Then she handed him a cup of tea and poured one for herself. On the tea table was the usual plate of cucumber sandwiches, crusts removed.

"My dear boy"—her voice was as husky as ever—"I know exactly how you feel." She wore the blue velvet house coat and gave off ever so faintly the scent he thought of as musk. "Do you remember the first time you played for me? You went through the whole *Poet and Peasant Overture*. I laughed, and you asked me what was so funny. Now you know." David smiled and sipped his tea.

Only one lamp was lit, bathing the room in a soft glow. Miss Parissot raised one hand to pat the blue-black mound of hair. "We've come a long way together, you and I. It's been exciting for me to watch you grow. Of course, if you feel you've had enough, nothing I might say would change your mind. But it's my duty as your teacher to tell you you're mistaken. Now that the foundation has been laid, you and I can build on it. I'm finally able to transform you into an artist. This is why you should think twice before you consider making a change."

He put down his teacup. "I only thought—" he began weakly.

"Silly boy, I know exactly what you thought." She gave him her most winning smile. "David, I know you through and through, both your strengths and weaknesses. Friedberg is a fine musician, he's an artist, but you would be going to a man whose main interest is in his career. Half the time he's so busy with his concerts that the lessons are given by his assistant. He simply won't have the time to get to understand you as I do."

David helped himself to a cucumber sandwich. It was

very quiet in the room; no sound from the outside penetrated the thick drapes. The world was far away; there was only this small space and the two of them in it.

"You must choose," she continued smoothly, "whatever is best for you, and not be swayed by any feeling of gratitude or loyalty. I did what I was supposed to do, and you owe me nothing. But you do owe it to yourself to make the right decision. In a year or two, if you should wish to change, I'd be the first to encourage you. But at this time, if you don't mind my saying so"—she sounded utterly objective—"you'd be making a mistake. Believe me, we've only scratched the surface."

David suddenly didn't mind her holding on to him. A change meant venturing into unfamiliar territory; it was easier to stay put. Her eyes were upon him, lustrous; she offered him a second cup of tea. "Well, what do you say? Are we still partners?"

"Of course we are," he exclaimed, as happily as if it were he who had won. He took the cup, more than a little flattered that she cared.

3

THE ocean changed from day to day, from a serene blue streaked with sunlight to a sullen steel-gray dappled with bursts of foam. Its music varied too, from the steady murmur that lulled David to sleep at night to the fierce boom of breakers against the shore. He had always loved the sea; now he was getting to know it.

He enjoyed the boardwalk. It took him little over an hour, at a brisk clip, to get to Sea Gate and back. The air had a salt tang; he wore a pullover and worked up a sweat. He would have liked to join the players on the handball courts, but his hands were too sensitive to the shock of the ball, even if he wore a glove. The walk was a good substitute.

As he approached Sea Gate he could see the great ocean liners—*Berengaria, Mauritania, Île de France, Queen Mary*—steaming in and out of the harbor. How graceful they were. Balzac said that no sight in the world was as beautiful as a woman dancing, a horse racing, or a boat sailing. He had a point.

David liked Brighton too because with very little effort on his part it gave him a living. His parents' friends, avid for culture, thought that the best way to introduce their youngsters to music was to teach them the piano. By giving a few lessons every day after school, he earned enough to cover his needs. "I'm teaching fifteen little girls," he informed Sidney, "all of whom are called Shirley. Every time I arrive for a lesson her mother says to me, 'What should I do with my Shirley, she don't want to practice.' "

"Why don't you tell her?" Sidney suggested.

"Look, I need the three dollars. Besides, you don't say things like that to the president of the Brighton Beach Hadassah."

"Why not?" Sidney wanted to know. He was happily enrolled in the law school of New York University. "What a relief," he told David, "not to have to worry whether I'll make it or not."

David, on the contrary, was worrying more and more. For the first time, as he sat practicing, he found it difficult to concentrate on the music. It was as if all the doubts that had been hiding at the back of his mind were finally leaping into the foreground. For years he seemed to have been moving toward a distant goal that, like the horizon, kept receding as he approached it. As on that summer afternoon when he went rowing with Abe, the weather had suddenly changed; the hopeful years had given way to Depression. "This," he told Deborah, "is no time to launch a concert career. It looks as if the world we prepared for has gone up in smoke."

"You're a damn good pianist," Debbie reminded him.

"Sure. But we're living at a time when it's no longer

enough to be good. Unless you're spectacular, you're nowhere. And spectacular I'm not."

"You've not done badly."

David considered this. "It's one thing to win prizes at school. It's another to face a tough concert manager who sells artists as other salesmen sell cars or refrigerators. The school world is a million miles away from the concert world. It was never easy to get from one to the other. Right now it's almost impossible."

"How d'you know?" Debbie persisted. "You haven't tried."

"I'm trying to see the picture clearly, and for that I have to be honest with myself. I was talented enough to reach a certain point, and I reached it. Many are called, Parissot always said, but few are chosen. Well, the chances are I'll not be one of them."

"Maybe it's just a question of self-confidence."

"It goes deeper than that, Debbie. Maybe I put my hopes on something that wasn't right for me from the start. I think I mixed up two separate issues. One has to do with loving music and wanting to be a musician. The other has to do with career and success, with becoming a famous artist and having the world at your feet. How come I confused them? Because everybody around me did. I'm a pretty good musician, no one can take that away from me. As for the hoopla about fame and fortune and Carnegie Hall crowded to the rafters, that was a delusion from the start. I finally discovered what I should have suspected all along, that I'm simply not meant for that kind of life."

Debbie was thoughtful. "I wish there were a magic word that would *solve* everything. Like 'abracadabra' or 'Open Sesame.' "

"Don't worry," David replied. "I'll work it out."

Sidney bought two tickets for the Carnegie Hall recital of a new Russian pianist named Vladimir Horowitz. He invited David. Half the pianists from the school were there.

By the time the intermission rolled around, most of them were in a state of shock. This was a new standard of piano playing, a style dazzling in its color, brilliance, verve. The concert seemed to point up everything David and Sidney had been talking about. They stopped afterward in a coffee shop on Seventh Avenue.

"My God, how he played!" David said. "What chance is there for us?"

"That's why I got out," Sidney said.

"Someone should have warned us. Sooner."

"We wouldn't have listened." Sidney ordered his usual pineapple cheese cake and milk. "You see a movie with the star up front and a hundred extras behind him. Each of them came to Hollywood thinking he'd be a star."

"You mean we're the extras?" David made a face.

Sidney took a mouthful of cake and waved his fork for emphasis. "Every time you shoot a load there's a million sperm in it. Only one of them is going to make it to the egg. The rest . . ." A downward jab of the fork signaled their extinction. "Art is as cruel as nature. For every one who makes it to the top a thousand drop out. Or is it ten thousand?"

"You dropped into law. Where am I supposed to go?"

"You'll find something. We all do." Sidney washed down the cake. "How do people get into this mess?"

David thought hard, creasing his forehead with the effort. "You begin by being the only kid on the block who plays an instrument, so you're outstanding. Then you go forward, and your parents and friends all believe you're on your way to Carnegie Hall. You win a scholarship, a prize, a concert with the orchestra—each is a step up the ladder that leads There. All of a sudden, like in one of those surrealist paintings on Madison Avenue, the ladder comes to an end in the middle of the canvas. You've reached the top step and you're nowhere!"

"I've been trying to tell you this all along," Sidney said. "I guess you had to come to it by yourself."

"The trouble is"—David spoke slowly, feeling his way—"that when we're young we don't question the goals our parents and teachers put before us. We try to become what they think we should be. And so we accumulate all kinds of illusions about ourselves that have nothing to do with what we're really like. Then comes the awful moment when we have to shake them off."

On the subway home, he remembered a story by Somerset Maugham about a young pianist who hoped to become a concert artist. When he realized that he couldn't, he went out and shot himself. Such an ending, it seemed to David, made no sense at all. Surely there were other ways of being a musician than trying to be a Horowitz. Somerset Maugham's fellow must have had a lot more wrong with him than his piano playing. He didn't really care about music—what he wanted was the glory that was supposed to go with it. The fool!

David slouched in his seat, resting his legs on the seat in front. The world would think of him as having failed; his mother would, too. He had let himself be influenced by her ambition, her overriding need to have a son who did extraordinary things. And he had let himself be flattered by Miss Parissot's big plans for him. But why did he have to accept their judgment, or anyone else's? The answer was simple. He didn't.

The train pulled into Brighton Beach. The boardwalk was deserted. A salty breeze floated in from the sea. A dark immensity hung over the Atlantic. Against that vast background the picture he had conjured up for Sidney came vividly alive: an endless staircase with himself on top, teetering on one leg while the other groped for the step that wasn't there. He refused to let the image dampen his spirit. What he needed was a little time to get to know himself better, and the honesty to find his own path, and the courage to follow it. Wasn't that what growing up was all about?

4

HE faced his parents. "I have something to tell you."

Lisa settled against one side of the armchair in the living room. "So tell us." She never sat back in the chair as it made her feet dangle.

Where to begin? He plunged in boldly. "I'm not getting anywhere with the piano, so I've decided to give it up." There, he had said it!

Lisa stared at him, puzzled. "What are you saying?"

"I'm saying," David replied, "that things have changed. Both in the world and in me. I now know that I won't make it as a concert artist, so I have to give up the idea and try something else."

Lisa leaned forward in an effort to understand his words. "Why now, all of a sudden?"

"Because my student days are over, and I finally realized what I'm up against."

"It took you all this time to find out?"

"How was I to know?"

Her face was grave. "Are you sure?"

"Quite."

She turned to Joel. "What d'you say to this?"

"What can I say?" Joel made his usual appeal to reason. "A person must want to do what he's doing, otherwise, how can he?"

Lisa rose and walked over to David. "My son, it's easy to get discouraged . . . to think that you can't do it. But you're as good as the best. I know it for a fact."

"That's just it, Mama, I don't. And that's what counts."

Her eyes were upon him, loving and luminous, as if she were fighting to save him from himself. "All those years you did think you could do it."

"Maybe. But I know better now."

"What if this is just a mood that will pass?" She sat down again. "All the work you put in, you mean to say you can throw it away because of a whim?" She made the word *ka-preez* sound not only capricious but sinful.

"It's not a whim, Ma. The concert thing is out. I'm just not made for it."

"How can you tell?" Her voice rose in disbelief.

"Maybe I suspected the truth long ago but didn't want to face it."

She appealed to Joel. "Speak to him, you're his father. Tell him that such moods come and go."

Joel raised his hand uncertainly, as though he knew in advance that his words would have no effect. "If he doesn't know at his age what he wants to be, who can tell him?"

"Don't answer with a question. Say something!"

"What will you do instead?" Joel asked. "You can't just *not* be something."

"I don't yet know. I'll teach for now."

"A piano teacher?" Lisa said bitterly. "With all those prizes you won, and a scholarship in France yet. How can it be?"

"It can be," David answered. "School is one thing, and the music world is another."

"What can we do with him?" Lisa demanded.

Joel turned his hands palms up. "We can't force him."

"There you go. Your only son is throwing his life away, and you tell him he's right."

Joel looked from one to the other as if he were trying to decide who needed his advice more. "I regret what you're doing, David," he finally said. "For your sake. I think you'll regret it too."

Lisa's face was gray with disappointment. "The eagle flew too high."

"What's that supposed to mean?" David asked.

"You know perfectly well what it means. I was so proud of you, I had such great dreams for you. I guess it wasn't written that they should come true."

A great sorrow crested in David at the anguish he was causing her. He walked over to her and put his hand on her shoulder. "Look, Mama, there's nothing I wanted so much as to make you proud of me. But I can't live my life according to your ideas. I have to live it as seems right to me. Surely you understand that."

"I understand." She shook her hand to and fro, and sighed. "The trouble is, my son, you want it all on a silver platter from heaven. Right away."

"You're saying I'm spoiled. Maybe I am. But I'm trying to be realistic."

"And when life gets difficult," she continued, "you lose heart."

How could he make her see it his way? "Maybe I spoiled you, too. I led you to expect an eagle for a son. From the time I was little you made me feel I had to be somebody special, somebody great. But do I have to be? Isn't it enough for me just to be me?"

"Just to be you? And who is that, may I ask?"

"I'm not sure, but I'll find out." David was still bent over her chair. He straightened up. "Don't think I don't appreciate everything you did for me. I know how much I owe you."

"The point is not what you owe us," Lisa replied, "but what you owe yourself. If I wanted you to be somebody it was not only for my sake but for your own." She stood up, her chin jutting forward, lips pressed together. Then her lips parted in a smile half playful, half sad. "You remember the time you stole your cousin Arthur's ball? I knew then, Dovid'l, that I'd have trouble with you."

"Maybe you expected too much, Mama."

"I wanted you to achieve everything I hadn't. Is that a crime?"

"No, only a mistake."

"Small ones press the knee, and big ones the heart." With a mournful look at David she walked slowly across the room and shut the door behind her.

His eyes misted over. He wished he could think of a word that would bring her back. The magic word, as Debbie called it, that was supposed to solve all problems. He had failed her, and all he could hope for now was that she would forgive him for it.

5

MISS Parissot dropped two lumps of sugar into the cup, added a slice of lemon, and handed David his tea. "My dear boy, the decisions that change our lives are taken for us deep down. We may think we're choosing them. As a matter of fact, they choose us."

David heaved a sigh of relief. This was so much less painful than the confrontation with his mother. He could see why. His mother was fighting—as she saw it—for his life, whereas this woman was basically indifferent. She had been involved with him as long as he served her purpose. Now that he no longer would, she was able to relinquish him.

"I do not try to change your mind," she continued, "for a very good reason. It is so difficult to make a concert career. You might think the world would be on your side. On the contrary, every obstacle is put in your way. You have to be able to take the disappointments, the rejections, and you can do that only if you want it desperately. Once you have doubts, there's no point in even trying. When," she inquired, "did all this occur to you?"

"I'm not sure. I never asked myself too many questions about my future, it seemed such a long way off. Suddenly I was getting close to it, I had to sit down and figure things out. Once I did, what I was doing made no sense at all."

"Where do you go from here?"

"At the moment I'm teaching. I've enough students to get by. Later on I'll see."

"What good times we've had together, you and I." She assumed her tea-party manner, and he knew she was saying good-bye. "Oh, those fingers of yours"—she wiggled her own in the air—"and how you loved the pedal. But I knew right away you had talent."

She glanced at her wrist watch. "I almost forgot, I've a dinner engagement." She accompanied him to the door. "It was fun, making a musician out of you. We came a long way together."

He glanced round the room as if to impress each detail on his mind. The soft glow of the lamps. The green velvet drapes that fell to the floor. The batik shawl on the piano, with the signed photographs of Kreisler and the rest. The ugly sofa and overstuffed armchairs. And Elena Parissot with her mound of blue-black hair, her heavily rouged face with its jowls and imperious features, her heavy perfume.

She held out her hand. "Good luck, dear boy. And remember—not too much pedal." She bent forward, kissed the air near his left ear and repeated the ritual on his right. "Don't forget me. We'll keep in touch."

"Of course we will," he said, knowing full well that she had no such intention.

The coffee shop on Seventh Avenue was crowded, as was the delicatessen next to it. A taxi honked its horn; that early-evening expectancy hung in the air. Some passers-by clustered around a man who was selling balloons. At Carnegie Hall the billboard announced forthcoming concerts by Moritz Rosenthal and Rachmaninoff. David looked at the two posters showing their blown-up faces. Had he really expected that his picture would be up there one day for all the world to see? He could not possibly have been that naïve. He remembered Professor Capaccio's concert at Palm Garden and his Aunt Bessie saying in that loud voice of hers, "Mark my word, he'll play in Carnegie Hall yet." He was ten, Bessie sounded quite sure of herself, how was he to suspect that she didn't know her fat ass from a hole in the ground? And so he, and a thousand youngsters like him, spent the next fifteen years trying to realize their Aunt Bessie's prophecy. Like them, he had enjoyed a pleasant dream. Well, the dream was over.

He turned the corner and stepped under the ornate canopy that guarded the entrance to the hall. Toscanini looked down at him benignly. David scowled. There was a promise somewhere that had not been kept. Someone had deceived him, he didn't know who. The hell with it!

He returned to the corner. At the curb, a man was selling roasted peanuts. David bought a bagful and walked down the stairs to the subway, feeling as if he were leaving a part of his life behind him.

It was a relief, during the next weeks, not to have to go near the piano. He took long walks in Manhattan Beach where houses, sea, and sky had a fresh, shiny look. Walking along the esplanade was like pacing the deck of a ship. The ocean came splashing over the rocks that had been piled up to contain it, shooting streamers of spray into the air. The two-story homes soaked up the November sunshine; well-kept lawns seemed to protect them against the turmoil that was rocking less affluent neighborhoods. A stiff breeze sent dead leaves scraping along the pavement with a soft hiss. David remembered Professor Sheldon perched on his desk, one leg across the other, nursing his ankle as he declaimed his favorite lines from Shelley's invocation to the west wind:

> Thou, from whose unseen presence the leaves dead
> Are driven, like ghosts from an enchanter fleeing,
> Yellow, and black, and pale, and hectic red . . .

Afternoons passed in giving lessons. In the evening a new life opened to him in Manhattan. Through Sidney he met Nat Bender, a tall, cadaverous man with a large nose and glittery eyes who held forth at a corner table in Stewart's Cafeteria on Eighth Street. Nat was a writer of sorts who talked his books instead of writing them. "The minute you put pen to paper," he explained, "you compromise." Therefore the best books were those that were never written, the best paintings were those that remained unpainted,

and the best symphonies never composed. This novel view
he expounded eloquently at his nightly seances.

David was fascinated by the names Nat dropped: Plato,
Nietzsche, da Vinci, Marx, Freud, Hegel. Nat's ency-
clopedic knowledge came from the main reading room of
the public library on Fifth Avenue, where he spent his days.
He was able to do so because Gladys, his girl friend, paid
the rent. She was a blowsy, round-shouldered woman who
kept her arms folded across her belly in a vain attempt to
hide the fact that she was twenty pounds overweight. She
sold brassieres at Macy's eight hours a day and considered
this a small price to pay for the privilege of supporting a
genius. She agreed with Nat that he should not take a job
unless it was worthy of him. In any case, there were no
jobs at the moment. Nat's nimble mind leaped from one
subject to the next. "My philosophical orientation," he
explained to David, "stems from logical positivism. At heart
I'm a nihilist." David did not know enough about either
positivism or nihilism to be able to gauge Nat's position,
but he thought the statement sounded great.

On Friday nights, when Gladys was paid, Nat moved
his coterie from the cafeteria to Ella's Corner on Mac-
Dougal Street. This was a basement where the lights were
dim and the air pleasantly hazy with cigarette smoke. Ella's
patrons huddled around little tables that were illumined by
a candle stuck into a mound of tallow drippings; their
unpredictable shapes could not but stimulate the imagination. Ella's Corner had one advantage over Stewart's: you
could buy drinks. Nat responded brilliantly to alchohol; one
Scotch on the rocks, and he was off on a fanciful improvi-
sation. His big number was Dr. Bulgakoff's lecture on the
virtues of Bulgarian buttermilk. Assuming an accent that
sounded authentically Bulgarian to anyone who had never
heard the language, he explained in detail how Bulgarian
buttermilk stimulated the sex glands. "De proh-cess is see-
meelehr to osmosis but not quite. Eet wahrmz you up inside

until you doo not know eef you are going or coming." Nat piously rolled his eyes toward the ceiling.

Gladys shook with laughter, her belly registering the tremors within like a seismograph. Sid roared, as did David. Nat's gaze wandered from face to face, his lips parted in a broad grin that revealed teeth missing on either side. His irregular features shone under a thin film of perspiration. Like Cousin Laibel long ago, he had the entertainer's eager look, the need to please and dazzle. By the standards of the bourgeois world he might be judged a failure, but in Ella's Corner he was a howling success.

David sometimes stayed over with Nat and Gladys. They lived on the top floor of a tenement on Grove Street. You had to walk up five flights. When the light in the kitchen was turned on, several cockroaches scurried away. The living room held an extra cot; Gladys brought out sheets and a pillow, and David was set for the night. He threw off his clothes, made his way to the bathroom, and looked at his face in the mirror. His eyes were tired, but there were flecks of light in their dark brown depths. His mop of curly brown hair stood up defiantly; when he ran his comb through it there was a crackling sound as if he were giving off sparks. He felt exhilarated from the talk and laughter of the evening. How pleasant it was to be in an atmosphere where no one worried about Chopin études or Horowitz's playing. He felt as if, after years of being locked in a windowless room, he had finally been let out.

In the morning Gladys left for Macy's; Nat and David roamed through the Village. The narrow streets, so determinedly picturesque at night, took on a normal appearance in daylight. Bars and restaurants were not yet open; houses looked neat and humdrum, like houses in which people got up in the morning, ate corn flakes, and raised children. The little park in Washington Square looked like a painting, as did the piers along the Hudson. David was astonished by the depth of his attachment to the city, its crowded streets, its composite smells and noises. He was a New Yorker through and through, and could not understand how anybody would want to live anywhere else.

On the nights when he did take the subway back to Brighton, he settled down to an hour of reading. He did not waste time on newspapers; the daily bundle of world events seemed to have little connection with him. He preferred a book, and was now well into *Of Human Bondage*. One incident in the novel struck close to home. Philip Carey, after a year of study in Paris, realizes that he lacks the talent to be a painter; yet he does not regret the time he spent trying to become one. He knows that for the rest of his life he will look at paintings differently from people who never studied art. In the same way, David decided, the years he had spent trying to become a pianist were a permanent part of his life. He would always hear music differently from the non-musician—from the inside, as if he were playing it.

When he reached home he found his mother at the kitchen table. "Why aren't you in bed, Ma? You know I don't like you to wait up for me."

"Who's waiting up for you? I was having a glass tea."

"You know you were."

"Maybe if you telephoned and said you'd be late, I wouldn't have to worry."

David made a gesture of impatience. "Look, Ma, I'm not a little boy any more. I should be able to come and go without reporting."

"Is it such a big thing to go over to a phone?"

"If you must know, it is. In the middle of a discussion it's hard for me to break away, and when I get to the subway I may not have a nickel or there are no phones around."

"Or you don't think of it. I know, it's easy for you to forget your mother." She paused, to give the reproach a chance to sink in. "Besides, why would you want me to know how you waste your nights. My son has to be a bohemian. A nothing."

"They're not the same thing, Ma."

"Don't give me your smart answers. You think I don't see how you're throwing your life away? With companions as worthless as you."

"Leave my friends out of this."

"Better you should leave them out."

"Why," he pleaded, "can't you accept me as I am?"

She pressed her lips together, as though to keep them from saying something she might regret. Then, "I cannot accept what I don't admire," she said softly. "I tried my best with you. Where did I fail? The older you grow, the more you remind me of your Uncle Adolph. God forbid you should end up as he did."

The mention of his unfortunate uncle made David smile. "C'mon, Ma, let's not quarrel. How about a kiss?"

"I should kiss you after you've run around with prostitutes all night?"

"Where does it say I ran around with prostitutes? Maybe I was having a serious discussion with a nice Jewish girl. Is it my fault you have a dirty mind?" He put his arm around her.

She let it stay. "I hate to upset you, my son. But it's my duty to tell you the truth." Her face was stern now. When she was in this mood her nose seemed to grow a trifle longer.

"You're judging me, Ma, and you have no right to do that."

"I have no right? Listen to him . . ."

David gave up. No matter what he said, she twisted it into something that fed her disapproval.

A dull pain pressed against his temples; his eyelids burned. Very well, he told himself, he would do without her approval. He neither needed it nor wanted it.

The trouble was that he did.

6

THE father of one of his students taught sociology at Hunter College. One Saturday night in January he gave a party for his colleagues to which he invited David.

The evening began on a high level. Names were mentioned that David had not heard before—Malinowski, Edward Sapir, the Beards, Margaret Mead. Vistas were opening before him whose existence he had never even suspected. Before long the professors turned to more mundane matters; what the dean said to the president, and who was going to be promoted the following semester.

The host asked David to play. Two months earlier, when he still thought of himself as a pianist, he would have refused if he had missed a few days of practice. Now he sat down at the piano without hesitation and launched into the Barcarolle of Chopin. Nor was he unduly disturbed by an occasional wrong note. By abandoning his career as a pianist he no longer had to be concerned about playing impeccably. He was free, in a curious way, to concentrate on the music itself, its nature and meaning. He shaped the broad curve of melody as it moved relentlessly from a dark pianissimo—through all the shimmering gradations between—to the brilliant climax. What a long line Chopin had fashioned, and what a joy it was to unravel.

When he finished, several people came up to tell him how much they had enjoyed his playing. Among them was Judith Sonnenberg, a woman he judged to be in her middle thirties. She was not especially pretty, but when she smiled, her face lit up. "Music is a mystery to me," she told him. "I enjoy it, but I always imagine it has some deeper meaning that I've failed to grasp."

"Whatever it means to you," David replied, "is what it means."

"My mistake, I guess, is to think it has a specific meaning. I'm not equipped to handle any other kind."

"There is none in music," David said. "That's what makes it music."

When the party was over, David found himself walking beside her. He accompanied her to the door of a brownstone in the East Fifties. "I've an old Steinway," she said. "Will you come and play for me sometime?"

"Sure. You teach at Hunter?"

"Anthropology."

"What's that?"

"Shall I give you Malinowski's definition? It's the study of man, embracing woman."

"How's that different from sociology?"

"Anthropologists study primitive societies. In the process they discover interesting facts about our own."

"Sounds great," he said, and realized that this was the kind of silly remark people made when they felt they had to say something but didn't know what.

She held out her hand. "I hope we'll meet again."

"As we say in Brooklyn, likewise I'm sure." He grinned.

On his way to the subway he felt pleased with the encounter. It was fun to be with someone who knew so much more than he.

Some days later he received an invitation to a cocktail party that Judith was giving the following Sunday. David looked forward to seeing her again, and came early. Her apartment on Fifty-second Street consisted of two large rooms and a kitchen. The bedroom-study was lined with books; the other room contained her piano, a square grand with old-fashioned legs. Three African masks hung on the wall, flanking a hand-woven tapestry with an unusual design; what looked like a mouth with very thick lips, parted to reveal two rows of enormous teeth. "What's that supposed to be?" David asked a sociologist whom he had met at the other party.

"*Vagina dentata*, the vagina with teeth. It's a concept that figures very much in the thinking of primitive man. The idea is that it's easy to find your way in but hard to get out."

David studied the tapestry. "Where's it from?"

"New Guinea. Judith brought it back with her."

"She was there?"

"Yes, she wrote a book about it."

As at the previous party, the conversation moved on two levels. On the one hand, there was much discussion of sociological theories. On the other, David heard a lot of professional gossip: why the chairman of the sociology department was unhappy over the dean's attitude; who was to get a coveted appointment at City College; who had done whom out of a handsome grant; why the new chairman at Yale was a terrible choice. Judith's guests, David noticed, discussed their colleagues in the same disparaging tone as Miss Parissot used to discuss hers. Backbiting obviously was a basic element of professional life, no matter in what field.

Judith wore a rose-colored hostess gown that made her seem taller and more graceful. Her habit of pursing her lips gave her face a prissy look. But her dark eyes were extremely intelligent and her hair, which was black with a sheen to it, was combed straight back to reveal her forehead. She wore it coiled on top of her head, as his mother used to.

He found her book on an end table near the piano— *Courtship Patterns in New Guinea*—and leafed through it. It seemed incredible that the eminently civilized woman who was exchanging pleasantries with her guests could have spent two years alone with the aborigines of a Polynesian village; yet this was precisely what the preface said she had done. As he watched her move about the room he wondered about her. What kind of woman would accept an assignment like that?

She felt his glance upon her and came over to him. "I see you found my book."

"I'd love to read it."

"By all means. I'll give you a copy."

"Autographed?"

"Of course." She paused, and added casually, "Why don't you stay after the party? I'll rustle up some food."

"Good." David was flattered that she had singled him out.

People began to drift off. When the last guest had gone Judith poured herself a drink, sank into an armchair and kicked off her shoes. "I'm bushed. I love having my friends in, but it takes doing."

"It was a nice party," he said.

"You enjoyed it?"

"Very much. It was different."

"Different from what?"

"From what I'm used to."

She slumped in her chair. "Why don't you play something? I'd love it."

He sat down at the piano and struck a few chords. "It's in tune," he said, surprised.

"Yes. I play a little and try to practice when I have time. This is the piano I grew up with."

He played an intermezzo of Brahms, the introspective one in B-flat minor. "Beautiful," she murmured. Touched by her response, David continued with his favorite nocturne of Chopin, the posthumous one in E minor. "I feel like an Esterházy," Judith said, "having a performance all to myself."

Presently she brought out some supper: cold chicken, tomatoes, and a bottle of wine. He asked her about her stay in New Guinea. "What was it like to be the only white woman in a primitive village?"

"I stepped back into the Stone Age. It was fascinating."

"Weren't you afraid?"

"Primitive people have a high moral sense. Besides, their concept of hospitality is much stronger than ours. I came to the tribe as a friend, bringing all kinds of trinkets as gifts, and was accepted as a friend. When it comes to sex, their system of taboos is so strong that I was totally off bounds for them. I don't think I was ever in danger. It did get lonely at night, but . . ." She shrugged. "You get used to loneliness."

"That was a tough job you took on."

"It's the only kind that interests me."

She spoke slowly, stopping frequently to find the word or phrase that would best express her meaning. He did not think she was bright in the way, for example, that his mother was; hers was not the intuitive sort of mind that leaped nimbly from one idea to the next. It was, on the contrary, a well-stocked mind that was trained to analyze concepts, thinking each one through before reaching a conclusion. She spoke with authority, as one accustomed to having people listen when she gave an opinion. They got on the subject of courtship patterns among the aborigines. She described one.

"Suppose a young Polynesian takes out a girl. If they like each other, they end their date searching in each other's hair for lice. When they find one they place it daintily between their lips and bite it. That's a sure sign they're serious."

"They'd have to be." David smiled, and asked if the book did well.

"You mean, did it sell? No, it's too specialized. But those in the field read it, and it had a sale in colleges and libraries. It appeared at the wrong time, too soon after Margaret Mead's *Coming of Age in Samoa*." She held out her hands. "Timing is important. But I can't complain."

It was past midnight when he got up to go. "You promised me a copy."

"Of course." She picked up the book from the end table and autographed it: "For David, in admiration of his beautiful talent. Judith Sonnenberg."

"Call me when you finish it," she said. "I'll be interested in your reaction."

He promised to do so. He had never known anyone who had written a book, much less inscribed a copy to him. It was exciting.

7

HE did not telephone Judith when he finished her book, not wishing to appear too eager. She called him. She was giving a lecture at the Museum of Natural History and asked him to come. He told her how much he had enjoyed the book. "If I'd had professors like you in college," he said into the telephone, "I might have learned something."

"What kind did you have?"

"They were old and crabby. They didn't like us and we felt the same way about them." He remembered little old Professor Sheldon. "All except one, in English lit. He used to recite Shelley and Keats to us. The others bored the hell out of me."

"I hope I don't," she replied.

The lecture took place on the second floor of the museum. By the time David arrived the room was almost full; he took a seat toward the back. He recognized several faces from Judith's party; the sociologist who had told him about *vagina dentata* waved to him. Judith appeared promptly at eight thirty, accompanied by a member of the museum staff who introduced her by listing her accomplishments. She began to speak in a low voice; David could see that she was nervous. As she gained composure her voice became resonant, she no longer consulted her notes. She was discussing the structure of the Polynesian family and managed to enliven her talk with a few humorous details, including the court-ship pattern that David had found so amusing.

Her lecture was followed by a question-and-answer period. Some of the questions, like her answers, were technical, but David was surprised at how well he followed the discussion. No one disputed her facts. What they argued about was her interpretation of them, especially her tendency to view primitive cultures in terms of psychoanalytic theory. According to her, society reflected the individuals who composed it rather than the other way around, as the Marxists believed. Whatever, therefore, deepened our understanding of the individual, as the writings of Freud did, enlarged our understanding of primitive society. The Marxists in the audience objected, as did the Darwinians. Judith held her ground. Marx's analysis of capitalism, she maintained, could hardly be applied to a tribal society in which individuals either owned no property or owned it collectively. As for Darwin, keen though his insights were, he came long before Freud and lacked the tools with which to analyze the primitive psyche.

David listened intently. There was much applause at the end of the lecture. Judith responded with a wave of her hand and gathered her notes. The audience filtered down to the great hall on the first floor; David fell behind to examine the cases filled with artifacts from Africa and Australia. When he came out of the museum, Judith was saying good night to some friends. He joined her.

The wide terrace of the museum was deserted. Judith glanced up at the equestrian statue that loomed above them and read aloud the attributes carved in the stone wall behind it: "Statesman . . . Historian . . . Humanitarian . . . Author." She stopped, and added, "Teddy Roosevelt was all of these, I guess, yet he wasn't much of any one of them.

"I have a theory that each of our presidents expressed another side of the American character. When things went smoothly we got mediocre ones like Harding or Coolidge. In a crisis the great ones appeared—Washington and Jefferson, Lincoln and Wilson. Now we're in crisis again and we have FDR. People think that great men make history. Actually it's history that calls forth the great men."

They walked down Central Park West. "Were you bored?" she asked.

"Oh, no. There was so much I had never thought about before. Would you believe it, I've lived all my life in New York and was never in the museum."

"I'm glad I brought you to it. Did I look all right?"

"You looked fine to me." He was surprised that anyone as sure of herself as Judith would need reassuring.

It was a pleasant winter night; the stars hung in tiers across the sky. A hundred lights blinked in the park; the tall buildings beyond formed a wall of light. They boarded the bus to the East Side. When they passed Carnegie Hall, David said, "This is my territory."

"Here," she replied, "I'd be the stranger." This reminded her of the overspecialization typical of our society. In tribal life, she pointed out, the same individuals who fished, hunted, and fought also created the songs and dances, played the drums, carved the masks, and acted out the ceremonies. But society advanced only when people specialized, thereby reaching a level of skill they couldn't attain in any other way. "It was possible for Leonardo da Vinci to be scientist and artist, painter, sculptor and architect, inventor and engineer all in one. In short, the Renaissance man. Today this can't happen any more, there's just too much to know. As a result, people know more about their specialty than ever before, but very little about anything else."

They reached her house. She had not had dinner, as she was too tense to eat before a lecture. "Come up," she said, "and we'll have a bite." She changed into a housecoat and whipped up an omelette while he glanced through her notes, which cleared up some points that had puzzled him. She found a bottle of white wine in the Frigidaire and brought out some fruit and cheese.

When they finished eating she sat down in the armchair near the piano. "I'd love to hear that Brahms Intermezzo again," she said. She slouched in the chair as he played, nuzzling her forehead against the arm, and smiled to him when he finished. "Something else?"

"I better get going." He glanced at his watch. "I've a long trip ahead of me."

She looked at hers. "It's almost midnight. Why don't you stay over?"

She made it sound casual, but he detected a clutch of

nervousness in her voice. It was the same cluttered sound he had heard when she began her lecture.

"Would you like to?" she asked.

She was moving a little too fast for him, he thought, yet it would not be friendly to tell her so. Besides, what had he to lose? "Of course," he answered, putting more enthusiasm into the words than he felt.

She relaxed. It was only then that David realized how much courage it had taken for her to extend the invitation. She sat up in the chair. "I don't have any pajamas for you."

"I won't need any."

"Or a toothbrush."

He grinned. "I'll gargle."

While she was out of the room he reassessed the situation. What had he to offer her in return for the enormous intellectual stimulation she gave him? Not much, really. A bit of piano playing . . . and some sex. Fair exchange. He had not thought of her in this connection, yet there was no reason why he couldn't. Why shouldn't the pleasures of the mind be united with those of the body? He had never yet succeeded in bringing them together, but this did not mean they couldn't be. It flattered him to be wanted by someone as distinguished as Judith, and he might even in time have gotten around to taking the initiative. That she had done so made it much easier for him; but also, curiously, a little more difficult.

"Bed's made," she called. He stood up, as if on command, and went into the other room.

It was a large comfortable bed, but from the moment David stretched out on it he was aware that something was missing. As had happened to him in the past, a part of him detached itself and seemed to be looking on from somewhere near the door. He remembered all he had learned from Val about lovemaking; but with Val whatever he did was simple and spontaneous. Here he watched himself take

Judith in his arms, watched himself kiss and caress her; he saw himself doing all this because she needed it, yet he remained curiously on the outside, as if he were playing a role that was expected of him.

In the end it was her desire that aroused him. Sex for him was still the mystery it had always been, a thing all its own that was impossible to describe in words or equate with any other feeling, that once started could not be stopped until it had poured itself out of him, leaving him happily exhausted and relaxed. But what she knew as passion was a seething, almost a suffering that threatened to rend her apart. Suddenly the scholarly intellectual was driven to fury, a demon impelled to suck him into her and imprison him there. She threw herself upon him, clutching him to her, tearing at him with her fingernails; she was insatiable. Amid the pushing and pulling that was both like a dance between them and a struggle, her face was transfigured yet agonized; she looked almost as if she were suffering—until the orgasm released her.

She lay back, breathed a deep sigh, and murmured, "Beautiful." She said this in exactly the same tone she had used when he finished the Brahms Intermezzo. He remembered one of those minor details that, once lodged in his mind, never left it. Professor Burke used to point out that *passion* came from the Latin word for suffering, for example, *The Passion According to St. Matthew.*

She took a cigarette from the little table by the bed and lit it. "Whoever invented sex," she said, "knew what he was doing."

"How do you know it was a he?"

"I've always assumed God is masculine."

"In Hebrew the word is plural, so he could be either. Or, like some of the Hindu gods, both."

"A bisexual god? I like the idea." She puffed on her cigarette. "I had an affair for three years with a very attractive man. When Hitler came to power, I realized my lover was antisemitic, and I could no longer have an orgasm with him. It was terrible to have sex and not be able to reach a climax. I came twice with you." She stroked his shoulder. "I have to admire a man before I can have sex with him. Or at least respect him."

"Men are different."

"In what way?"

"A man can enjoy sex with someone he's never seen before and will never see again."

"A woman can, too," Judith said, "if she's not mature. The physical part is fun, but in the long run it has no meaning by itself."

"You like to think men and women are equal."

"Aren't they?"

"No," David said. "The woman is stuck with the consequences, while the man can walk away. The difference between them is nine months."

"I'm not convinced the difference is biological," she said. "More likely it's socially conditioned. But that's a big subject for one A.M." She turned and kissed him. "We'll argue about it some other time."

She fell asleep almost at once. He eased himself off the bed and made his way to the bathroom. Then he lay down beside her. In a curious way she had left him unsatisfied. It occurred to him that if Val had walked into the room at this moment, he'd have leaped into bed with her. Turning on his side, David listened to the quiet rise and fall of Judith's breathing. She was easily the most brilliant woman he had ever met. What a pity she wasn't his type.

TWO

1

To carry on her work properly, Judith needed peace of mind. That in turn depended on her having a stable relationship with someone who could satisfy her emotional needs. Was this asking too much? If it wasn't, why she had such trouble finding it?

Time and again she thought she had; then problems arose. The problems were usually on the man's side; she herself was only too eager to give and receive love. After each breakup the search began anew. How was she supposed to keep her mind on her work when a restlessness churned inside her? She knew she was as capable of distinguished research as Ruth Benedict or Margaret Mead. What she lacked was the inner serenity that would enable her to concentrate on her scientific projects. Hence David had stepped into a situation that was all set up for him. There was an emptiness in her life, and he had come along just at the right time to fill it.

She never tired of analyzing their relationship and plotting its course. She thought of love as a process of continual growth, a need to search out the thoughts and feelings of the beloved. In her estimation David was not sufficiently aware of himself as a person; one way to overcome this deficiency was to get him to talk about himself.

"Some people," he told her, "like to ride forward on a train. They've got to see where they're going. Others prefer to ride backward, as if they were being carried somewhere without any effort on their part. I'll let you guess in which category I belong."

She smiled. "I can't imagine."

"It's been a month since we met," he said, "and I've found out all kinds of things about myself."

"Such as—?"

"That I hate making decisions. I'd rather let someone make them for me."

"You didn't know that?" She sounded surprised.

"And I've found out some things about you," he continued.

"For instance?"

"You like to run things. You're the kind who sits facing forward."

"I have to know where I'm going."

"Anyhow, if someone who likes to take over meets someone who doesn't mind being taken over, it's a perfect match."

"Are you proposing?" She laughed.

"I'm not ready yet."

"The way to get ready is simple. All you have to do is grow up."

"I know. Character, principles, maturity. Don't preach to me. That's my mother's specialty."

"I'm not your mother, and I have no wish to be."

"That's fine with me."

Like his mother, she tended to put the one she loved on a pedestal, endowing him with all sorts of qualities that served to make him not only more desirable but also unattainable. Once she had raised him high above her, her humility was touching. "Beware," she told David, "of a woman in love who's over thirty-five. She feels it's her last chance, therefore she's desperate."

It was not normal, David objected, to be so fearful about love. She silenced him. "*Normal* is a silly word. The only normal people are the ones we don't know."

Her boundless confidence in her intellectual powers went hand in hand with her total lack of confidence as a woman. Like most people who lack physical beauty, she exaggerated its importance. As a matter of fact, when she became absorbed in a discussion her face took on an animation that was charming; you forgot that her features were not prepossessing. David was glad that she was older than he. Confused as he was about himself and the world, it would have been impossible for him at this point to take up with someone younger. Judith nevertheless was sensitive about her age. "There are times when I don't understand you," she told David. "I suddenly feel I belong to another generation."

He was fascinated by the contradictions in her nature. On the one hand, she prided herself on her ability to interpret facts objectively. On the other, her intensely subjective nature led her to shape the facts according to her preconceptions, to such a degree that she was able to reach almost any conclusion she wished. She did not lie, either to herself or to others; instead she persuaded herself of the truth of what she wanted to believe. In this fashion, the scientist and the woman were inextricably intermingled. Now that she had found David, she was able to convince herself that he could give her the emotional stability she needed, and adhered to this view despite all evidence to the contrary.

Although trained as a scientist, Judith had always been attracted to the arts. Among them she ranked music highest because it was the most abstract. She liked to quote Walter Pater's famous statement that "all art constantly aspires to the condition of music," and regarded it as her good fortune to have fallen in love with a musician. His predecessor, the Nazi sympathizer, had been a businessman, and the one before was a psychoanalyst. She considered David infinitely more interesting than either of them, and never tired of hearing him play. "That was exquisite!" she would exclaim when he finished a piece. "You get into the very soul of the music."

He tried to bring her to a more realistic view. "Honey, it's perfectly good playing, nothing more."

"Yes it is," she asserted. "You don't know how good you are."

He was touched by her enthusiasm in spite of himself. "If I told you what I thought of some anthropologist, you'd say I wasn't qualified to form an opinion. The same goes here. You enjoy my playing? Fine. But as to how good it is, you must let me judge."

Judith didn't give in that easily. "I know real talent when I hear it. If you only had more confidence in yourself you could have a wonderful career."

"You'd have to know much more than you do about the music world to know what it takes to have a concert career. Talent. Luck. Being at the right place at the right time. Knowing the right people. And you'd have to know much more about me to understand why I don't want to face that kind of rat race."

"What made you change your mind?"

"Growing up, I guess. Up till a certain point you ride along with it. One fine day you wake up and ask yourself, 'Where the hell am I going?' And you jump off as fast as you can."

"All I can say is I've gone to enough concerts and heard enough pianists to know what I'm talking about."

"I'm not a public performer. I'm a private guy and I want to live a private life." However, he was flattered by her inflated opinion of him even if he was too sensible to share it.

Her anxiety showed itself whenever they parted. "Don't forget, you're coming Friday night," she would remind him, or "Call me tomorrow." It was as if she could not bear to let him go without establishing the next link between them.

"You sound as if you're afraid you'll never see me again," he said.

"When someone's in love, every good-bye may be the last."

"How can you think like that? It's not logical."

"What has logic to do with it?"

"Silly!" It was touching, how much she needed him. And just a bit frightening.

2

THINGS at home grew worse as Lisa expressed disapproval of David's ways more and more openly. Their relationship was so fraught with tension that a word could cause it to explode. The quarrel might begin with as innocent a question as, "Will you eat home tonight?"

"No, Ma, I have to be in the city."

"Sure. Why would you eat a decent meal with your parents if you can run around all night with your *bummerkehs?*"

"Look, Ma, I don't interfere in your life, don't interfere in mine."

"Who's interfering? When I see a child of mine on the wrong path, I shouldn't tell him?"

"I'm not harming anyone—"

"Except yourself!"

"—and I'm living the way I see fit. It may not be right for you but it is for me. We're different."

"That you can say again. You know what your father said to me the other day. Of course he wouldn't say it to you. 'You have ten minutes of pleasure, and you're stuck with them for the rest of your life.' "

David remembered Sidney raising his hand in the gym class to ask the professor, "How d'you make it last ten minutes?" He thought a moment. "You told me that," he said, "in order to hurt me. Why would you want to do that?"

"Because it's my duty to tell you the truth," she said sternly.

He was getting angry. "If you're going to preach to me, I'll leave."

"That's right, bury your head in the sand so you don't have to see what you don't want to."

He slammed his hand on the table and made for the door as she fired her parting shot: "The eagle flew too high!"

One quarrel got out of hand. As usual, it took place in the kitchen, and began innocently enough when David finally told his mother about Judith. "Why haven't you invited her here to meet us?" she asked.

"I didn't think of it," he answered lamely, and corrected himself. "Maybe I did, but I just didn't get around to it."

"What's the matter, you're ashamed of your parents?" Lisa asked.

"What kind of a question is that?"

"You turned your back on your music, you could turn your back on us too."

"C'mon, Ma, stop being dramatic."

"That she's older than you I like. And that she's a *professorkeh* I like even more. Who knows, maybe she'll put some sense into your head."

"What right have you to talk to me like that?" The accumulated resentment of months suddenly rose up, triggering a response out of all proportion to what Lisa had said. "For God's sake, can't a person have a decent conversation in this house?" he shouted. Instead of bringing his hand down on the kitchen table with a resounding slap, as he usually did when he lost his temper, he grabbed the bread knife that lay directly in front of him and hurled it against the smooth white top. It bounced back, traced a somersault in the air, struck Lisa in the throat and fell to the floor.

She raised her hand and stroked the spot where the knife had hit her. Then she bent down, picked up the knife and put it back on the table. Finally, "So you want to kill your mother?" she asked.

He stared at her, horrified. "You know I didn't mean it. I just grabbed the first thing that lay there. It was an accident."

"I only know what I saw, my son. We live in a strange time. When I was young, children had respect for their parents. When you were a child you had respect too. Now it's different." She let out a sigh. "We talk to each other across a far distance, and neither one hears the other."

He came beside her. "I'm sorry, Ma. Really. Forgive me." He put his arms around her and kissed her.

She turned her face away. "I forgive you, my son, but it doesn't change anything. When you were a baby I used to bind your arms and legs as we did in Russia, so that they would grow straight. And now you throw a knife at me." Two tears rolled down her cheeks. Lifting her apron, she wiped her eyes.

David stared at her, engulfed by shame. How could he reach her? How bring her back to him? The answer was short and decisive. He couldn't.

That night his father said to him, "Let's have a talk, David. In your room." He led the way and sat down in the only chair, near the piano. There was a long silence, during which he seemed to be studying the pattern on the rug. At length he said, "Something is wrong between us."

"Like what?"

"How should I know? Am I a philosopher? We did the best we could, your mother and I. We thought we were preparing you for a happy life. It looks as if we were mistaken."

"What has happiness to do with it?"

Joel ignored the question. "I'm beginning to think that no matter what parents do for their children, it's wrong. If they don't love them enough it's wrong, and if they love them too much, it's also wrong."

"How can you love someone too much?"

"By protecting him and giving in to him all the time. I made that mistake with you."

"You give in to Mama all the time. Is that a mistake?"

"Your mother is a remarkable woman, David. With a very strong will and a very strong sense of right and wrong. Is that bad?"

"No. But it's not very easy to live with, especially if she thinks you're wrong."

"I didn't come here to scold you. You're a man now, you're supposed to know what you're doing. What happened today between your mother and you should not have happened."

David felt himself turn red. "I'm sorry I lost my temper, Papa. Believe me. If only she wouldn't criticize me all the time."

"She does it for your own good."

David made a gesture of distaste. "The problem goes deeper. Basically she doesn't approve of me. She sees life in one way, I see it in another, and so the conflict between us is"—he hunted the right word—"unavoidable."

Joel thought awhile. "I don't know how to say this, but I'll try. Your mother and I have had our share of troubles. It was not easy to come to a new country and build a new life. We were lucky, we didn't do badly. Now is the time for us to relax and enjoy what we have. We shouldn't have to lose sleep over you, to have quarrels in our house, to be yelled at by our child because we tell him what we think. You say you want to live as you see fit. But as long as you're with us we can't help giving you our opinion. What you call interfering. If you were on your own, you'd be free to do anything you please." He stopped and finished quietly. "You want to be your own man? Fine. Then go live as your own man."

The idea had occurred to David more than once, yet now that his father suggested it, he felt hurt. "Pa, are you telling me to get out?"

Joel's face darkened. "I would never tell you that, David. All I'm saying is, since you and your mother don't get on, it might be better if you lived somewhere else for a while."

David looked away. His glance reached the window and the darkness outside, a darkness vast and forbidding. His gaze returned to Joel. Apropos of nothing at all, David said, "Mama told me what you said to her. You shouldn't have said it."

"What are you talking about?"

" 'Ten minutes of pleasure, and you're stuck with them for the rest of your life.' "

Joel's face showed his embarrassment. "All I meant was—"

"What?"

"A person expects all kinds of things. When they don't happen, he's disappointed."

"I never told you to expect anything."

"True. The disappointment is there all the same."

The statement egged David on to greater severity than he would have liked. "In a way you used me. I was supposed to be a *wunderkind* so you could boast about me to your friends and enjoy being the father of a genius. That's always a risk."

"If I boasted, it was only because I had something to boast about. Now I don't, so I'm quiet."

"You shouldn't have to boast at all," David said. "Or if you must, boast about yourself. Why should you push your needs on me?"

"Someday," Joel said gently, "when you're a father yourself, you'll find out how hard it is to strike the right balance. Then you won't judge me so harshly."

"I don't judge you harshly. I only know what your ambition cost me. The price was too high."

"I meant well. What more can I say?" He got up.

David's anger melted. "It doesn't matter, Pa. No hard feelings."

"We love you very much, David. I'm sure you love us too. Yet we go on hurting each other. It puzzles me."

"Me too."

"I always believed," Joel said slowly, "that if people used

their heads they could solve any problem. It's not true. The mind can do only so much, but it has no control over our feelings." He raised his hands in perplexity.

On an impulse David bent forward, pressed his cheek against Joel's and kissed him. He felt like crying.

3

HE lay on his back and stared into the dark. Moving out meant a change in his life for which he was not prepared. He tried to formulate a plan, but his thoughts were muddled. He pictured himself installed in his own apartment, attending to a host of tiresome chores like disposing of the garbage and seeing to it that the laundry was sent out. Freedom obviously had its price. The trouble was that he didn't earn enough to rent an apartment; he would have to make do with a furnished room.

Layers of pale light filtered into the room, heralding the dawn. That summer night long ago in Luna Park: he sat on the low, white plaster fence near a colored fountain and sobbed his heart out because they had gone off without him, they had purposely left him behind. It had taken them a long time, he thought wryly, but they were finally getting rid of him. The old sense of betrayal returned with a vividness that astonished him. Didn't these childish feelings ever die?

He looked out the window. The sea was calm, its satiny surface a pale blue in the east, deepening to maroon where the sky was still dark. Careful not to wake his parents, he shaved, dressed, and tiptoed to the closet. On the upper shelf stood the black handbag his mother had given him for his trip to France. Next to it was his father's battered valise. David took it down and filled it with shirts, socks, underwear, and his shaving kit.

Where to? He went back to the window. The sun had come up, covering the ocean with a golden patina. Two seagulls swooped down to breakfast on a fish. He thought of the fantasy that had haunted his childhood, of a subterranean garden filled with trees that shone and with gentle music. This was the enchanted garden where you were young and protected, and your every need was taken care of. Then you grew up and ate of the tree of knowledge, you lost your innocence; finally you were thrown out and told to make your way in the world. The myth had only one moral. No matter how much you wanted to return to the garden, you never found it again.

It occurred to David that he was thinking like Judith. The instant her name crossed his mind he knew his problem was solved. Why hadn't he thought of her at once?

That evening he told her what had happened, concluding his account with "I guess I'm just not her kind of person."

"That's her problem," Judith said.

"Still, it upsets me."

"Aren't you making too much of this? It was another family quarrel. That's what families are for." She pursued her line of thought. "Of all the animals, man takes the longest to learn to fend for himself. The family helps survival. Baby is fed and washed and encouraged to stay alive. As society developed the family became an educational unit. Ritual, tradition, social attitudes were handed down from father to son. But in our time, the family became—" She stopped.

"What?"

"A place where parents and children can torment each other. No wonder Freud saw the family as the perfect breeding ground for neurosis."

"Does it have to be that way?"

"Probably. In our society the family has become too tightly knit. As a result, parents and children are much too intense about each other. It's different in primitive society, where all the adults love all the children as well as their own. There the tribe takes the place of family, which is much healthier."

"So let's all go to New Guinea. Don't they have problems too?"

"Of course they have, but of a different kind. Anyway, moving out is a step forward for you. It's about time you cut the umbilical cord."

The umbilical cord figured prominently in Judith's conversation; she made it sound like something damp and smelly. He pictured her, scissors in hand, snipping it with great satisfaction, whereupon a dirty gray fluid oozed out.

Later, she emptied two shelves in the closet, on which he arranged his things while she prepared dinner. When they finished eating, he played for her; then they went to bed and made love. Afterward they lay side by side, quietly talking until she wanted to have sex again. "Once I've shot, I'm through," he said, then added, "I was always that way," lest she think she did not arouse him sufficiently.

He put on the trousers of his pajamas when he had to go to the bathroom.

"You don't have to cover up," Judith said. "I know what you look like."

"I'm not used to walking around naked. In my house we didn't."

"You can take the boy out of Brighton Beach," she answered, smiling, "but you can't take Brighton Beach out of the boy."

Before falling asleep a disturbing thought flitted through his mind. Could it be that he had exchanged one mother for another?

4

JUDITH spent her vacation in Provincetown. Since David's students stopped their lessons for the summer, he was free to accompany her. She rented a small cottage; they left for Massachusetts toward the end of June. David had never been to Cape Cod and found the combination of sea and dunes very much to his taste. With its rickety wharves and jetties, its Colonial houses and winding alleys, the town cultivated the quaintness that tourists expected. A shop was a shoppe, a bar was ye olde taverne, and a bronze tablet marked the spot where the Pilgrims landed. Judith's cottage was at the far end of what was appropriately named Commercial Street. For swimming there was a choice between the bay, which was warm and shallow, and the ocean, which was cold and deep.

The fixed population was a curious mixture: an overlay of middle-class WASPs on a base of olive-skinned Portuguese fishermen. The two groups had not yet begun to mix, although an occasional intermarriage took place despite all taboos. The first of July brought the summer visitors from New York, an invasion augmented by the daily load on the excursion boat from Boston. The boat people crowded into the eating places for lunch, gorged themselves on the lobsters for which the Cape was famous, and hurried back to the central pier in time for the three o'clock departure. The painters and psychoanalysts who came for the summer, along with the theater whose roots went back to Eugene O'Neill, gave the town a cultural atmosphere that the natives mistrusted. They would have preferred the visitors to pay for their rooms by mail and stay home. The cottage next to Judith's was occupied by a painter named Bud Morrisey, who summed up the situation: "This place is anti–New York, anti-Jew, anti-Communist, and anti-queer."

To which Judith replied, "What if you belong to all four minorities?"

During the morning she worked on her material while David read or swam in the bay. After lunch they took the bus to the oceanside, where a group of her friends gathered daily. The psychoanalysts argued about fine points of Freudian theory, their discussions as doctrinaire as those farther down the beach among Stalinists, Trotzkyites, and Lovestonites. Whoever spoke seemed to regard his doctrine as the only true one, all others being heresy.

Judith's friends were delighted to have a musician in their midst. They did not know much about music, but this did not prevent them from holding strong opinions about it. Most of them attended concerts, bought records, and had all sorts of questions to put to David. Wasn't Bruno Walter's Mozart better than Toscanini's? Didn't Schnabel play the Appassionata better than Hofmann? Why didn't Backhaus, whose records were marvelous, play in this country? David was amused at the way they deferred to his opinions. Being an oracle was a new role for him.

He had the same sense of venturing into new fields as he had had with Nat in the Village, except that Judith's friends were professional in a way that Nat was not. Conversation for them was more than a way to pass time. It involved an exchange of ideas, a sharpening of wits and flexing of minds. Their talk ranged over a variety of subjects. Which was more decisive in shaping an individual's development, heredity or environment? Was economics as decisive a force in society as Marx claimed? Would a socialist system obviate neurosis or merely substitute other kinds for the ones we knew? Would Tolstoi have developed his outlook on life and art if he had lived in Germany instead of Russia? David had never before been exposed to a milieu where ideas were pursued with such passion. He listened avidly. An intellectual, according to Judith, was someone who was as excited by ideas as a gourmet was by food and drink. Could it be, he wondered, that he was becoming one?

The shadows gradually lengthened across the beach. The aquamarine of sea and sky turned a deep blue, and the air took on the transparent quality that every painter prized. They gathered up their things and took the road back to town. An enormous stillness hung over the dunes, punctuated by the cawing of gulls. This was a Puritan landscape remote from the world, untouched by it. Pastel shades flowed over the mounds of sand—warm yellows, pinks, and lavenders. "Look at the colors," Bud exclaimed. "All you need is a pair of eyes to see how they mix."

Evenings were enlivened by a round of parties. Since David saw the same people, ate the same food, and heard the same talk at each, these gatherings flowed into one continuous festivity. He enjoyed this carefree existence even though it disturbed him that, at least for the summer, he was living on Judith's money. She ridiculed his concern, ascribing it to his "petit-bourgeois upbringing." Her earnings, supplemented by a small trust fund, were more than adequate for their needs. She would have taken the cottage in any case, she assured him; his being there added very little expense. All the same, he felt uncomfortable at accepting a hospitality he could not repay.

Touched by her kindness and generosity, he was eager to please her. The fact remained, however, that she was in love with him and he was not in love with her. He tried to make her feel wanted, but the constant effort this entailed introduced a certain amount of pretense into their relations, so that he sometimes felt like an actor playing a part. His uncertainty only exacerbated hers, with the result that he sometimes wounded her without meaning to. One Saturday night in August after they returned from a party at Bud's, Judith was strangely silent.

"What's wrong?" David asked, although he knew. She was annoyed because he had danced a good part of the evening with a young blonde named Mitzi, whose charm was as synthetic as her name. Mitzi was typical of the girls who floated through Provincetown in search of a suntan, a little sex, and some lessons with Hans Hoffman. That summer they were following Picasso.

"Nothing at all," Judith replied, "although I'd prefer it if you didn't make a fool of yourself in public."

"How was I a bigger fool than anyone else?"

"You kept dragging that creature around for at least an hour."

"What could I do? Whenever the record ended, Bud pushed the needle back to the beginning."

"And the way you two hugged each other. Disgusting!" She pursed her lips in distaste.

"Judith, you're jealous!"

"Of course I am."

"Look, honey, we're arguing over someone I probably wouldn't recognize if I ever saw her again."

"I'd never have guessed it from the way you fawned over her."

"How can anyone as brilliant as you be jealous of someone like her?"

"It's easy. She's prettier than I am."

This was a statement he could hardly contradict. "You put too much importance on good looks. After all, we're not living in a movie."

Judith suddenly became the social scientist. "It's because our whole environment is oriented to youth and good looks. No individual can be more mature than his society."

Once she was back in the realm of ideas, her insecurities disappeared. Now she began to develop one of her favorite ideas: the individual recapitulates the development of the race, and is therefore unable to move too far ahead of his fellow men. "Except, of course, the genius. A Darwin or Marx, a Freud or Einstein leads the world to new ways of thinking. No wonder such men are rare."

By the time they got to bed Judith had forgotten her irritation; she was all affection. As always, David was astonished at her sexual appetite; he had never known a woman who enjoyed men in so savage a manner. Finally sated, she dropped off to sleep. The rise and fall of her breathing traced a gentle rhythm against the stillness. In the half light her features took on a softness they did not normally possess. This remarkable woman loved him with utter devotion, he told himself, and expected so little in return. The thought should have pleased him; instead it disturbed him. How had he gotten into this situation? More important, how would he get out?

5

ON the morning after Labor Day the summer visitors left. Sidewalks were suddenly empty, the town reverted to its rightful owners. As neither Judith nor David had to be back in New York for another two weeks, they stayed on. The weather was glorious, the air crisp with that foretaste of autumn. Dazzling sunlight fell on a sea as blue as the sky. Their group on the beach had dwindled, and when they came out of the water they shivered a little; but in the late-afternoon light the dunes were lovelier than ever. David reluctantly watched the last days of summer slip away. He accompanied Judith to the city the day before she was due back at the college.

His first concern was to seek a reconciliation with Lisa. He had written his parents from Provincetown, to let them know where he was, and Joel had responded with a friendly note. He hoped they were ready to see him. Joel answered the telephone and made it plain that they were.

The following Sunday, David took the subway to Brighton. He was strangely moved by the familiar sights and sounds—the hubbub along Brighton Beach Avenue, the handball courts on the ocean front, the sun bathers and discussion groups on the boardwalk. He felt tense as he rang the bell of their apartment, but relaxed when his father opened the door and embraced him. Lisa was waiting in the living room. "Dovid'l! You look so healthy!" she exclaimed. "So brown!"

He took her in his arms and for an instant was over-powered by the realization—almost like a clench of pain—of how much his parents meant to him. Adopting the same conversational tone as Lisa, "I had a wonderful summer," he said.

She seemed littler than ever but more fiery. Her staccato gestures practically gave off sparks, her cavernous eyes glowed; she managed as always to fill the room with excitement. She put herself out to be charming. She asked about Provincetown and its people, and wanted especially to know how the place looked.

"Would we like it?" she asked, meaning Cape Cod.

He grinned. "I don't think so. Too many goyim."

She asked him to play some Chopin. He went through two of her favorites—the Nocturne in E-flat and the melancholy Waltz in A minor. When he finished, Lisa let out a long sigh. "Ekh, such a talent and he lets it go to waste. I could weep."

"I thought we decided," Joel cautioned her, "no personal remarks."

"All remarks are personal," Lisa countered. "If they're not, they don't mean a thing."

"You talk like that," Joel said, "and you'll upset him."

"So I'll upset him," Lisa burst out with something of the old fire. "What is he, a prince, that I have to weigh my words?"

"Why don't you say all this in Russian," David suggested, "so I won't understand."

It was time for a bite. Lisa whipped up an omelette which she smothered in sour cream and served with pumpernickel bread thickly buttered and covered with pot cheese. "So you like goy cooking?" she inquired, in a tone that was half question, half accusation.

David assured her that in matters of cuisine, Brighton Beach was miles ahead of the Cape.

"I'm glad to hear it." Out of the blue she added, "How is your *professerkeh?*"

"She's writing a book," David said. He knew this would impress her.

Lisa leaned forward. "I'll give you some advice, my son.

Free love is for anarchists like Emma Goldman and Alexander Berkman. For ordinary people it's not enough to live together. Your friend may be a *professerkeh*, but I'm sure she wants to get married. Every woman does." Having shot her bolt, she relaxed against the side of the chair. "So when do we meet her? Or are you ashamed of your parents?"

"Stop that, Ma. It's silly for me to drag her out here. When you're in Manhattan you'll drop in."

"That reminds me," Joel said, "of the way Mr. Elman used to invite us—"

"May he rest in peace," Lisa interjected.

"We're not dropping in on anybody," Joel continued. "If you'll ask us for a definite time we'll be glad to come."

"Good. How about Friday? Around five."

One more matter remained to be discussed. David's pupils had been asking when he would resume his lessons. He decided to begin the following weekend. This settled, he was ready to leave. Lisa put her arms around him. "It warms my heart to see you again, Dovid'l. I missed you."

"I missed you too." They kissed, and for a moment it was as if no shadow had ever fallen between them.

He announced the impending visit to Judith. "Do I have to meet them?" she asked.

"Not really. What's your objection?"

"Your father sounds like fun, but I'm too jealous of your mother. After all, she's my chief rival."

David laughed, and Judith gave in.

He looked forward to Friday, yet not without apprehension. He was ashamed, not of his parents—as Lisa maintained—but of his dependence upon them, his childish need to win their approval. It would embarrass him, he knew, to have Judith see how juvenile he became in their presence. Several of his friends, he had noticed, showed a similar embarrassment when he met their parents, as if they were revealing a side of themselves they didn't want him to see.

He knew his parents would be prompt. Sure enough, on Friday the bell rang on the stroke of five. They had dressed up for the occasion. Lisa wore her best dress, a dark blue silk with a pink collar. Her boyish bob, freshly trimmed, was at variance with the severe cut of her pince-nez. Joel was in his new suit, a navy-blue worsted. David made the introductions, and Judith offered his parents a drink. They preferred tea. David, grateful for something to do, went into the kitchen to heat water and brought out a plate of crackers and cheese. He knew his mother was ill at ease. It was not like her to be silent.

The *vagina dentata* on the wall caught Joel's eye. "What's that?" He got up to examine the tapestry.

"Primitive people," Judith explained, "believe that the female sex organ has teeth. At least their artists do."

The idea delighted Joel. "Did you hear that?" he asked Lisa.

"I heard, I heard," she answered, less than amused.

Conversation proceeded slowly because of the language barrier. After almost a quarter century in America, David's parents were still not fluent in English. They spoke it when they had to but were painfully aware of their limitations, and reverted to Yiddish at the first opportunity. Judith, with her German-Jewish background, understood most of what they said; David translated the rest. To get things moving he suggested that she tell them about the time she spent in the South Pacific.

Joel was fascinated and asked all sorts of questions. Lisa, on the contrary, kept her eyes fixed on her teacup, as though afraid it might at any moment jump out of her lap.

David drew Judith out. "Tell them about my favorite courtship pattern."

She described how the young man and his lady love bit into each other's lice.

At this Lisa came alive. "That's how they make love?" She grimaced. "Tfui! Good for the health it's not."

Judith laughed and described her encounter with a chieftain of the Maori tribe.

"They're like children," Lisa said.

"No, he had a fine mind," Judith replied. "He could explain everything that happened in his world. His explanations were wrong not because his thinking was childish, but because his knowledge was limited."

"Aha." Lisa nodded to indicate that she caught the distinction. "Tell me, a nice Jewish girl from a good family goes to live alone among savages. You weren't afraid?"

"If I was, I got over it."

"And now you write books about it. I like that!" Lisa shook her head for emphasis. "It's good for a woman to write books, otherwise men think the world belongs to them."

"You'll be happy to know," Judith said, "that some primitive societies are matriarchal. The power rests with the woman."

"Ekh, I was born too late," Lisa said. "Or too soon."

Judith's remark seemed to have established a bond between her and Lisa. David was delighted to see his mother gradually recapture her usual ebullience. His father, too, seemed to be at ease. Judith's encounter with the chieftain reminded him of the time he had met the rabbi of Lvov. "The rabbi felt he could explain everything in the world because his God told him the truth. Your chieftain probably felt the same way."

"Don't listen to him," Lisa warned Judith, and added, as one believer to another, "He doesn't believe in anything. Can you imagine!"

The visit ended at seven. As they left, Lisa said to Judith, "You must come to see us. Will you?"

"Of course, if David'll bring me."

"Did you hear that?" Lisa asked David.

Joel seconded the invitation with enthusiasm. Suddenly bold, he leaned forward and kissed Judith on the cheek.

They left. "I hope your mother liked me," Judith said uncertainly.

"She was probably afraid of you."

"Not as much as I was of her."

"I was surprised to see how shy she is. At home she burbles on from one thing to the next while my father and I listen. Here it took her quite a while to get her bearings. My father felt at home from the start."

"He's delightful. Seems to enjoy life. Your mother is much the stronger personality."

"You're telling *me?*"

"She must have been very beautiful. Those intense eyes and high cheekbones. Like a portrait from the past. He adores her."

"She used to torment the hell out of him. Much less now. As a matter of fact, she's mellowed. Even toward me."

"She certainly has you under her thumb." Judith sighed. "I wish I did."

The next day, when David arrived to give his lessons, his parents were eager to discuss the visit. "Pa, you made a great hit with her," David said.

"And she with me. A very interesting woman."

Lisa didn't think she had made a good impression. David reassured her.

"Still," Lisa said, "she's a professor. Suddenly I realize how much more she knows, and my tongue becomes heavy like lead."

"What you don't realize, Ma, is that your opinions are just as interesting as hers, and your way of putting things maybe even more."

Her glance showed that she appreciated the compliment. "She's quite a bit older than you."

"Is what?"

Lisa was thoughtful. Then, shaking her forefinger from side to side, "It's not easy to be the older woman," she said. "Your Judith should ask me. I know."

6

WHY, David wondered, couldn't he allow himself to enjoy his good fortune? He was settled in an attractive apartment where Judith did everything possible to make him comfortable. For the better part of the day he had the place to himself. He could browse among her books; they were on a variety of subjects—sociology, anthropology, psychology, history—that would certainly broaden his view of the world. If he tired of reading, he could play the piano when the spirit moved him, which was not often. In the afternoon he went out to Brighton to teach. When he got back, he did the necessary shopping; Judith was teaching him how to cook. On the days when she had to work late, he prepared dinner, which she always praised to the sky. In short, a more satisfying existence it would be difficult to imagine.

At a deeper level, however, he was consumed with restlessness. He could not put a name to his discontent, but it was there, nagging at him like a toothache. He was fond of Judith and genuinely enjoyed her mind; but as things stood between them, he kept wanting out. When he considered how hard she tried to please him, he saw himself as a monster of ingratitude. The fact remained that she expected to be paid for her efforts; as his mother liked to say, there was always a price, and the price in this case was himself, all of him. He should have felt uplifted by her love; instead he felt imprisoned. He had become her chief preoccupation; it was a greater responsibility than he could bear. The *vagina dentata* on the wall of her living room summed up his situation. Those Polynesians were no fools.

He was happy to be teaching again, which made it possible for him to contribute his share to the household. Money was not their problem; neither he nor Judith attached much importance to it. The problem was *them*. Judith's solution was to go on at such length about their "relationship" that he began to hate the word. It made him think of a thick black ooze, like the lava that buried Pompeii. He felt that instead of living their relationship, they were talking it to death. Yet how could Judith keep from talking about a subject that was continually on her mind?

What he had to do, according to her, was to change his personality and to achieve emotional maturity. "I don't get it," he told her. "When a woman falls in love with someone, you'd think she'd want him to stay as he is. Not at all. The first thing she does is try to change him." First his mother had tried to change him into her kind of person, now Judith was trying to transform him into the kind of man who could love her. This attempt, he suspected, was doomed to fail even as the other had.

Why did he stay? Inertia? The need for someone to hold on to? From time to time, when he awoke in the middle of the night and looked at Judith sleeping beside him, he asked himself, "What the hell am I doing here?" It occurred to him that there must be thousands of men and women who, perhaps at that very moment, were asking themselves the same question. Sooner or later, he knew, he would have to break away. In the meantime he tried to be as kind as he could. Yet the kind thing, he dimly suspected, would be to end the affair as quickly as possible.

Judith did not share the romantic view of love as a flame that warms, a music that enchants. To her way of thinking, love was something you had to work for, that you achieved through profound effort. Making that effort lifted you above yourself to the highest plane of human awareness. David could hardly take issue with so noble a view; nor could he tell her that, where she was concerned, he had made the effort and failed. How could he be honest with her when honesty demanded that he pack his bag and leave? He found it easier to spare her feelings, but the deception only made him feel guiltier.

Underneath the words they spoke, another conversation

went on. Assertion on her part called forth reluctance on his, her constant demands that he satisfy her needs answered by his half-hearted attempts to do so. This unspoken conflict steadily gathered momentum until the moment when they lay in each other's arms. It was a moment he sought to postpone even as she sought to hasten it. Just as long ago he had stimulated his imagination by conjuring up the anonymous women of Danny Friedman's French pictures, so he now summoned to his assistance memories of Val, with whom sex had been such fun. How lovingly he envisioned her full breasts with the large nipples, her smooth thighs, her velvety skin. Never before had he found it so pleasant to substitute fantasy for reality. Luckily, Judith had no way of finding out how unfaithful he was.

Meanwhile he was falling in love with Manhattan. November was clear and nippy; in the weeks before Christmas an excitement hung in the air. The trees on Park Avenue were lighted; shops were decked out in holiday finery. People rushed on all sides; they were going somewhere, they belonged. He was fascinated by the city even as it overwhelmed him. Would he ever fit in . . . make a place for himself? He wondered. He confided his fears to Judith, who assured him that those strangers in the street were not as stable as he thought; they had their problems too. She quoted her favorite maxim: "The only normal people are the ones we don't know."

Matters came to a head between them on New Year's Eve. The night began pleasantly enough with a party at the home of one of Judith's colleagues. Talk centered about Hitler, who had just proclaimed himself Fuehrer. Judith was reading *Mein Kampf* and warned against dismissing the book as the raving of a lunatic. On the contrary, she found it to be a viable blueprint for the seizure of power if conditions were favorable, which they would be as long as men like Chamberlain and Daladier remained in power. She went on to discuss the circumstances that brought about the decline of a civilization. Rome, despite its strength, had fallen before an influx of barbarians who were not as well armed as the imperial legions but were more highly motivated. It could happen again.

She presented her ideas with utter clarity, in a low pleasant voice that faltered occasionally as she stopped to hunt for the right expression. This was the side of her that her students and colleagues knew: a scholar in full control of her material, trenchant and objective, and thoroughly at home in the world of ideas. David listened in admiration. There seemed to be no connection between this authoritative college professor and the passionate woman who had lain in his arms the night before; nor was there any way in which he could make the two sides of her fit together. Was this split between public image and private self true of everyone in the room? Would he have been aware of it if he were not her lover? He suddenly realized to what extent her infatuation with him was cutting into her work, taking up time and energy that should have been spent on her intellectual pursuits. The thought only deepened his feeling of guilt.

It was snowing when they left. The city was touched with magic; snowflakes danced in the air, glistening as they floated into the pools of light around street lamps. They were only a few blocks from Judith's apartment. She took his arm. "It's so lovely out, let's walk. I just bought these shoes, but what the hell." She went on brightly about the people at the party. Once they reached home, her mood changed.

"I'm depressed," she said, and poured herself a drink.

"What about?" David asked, as if he didn't know.

"About us."

"Meaning—?"

"Our relationship isn't getting anywhere."

That word again! He scowled. "Where do you want it to get?"

"I'd like it to be mature and honest. It's neither."

"I suppose I'm to blame."

"It's not a question of blame. It's a question of making the effort—"

"Do we have to talk about this again?"

"There's only one way for people to be honest with each other, and that's by talking things out."

"Talking makes sense only if it brings them closer together. Otherwise it's only a cover-up."

"Are you implying ours is?"

"I'm not implying anything." His good spirits evaporated.

"If you wanted to," Judith said, "we could have a wonderful relationship. If only you were able to love."

"Maybe it's a talent like musical talent, that not everybody has." Despite all her talk of honesty, she was not honest herself. She pretended that he was incapable of loving just because he was incapable of loving her.

"You're wrong," Judith said firmly. "The ability to give and receive love is not like musical talent. Everyone is born with it, it's programmed into our genes for survival. In some people it grows weaker and atrophies. From fear, selfishness, immaturity, God knows what."

"What are they supposed to do? Kill themselves?" He hated it when she sounded like a teacher correcting an unruly pupil.

"No, they're supposed to gain some insight into themselves and to overcome whatever it is that prevents them from loving."

"I do the best I can," he said, trying not to show his irritation.

She assumed a reasonable tone. "I have no right to make demands on you. But how I wish you could give more of yourself. Can you blame me?"

Now it was David who was depressed. His head ached, the overheated room pressed in on him; their conversation was going nowhere. "I need some air," he said abruptly and, jumping up, threw on his coat. "I'll be right back."

A strained smile crossed her lips. "Strange, every time you leave me I have the irrational feeling I'll never see you again."

"See, I'm not the only one who's irrational."

Judith glanced out the window. "It's still snowing. Put on your rubbers." He smiled in spite of himself, she sounded so much like his mother.

Outside, the snow crunched under his feet; he headed for the river. The cold air was bracing. He breathed deeply and brushed the snowflakes from his hair. First Avenue was deserted; he crossed and made his way to the dead end. The river lay below, a shiny black ribbon at the bottom of the world. Queensboro Bridge floated behind the snow, its outlines veiled, its massive pillars crouching in the dark. Even the Pepsi-Cola sign on the Long Island shore was muted to a reddish blur. David remembered the title of Debussy's prelude *The Snow Is Dancing*. What lovely music.

He felt calmer and retraced his steps; Judith had changed into a pale-yellow nightgown and had let down her hair. She was contrite. "I'm sorry if I upset you."

In a forgiving mood, he put his arm around her. "Forget it." And when they went to bed, she was all tenderness. David suddenly recalled a statement by some movie star that all problems were solved in bed. Were they?

7

IN the next weeks, he became increasingly irritable. A book he was looking for and couldn't find, a telephone number he needed and mislaid—any trifle sufficed to bring on an outburst totally out of proportion to its cause. One evening he was in the kitchen cooking a lamb stew. Judith had just come home and was at her desk going through her mail. She had taught him to use herbs; he tasted a spoonful of the broth and was delighted with his concoction. As he turned to reach for a ladle, his elbow hit the pot; it tipped over and crashed to the floor. The precious stew oozed into a puddle. In a rage over his own awkwardness, he grabbed the plate nearest him and hurled it to the floor. The plate splintered, its white shards settling into the brownish stew. Judith came running.

"What happened?" She took in the scene. Relieved, she said, "I thought the world had exploded."

David stared at the mess, overwhelmed by the senselessness of his tantrum. "Damnit! Such a lovely dinner."

"So what?" She put her hand on his arm. "We'll eat out."

He sent her back to her desk and brought out a mop. As he pushed the mop across the floor it came to him that the moment of truth had finally arrived. He had to regain his freedom, and he could do so only by taking a firm stand. If he didn't, he would only grow more and more hostile to her. He finished his task and went into the other room. Facing her desk, "There's something I've been meaning to tell you," he said, sounding as decisive as he could.

"What?"

Couldn't she guess? He looked away and forced himself to continue. "It's just not working out between us."

She raised one hand, palm against her throat. Hesitant, "Is there someone else?" she asked.

"No, I just want to leave."

"Where will you go?"

"I haven't decided yet. Is that important?"

"Yes. If there is no one else," she said evenly, "and there's no other place you want to be, all you're doing is running away. Not from me, as you think, but from yourself." She suddenly sounded as objective as if she were analyzing a problem for her Polynesians. "You're dissatisfied with yourself, so you take it out on me."

"Meaning—?"

"If you were working at something you loved, you'd be quite content with the way things are. But you don't know where you're going, you have no respect for what you're doing, therefore you imagine that if you only got out of here your problems would be solved."

David's resolve weakened under the hammer blows of her logic. He said nothing. Judith rose and came over to him. "Going away from a situation never solves anything unless you go toward something." She looked into his eyes. "Why don't you try going back to the piano?"

"I've told you, that's all behind me."

She took his arm. "David, how I wish you'd find yourself. How I wish I could help you." Her voice grew tense with emotion. "It's meant so much to me to have you in my life, to care about you and know you're there.

"I sometimes wonder," she continued, "what it would be like to lose you, to have to go on without you. I can't imagine it. I know I spent a good part of my life without you, but all that seems so far away. You gave me the direction I needed. Perhaps I should have found it in my work, but I didn't. I might have gone much farther if I'd been completely the scholar, but my work was only something to do until I found what I was really looking for. I'm too much of a woman to be a scientist. You're far more important to me than any book I might write."

David had the sensation of a hand clutching at his throat, choking him. "What if I hadn't gone to the party where we met?" he asked. "You'd have never known I existed."

"There is no 'if' in history. What if Napoleon had been happy at home with Josephine? We know only what happened, not what might have happened. You did go to the party and I did meet you. It had to be."

David took her in his arms. She had won again.

The final break between them came sooner and more violently than he anticipated. They had dined with some of Judith's colleagues; David had enjoyed the evening. But as soon as the others made off, his high spirits left him.

Judith could not help noticing the change. "You were having a fine time with my friends," she said as they went up the stairs to her apartment, "but as soon as we're alone—" She turned on the light without completing her reproach.

"It's just that they don't face me with a problem"—why did he defend himself?—"and you do."

"Naturally. They don't mean anything to you and I do."

He noticed that she had twisted his words to mean something he didn't intend. "The problem is," he blurted out, "I want to stay with you and I don't." Once again he had softened the truth so as not to hurt her; he didn't want to stay with her at all.

"What makes you think you're the only one who's ambivalent? Everybody is, more or less."

He resented her tone of sweet reasonableness and the way she forced him to go along with her fiction. "You keep saying you understand me. As a matter of fact, you don't understand me at all."

"We're both complex people, David. No one can hope to understand another person completely. But I think I've a pretty good idea of what you're like."

"No, you don't," he cried, his anger rising, "or you'd know what you're putting me through. I feel guilty because you've done so much for me and I'm not grateful."

"You don't have to feel grateful," she said evenly. "Whatever I did, I did because I wanted to."

Her calm tone only fed his wrath. "I feel guilty because you want me to love you and I don't." There, he had said it! "And there's nothing I can do about it."

The blood rushed to her face in splotches. "Don't say that." There was fear in her voice. "I can't bear to hear it."

"But it's the truth!" For some reason her helplessness made him more angry. "You keep talking about honesty. Well, now I'm being honest!" Repelled by her hangdog look, he glowered at her. "All these months I've tried to make this work. I keep thinking of all you've done for me and try all the harder. But it always adds up to the same thing." Now that he had plunged the knife in, he had to twist it so that it would hurt. He felt a terrible remorse at what he was doing, and fought it off by working himself into a fury. "This is more than I can handle, I want out! D'you hear me? Out!" he shouted, amazed at his cruelty yet finding a strange pleasure in it.

She took a step toward him. "Don't leave me, David," she begged. "Please . . ." She bent forward, one hand lifted in supplication.

He stiffened. This time she must not talk him out of his decision. There was only one way to protect himself—to strike harder. "You keep telling yourself that I love you. But I don't and never did! You want to know the truth? I hate you for what you're doing to me. For the whole damn mess!" Abandoning all efforts to control himself, "I hope I never see you again!" he screamed at her.

She stood with head bent, mouth abjectly open, looking as if she had been whipped. David, appalled at what he had done, could bear the sight of her no longer. He ran into the bedroom, emptied the shelves where he kept his shirts, underwear, and socks, and crammed them into his father's battered valise. As he did, a childhood memory crossed his mind of his father grabbing the valise after a quarrel with his mother and running out of the house. But this was different. His father loved his mother and always came back. He never would.

Judith was standing where he had left her. Her arms hung limply, her lips were trembling and tears flowed down her cheeks. She raised one hand to brush them away. "Please, David," she whimpered, "don't go . . ."

"I'm getting out, goddamnit! And I won't be back." Valise in hand, he ran down the stairs and turned toward First Avenue. He crossed over and continued to the dead end, where a solitary bench faced the river. Sitting down, he rested the valise beside him.

The city was asleep. A dampness rose from below like an exhalation; the Pepsi-Cola sign on the opposite shore cast a red trail across the water. The bridge loomed to his left.

His anger subsided; he knew only that he was free of her at last, and it was a wonderful feeling. He unbuttoned his coat, stretched out his arms and, letting them rest on top of the bench, threw back his head. The sky was overcast. He sucked in the moist air and felt his lungs expand. The little iron fence in front of him ended in a series of semicircular loops that curved away from the river, presumably to keep people from jumping. Well, he had no such intention.

Sounds floated out of the night to tease his ear. An automobile horn on First Avenue. A bell. A steam whistle. A foghorn that sounded like a trombone; it came from a tugboat threading its way past Ward's Island. Followed by a sound he could not identify, as though a huge cork had popped out of a bottle. A sound, dull and hollow, that disturbed him. He tried to hold on to his new-found freedom, to taste it, enjoy it, but his disquiet would not be allayed. It grew by leaps and bounds, until it became an overriding fear. Something was summoning him back to her apartment. He tried to ignore it, he tried to shake it off, but the fear grew ever more insistent. Unable to fight it any longer, he jumped up, grabbed the valise and broke into a run.

Faster and faster, the fear mounting, across the avenue without stopping for the light. He bounded up the two flights of stairs and rang the bell. A sweet unpleasant smell hit his nostrils, like the damp smell of the river but more acrid. He kept ringing. There was no answer. He slammed the valise as hard as he could against the door, remembered that he had the key in his pocket, and let himself in.

The sweetish reek of gas made his nose tingle. He ran into the kitchen. Judith was stretched on the floor, face up. He held his breath, ran to the gas range and turned off its burners; then to the window. She had locked it and stuffed a towel against the sill. He unlocked the window; a stream of air rushed in. Grabbing her under the arms, he pulled her to the window, propped her up on the sill and shoved her head out. It rolled to one side as if about to snap off.

"Please don't die . . . please!" Her face was green. He

slapped her cheeks and pushed the upper part of her body onto the fire escape, shaking her repeatedly. He moved swiftly, efficiently, as if part of him were watching from the outside and directing him; at the same time he saw everything about him with unnatural clarity. He noticed the coffeepot on the range and made a mental note to pour out its contents. Turning Judith over, he pounded her on the back to clear her lungs. She began to breathe.

Her lips opened; she vomited over the fire escape. Reaching down for the towel, he wiped her mouth, and tried to clean up the mess. He turned her on her back so that her head rested on the outside sill, and fetched a pillow from the bedroom. Raising her head, he pushed the pillow underneath it.

What next? A doctor. He went to the telephone, asked Information for the emergency ward of the nearest hospital, and dialed. Abruptly he hung up. The publicity. HUNTER COLLEGE PROFESSOR ATTEMPTS SUICIDE. The disgrace. Someone said you spent the first half of your life trying to get your name in the paper and the second half trying to keep it out. He decided to call Judith's doctor instead. He had met him at several of her parties but could not recall his name. He leafed through her little telephone book but realized that he would not recognize the name even if he saw it. The closet door was open. He caught sight of a small gas stove that she used on winter nights when the steam heat was insufficient. He dialed Lenox Hill Hospital and reported that a friend had been overcome by gas escaping from a defective heater. Why would they check his story at two in the morning?

Judith was breathing regularly now, although she still had not come to. If he had returned ten minutes later she'd have been dead. Because of him. He tried to push the thought out of his mind but could not. Would they have arrested him as her murderer? What would prison have been like? A bell clanged; he rushed to the window. The ambulance slid to a halt directly below. Seen from above, its sleek oblong top looked like a hearse. Two orderlies dressed in white jumped out. David pressed the buzzer to let them in.

He led them into the kitchen where they unfurled a stretcher, laid Judith upon it, and covered her body with a white sheet tucked under her chin. She opened her eyes and looked at David, as though trying to remember where she was. "You . . . you came back?" she murmured.

He followed the stretcher down the stairs. One orderly climbed into the ambulance, the other made for the driver's seat and beckoned David to join him. The car sped through deserted streets, its bell clanging as they approached each intersection. At the hospital, the orderlies carried the stretcher into a narrow hallway while David gave the details of the accident to the man at the desk. He sat down in a corner of the waiting room, on a long wooden bench with curved slats for a back.

On the opposite wall there was a mirror. A drawn, frightened face stared back at him. Brown eyes. Curly hair. His father's full lips. His mother's firm chin, though he had so little firmness to go with it. A pleasant face, not especially handsome but not bad-looking either. And scrawled beneath it in large red letters, as though with a lipstick—or blood—he saw a single word. Murderer!

One of the orderlies came toward him. "She'll be all right," he said, with a nod. "You'll be able to see her in the morning."

David thanked him and went out. Lexington Avenue was very quiet; the winter night still had several hours to go. The calm that had held him in its grip snapped; he thought he was going to cry, but no tears came. Burying his face in his hands, he surrendered to the feeling of loathing that spread over him. He hated his callousness, his cruelty. He hated what he had done to her. Worst of all he hated himself.

8

DAVID snuggled against the pillow, relishing his drowsiness yet feeling a little dazed. Then he remembered, and came awake. The world was going about its affairs, unaware of what had taken place. One good thing about living in Manhattan: people minded their own business. You hardly knew your neighbors and didn't much care what happened to them. He reached for the telephone and dialed the hospital. A woman's voice informed him that Judith was much better and would be released that afternoon. At three.

He filled an overnight bag with toilet articles, took three ten-dollar bills from the drawer where she kept money and sealed them in an envelope. With her cloth coat folded over his arm, he set out for the hospital.

The young nurse at the receiving desk asked if he wished to see the patient.

"No." Some explanation was necessary. "I'm on my way to work, I'll be back later. Could I leave these for her?"

Back at the apartment, he drank some orange juice and scrambled two eggs. The dazed feeling persisted, as if someone had hit him on the head. He drank two cups of coffee and tried to assemble his thoughts. The first thing was to get out of the apartment. He could not go home; his parents would ask questions. Yet there was nothing to keep him in the city now. Since most of his pupils lived in Brighton, the sensible thing was to find a furnished room near the ocean, but away from his parents. He made the bed, sat down, and let his eyes wander over the room.

He knew that he had to bring Judith home; this was the least he could do. Yet he did not stir. How could he face her? Perhaps if he sat quietly enough, everything would take care of itself. He glanced at the clock; it was almost two. He pulled himself to his feet, took his valise, locked the door, and left the key in its usual place under the mat.

The city was at lunch. A new building was going up on Lexington Avenue. The construction workers sat on the sidewalk, their hard hats beside them, sandwich in one hand and a bottle of Coke in the other. David deposited the valise in a locker at the subway station and took the uptown local. He got off at Seventy-seventh Street and walked a block to the hospital.

A gray-haired woman in black shuffled out of the entrance, supported by a youngish man, probably her son. Families could be a pain in the neck, but they were something to fall back on when you were in trouble. If only Judith had a relative she could depend on. David stopped a moment, trying to muster up the courage to face her. *You're a coward, David Gordin. You're a shit!* He forced himself to continue and went inside.

The young nurse at the receiving desk recognized him. "I sent those things up."

He nodded.

"I'll see if she's ready." The nurse lifted the phone. Her long fingernails were shaped into points and painted red. She said a few words, listened to Judith's reply, and put down the phone. "She doesn't want to see you." She made it sound like an accusation.

"Wha—?"

The nurse glanced at her nails. "That's all she said."

"You mean—?" He glanced uncertainly around the lobby. No one was aware of the situation. No one cared.

The nurse turned her attention to a short fat man who wheezed. He wore a sports jacket that was too tight for him, in a loud pattern that alternated little green squares with various shades of gray. He asked a question, and the nurse shook her head.

David walked into the street, puzzled yet relieved. Could he blame Judith? It was the first time she had ever said no to him, and he was glad she had had the guts to do so. Things might have turned out differently if she had been able to say no occasionally. Now that she finally could, it no longer mattered. Her decision made it easier for him to get away, but it changed nothing.

He stopped at the corner and waited for the light to change, resting his head against a lamppost. The iron felt cool and soothing against his cheek. When he was a kid on South Fourth Street, if he pressed his ear against a lamppost he could hear the hum of an approaching trolley long before it appeared. The trolley had a little black sign in front on which was printed, in white letters, a single word: Maspeth. How he wanted to go there, but he never found out where Maspeth was.

He retrieved his valise from the subway locker, rode down to Fourteenth Street, and changed for the Brooklyn train. Settling at the back of the car, he leaned against the wall. Presently he dozed off. He did not have to worry about riding past his station. Brighton Beach was the last stop.

THREE

1

THE street was lined with two-family houses. They all looked alike. The sidewalks were wide but the middle of the street was still unpaved. July and August brought hordes of visitors and their children. Now it was off-season and the rent was cheap.

His room—it was called a studio—had a single window that looked out on a back yard, another window, and a patch of sky. The bed became a couch in the daytime. David hated everything about the room—the pale-yellow walls, the chintzy curtains, the hideous linoleum on the floor. But there was a tiny kitchenette where he could prepare his meals, which was cheaper than eating at the cafeteria on Brighton Beach Avenue.

It was ten past one. His first lesson was at three. Which meant he had to pull himself together. It was like putting on make-up: you painted a face over your real face, and that was the one the world saw. Fortunately, no one knew what had taken place between him and Judith. If he was to safeguard his secret, he had to hide what was going on inside him. That took doing.

He pulled himself off the bed and surveyed the room.

Shirts, socks, trousers lay on the floor alongside old newspapers and several books. His mother considered neatness a sign of character. Was this his way of showing her that he had none? If so, what a pity she wasn't here to see it. One good thing about living alone: he was free to do as he pleased. It was obvious he had no talent for housekeeping; yesterday's dishes were piled in the sink. He did remember to carry out the garbage; he was afraid of roaches. During the six weeks that he had lived here, he had called in a cleaning woman twice; but it took no more than a day or two for the mess to return. Sloppiness, David decided, was a form of freedom. He smiled, remembering from some forgotten history course what Mme. Roland said on her way to the guillotine. *Freedom, what crimes are committed in thy name.*

The bad thing about living alone was the loneliness; there was no one to talk to. David felt as if a wall was going up around him. The wall shut out the world, which was to the good, but it also shut him in. He had no choice at the moment; he could not bear to be with others, to listen to their chatter or face their prying eyes. He needed to figure things out, and for that he had to be by himself.

He took a shower, shaved, and dressed. He found a shirt, looked for a tie; at last he was ready to leave. He stopped for a sandwich and coffee at the cafeteria and proceeded to his parents' house.

They were in the living room. After a bit of small talk Lisa asked, "How's your *professerkeh?*"

"Judith? She's fine," he answered smoothly.

"Why don't we ever hear from her?"

"She's busy finishing a book."

"About what?"

"About the Negroes in the South. Two years ago she studied a community in Alabama. Now she's writing it up." By introducing a bit of truth into his lie, perhaps the lie would ring true.

"To be able to write a book . . ." Lisa sighed. "Ekh, that

must be wonderful. And when it's finished, it's there, black on white for the whole world to see. Bring her sometime, I'll make dinner."

"She has to go south for a few weeks," David said. "When she comes back, I'll ask her."

Was it wrong, David asked himself, to deceive his parents like this? Whom did it harm? He would bring Judith back from the South, then give her an illness or two. After that he could send her on a trip to the Far East from which, for one reason or another, she didn't return. Wasn't this what writers did all the time? They made up stories about things that never happened to people who never existed, and if they were good at it, they were praised to the skies. He at least had a reason for inventing his story. If his parents found out the truth . . . the thought made him shudder.

His pupil arrived. Shirley, age twelve, was short and fat. She lacked a sense of rhythm; otherwise she played not badly. "Count, Shirley," David advised, not that it did much good. Shirley was studying Beethoven's Sonatina in G major. The first movement bored her, but she liked the Minuet. Beethoven probably wrote the piece for a student not much older than Shirley, perhaps a young countess who was not so fat because she rode horses. Would the countess's sense of rhythm have been any better than Shirley's? Of course not. Was Beethoven paid more than the three dollars he received for Shirley's lesson? Most likely. The Viennese aristocrats were not overly generous, but they recognized a genius when they met one. David pictured the short stocky man with the beetling brow strolling through the woods around Vienna, no longer able to hear the song of the birds but intent upon the sounds within. "I will take fate by the throat, it shall not overcome me. . . . He who truly understands my music will be free of the sorrows that others carry around in them."

Shirley played an F-natural. "Darling, you're in G major," David said. "Has to be F-sharp. Try it again." How the devil was he supposed to concentrate on what Shirley was doing when his mind kept wandering off in all directions? The answer was simple. He couldn't.

His mother opened the door. "Telephone for you."

"Who it it?" he asked as he made for the kitchen.

Lisa shrugged. "I think it's Judith, but she didn't say."

David repressed a start, then picked up the phone. "Hello?" She had hung up. He remembered that his mother was listening. "Yes, dear," he said into the mouthpiece, "I won't forget." He put down the phone, puzzled, and returned to Shirley.

It was after six when he finished his third lesson. His parents had gone out. There was a plate of cold chicken for him on the kitchen table and a dish of applesauce. David ate, threw on his coat, and went downstairs. He came into the street. She was waiting.

"Judith! What the hell are you doing here?"

"I—I had to see you."

He glanced toward the boardwalk. What if his parents appeared? "Let's walk." He led the way toward Ocean Avenue, where the boardwalk began. "Did you call and hang up?"

"Yes. I wanted to make sure I'd find you."

"You should have said hello to my mother."

She shook her head. "I'm sorry. I didn't think of it."

"Yes you did." His voice became hard. "You were afraid that if you said who you were I wouldn't come to the phone."

"Perhaps."

They walked in silence. Then, "Thanks for bringing those things to the hospital," she said.

"Did you get home all right?" What an idiotic thing to ask. As if he were inquiring whether she had had a pleasant return from a vacation. Defensively he added, "I was all set to bring you back."

"I know. But I didn't want you to see me there. I couldn't bear the thought. Besides . . ." She fell silent.

Changing his tone, "Why did you come?" he asked.

"I kept remembering all the horrible things you said. I wanted to carry away a different memory of you."

He could not shake off his feeling of guilt. "Judith, haven't I harmed you enough? How much of this do you need?"

"You didn't harm me, David. You gave me great happiness."

"But there was a terrible price to pay. You almost paid it." He remembered the dreadful moment by the river when he jumped up and ran back to her. "Judith, it's over. Finished." His voice was low and without rancor.

"We were so happy with each other at first. Why couldn't we start again?"

To see her humble herself in this way was more than he could bear. A great sorrow came over him, for her, for the mess they had made. At the same time he knew he must be firm. No matter what she said, he had to be the stronger. "Look, Judith, the time for sweet talk is over. Don't you understand? All I want now is for you to go your way and let me go mine."

She said nothing.

"I'm not a bad sort," he continued. "Neither are you. We were just bad for each other. The chemistry was wrong. I knew it right away but didn't know how to tell you. And when I finally did, I almost killed you."

She thought awhile. "What did I do to make you hate me so?"

"At first you brought out the best in me, the part that's curious about things and wants to learn. Then you fell in love with me and began to make demands I couldn't meet. That brought out the worst in me, the part that's mean and cruel. I hated what I was doing to you, especially since I admired you so. But you're wrong to think I hate you. Why would I?" Why indeed?

They had reached the boardwalk. It was warm for February. High in the turquoise sky Venus shone with a steadfast glow. Below, the horizon was shrouded in shadow. They sat down on a bench facing the ocean. "Why can't we be friends?" she asked.

"Because you don't want me for a friend, you want me for a lover. When people break up and say, 'Let's be friends,' they're kidding each other. They're just trying to hold on, to prolong the agony." He turned to her. "Judith, it's time to let go." He said it gently, as if he were explaining something to an unreasonable child. She did not answer.

The ocean took on a wine-dark color. "There should be a vaccine against love," David said, "just as there is against smallpox or diphtheria. You could have loved ten other people if you had met them instead of me."

"You told me that."

"You want to know something? If I had loved you as you wanted me to, I'd have ended up like the others, just another man in your life. But once you realized you couldn't have me, I became the one you had to have. You may call it love, I call it obsession."

"Aren't they the same? Whatever you call it, I loved you very much."

David noticed the past tense and was grateful. "One more thing. When I think of what almost happened, I could go out of my mind. Please don't try to see me again. If you phone, I'll hang up. If you wait for me, I'll run like hell. I can't take it anymore, and you shouldn't."

"Why are you so cruel to me?"

"That's where you're wrong," he said firmly. "I tried to be kind, and that was cruel. I'll never make that mistake again. The kind thing would have been to make a clean break and set you free. I understand that now, and you must too."

He was astonished at his firmness. So was she. "You keep saying it's hard for you to reach a decision. But once you make your mind up you're as determined as anyone I ever knew."

"I have to be desperate first."

The stars had come out. Far on the horizon a ship sailed to sea, its decks limned in light.

"All my life," Judith said, "I tackled the impossible. That's what got me to New Guinea in the first place. I must say," she added with a rueful smile, "those two years were not as tough an assignment as you."

He walked her to the station. They stopped at the foot of the stairs. "Forgive me, Judith," he said.

"There's nothing to forgive."

In repose her face took on a sorrowful dignity. He recaptured something of the admiration he had felt when he first knew her. "I wish things could have been different between us."

"For that," she answered, "you and I would have had to be different."

He leaned forward, put his arms around her and kissed her. She trembled in his embrace, and he knew that she was crying. As she turned to leave, "Good-bye, David," she whispered.

He walked away.

2

SOMETHING had gone wrong inside him. He became aware of this gradually, and was not even sure what it was. He thought of it simply as That Thing.

It took a number of shapes. For one, he was more irritable. Trifles he ordinarily would not have noticed fixed themselves in his mind and blew up out of all proportion. What had the clerk in the store meant by that remark? Why was everybody against him? He returned to the imagined injury again and again, examining it from every angle. The irritation passed as suddenly as it had begun, leaving him free for the next disturbance.

He felt anxious in a way he never had before. A vague

fear floated through his consciousness, attaching itself to anything that came along. A racking headache pressed against his temples until the world seemed blurred. What if he was developing a brain tumor? For days on end he was obsessed with thoughts of the horrible death awaiting him. He was eager to consult the family doctor but decided against it. The news might get back to his parents, and he wanted none of their sympathy. Some other doctor? The prospect of confiding in a stranger stopped him. And what if his fears were confirmed? That would be even worse. Suddenly the headache lifted and he felt fine again, until the next cycle of worry.

Every choice presented itself to him along with its opposite. Should he buy a new sports coat or shouldn't he? Should he cook dinner for himself or eat out? By focusing on small things, he kept himself from confronting the larger issues he couldn't face. Somewhere along the line the connection between thought and action had been broken: he would keep postponing the action until it was no longer possible to act. In this way his paralysis of will and his anxiety fed one another, imprisoning him ever more deeply in the morass of That Thing.

His moods followed some mysterious law of their own whose workings were hidden from him, therefore all the more frightening. He would suddenly feel elated: the sun shone, the sky was blue, he was on top of the world. Just as suddenly he would plunge into a deep depression from which, try as he might, he could not extricate himself. He told himself again and again that he was not responsible for someone else's neurotic behavior, he could not be blamed for Judith's mental quirks. It didn't help. He tormented himself with vain regrets. Why hadn't he managed his life better? Why had he driven Judith to her desperate decision? Why hadn't he foreseen the consequences of his behavior? Above all, why wasn't he someone else?

His main concern was to hide That Thing from others. This demanded constant vigilance on his part. He covered his fears so well that no one seemed to notice anything amiss. He was delighted to come through each day without a mishap. Whe would suspect from his outward behavior that he was going to pieces inside? Dissimulation, he decided, was like playing scales. With practice you improved.

Increasingly he found it easier to be alone; only then could he relax and be himself. He did not mind solitude; most people were boring. They chattered and gossiped, they wasted time. How much wiser to stay home with a good book. There was so much to learn, and so little time to learn it. He had only to step into the public library on Ocean Avenue to find himself in the presence of the greatest minds that ever were. He was re-reading *War and Peace*. It was Abe who had persuaded him to read the novel for the first time; he was getting much more out of it now. What fascinated him was the way Tolstoi was able to tie in the personal life of his characters with the great historic events that surrounded them. Was there always a connection between the individual's fate and society? For example, between his depression and the greater Depression around him?

He read mostly history and biography. Burckhardt's book on the Renaissance made a deep impression on him, as did Emil Ludwig's *Napoleon*. Except for a few great novelists, he stayed away from fiction. What was the use, he asked himself, of reading a novel, supposedly a slice of reality, by someone who was probably no closer to reality than most of his readers? He was turned off by the overgrown boy scouts who swaggered through Hemingway's stories, but responded to Steinbeck; also to the jeweled prose of Thornton Wilder. Reading not only taught him things but lifted him out of himself. Every once in a while he came upon a text on psychology that looked interesting, and brought the volume home hoping it would shed some light on what he was going through. He soon gave up. Every symptom in the book seemed to apply to him.

At night he went for a walk. He kept to the back streets so as not to run into anyone he knew. He ended up on the boardwalk, which at that hour was deserted. It stretched before him like a shiny ribbon between two rows of lights that merged in the distance. He walked briskly, filling his lungs. The wind from the Atlantic took on a fragrance in March; waves surged along the beach and broke with a roar. As he approached Sea Gate he passed the string of buoys that served to guide ocean liners into the harbor. The bouys rocked with the waves, the bells attached to them making a dark, mournful sound. At the end of the boardwalk not a soul was to be seen. He felt altogether content in this vast emptiness. Safe. Yet somewhere in the dark That Thing lurked, waiting to act up again.

3

HE needed someone to talk to. He telephoned his friend Sidney, whom he had not seen in over a year.

They met in midtown. Sidney was as thin, his shock of red hair as unruly, his gestures as staccato as ever. He launched into a detailed account of his activities; he would soon be finishing law school. "Am I glad I switched," he said. "Smartest thing I ever did."

"What about the violin?" David asked. "You ever play?"

Sidney shook his head. "When I'm all set I'll pick it up again. Until then . . ." A brusque downward gesture completed the sentence.

His sex life was booming too. Her name was Nathalie, and she was a divorcee. "She had a lousy marriage, so she's not eager to try it again. Suits me fine." Sidney sang her praises. Then, "Enough about me. What are you up to?"

"Nothing much. I'm teaching a bit and . . ." David's voice trailed off. How could he report anything when his chief aim was to conceal? He turned back to the past. "That was some summer we spent in Ferndale." It seemed like a lifetime ago.

Sidney grinned. "The night you tried to get into Elsie's room."

"And Val."

"How you managed that with me around, I'll never know. Did I envy you."

"The night we visited Professor Sheldon and you got into an argument."

"He was a dud."

"No, he was a sweet little man. 'Grow old along with me,' " David declaimed in his most stentorian manner, " 'the best is yet to be.' "

"*In Memoriam.*"

"No, *Rabbi Ben Ezra*," David said. "And the way you'd look down at your cock and say, 'Just think, a Beethoven may come out of here.' "

"He still may," Sidney said.

They were sitting in a cafeteria on Times Square. Sidney's favorite dessert was still pineapple cheese cake washed down by a glass of milk. When they ran out of memories it was time to part. Sidney returned to the Bronx, David to Brighton Beach. They had drifted too far apart, he realized, for them to be able to pick up where they had left off.

His visit with Deborah, on the last Saturday night in March, was more rewarding. She was living in the Village, on Perry Street, and taught piano at the Third Street Music School. She looked as fragile, as vulnerable as she always had, with her delicate features and olive complexion. Her gentle gray eyes had retained their expression of wonder. He put his arms around her and held her close. "What a lovely girl you are," he said. The woman she was living with came into the room. She was older and on the masculine side. Her iron-gray hair was cropped short; she wore a tailored suit. "This is my friend Angela Ward," Debbie said. Angela, it turned out, taught English at Stuyvesant High School.

He remembered Deborah's piano from the Bronx. She brought out the four-hand music they used to play. They went through several of the Hungarian Dances and the Schubert Fantasy, then they sat around and talked. The room had a cheerful look. Two Japanese lanterns formed bowls of light; the chairs, table, and bookshelves were of blond oak. Debbie sat next to Angela on the couch. They held hands, David noticed, much more than married couples generally did, as if they had to make their relationship clear to the world, or to each other. Presently they were joined by a middle-aged man who owned an antique shop in the Village and his lover, a young poet who had just had a piece accepted by *Poetry* magazine. The four of them gossiped about their friends and laughed a lot.

If he had come in the hope of unburdening himself to a sympathetic ear, he soon realized that Debbie had no time for that. She was fond of him, she made him feel welcome, but she had moved into a world of her own in which he had no place. He wondered once more if there had been anything between her and Miss Parissot, but dismissed the thought. Who cared? When the time came for him to leave, Debbie walked him to the door. She kissed him. "It was *wonderful* of you to look me up," she said. "Will you come again soon?"

"Of course I will," he promised, knowing that he wouldn't. He walked to the subway station. Sheridan Square was jumping. He returned to his loneliness.

His evening with Nat Bender and Gladys was less pleasant. Nat still held forth in Stewart's Cafeteria on Eighth Street. His tousled black hair still looked as if it might emit sparks. He had bagged a job on the W.P.A. Writer's Project. Having a regular job was a new experience for Nat and stimulated his imagination. The saga of Dr. Bulgakoff and his Bulgarian buttermilk had expanded considerably. The good doctor was now trying to sell his product to the Chinese, on the ground that it was the most potent aphrodisiac known to man. As the Chinese believed him, the buttermilk was having stupendous effects. These Nat gleefully detailed, while his coterie was convulsed with laughter.

David smiled out of politeness, but he no longer had the heart to enjoy Nat's fantasies. The realization saddened him.

It was well past midnight when he returned to Brighton. The boardwalk was deserted, its lights stretching before him like blank faces in the night. A profound sadness seized him; he seemed to be alone in the world, cut off from the people he had known and loved. Everywhere men and women were sitting in lighted rooms, talking and laughing together. Only he was alone on this godforsaken boardwalk, an outcast.

The darkness hung over him, endless, impenetrable. It seemed to him that the wall around him was higher, thicker than ever. A blank wall that cut him off from the world. How had he been trapped inside it? He could not find the answer.

4

LISA glared at David. "You lied to us!"

"How?" He tried to sound defiant, but under that searching look his defenses crumbled.

"You let us believe that you're still with Judith. You're not!"

"How would you know?"

"Very simple. I telephoned her and she said she hadn't seen you in a month."

Now he was angry. "Why did you call her?"

"I knew something was wrong. I felt it in my bones."

"What right have you to meddle in my affairs?"

She turned to Joel. "Listen to him!" Back to David: "If you have a right to lie to me, I have a right to find out."

"David," Joel said, "it's not a question of whether we have the right. We worry about you, we want to know if anything is wrong. Surely you can understand that."

"I understand only that you're meddling in my affairs." His voice was surly. "I forbid you to do that."

"You forbid us?" Lisa cried. "That yet I had to hear."

"Why did you leave Judith?" Joel asked. "She's a sensible woman. I was hoping she would straighten you out."

"It's a long story. I don't want to go into it." He realized that Judith had not told his mother the whole truth. Something to be thankful for. "Besides, I don't like you to pry." He used the Yiddish idiom "to creep into my bones."

Lisa lost patience. "Then why do you come here and worry us with the way you look and the way you act? If you don't want us to bother you, why don't you just stay away?"

"Because I have to *support* myself, and the only way I can do that is by giving lessons, and for that I need a piano, and the piano is here. That's why!" He was not going to tell them that he was sick and lonely and falling apart, that he needed their love and encouragement, not their anger and accusations.

"David, you're welcome to come whenever you like," Joel said, "and the piano is yours whenever you need it. Please understand that we'd like to help you, but we don't know how. Where are you living?"

He pictured the look on his mother's face if she saw the mess in his room. "I won't tell you."

"At least give us the phone number," Joel continued, "in case we have to reach you."

David recited the number. His father wrote it down.

"Who's taking care of you?" Lisa asked. "Who feeds you?"

"I do the cooking."

Lisa turned to Joel. "Woe is me. He'll starve to death."

"David, why don't you come back to us?" Joel said. "You'd be better off here."

The pleading look on his father's face unnerved him. "I have to go," he brought out uncertainly.

"Something happened between you and Judith," Liza said. She gazed straight before her, like a fortune teller sorting out in her mind what the tea leaves had told her. "I don't know what it was, but it was not good."

David grabbed his coat and made for the door, but not before Lisa aimed her parting shot. "Father in heaven, what did I do to deserve this?"

David took off almost at a run. Their offer to help him could only mean that they had noticed he was in bad shape. He was infuriated that they had so easily seen through his defenses. His mind whirled in that mouse-in-the-trap way, faster and faster until his head ached. He reached the boardwalk, sank down on a bench, and buried his face in his hands.

A sense of failure weighed him down. Failure on every level: As a son. As a friend. As a lover. As a pianist. As a human being. His despair rose like a cry inside his head from which there was no escaping. He sat up and stared in bewilderment at the sea. Shapes and patterns swirled crazily in the dark. "For heaven's sake," he whispered to himself, "you're having a nervous breakdown."

At last That Thing had found a name. He was surprised it hadn't occurred to him before.

5

APRIL was lovely at the shore. A soft breeze blew in from the sea and a lavender haze veiled the horizon. The days grew longer; so did his bouts with depression. Hours passed before the black mood lifted, leaving him listless and exhausted. Hardly less unnerving were the attacks of fear. A vague anxiety churned inside him, without shape or name, looking for some object to which it could attach itself. Sooner or later it manufactured one, no matter how illogical. He might be walking down a street; an auto passed. He was suddenly convinced that if the car turned left at the corner something terrible would happen to him. His heart beat wildly, a cold sweat poured over him. The automobile reached the corner and did turn left, yet nothing untoward came to pass. He breathed a sigh of relief; how foolish of him to have yielded to fear in this fashion. Despite this sensible thought, he remained just as defenseless against the next attack.

Headaches plagued him with increasing frequency. He became convinced that he was going blind. He peered at objects as though he could no longer see them; little worms, red and yellow, crawled across his field of vision. He pictured himself, cup in one hand, cane in the other, picking his way through total darkness as he begged for alms. He finally consulted an eye doctor, who assured him there was nothing wrong with his eyes. All he needed was a pair of glasses.

He had difficulty in falling asleep. He would get to bed dead tired but the instant his head touched the pillow he came wide awake. After tossing from side to side, he settled down to read through the night. He was discovering the French writers—Balzac, Flaubert, Anatole France. Finally he got to Proust. The long involuted sentences in *Swann's Way* were more effective than any sleeping pill; after a page or two he fell fast asleep. Within a few weeks he had dipped into the novel here and there without being able to focus on it. Then, one night, he read the scene where Marcel, despite his parents' stern injunction, decides to summon his mother once more to his bedside. The boy runs to the top of the staircase, picturing her anger, and when he catches sight of her bursts into sobs. Suddenly it was as if a door had opened and David had finally stepped into Proust's special world. He caught the flavor of the prose and the majesty of its rhythm. "It is a long time, too, since my father has been able to tell Mamma to 'Go with the child.' Never again will such hours be possible for me. But of late I have been increasingly able to catch, if I listen attentively, the sound of the sobs which I had the strength to control in my father's presence, and which broke out only when I found myself alone with Mamma. Acutally, their echo has never ceased . . ." David read through the night, transfixed. But this was one of the great novelists! How strange that he hadn't realized it before.

His dreams were disturbing. Two of them came back again and again. He was rowing a dinghy, the kind that lifeguards used, past the buoys that marked the entrance to the harbor. He was standing because the two seats were occupied by Judith and his mother. The dinghy had sprung a leak, air was escaping from one of its pontoons; soon, he knew, they would all be in the water. He covered the leak with his foot and thrust the oar forward with a firm stroke to either side, as Venetian gondoliers did. "Row harder," his mother said, "or we'll drown." He did as she said, but the dinghy was sinking. "It's no use," Judith said quietly, "we won't make it." He awoke in a sweat.

He had to play a concert in Carnegie Hall; he put on his tails and set out. They were paving Seventh Avenue. He tried to cross over to the hall but his shoes sank into the freshly laid tar. He pulled one foot out with the greatest difficulty, only to have it sink again at the next step. It took enormous effort to reach the opposite side of the street. He looked around for a shoeshine man to remove the tar; none was in sight. He fished a newspaper out of the trashcan on the corner and cleaned off his shoes as well as he could. Some of the tar came off on his hands, also on the cuffs of his shirt. He stopped at the men's room, washed his hands and pulled up his sleeves so that the dirtied cuffs wouldn't show. There was a burst of applause as he came on stage; the hall was filled. He bowed, sat down at the piano and launched into Chopin's A-flat Polonaise. The piano, to his surprise, was not a Steinway; its name was printed in a language he could not read, that looked like Russian. As he played, the cuffs worked their way out of his coat sleeves so that everyone could see they were soiled; he was terribly embarrassed. The opening section of the piece ended in an ascending scale that both hands had to play as fast as possible, arriving at the top together. Unfortunately his left hand fell behind and ended a split second behind the right.

This was not the kind of mistake that could go unnoticed. People began to whisper and laugh, pointing at him; some got up to leave. He had never felt so ashamed.

The occupants of the first-tier boxes rose as one man; they were wearing, of all things, academic caps and gowns. They repeated one word over and over, which he could not hear because he was playing loud. When he reached the lyrical soft section he heard it only too well. "Guilty!" they cried above the music. In the center box sat a gray-haired woman—the judge. Her face was turned away from him because she was reading an official document. He saw the mortarboard of her academic cap, with a gold tassel that swung over her shoulder. "And the punishment?" she asked, her face still averted. He stopped playing and shouted, "For what?"

"For murdering the music, of course," she replied. The others shook their heads in approval, the tassels on their caps bobbing up and down. He wanted to shout, "It's unfair!" but was unable to utter a sound. "The punishment!" the judge insisted, and prepared to pass sentence. David did not hear it because he awoke.

He stared about in terror; his heart was racing. He turned on his back so as not to hear his pulse beat against the pillow.

6

THERE had been a time in his life when he was well. Why couldn't he go back to it, if only for an afternoon? A powerful longing took shape inside him to revisit the streets of his childhood. They were only an hour away.

His pilgrimage to the past began at the Manhattan end of the Williamsburg Bridge. He wandered through the East Side, remembering. There were no longer any pushcarts on Hester Street. The entrance to the bridge was considerably less impressive than he recalled. What had once seemed like a majestic staircase was not majestic at all; in fact, it was dilapidated. He followed the steep ascent of the pedestrian walk; something of his old exhilaration returned when he found himself higher than the rooftops. The two bridges to the south hung gracefully from their cables; toylike vehicles moved slowly across. He remembered the Saturday afternoon walk across the bridge while his mother performed her favorite set piece—the horrendous account of her trip across the Atlantic. He reached the center of the span and saw himself standing there, making ready to throw the reddish-brown sponge ball into the river so that she would love him again. The path began to slope down. Soon the dome of the Williamsburg Savings Bank came into view; the building needed cleaning. Now Bridge Plaza opened before him. He turned to the left, past the bronze horseman whose name was not Valley Forge. The benches in front of the statue were empty. This was where she had waited for him after school, holding a brown paper bag with a gooey napoleon inside.

He walked along South Fourth Street. The blocks seemed shorter, the buildings not nearly as tall. He crossed Hewes Street and caught sight of the house, as brown and friendly as ever, with its tiny stoop and the stone stairs leading down to the cellar where Stella Rabinowitz and he had explored each other. A thousand memories, stored away for the better part of twenty years, leaped to his mind. The morning smell of chalk and blackboard. The sound of the church bells on Sunday morning. The Saturday afternoon chess game between his father and Mr. Levine. The party to celebrate the arrival of the piano, with platefuls of dates stuffed with walnuts, his mother reciting Pushkin, and Uncle Isaac pulling out his gold watch to announce that it was time to go home.

He turned the corner, crossed Broadway and headed for Ross Street. Here and there an abandoned building gazed with a vacant stare, its windows covered with tin. On Marcy

Avenue he passed the high school; it still looked like something out of *Kenilworth*. Ross Street had come down in the world since he lived there, but it was still a cut above South Fourth. He reached Lee Avenue and the ice cream parlor where his group had their nightly hot chocolate. Carl, who forgot his lines in the middle of Kipling's "If." Bill, the comedian. Solly, the future accountant. Hymie, the future politician. And Abe. Where were they now? They had promised to have a reunion in ten years. What a grim evening that would have been! The Lee Avenue trolley passed, the one he used to take when he went to visit Henny Jershow. She would be married by now, with a couple of kids; probably a little plumper. He came to the old oak on the corner where Abe and he used to say goodnight. It had all happened so long ago. Why then did it seem so close?

The sun moved westward toward the bridge. He reached the gray synagogue on Bedford Avenue and sat down on the steps. He had been walking for hours and was tired as he never had been before. Tired of his loneliness, his sadness, his guilt. Why had he come back to Williamsburg? To recapture the peace he had lost? Or simply to say goodbye? Whatever the reason, he had not found what he was looking for. Thomas Wolfe was right: you couldn't go home again.

David shut his eyes and felt the energy drain from his body. He wished he never had to stand up again. Or take another step.

7

IT was past midnight; the boardwalk was empty. He went down the steps that led to the beach; the sand crunched under his feet. He walked toward the water.

Before him stretched the immense black space of the sea. He turned to look back. The lights on the boardwalk curved to either side in a kind of semicircle. He felt wonderfully free, almost light-headed. He listened to the sound of the bells as they moved up and down on the buoys. Why had he ever thought their tolling mournful? Actually the sound was quite pleasant.

His mind was whirling, jumping from one thought to the next with a speed and clarity that amazed him. Or was it the darkness that was whirling around him, pressing against the back of his head, gently pushing, urging him on? He took a step forward, almost as though to test himself. A million years ago mankind had come up out of the water. The black space beckoned to him. If he swam out only a little way . . . It was like returning to a place he had once lived in.

He looked around to make sure no one was watching, took off his shoes and socks, and stripped to his shorts. At first, he left his clothes where they dropped. Reconsidering, he arranged trousers, jacket and shirt in an orderly pile. For once in his life he would be neat. The things that had worried him seemed so far away, so trivial. He seemed to have thrown them off along with his clothes. He was on a higher plane now, from which he was able to look down calmly on the petty annoyances of life. It was not only possible to escape That Thing, it was easy. All you had to do was to slip out through the back door.

The darkness flowed around him, mild and sweet. He thought of the books he had read in his hope of acquiring wisdom. Why had they taught him so little? Or was it that he was incapable of learning the right things? As he reached the water's edge, his vision blurred; tears ran down his cheeks. What was he crying for? He stepped into the water. An icy chill struck his ankles. He sucked in his breath and pushed forward until the water rose to his knees, thighs, testicles. Goose-pimples raced across his skin; he felt himself turn blue. This was no time for indecision. He jumped.

The shock knocked the breath out of him. He swam out, turning his head sideways and opening his mouth as wide as he could to suck in air. The numbness passed; he picked up speed, kicking the water behind him. His body felt wonderfully light; the old sense of weightlessness, of oneness with the sea. The waves were larger than he had expected. As one came along it lifted him up before it let him slide down its back, blotting out the lights on the boardwalk as it moved toward shore. For an instant he was in total darkness. Then the next wave caught him up, and the lights went on again. Once he had been afraid of the dark. Now it was no longer frightening. On the contrary, it was calm and restful; it promised good things.

David pulled at the water with powerful strokes. He took a last look at the sky, ducked his head, and dived. Toward the subterranean garden where the trees glistened and a soft music filled the air. A wild expectancy surged through him. The sea pressed in on him until he no longer felt the cold, only the weight of the water. His head felt like a balloon that had been blown up to bursting. The sensation long ago of burying his face in the pillow and watching stars float out of a pink-gray void. The stars were floating before him, he was touching the bottom of the Atlantic with a million gallons on top of him, he was about to enter the subterranean garden when a great No! tore through his brain, booming in his ears like a giant bell, commanding him to shake off the darkness before it was too late. A hunger stronger than thought or will, stronger even than despair—the blind animal hunger of his body to stay alive—took over for him and with a last desperate thrust forced him to the surface.

Floating on his back, gasping and sputtering, he filled his lungs with air. It had a sweetness he had never tasted before. The pain in his head was so great he couldn't think; his body thought for him. As he turned to a swimming position, his arms and legs flailed the water and pulled toward the light, ever toward the light. Near shore, still gasping, he tried to stand up and touched bottom. He staggered out of the water, reached dry sand, and dropped down.

He was shaking all over, his teeth chattered, his thoughts froze inside his head. But he knew. His body had been wiser, stronger than he. It had brought him back alive and he was glad of it. Alive!

Words floated sluggishly through his brain, shaping a question. Why had he imitated Judith? Was this his way of expiating what he had done to her? It came to him that he hadn't imitated her at all. She had turned on the gas because she wanted to die; he had walked into the sea in order to convince himself that he wanted to live. Deep inside, he must have known that no matter how far out he swam he would be able to get back.

He had touched bottom and made it back. What else mattered? David tried to shape a smile. He passed out instead.

8

WHEN he opened his eyes, everything was white—the walls, the doctor's jacket, the nurse's uniform. The doctor assured him he would be all right, from which David inferred that he had been sick; he had the sensation of struggling out of a deep sleep.

"Woe is me, we almost lost him!" Lisa exclaimed, clasping her hands to her breast. She had said the same words after Abe and he had almost drowned. He wondered what had happened after he fell down on the sand. Dimly he recalled being awakened at dawn by the man who cleaned the beach. He had put on his clothes and walked along the boardwalk; he was sweating and shaking with cold at the same time. He had managed to reach his room, and dropped down on the bed fully dressed. That was the last thing he remembered.

"A person should come down with pneumonia in the

summer?" his mother wondered. "I never heard of such a thing."

David looked at his parents. How much did they suspect? He knew enough not to ask.

"When you didn't come to give your lessons," his father said, "we knew something was wrong. Your landlady found you burning up with fever and called a doctor. He took one look and ordered an ambulance. For six days they wouldn't let us see you, that's how sick you were. Today they said yes."

David closed his eyes. All he had to do was keep his mouth shut, and no one would ever know. What a stroke of luck that he had been able to get off the beach.

Lisa came to visit him every day. Sometimes she brought a napoleon that bulged with creamy custard. "Eat, my son, it'll do you good."

David smiled. "This is what you used to bring me after school when we went to the movies. Remember?"

"As if it were yesterday," she sighed. "It was a dream. A beautiful dream."

The afternoons passed quietly. They chatted about a variety of subjects. David remembered the quality of afternoons long ago when she made him stay home from school because he had a cold: the cozy feeling of lying in bed knowing that everyone else was in class. They were gentler with each other now, and able to talk about themselves freely, easily. One day he asked her if she believed in life after death.

"What sort of a question is that?"

"Well, do you believe the Messiah will blow his trumpet on the Day of Judgment and we'll all rise from our graves?"

"That's a hard one to answer."

"What it boils down to is, do you believe in heaven or hell?"

She thought awhile. Then, "Shall I tell you the truth? Those are grandmothers' tales. What's here on earth is all there is. Once we die there's nothing."

"What about God? Where do you suppose He is?"

She hedged. "Do I know?"

"You must have some idea if you believe in Him. Is He up there"—David pointed to the ceiling—"or down below?"

"You know where He is?" She tapped her forefinger against her heart. "Here."

"Pa says you grow more religious each year. You make up rules that aren't even in the Bible."

"How would he know? He hasn't read it since he was a boy." She smiled. "As you grow older there's more to believe."

A change had come over her. She never corrected or reproached him, she no longer preached at him, and she asked no questions. "I hate to admit it," she said to him, "but I was too hard on you. I wanted to make you over. That was a mistake."

He knew what it cost her, given her pride, to acknowledge that she had been wrong. "It's all right, Ma. I'm glad we're friends again."

"When you almost lose someone you love," she said, "you look at him differently. The things you quarreled about no longer seem important. Shall I tell you the truth? I don't care what you do or don't do. All I want is for you to stay in this world."

"Thanks, Ma." David smiled. For the first time in months he felt at peace.

V

The
Road
Back

ONE

1

s he picked his way through the Sunday crowd,
enjoying the hubbub around him, he suddenly
heard "Davey!" Nobody had called him that in
years.

"Abe! I can't believe it!"

Abe hadn't changed much: the same flat nose, big brown
eyes behind thick glasses, and fuzzy voice. A neat mustache
had taken the place of the fuzz over his upper lip, and he
was no longer skinny.

"What are you doing here?" Abe asked.

"I live close by." David pointed behind him, toward
Brighton. "And you?"

"I'm interning at Kings County."

"Funny that we've never run into each other," David said,
trying to sound casual. Abe belonged to that time in his life
when everything was simple and clear: B.C.—before con-
fusion. He had to be careful not to reveal this.

Abe explained that when he was unable to get into an
American medical school, he had gone to Edinburgh and
had stayed on for graduate work in psychiatry. "What about
you, Davey? What are you doing?"

"I teach."

"Where?"

"Privately. The kids are still on vacation," he added irrelevantly, "so I'm free." It really didn't sound like much.

Abe was puzzled. "What about the piano? You were so
talented."

How to explain to someone else what seemed so simple
and clear to him? "There's a Depression on, it's a bad time
for a musician." David wondered, even as he said it, whether
the fault was in the time or in him.

"I guess so," Abe said, looking unconvinced.

"What about our friends?" David asked. "Do you see any
of them?"

Abe brought David up to date. Bill and Hymie were lawyers, Carl had gone into his father's cloak-and-suit business, Solly was something or other in the city administration. "They keep saying we should have a reunion. Would you come?"

"Yukh!" David made a gesture of distaste.

They were walking now. They might have been back on
Lee Avenue, walking toward the old oak on the corner of
Rodney Street, Abe leading the way into their private world
and David eagerly following.

Abe glanced at his watch. "We better turn back. I have
to be at the hospital."

"I'll walk you back," David said, as in the old days.

"What was that girl's name?" Abe asked.

"Who?"

"The blonde. Don't you remember?"

"You mean Henny? Henny Jershow."

"You ever see her?"

"Oh, no. That's a million miles back." Henny seemed so
remote, with her golden curls and blue hair ribbons. Would
Judith, David wondered, seem as remote ten years hence?

They reached Abe's car. "Strange," David said, "it's as if
you'd never been away."

Abe grinned. "What's a couple of years between friends?" He held out his hand.

"Can I—" David stopped, embarrassed at appearing too eager, and began again. "Can I see you sometime?"

"What a foolish question." Abe laughed. "Come to dinner tomorrow. You'll meet Gwen."

Although David was usually late for appointments, the next day he arrived at Abe's house—it was part of a huge complex called London Terrace—fifteen minutes early. He walked around the block. It was a long time since he had looked forward to an evening so keenly.

Gwen greeted him like an old friend. "Abe's told me so much about you," she said. She was a pretty girl whose diminutive features reminded him of Debbie, except that her coloring was fair and her hair was a light brown. He liked the sound of her voice and was fascinated by her clipped Scottish accent. She gave an impression of fragility, yet she obviously had a mind of her own. Her father, who owned a bar in Edinburgh, had been horrified at her wanting to marry a Jew, but had been unable to change her mind. "The way my folks carried on," she said, "you'd have thought the world was coming to an end. Now they love him. Can you figure people out?" She smiled. "And *his* parents! The first time they visited, I went to all kinds of trouble to prepare a kosher meal. How was I to know they eat ham when nobody's looking."

David did not talk much. He felt no desire to assert himself or to make an impression. On the contrary, it was enough for him to be with Abe and Gwen, feeling protected and content. The living room was furnished in what Abe called Swedish modern—walnut cut in straight lines and planes. The wall over the couch was enlivened by a reproduction of Toulouse-Lautrec's poster of Jane Avril. There were no curtains. "Abe doesn't like them," Gwen explained. "He says they gather dust."

At one point, David could feel Abe's eyes on him, probing. "You've changed," Abe said. "You're quieter now."

"Maybe I'm more serious," David replied. "Besides, I have to get used to you again."

It was past eleven when he got up to go. He wanted very much to come back, but did not know how to say it.

Abe said it for him. "Some friends are coming Saturday night. Why don't you join us? Around eight."

"Sure." It occurred to David that Abe would never know how glad he was to come.

The party on Saturday consisted of several young psychiatrists and psychoanalysts—David was not too sure of the distinction, but knew that there was one—and their wives or girl friends. The talk revolved around Freud and his doctrines, reminding him of what he used to hear in Judith's circle, except that the point of view here was clinical rather than academic.

The evening revolved around Dr. Adrian Kline, a short dynamic man in his early fifties who dominated the discussion. David could see that Abe and his friends looked up to him with a respect that bordered on veneration. Kline was a follower of Alfred Adler, the first of Freud's pupils to break with the master, and was spokesman for the Adlerian view that the central drive of the human personality was toward power—more accurately, ego affirmation—rather than sex. Kline's talent for presenting his ideas in terms accessible to the layman had enabled him to write several popular books on how to achieve happiness in our society. Happiness in his view depended on the degree to which an individual identified himself with his fellows. This, of course, was not easy to do in a society based on rugged individualism, where it was every man for himself. Rugged individualism, according to Kline, was not rugged at all. On the contrary, it was a neurotic concept that exposed all of us to that alienation from the group which had become the malady of the age.

Kline consequently rejected capitalism on psychological rather than moral grounds. A competitive society based on private property could only foster the most aggressive—that is, egotistical—impulses in human nature. Such a society afforded its members freedom, but the price was loneliness. Kline viewed the various types of mental illness as so many mechanisms of flight from the unbearable burden of man's aloneness. There could be no true happiness where each individual tried to get ahead at the expense of his fellows and of necessity remained indifferent to their fate.

The solution was simple: society had to find its way back to the collective goal. Only then would the gulf between the individual and the group, between the "I" and the "they" be bridged. This demanded the emergence of a new type— the social man whose personal destiny was inseparable from the destiny of the group, who found his highest fulfillment in serving his fellows. Such men were not unknown to history, from Isaiah and Christ to Gandhi and Schweitzer. Only when society consciously aimed at the development of the social man would the world rise above the sorry state it was in.

David listened, fascinated. "What about human nature?" he asked.

Kline had no patience with those who insisted that it never changed. Human nature was constantly changing. "You've only to look at Nazi Germany," Kline stated, "to see how easy it is to change people. After two thousand years of Judaeo-Christian morality, Hitler is raising a new generation of monsters who stand completely outside its teachings, and who will be capable of deeds such as the world has never known. If mankind is to have a future," Kline concluded his disquisition, "we'll have to find a way to combine the best features of socialism and bourgeois democracy. On the one hand economic security, on the other personal freedom."

"That's a big order," David said. "Can it ever be attained?"

Kline shrugged. "Could a peasant of the tenth century in his wildest dreams have imagined what our world would be like? That's how little we can imagine what the world will be like five hundred years from now. I'm an optimist. I believe anything is possible for man to achieve."

Abe's friends, David noticed, were not a drinking crowd. They helped themselves to a punch of fruit juice spiked with brandy and benedictine. At eleven Gwen brought out platters with cold cuts, cole slaw, and rye bread. Shortly before midnight, Dr. Kline left, and the others soon followed. Abe walked David to the subway. "Did you enjoy yourself?" he asked.

David nodded. "I liked your friends. Especially Dr. Kline." Overcoming his shyness, he added, "What I really liked was being with you and Gwen."

He wanted Abe to invite him again; it occurred to him that he could do the inviting. "How about both of you coming out to the beach tomorrow? It'll be a hot day," he added, as if that were the reason for the invitation. "My parents'll want to see you too."

"Fine. I've some time off in the afternoon, and Gwen loves to swim." Abe thought a moment. "Davey, it's good to see you again. I often wondered what happened to you all these years."

"Nothing happened. At least, not much." David had a sense of pulling down the shade so that no outsider could peep in.

2

LISA scrutinized Abe. "How you've changed. The boy became a man."

Abe looked sheepish. "And such a pretty wife," Lisa continued, looking Gwen over. "A nice Jewish girl. I'm glad you didn't marry a *shiksa*."

It was too late to warn Lisa that Gwen was not Jewish. Fortunately she was speaking Yiddish. "I don't believe in mixed marriages. At first everything is sweet and rosy. Just one quarrel, and she'll call you a dirty Jew."

"Ma, Gwen isn't Jewish."

"So why didn't you tell me?" Lisa asked, undaunted.

Abe turned to Gwen. "David's mother doesn't think mixed marriages can last."

Gwen laughed. "Tell her ours is an exception."

Lisa changed to English, choosing the words carefully. "How you say?—from your mouth to God's ears." Having cleared up the gaffe, she reverted to Yiddish. "A doctor? Your mother must be proud of you."

Abe shrugged. "I guess."

"Are there many Jews in Edinburgh?" Joel asked.

"Not as many as in New York."

"They speak Yiddish?"

"I didn't hear any."

"Do the people there hate Jews?" Lisa asked.

"Not at all."

She looked pleased at this bit of information, but started off on a new tack. "I'm glad you've come back," she said to Abe. "I remember how upset David was when you weren't his friend any more."

"Ma, you're embarrassing me."

"What's so embarrassing about missing a friend? He must have missed you too." To Abe, "Am I right?"

Abe grinned. "Of course."

"You see? Right away he's embarrassed."

Later, David rounded up some towels for the beach. They settled by the breakwater, where it was less crowded. Gwen, rubbed suntan oil on her arms and legs, and stretched out on her towel.

"Your mother's amazing," Abe said. "A bundle of energy."

"She can wear you out," David answered, "if you let her."

"The years haven't changed her, except her hair's grayer."

"Each year she finds another remedy against aging. The latest is raw carrots."

"Your dad's as gentle as ever. How she dominates him."

"She leads, and he follows. It's a perfect match."

"Dr. Kline had an idea." Abe began quietly. "He runs a clinic for disturbed children, I help out too. For some time we've been saying the kids ought to have music in some form or other. He thinks you could do it for us. Would you?"

David was about to say, "I'm not up to it," but changed to "It's not anything I know about."

"What's your objection?"

"It's that I've been—" David stopped. "I just don't feel like getting involved."

"You have to get involved," Abe said, "otherwise you're not alive. Besides, it'll give us a chance to see each other."

"And when you're through I'll give you dinner," Gwen added.

David was touched by her friendliness. "In that case . . ." He was suddenly glad to give in.

That week Abe introduced him to the clinic, which was housed in a dilapidated brownstone on East Seventeenth Street. Here Dr. Kline applied his theories about the social man. Toys were shared by several youngsters together. Everything possible was done to connect the individual with the group. Dr. Kline spent an hour with David outlining his plan. "Abe tells me you've been teaching the piano. That's not what I have in mind. I want to use music as a group activity. How can we go about it?"

David suggested that they form a rhythm band. He described the various noisemakers available, from triangles and toy cymbals to small drums and bells. Dr. Kline was delighted. He promised to have the instruments ordered, and showed David a fair-sized room on the second floor with a piano in it, that could serve as a classroom. The first session was set for the following Friday.

While he was with Kline, the prospect of the rhythm band had exhilarated David, but by the time he reached home the glow had faded. Why had he allowed himself to be talked into this scheme? He really didn't have any interest in facing a roomful of crazy kids. The old disquiet came over him. Whichever way he turned he faced an impasse. If he said no, he would be letting Abe down. If he said yes, he would be taking on a host of obligations he dreaded. The sense of peace he had enjoyed in the past weeks was destroyed. Self-reproach was followed by guilt, which in turn brought on depression. It was an unnerving experience to find himself traveling that familiar road. Finally, on Thursday, he could hold out no longer. He telephoned Abe to say that, so far as he was concerned, the project was off. Abe listened and asked him to come over that evening.

Gwen was out when David arrived. He tried not to show Abe how upset he was. They settled in the living room, and David reiterated his stand. He had hoped to keep the less wholesome side of himself hidden from Abe; now he had been put in a position where he could no longer conceal it. He resented Abe's role in this and for the first time since their reunion felt unfriendly toward him.

Abe heard him out. "Look, Davey," he said when David had finished stating his case, "no one's trying to force you into anything you don't want to do. Though I would like to say, as your friend, that it might do you a lot of good to get involved. It would pull you out of yourself."

"Do I strike you as needing that?"

Abe was diplomatic. "All of us do, we're too much concerned with ourselves." His tone was disarming. "All I can tell you is that it would be a defeat for you to withdraw."

"Why?"

"You've fallen into the habit of saying no to things. You should try saying yes for a change. You think you're giving me logical reasons for refusing. Actually you're just having an anxiety attack. You get rid of anxiety by overcoming it, not by giving in. As your doctor I can tell you—"

"You're not my doctor."

"True. All the same, you're thinking only that Kline needs you for this, which he does. You're forgetting that you need him just as much."

"Meaning—?"

"Meaning that people need each other." Abe leaned forward, his face intent. "Look, Davey, you're not signing a contract. If you don't like it, you can always pull out. But you shouldn't say no before you've even given it a try."

David said nothing. Abe gripped his hand. "I'd ask you to do this for me, but it wouldn't be right. Whatever you do, you should do for your sake, not mine."

Abe's deep fuzzy voice had a calming effect, as did his reasoning. David heard himself say, "I appreciate your interest."

"What kind of a remark is that?" Abe muttered. "It's like people saying, 'Thank you for thinking of me.'"

"It's wallpaper talk," David apologized. "Just covers space."

"Well, cut it out. I'll tell you what," he said in a tone of summing up. "Come to my office tomorrow at noon, we'll go over to the clinic. If you don't show up I'll be disappointed, but I'll understand. Fair enough?"

This was a reasonable offer. All the same, David was condemned to a sleepless night. He lay tossing about, torn between familiar pros and cons. Finally, when it was almost dawn, he reached some kind of equilibrium. If he awoke in time, he would go to Abe's office. If he slept through the appointed hour, that would be a decision of sorts too. He fell into a deep sleep, awoke at ten, and reached Abe's office just before noon.

Abe showed his delight. "I knew you'd make it," he said with a smile. "That's not quite true," he added. "I was hoping you would, which is not the same."

As it turned out, the moment David entered the classroom his apprehension vanished. He faced a dozen youngsters ranging in age from eight to thirteen; seven boys and five girls. Several watched him with interest, the rest were apathetic. The first thing, he decided, was to try to win them over. "How about listening to some music?" he asked, and sat down at the piano. He launched into *Columbia the Gem of the Ocean* in a vigorous march time, and asked them to count the beats while he played: One two three four, One two three four, with an accent on the first beat. At first only the older children did as he asked, but when he repeated the song, the younger ones joined in. Counting led to clapping, first on every beat, then on every other beat, finally on only the ONE. The clapping gathered strength, especially when it became part of a game: he divided the class into two teams, boys against girls, the girls clapping every other beat while the boys marked the ONE. This took a little practice, but in the end the rhythmic patterns were performed with gusto. Excitement mounted when David distributed the percussion instruments that Dr. Kline had ordered and the rhythm band took off on its initial flight. The session lasted for an hour and a quarter, at the end of which David was as buoyed up as his pupils.

"How did it go?" Abe asked afterward.

"I had a grand time," David confessed, "and I think they did too. I hate to think I almost passed it up."

Abe still had the habit of sucking in his lower lip when he was pleased. "So what did I tell you?"

"Doctor, I'm sorry I made all the fuss. And I promise," David added contritely, "not to do it again."

Abe grinned. "You will. But I won't pay attention."

3

EVENTUALLY David expanded the rhythm band and added a small chorus that sang folk songs from around the world. The youngsters responded with enthusiasm, which encouraged him to add a listening group once a week; the half hour was devoted to a piano piece that he played himself, prefac-

ing it with remarks about the composer and the music. Dr.
Kline came by one afternoon and told David that this was
precisely the kind of program he had envisioned.

In the evening, David often joined Abe and Gwen for
dinner. They also began to see each other over the weekend. Much of their talk was devoted to the clinic, but Abe
also liked to hold forth on the state of the world. His political outlook had been shaped by Dr. Kline, who divided
the legacy of Freud and his disciples—like Gaul—into three
parts. Central was the work of the master who so brilliantly
uncovered the nature of the bourgeois family. To the right
was the mysticism of Jung, whose emphasis on the racial
unconscious fit in, whether he intended it or not, with Nazi
thinking. To the left was the teaching of Adler, whose view
of the individual in society led from Freud, in a roundabout
way, to Marx.

Abe was the typical fellow traveler. He saw the world as
a perpetual battleground between the haves and the have-
nots. Since he had very little contact with workers, he did
not have to reckon with the realities of the class struggle.
Instead he gave himself with a kind of messianic fervor to
the vision of a society that took from each according to his
ability and gave to each according to his need. The most
attractive feature of this community, once the dictatorship
of the proletariat had accomplished its aim, was the gradual
withering away of the state. Abe's convictions verged on
religious faith, combining as they did Isaiah's prophecies
concerning the lion and the lamb with Christ's strictures
against the rich, and leavening both with the dream that
had engaged utopian writers from Sir Thomas More to
Edward Bellamy. He considered Lenin one of history's great
men, but mistrusted Stalin and was shocked by the assas-
sination of Trotzky. "Lenin would turn over in his grave,"
he announced sadly.

David loved to listen to his harangues, even if every so
often he let himself be lulled by the drone of Abe's voice
instead of attending to what he was saying. "There's one

big difference between us," he told Abe. "You're a political animal and I'm not."

"You should be. How else d'you expect to understand what's going on around you?"

"I first have to solve my own problems, then I'll tackle the world's." He smiled at Abe. "You know why we don't agree on politics? You're religious and I'm a non-believer."

Despite his conviction that capitalism was on its last legs, Abe was extremely career-minded. David considered this a contradiction. "If the system's going to pot, why do we have to adjust to it?"

"It'll probably last our lifetime, so we might as well be comfortable. Look, Davey, there's only two ways for a man to fulfill himself. Through love and through work. I don't see you doing either."

"I'm resting."

"From what?"

For once it did not seem important to David to hide the fact that he had been ill. "I've had a bad time, Abe, so I'm taking it easy."

"I realize that. But it's also important to get back into things."

"You don't seem surprised."

"We never tell a friend what he hasn't already figured out for himself. You want to talk about it?"

"Not particularly."

"Did you have someone to help you?"

"Not till you came along. That was my lucky day."

Abe smiled. "We'll do better yet."

"Don't push me."

October was the time of year when David began to worry about the coming season. Would his students come back to him? Would he find new ones? He expected he would muddle through somehow; however, Abe was hectoring him to seek a teaching post in a college or university. "It's ridiculous for you to be teaching little girls in Brighton Beach."

"They're not all girls. It leaves me free to read, to think, to do as I like. Why tie myself down?"

Abe attacked from another angle. "You're traveling third class, and you could do better. If you had a job, you could get out of Brighton Beach. You shouldn't be living at home any more."

David protested that he wasn't living at home.

"But you haven't broken away," Abe countered. "You teach there, you have meals there, it's still your base. You've got to learn to stand on your own feet."

"My feet ache."

"Very funny. Everybody's feet ache. We still have to stand on them."

After much discussion, David agreed to ask Elena Parissot if she could help him get on the staff of the music school. He was distressed at the prospect of asking a favor of his old teacher, but Abe hammered away at him until he telephoned her.

She received him in the blue-velvet housecoat he remembered so well. Except that she was a trifle stouter, she had not changed. Her blue-black hair was piled in its usual mound, she was heavily rouged, her aquiline features more than ever resembled a Roman emperor of the decadence. She took his hand and leaned forward to be kissed, meanwhile kissing the air near his left ear.

"David, what a pleasure to see you! I've thought of you so often." She smiled coquettishly. "And what have you been doing?"

He went on a bit about the work he was doing at the clinic, but could see that she was not interested.

"You were very talented," she finally said. "I was so disappointed when you decided not to go ahead."

"The odds were too great," he replied. "After all, who of your students has made a career?" This was the wrong thing to say, but she had put him on the defensive and he could not help striking back.

"My dear," she said smoothly, "one can never guarantee

these things. It's not only the talent that decides. You have to have luck and a hundred other things. Having some money behind you doesn't harm either. And you have to want it so badly that you'll keep trying no matter what. Well, it's over and done with"—she threw up her hands in a Gallic gesture—"so we'll never know what you might have achieved. Let me give you some tea."

She reappeared wheeling the little serving table that was laden with her pretty tea things and a plate of French pastries. David inquired after Maman.

"She's getting on. Aren't we all?" Miss Parissot sighed, and poured.

It was time to come to the point. David drew a breath. "The reason I asked to see you—" he began.

"Whatever it was," she interrupted, "I'm so pleased you did. We had such lovely times together, you and I."

This lady was a tough customer, David decided, but he was determined not to let her deflect him. "I need a job," he said quietly, "and I thought you might recommend me for one at the school."

"I'll be delighted," she answered in her most sincere manner, and smiled lovingly. David knew then and there that she had no intention of helping him. "Of course, it won't be easy. We have a new director and he's brought in his own people. I'll try, naturally, but you must not expect too much." She lifted the plate of pastries. "Have one, my dear. They're delicious."

Long ago she had appealed to his loyalty when he thought of leaving her for another teacher. But that was when there was still a possibility that he might be useful to her. She was obviously not one to waste her affection where she would get no return. Yet he realized that he must not judge her too harshly. With a new director in charge, she was probably too unsure of her own position to intercede for him.

They chatted until she glanced at her wrist watch. "Oh, I've a dinner engagement!" She sounded exactly as she had years ago. David rose; she accompanied him to the door. "It was wonderful of you not to forget me. You *will* come again soon, no?" Her unnatural emphasis on *will* made it plain that the invitation was not to be taken too seriously.

They embraced. David walked down Broadway, reviewing the visit. Apart from her music, he decided, she was a complete phony. How strange that he had never realized it before.

At Abe's insistence he wrote two dozen letters to the music departments of various colleges, setting forth his qualifications and applying for a job. He considered this effort as unlikely to produce results as his visit to Miss Parissot, but wanted Abe to feel that he was trying.

He received a number of form letters advising him that there were no openings at present but his application would be put on file. Suddenly an answer came from a junior college in Montana that he was being considered.

Abe was jubilant. "I told you something would come of it!"

"Montana?" David made a face. "Where's that?"

"What's the difference?"

"But it's so far."

"Far from where?"

"From New York, of course."

"What's so wonderful about New York. It's not as if you've been so happy here."

David was about to say, "How d'you know?" but decided to ignore the remark. "New York is the only country I have. Besides, Gwen and you are here."

"Then look for a job in New York," Abe said. "Maybe one of your professors at college could help."

"They were old farts." David remembered his little English professor. "All except one. He sat on his desk holding his ankle and spouting Browning. I played at his house a couple of times."

"Well, try him."

The letter to Professor Sheldon began in time-honored fashion with "I don't think you'll remember me but . . ." Abe read it through and said, "Send it. All you can lose is a two-cent stamp."

To David's amazement, the professor wrote back. He remembered David very well, he said, and would very much like to see him. When they met, he peered up at David. "I wouldn't have recognized you," he said softly, "but I remember you wrote a nice composition about Isaiah."

He looked browner and more wrinkled than David remembered, and seemed littler; but his eyes were as bright as ever. He led the way into the living room, where nothing had changed. The overstuffed sofa and chairs looked as heavy as ever, and on the huge sideboard the Chinese courtier and lady in their ivory costumes maintained their obsequious stance.

"It's been a long time," the professor said as they sat down. "How old are you now?"

"Twenty-six."

"You were eighteen then. What have you been up to?"

"It's a long story," David said with a smile. "I remember the last time I was here. I came with a violinist friend of mine, we played chamber music."

"He was not pleasant," the professor said. "What happened to him?"

"We lost track of each other."

"That's just as well," the professor said. "This is my last semester at the college. I'm retiring. Would you believe it, I've been there forty years."

David nodded.

"Success is doing what you enjoy and getting paid for it," the professor continued. "I loved English literature, I loved teaching, and I made a living at it. What more could I ask?" He mused a moment. "Besides, some of my students became pretty good writers. It's nice to know I helped get them started. I was reading Santayana's essay on beauty this afternoon. He makes some interesting points." Without a transition, "I remember your music," the professor said. "Why don't you play for me?"

David was about to explain that he was out of practice, but changed his mind. "What would you like to hear?" he asked, and struck some chords on the square grand. It was still a trifle out of tune.

"Beethoven."

He had not seen the notes of the *Pathétique* in two years, but they came back to him as he played. Except for an occasional slip, he went through the first movement smoothly enough and followed it with the soulful Adagio. "It's lovely to hear music in a room," the professor said. "So much more personal than in a concert hall." Changing the subject, "You asked to see me. What about?"

Caught off guard, David blurted out, "I need a job. And thought you might help me."

The professor showed no surprise. "There's not much music at the college. Should be more," he mused. "Let me call Professor Heinz and ask him to see you."

"Would you?"

"Why not? We need talented young men. You're talented, aren't you?"

David smiled. "I'm not so sure."

"Well, I am."

When David described the visit to Abe, he said, "Sheldon was so much more real than Parissot. That bitch!"

"You were reluctant to go." Abe's face showed his pleasure. "See how well it turned out?"

"I've been meaning to tell you something," David said.

"What?"

"Thanks."

"For what?"

"For . . . everything."

"Not so fast. You'll thank me if something comes of it."

"That's not what I'm thanking you for."

Abe grinned. "What did I do?"

David thought a moment. "You want to know what you did? There was a wall around me. It had gone up a long time ago. You put out your hand, and the wall came tumbling down."

"That's the name of a song, no?"

"A Negro spiritual."

"It's my turn to tell you something, Davey. When I ran into you on the boardwalk and asked you over, I didn't think you'd show up. Then when I asked you to come to the clinic, I didn't think you would. If you hadn't, the wall would still be there, because I couldn't have reached you. So it's you who did it, not me."

"Thanks anyway."

"You're welcome," Abe said, and sucked in his lower lip.

TWO

1

Now that she had left youth behind, Lisa strove for the mellowness she associated with middle age. There was a wisdom that came with relinquishing people and things. Her two older sons were married—that meant, in the hands of the enemy. Her youngest, the child of her love, had failed her, but she had made her peace with that. Her husband, she was finally convinced, loved her and had eyes for no other, although he still needed a firm hand to guide him. Only her daughter, her Aniushka, was wholly hers. Of her grandchildren, only Annie's offspring really interested her; the others belonged to their mothers, with whom her relations were on the order of an armed truce. The wives of Joel's cronies were still a pain in the neck. When they met her on the boardwalk, they would say, "We give you credit, Mrs. Gordin," especially when she wore an outfit that was a shade youthful. "What do they think I am, ninety years old?" Lisa hurled the rhetorical question at Annie and indulged in one of her rare vulgarisms: "They can kiss me where the Jews had a blister."

She treated David, as she put it, with silk gloves. Their quarrels had left a painful memory; that terrible time must never return. She loved him as much as ever, of course; a Jewish mother loved her children no matter what they did. But the time had come for each of them to leave the other in peace. He had his life to lead, and it was not up to her to tell him how. She never mentioned Judith to him, or his bout with pneumonia; she sensed that there was more to the story than she knew, and she preferred not to know it. It was fashionable nowadays to blame the parents, especially the mother, if a child didn't turn out as you expected. She had no patience with this kind of thinking.

The old fire was there; she still needed to dominate, to hold the loyalty and attention of those about her. But a new enemy faced her—insomnia. As soon as her head touched the pillow she came awake, no matter how tired she was. She tried all the accepted remedies—a glass of warm milk, a hot tub, counting sheep, pleasant thoughts—except, of course, a sleeping pill, which she considered as unwholesome as rouge and hair dye. She read through the night while Joel slept peacefully beside her, and did not doze off until dawn. Then she slept fitfully for a few hours and wandered through the next day in a haze. Mostly she read Russian, but of late she had turned to books in English, even though she still quoted Chekhov's dictum about its being a language for horses. Isadora Duncan's *My Life* made an indelible impression upon her. The great dancer struck her as the kind of free spirit every woman should aspire to be. She summed up Isadora's life tersely: "She felt much and suffered much."

Lisa gave much thought to the nature of love, although she now viewed the subject from the standpoint of the menopause. She had no patience with women who filled the air with lamentation over their change of life. The woman's role in sex, she held, should be veiled in mystery; that was the best way for her to retain her allure. It followed that the less she told the man about her problems, the better. The important thing was never to disappoint him. If you weren't in the mood, you pretended. How else prevent his fancy from straying? A woman's change of life therefore changed nothing as far as lovemaking was concerned. She couldn't have any more children, but that wasn't such a bad thing, come to think of it. In any case, love and the passion that went with it remained the same. Or almost.

She was growing more and more religious. Each year she added a few observances that she had been lax about before. She was deeply disturbed when she heard that a neighbor had died. "Why do you take on so?" Joel said, "you barely knew the woman." Lisa replied with a Russian proverb: "When the lambs are shorn, the sheep tremble." While Joel and she were young, no one of their acquaintance died; now it happened more and more often. "It's a strange thing," Lisa would say, "people are dying who never used to."

How would she manage the big leap into the hereafter? She tried to picture herself on her deathbed. What would she die of? When? Since she was older than Joel, she assumed that she would go first. Would he mourn her? How long would he remain a widower? And what sort of woman would he marry? She knew that such thoughts were morbid but couldn't help thinking them. A recurrent dream disturbed her. She came back from a journey wearing the long black dress with puffed sleeves that she had brought from Russia. When she reached the door of their house, Joel came out but failed to recognize her. "Who are you?" he asked. "Why don't you go away?" She awoke, sobbing.

She became increasingly prone to accidents; they were usually caused by her impetuosity in moving about. On one occasion she broke her ankle as she stepped off a sidewalk, and was laid up for a month. She reached up to the kitchen closet and opened the door too hastily, whereupon a plate fell out, struck her in the mouth, and injured her gums. As she entered the subway, a door swung open unexpectedly and hit her in the shoulder; she had to wear her arm in a sling. And so it went. "I could swear you're punishing yourself with all those accidents," Joel insisted. "What a crazy idea," Lisa retorted and gave him a fishy look.

After a bout with influenza she went off to regain her strength in Lakewood, then at the height of its popularity as a winter resort for New York Jews. Two days later Uncle Mischa died. There had been no contact between Lisa and her brother since her final quarrel with Aunt Bessie. Joel was in a quandary: should he summon her back for the funeral? He consulted David; they decided not to interrupt her convalescence. The pine-scented air would do her more good than the trip to the cemetery in Queens.

Uncle Mischa was buried on a raw day; the icy wind persuaded Joel and David that they had made the right decision. When Lisa returned from Lakewood neither of them mentioned what had occurred. It was a cousin who revealed the truth. Lisa exploded. "My brother dies, and you let me enjoy myself in Lakewood? Woe is me!" Her eyes flashed fire, her nostrils quivered with rage. "Idiots, both of you! You should have your heads examined!"

Joel had not foreseen this reaction. "We meant well," he answered feebly. "You were sick, we wanted you to get well. Was that so terrible?"

"He was my last surviving brother. And you let him be laid in the earth without my being there?"

"What if you had been? Would you have brought him back to life?"

"I'd have paid him the last respects, which because of you I didn't do. For shame!" (She used the Yiddish idiom, "A shame and a disgrace!") She pressed her hands together in anguish. "I will never forgive you. Or myself!"

For weeks she flagellated herself with reproaches, refusing to be consoled. She dragged out the picture album with the green plush cover and spent hours staring at the photographs of her kin. Her brother Yuri, the millionaire convert, whom she had not heard from since the war. Her brother Adolph, who fell apart on the esplanade beside the

Black Sea. Now poor Mischa, who had been so kind to her when she was a little girl. And the two idiots in her life did not realize that she would want to be at his funeral. How could anyone be so insensitive to her needs?

Joel was finally able to persuade her that he had meant no harm. She shook her head sadly. "You say you love me, you pretend to understand me. But you don't have the faintest notion of what I'm like. And you never will."

2

THE civil war in Spain had a devastating effect on Abe. "You don't understand what this means," he told David. "If Hitler and Mussolini win here, they'll think they can win everywhere. Spain is the dress rehearsal for what's coming."

People were beginning to go to parties to raise money for the Loyalists. Dr. Kline decided to organize a benefit at the clinic. He wanted some musical numbers on the program and asked David to participate.

"I couldn't say no to him," David confided to Abe, "but I really don't want to."

"Why not? It's a good cause."

"I know. But I don't feel like playing again. All that's behind me."

"Davey, stop giving me a hard time. You'll play, and what's more, after it's over you'll be glad I made you do it."

There was no wriggling out of the situation. David drew out three mazurkas of Chopin and the Ballade in G minor, and worked at them an hour each day.

Abe had persuaded a soprano he knew, Louise Kerner, to take part in the program. She lived in London Terrace, on the same floor as Abe and Gwen. David was to accompany her, and went to her apartment for a rehearsal. She was an attractive brunette who had the singer's habit of underlining what she said with the expression on her face, so that you saw what she meant even as you heard it. David judged her to be about thirty, the kind of bosomy girl who was always trying to lose five pounds. Her eyes were large and wide apart; drama lurked in their amber depths. She sang the final notes of Schubert's *Death and the Maiden* with a dark resonance that was positively spectral, and was equally at home with the gay lyricism of *Hark, Hark, the Lark!* The Schubert group was followed by two great songs of Schumann—*Ich Grolle Nicht* and *Am wunderschoenem monat Mai.* Never having accompanied singers before, David was surprised to find that he did it well. He enjoyed playing for Louise for the same reason he had enjoyed duets with Debbie: she had a fine sense of rhythm. She never dragged out a note for its own sake but felt it as part of the phrase.

The concert was scheduled for a Sunday evening. On the night before, David's mood changed; he was suddenly thrust back into the state of anxiety he remembered from his illness. He could not think clearly; depression pulled him down. He turned his resentment against Abe, who said, "Davey, listen to me. You keep wanting to run away, which is understandable. But you have to realize there's no place to run to. Except maybe death or insanity, and I don't think you want either."

"What I want is to be left alone. Is that too much to ask?"

"As a matter of fact, it is. Besides, it's not even what you want, or you'd never have stuck your head outside that wall."

"I want you to let me off having to play."

"I can't and I won't." Abe's fuzzy voice suddenly took on a firmness. David realized that one of them would have to give in, and it wasn't going to be Abe.

As it turned out, the concert went well. The main hall in the clinic was packed. To his astonishment, David felt no apprehension as he came out to play. He understood why. He was appearing for a cause that extended far beyond the confines of music. Thus his playing was no longer the issue.

He began with the three Mazurkas. There was a quality of caprice about these short pieces that verged on coquetry. The Ballade was another matter. Here Chopin became the epic poet who painted on a large canvas. David was no longer on top of the difficult passages; he missed a note here and there, yet he knew he was communicating the essence of what Chopin intended, which was all that mattered.

He relaxed once Louise came on. In the Schubert and Schumann songs she did everything as she had worked it out at their rehearsal, yet she managed to sound as if she were doing it on the spur of the moment. After each song she smiled to him, and he knew that she was pleased with his accompaniment.

The concert was a success. "I'm glad you talked me into it," David told Abe. "I hate to think I almost pulled out."

Abe grinned. "Just remember that," he said, "for the next time."

The next day Professor Sheldon telephoned to say that he had set up an appointment for David with the head of the music department. He advised him to bring along an outline of a course he was prepared to give. David outlined a course on the history of opera. As he walked up the hill to the college, he remembered how impressive its towers had looked when he saw them for the first time. They seemed as beautiful now. The campus was exactly as he had left it; he recaptured something of the brightness of spirit of his college years. The light was muted in the great hall, whose arches seemed as shadowy and remote as ever. Professor Heinz was practicing the organ. David took a seat toward the back.

The rhapsodic opening of Bach's Toccata and Fugue in D minor floated through the empty hall with that reedy sound of which only the organ is capable. The professor gave a recital every Wednesday and Sunday afternoon, rain or shine, and had done so for years; the printed program David picked up announced the 1,367th. When the professor finished practicing, another gentleman hurried up to him and shook his hand. The two ascended the steps that led to a narrow door at one side of the stage. Professor Heinz stepped back and with a courtly gesture motioned to his companion to precede him, whereupon the companion stepped back and motioned for the professor to go first. They stood bowing and gesturing in this Gaston-and Alphonse routine as David walked toward the stage. By the time he reached the door the two men had passed through.

Professor Heinz received him in his office. He was a tall, surly gentleman with cold blue eyes that darted about under pink lids. His blond eyebrows were practically invisible, and his tight little mouth gave his face a petulant expression. He glanced through David's outline and dropped it on a stack of papers on his desk. "I don't understand why Professor Sheldon sent you," he said in a squeaky voice. "Nobody likes music at this college. Nobody wants it. There are no jobs."

David apologized for having bothered the professor and took his leave. He sat on the stone bench that curled around the flagpole in the middle of the campus and surrendered to his disappointment. The thing to do, he decided, was to write to that college in Montana before it was too late.

He reported the failure of his mission to Professor Sheldon, who told him to prepare another outline and go back for a second try. This struck David as strange advice, but he followed it. He prepared an outline for a course in the symphony and returned to the college a week later.

This time Professor Heinz was practicing for his 1,369th recital. The massive harmonies of Bach's Fantasia and Fugue in G minor resounded through the hall. At the end of the piece the other little gentleman appeared and shook the professor's hand. The two men climbed the stairs at the back of the stage, came to the side door and went through their act. David followed them and confronted the monster in his lair.

"Why d'you bother me?" Professor Heinz squeaked, making a sour face. "Didn't I tell you there's nothing for you?"

"Professor Sheldon thought you might like to see this." He drew out the outline and placed it on the desk.

Professor Heinz glanced through the sheets. "It's not bad, young man, but I already told you . . . If you'll excuse me, I have an appointment." He fled.

David decided that it probably snowed in Montana six months a year, night fell early, and he'd have to get used to it. He pulled himself to his feet, found a telephone booth and reported his new defeat to his mentor.

Professor Sheldon was as optimistic as ever. "Bother him again," he advised. "Bring him a new outline."

For his third assault David brought along an outline of a course on the history of piano music. This time Professor Heinz was practicing Bach's Passacaglia in C minor for his 1,371st recital. The magnificent theme floated up from the darkest realm of the pedals, enmeshed in the flowing lines of Bach's counterpoint. David listened, entranced. He watched the two old men go through their routine, and followed them. "You here again?" Professor Heinz squeaked.

"Professor Sheldon thought you might like to see this." David presented the outline.

Heinz handed it back. "Will you stop wasting my time?"

"I only thought—"

"It doesn't matter what you thought," the professor muttered.

"I'm sorry." He was tempted to add, "Excuse me for being alive."

He retreated to the flagpole and relinquished the lovely dream. Professor Heinz could go fuck himself. He hoped the job was still open in Montana. This time he decided to wait a few days before reporting to Professor Sheldon. No more outlines.

Two days later the telephone rang. David was astonished to hear the squeaky voice announce, "This is Professor

Heinz." It turned out that Alphonse had fallen ill. Could David take over his classes? Plus a survey of nineteenth-century music. David called Professor Sheldon immediately, who crowed, "What did I tell you?"

Lisa was enchanted. "My son the college professor," she said.

"Stop making a fuss," David admonished her. "I have to get out my notes and read up on the stuff. I've been away from it for years."

Over the weekend he went through the material. It seemed to him that the more he studied, the less he knew. On Sunday the familiar symptoms had returned. A dull ache pressing against his temples. A shapeless anxiety dragging him down. And binding these into a desperate whole, a desire to run off somewhere and hide. By the middle of the day he had decided not to turn up at the college the following morning.

He telephoned Professor Sheldon to tell him of his decision; the professor was out. Then he called Abe, who exploded. "For God's sake, will I have to come and get you tomorrow morning? I won't be able to." There was a pause. "Tell you what," Abe said. "Come over tonight, bring your books, you'll spend the night here. See how you feel in the morning."

David laughed, embarrassed. "You mean you'll take me to school?"

"If I have to."

The couch in their living room opened into a bed; David studied half the night. In the morning he still did not feel like going. Gwen made breakfast and gave him a second cup of coffee. Then Abe said, "C'mon, I'll run you up. I want to be sure you get there."

They took the West Side Highway uptown. The Hudson displayed its silvery sheen; lilac clouds floated over the Jersey coast, and the air was crisp. They passed Grant's Tomb, where Debbie and he used to walk after her lesson with Miss Parissot, and turned off the highway at 125th

Street. Soon the car passed through the mullioned gate of the college.

"I'm not getting out," David announced.

"Will you stop carrying on?" Abe parked the car, walked around to the other side and opened the door. "Are you coming out or do I have to drag you?"

"I'm scared stiff. I don't know the stuff and I'm not prepared."

"Just stay one step ahead of them," Abe reassured him. "That's all you need. Come on, Davey, will you?"

The corridors were filled with students on their way to class. Abe went with David to his classroom on the second floor. "An hour from now you'll be wondering why you wanted out." They reached the door. "Okay," Abe said, "tell it to them good."

Thirty sophomores stared at David. He introduced himself and called the roll. "I'm supposed to tell you something about music," he said, and on an impulse added, "By the way, what is music?" That opened a discussion, from which David extracted a viable definition: music was an art whose medium was organized sound. "And what is art?" One of the students came up with Tolstoi's wonderful definition: "Art is a human activity having for its purpose the communication to others of the highest and best feelings to which man has risen." Warming to his subject, David suddenly remembered Stravinsky's statement that music was powerless to express anything except itself—in other words, it had nothing to do with the communication of human feeling. This led to a spirited argument about the function of art.

He was soon chatting with the students as if they were friends. He could not help recollecting how forbidding his own professors had appeared to him when he was a student—"the sniffing of the unwashed"—and the enormous distance that had separated them from their students. His attitude toward the young men before him was the opposite. He was one of them, he spoke their language, he understood them and they him without any difficulty.

One of the students interrupted the discussion with "Why don't we hear some music?" David played the three mazurkas and the ballade. It turned out Abe was right; he couldn't understand why he had been so apprehensive. He was taken by surprise when the bell rang, the hour had passed so quickly. The students left; several clustered around him for additional questions. When they had gone, David remained at his desk, staring at the empty classroom. He felt a deep and quiet satisfaction.

In the crowded hallway he remembered that when he was at the college, only the faculty were permitted to use the elevators; the students had to walk. For the next hour he rode up and down as often as he could.

"Well?" Abe asked later.

"It was beautiful," David reported. "I had the strongest feeling that I had finally found the place where I belonged."

Abe grinned. "You're lucky, Davey. Most people never do."

3

Dr. Kline did not know much about music, but he had a clear idea of the role it could play in psychotherapy. He often came to David's class and sat chatting with him afterward. Their talks rarely took a personal turn. One afternoon, however, Kline mentioned the feeling of guilt that haunted many people. David could not help applying the remark to himself. "To what extent, doctor," he asked, "is one person responsible for another?"

Kline considered the question, relating it to his theory of the social man. He pointed out that in the highest sense we were all responsible for one another, although only the rare individual acknowledged the responsibility in full. It was this awareness that made a Florence Nightingale or Albert Schweitzer devote their lives to helping others. Yet many people seemed to have this quality in some rudimentary form. "Look at the millions of dollars spent each year on charity. A person writes a check to help someone he's never seen and will never know. He feels a little better for doing so—in other words, a little less guilty. Of course, it's also tax-deductible."

Before he knew how it happened, David had launched into an account of his involvement with Judith. He spoke quickly, anxiously, as though afraid that the doctor might stop him before he got the whole story out. He told it from Judith's point of view rather than his own. "I should have broken it off right away but I didn't see what I was getting into." When he reached their final quarrel and Judith's desperate act, a feeling of shame overcame him, but it was too late to turn back. At the same time he felt a deep sense of relief at having had the courage to unburden himself. "You see, doctor," he said, "if Judith had died, I'd have been responsible."

"But she didn't," Kline said. "Don't you see how neurotic it is for you to go around feeling guilty for something that never happened?"

"What you say is logical, but logic has nothing to do with the way we feel."

"True. You never told Abe any of this. How come?"

David thought. "I feel too close to him. I'd be embarrassed. Maybe I don't want him to see this side of me. He broke off our friendship when we were boys because I didn't measure up to what he expected of me. I don't want him to judge me again."

"You're extremely honest with yourself, David. It's most unusual."

"You mean, I don't try to kid myself?"

"Most people do. It makes things easier. As for Judith," Kline continued, "you have to realize that suicide is an abnormal act. There has to be a deep disturbance in the personality for someone to overcome the basic wish to live. She probably didn't think she deserved to be loved in the first place, and needed to be convinced of it. You fed that need. That's why she couldn't let you go. You, on the other hand, needed to be bolstered up by having someone completely in your power. So the two of you held on to each other. What's the definition of a sadist? Someone who refuses to be cruel to a masochist."

"But did I have to explode that night with such violence? I'm not usually a violent person."

"You exploded because you had bottled up your resentments too long."

"So it was my fault after all."

"Put oxygen and hydrogen together and they make water. It's neither one's fault, that's the way they are."

"Anyway, I cracked up, so I was punished."

"Had you come to me while you were sick, I might have found a way to help you. At least I'd have speeded your recovery. However, you haven't done badly. Most problems," Kline added with a smile, "don't get solved. They just go away after a while, provided you live through them."

Kline was leaving on a three-week trip to Mexico. He was to attend a conference in Cuernavaca, then he wanted to visit the Mayan ruins in Chichen Itzá. Abe and Gwen gave a going-away party for him, to which they invited several of his disciples and his wife. Audrey Kline was what Abe called a cold potato: a tall, blondish woman, handsome in a conventional way, who wore black in the evening with a single strand of pearls. She was not so much unfriendly as aloof; with her left elbow cupped in the palm of her right hand, arm against her chest, she nonchalantly fingered her pearls. People wondered what Kline saw in her. Abe had the answer: money. The doctor needed a rich marriage at the start of his career, and she was it. Kline was conspicuously attentive to her that night, placating her with *hon* and *sweetie* and occasionally holding her hand. David wondered if they had had a quarrel on the way over.

As usual, the doctor held forth on his favorite theories. He measured mental health by three criteria—an individual's adjustment to sex, work, and society. Sex involved the capacity for love, by which he meant a mature commitment to a person of the opposite sex. (He followed orthodox Freudian doctrine in regarding homosexuality as an adolescent fixation that most of us outgrew.) Work included success or failure in a career, and an individual's need to feel productive and useful. Third was the handling of friendships and participation in social activities; the feeling of being accepted—or rejected—by one's environment. "I consider any man in reasonably good mental health," Kline asserted, "who has a wife and children he loves, a job he enjoys and makes a living at, and a circle of friends he likes. As a matter of fact, not many of us can pass the test on all three grounds. You get through life tolerably well by succeeding in two of the three areas. One out of three makes you a doubtful case."

Later, they trooped across the hall to Louise's apartment, where the piano was. David accompanied her in three songs of Brahms and Grieg's *Ich liebe dich*, which she sang in English. He liked her voice, expecially its warm caressing quality in the lower register. She gave Grieg's melody the simplicity it needed, shaping the repetition of the central thought with a mounting intensity that he echoed in the piano part: "I love you, dear—I love you, dear—I love you, dear, now and forever!"

At midnight, Abe proposed a toast to the doctor's successful journey and another to David's career at the college. All in all it was a pleasant evening.

When David arrived to have dinner with Abe and Gwen some days later, he found Louise there. He enjoyed the meal, but after she left he suddenly grew suspicious. "Hey, are you trying to be a *schadchan?*" he asked Gwen.

She turned to Abe. "What's that?"

"A matchmaker."

"Whatever put that idea into your head?" she exclaimed,

then added mischievously, "And what if I am? You like her and she likes you, what's so terrible about bringing the two of you together?"

David decided it would take too long to explain. "I'm not quite ready for that sort of thing," he said.

"Haven't you rested enough?" Abe asked.

Now they were both being mischievous. David responded with an emphatic no.

"Okay, let's confess," Abe said. "Gwen and I are trying to figure out how we can get you out of Brighton Beach. The easiest way would be for you to move in with Louise. She's divorced, she's free, and you'd be living in Manhattan where you belong."

"What's wrong with Brighton? As my mother says, the air is better."

"That's what's wrong—she's there. And your dad. It's time you got away from them. Look, Davey, you have a job. The next step is Manhattan."

"There's always a next step. All I want is to stay put."

"Davey, the time has come. Stop arguing."

"Very well, find me a place and I'll move. But it's got to be near you."

"Suppose Gwen and I were not around."

David was suddenly jolted. "You're not planning to go away, are you?"

"No."

He was immeasurably relieved. "Okay, I'll find my own apartment."

On several occasions he had seen a sign outside London Terrace announcing that apartments were available. He inquired the following afternoon, and was shown a studio on the second floor with kitchenette and bath. It looked out on a court, the light was poor, but the price was right— fifty-two a month. "I made up my mind like that," he told Abe, snapping his fingers.

He stood surveying the empty studio. When he brought in some furniture, he decided, the place wouldn't look at all bad. It was little more than a hole in the wall, really. But it was his.

4

HE had spent the evening studying the lesson he was supposed to teach his counterpoint class the next morning. It was almost midnight when the telephone rang.

"Davey." Abe's voice was barely audible.

"Abe. Anything wrong?"

"Yes." Then, "Dr. Kline was killed in Yucatán. In an auto accident."

The breath left him. "When?"

"This afternoon."

"I'll be right over."

"Please."

The Brighton express did not run at that hour; the subway ride seemed to take forever. He was alone in the car. Ever since his long talk with the doctor, he had felt very close to him. It was impossible not to respond to Kline's aliveness, his insatiable curiosity, his intellectual energy. David tried to absorb the news of his death but couldn't. It made no sense.

At the apartment, Gwen answered the door. Abe was in the bedroom, a bathrobe over his pajamas, hunched over the side of the bed. He was chewing his lower lip. When he saw David his eyes filled with tears. "He was a wonderful man," Abe said brokenly. "I loved him. We all did."

"How did it happen?"

"Head-on collision with a truck. Someone was with him in the car. She was killed too."

"A woman?" David was startled by this bit of information. It lent the tragedy another dimension.

"What difference does it make? He's dead." Abe suddenly straightened. "It's unfair! People who have nothing to give live to a ripe old age, and someone like that—"

David sat down on the bed. What was there to say? He put his arm around Abe's shoulder.

"Most people live too long," Abe continued bitterly. "Their life is over but they go on because their heart doesn't know when to stop. But a man like Kline was just coming into his own." He slapped the bed savagely. "Everything was opening up for him."

Gwen brought two glasses of white wine. Abe refused, but David took his. "If he hadn't gone to Mexico—" He stopped, remembering Judith's statement that there was no conditional in history. We knew only what happened, not what might have, could have, or should have happened.

Audrey Kline had asked Abe to meet the train that brought back the body. David went with him to Grand Central, and watched as the coffin was transferred to a hearse. Another coffin was taken away.

"I wonder what she was like," David said.

"The newspapers never mentioned her name," Abe replied. "Someone saw to that."

The funeral was private, but Abe arranged a memorial program at the clinic. David played the dirgelike movement from the Sonata in D minor that Beethoven marked "slow and sad." He accompanied Louise in Brahms's *Von ewiger Liebe* and Strauss's *Traum durch dämmerung*. Then Abe read several passages from Adrian Kline's writings. He was too shy to read well in public, and his voice, always fuzzy, cluttered with emotion; but the grace of Dr. Kline's thought came through nevertheless. Audrey Kline as usual wore black. She sat through the program, handsome and aloof, fingering her pearls.

David thought about the contradiction between Kline's beliefs and actions. The doctor exalted mature married love as the highest good of which the heart was capable, yet apparently his own marriage had been a sham. He preached honesty and sincerity in emotional matters, yet he was a deceiver. How could he have presumed to find answers for others when he didn't have them himself?

It was possible for Dr. Kline to keep his love secret, David reflected, just as it was possible for Judith to turn on the gas and for him to swim out into the ocean without anyone being the wiser. Did everybody, he wondered anew, carry around a secret that would never be revealed? He thought of Dr. Kline and his woman as they must have been during their last days together, happy with each other, all barriers down, secure in the knowledge that no one knew where they were or what they were doing. One turn of the wheel, and the whole world knew. And judged. He wondered what thought passed through their minds as the truck crashed into them.

After the memorial program, he walked Louise home. She wore a black leather jacket, and kept her hands thrust deep into her pockets. David felt like talking. "Abe is angry," he told her. "He believes life has to have a meaning, and Dr. Kline's death flies in the face of that. Abe thinks I'm full of illusions about myself and the world, yet he's up to his neck in illusions. Some day he'll realize there is no plan or meaning, except what we invent to help us stay alive. Or face death. God, the soul, life after death . . . pure hokum. My father's an atheist, so I never had to free myself from those myths. I just grew up without them. It's a great advantage."

"Abe's very devoted to you," Louise said.

"I saved his life once, and he's saved mine, so we have a right to like each other." He enjoyed talking to her because she was straightforward; also, she was very feminine, but not in an aggressive way. "You're a fine musician," he said, glancing at her. Her face in repose had a sadness, but when she turned her eyes to him they were flecked with light.

"So are you."

"Most singers are so busy with voice production they forget the music, they squeeze each note and drag the tempo. You never do. You sound as if you have absolute pitch."

"No, only relative. For the kind of music I sing it's good enough."

They came to Seventh Avenue, and she took his arm as they crossed. At the entrance to London Terrace, she said, "Would you like to come up for a nightcap?"

He tried to sound casual. "I've an early class tomorrow, and I have to prepare for it. I'm just one jump ahead of my students."

"Why are you afraid of me?"

"What makes you think I am?"

"You've never called me. I was hoping you would."

She was not the kind to lie to. "As a matter of fact I *am* afraid. I find myself thinking about you sometimes. And I put you out of my mind."

"Why?"

"I had a bad experience—"

"Hasn't everyone?" She smiled.

"I know. But mine was pretty awful, and I'm just coming out of it."

"What you're saying is, you don't feel ready to get involved."

He nodded.

"When you feel like it, call me."

"I will," he said.

"I'll be happy to see you, if I'm around." She was not given to coquetry, for she added very simply, "I probably will be."

"You're lovely," he said, and, leaning forward, kissed her on the cheek. He was glad he had.

THREE

1

I KNEW something would turn up," Professor Sheldon said.

"It was luck."

"That's all it takes."

"How can I ever thank you?"

"For what? I lifted a phone. That's all I did."

"Oh, no," David said. "You made me go back and beat my head against a wall. And you gave me the courage to do it. That's very much."

The professor thought. "Someday you'll be in a position to do the same for someone else. That's how you thank me."

"A lovely idea."

"Let me give you some advice. There are only three things you mustn't do."

"Like what?"

The wrinkles deepened in the professor's brown face. "Don't ever lead a Communist demonstration. Don't ever get involved with the little girls in your class. And don't ever get involved with the little boys in your class. Follow these three rules and you'll do fine."

David laughed. "I'll remember."

The professor, who had turned seventy, retired in January. The college had been the center of his life for the better part of forty years; suddenly it was no longer there. He could not read much—his eyes were poor—and he had nothing to do except wait for Miss Pratt to return from her school. He was bored and restless. David had an idea. "You always wanted to play the piano," he told his mentor. "Why don't I teach you? You'll have a great time with it, I promise."

Thus the lessons began. The professor practiced three or four hours daily, then he took a walk and a nap; by that time Miss Pratt was home. Having dabbled at the keyboard for years, he made quick progress. From the easy pieces that Bach wrote for Anna Magdalena's notebook to Mozart minuets, a Beethoven sonatina, before long a Chopin waltz. The professor was delighted.

The lessons took place every Thursday. David arrived at five, and they went on until dinner time, when Miss Pratt and the professor's daughter joined them. Conversation revolved around two topics—gossip about the college and politics. The professor was a staunch Republican, as was Miss Pratt. They hated Roosevelt not for personal reasons but because he was a menace to the country. He was a traitor not only to his class but to the sturdy American values that their Maine forebears had cherished. Why would anyone of FDR's background coddle the poor and make the masses feel that this country owed them a living? The New Deal would erode the virtues of self-reliance and individual initiative that had made America great. The country was obviously headed for destruction, from which only Tom Dewey could save it. Although their remedies for the nation's ills were very different from Abe's, they were as confident as he that they had the answers.

After dinner, they repaired to the living room where the windows had not been opened for years. The sturdy mahogany pieces stood their ground, mute witnesses of a way of life that had vanished. Miss Pratt sat in the overstuffed armchair opposite the piano, her head bent over her knitting. David played Beethoven or Chopin; Miss Pratt thought Debussy too modern. When he finished she always said, "Thank you, David, that was lovely."

One night, after he had played, David had an inspiration. Turning to the professor, he said, "Why don't you read us something?" That inaugurated a series of performances. In the same tone in which for forty years, seated on his desk in Room 110 and nursing his ankle, he had declaimed the great English poets, Professor Sheldon now unloosed his gravelly voice upon their masterworks.

> Grow old along with me,
> The best is yet to come . . .

And in the same spot where for forty years he had stopped to explain to generations of freshmen what Browning meant, he now interpreted the poet's meaning for Miss Pratt, David, and—on those evenings when she joined them—his daughter. His voice became more impassioned when he tackled the Romantic poets:

> Oh lift me as a wave, a leaf, a cloud,
> I fall upon the thorns of life, I bleed!

Pausing, he described how Byron burned Shelley's body on the beach beside the Mediterranean, then returned to the impetuous *terza rima* of the "Ode to the West Wind." Shelley, Keats, Byron, Wordsworth, Browning—these were the poets he loved and understood. According to him, they had no successors.

Now that David had become his friend, the professor revealed his secret. Miss Pratt was not Mrs. Sheldon, as David had assumed. Mrs. Sheldon had been confined to an asylum for the past twenty-four years, whereupon the professor had returned to Miss Pratt, his childhood sweetheart. She and her brother had shared the apartment with the professor and his daughter, which gave the menage the respectable appearance it needed. As the professor pointed out, anyone so minded could have harmed Miss Pratt and him by reporting that they were living in sin. The brother ultimately moved to California and the professor's daughter was busy with her patients, so that Miss Pratt and he were now alone in the apartment; but at their age it no longer mattered what people said.

David repeated the story to Abe and Gwen. "They're so conventional," he summed up, "and respectable. Yet here they are, living openly together. Would you believe it?"

The romantic tale took an unexpected turn. Early in March the wife died; the professor and Miss Pratt decided to get married. He asked David to be a witness to the wedding, along with his daughter. On a windy Wednesday morning they rode down to City Hall in a hired limousine. Miss Pratt looked extremely elegant in a light-gray tailored suit, her unruly gray curls peeping out beneath a smart felt hat. She wore a corsage of two orchids. "It's a bit late for me to wear white," she said to David and smiled.

"Do you, Harold Sheldon, take this woman to be your lawful wedded wife?"

"I do," the professor replied in a low voice.

"Do you, Charlotte Pratt, take this man to be your lawful wedded husband?"

"I do," she said firmly.

David embraced the professor and kissed the bride. "Congratulations, Mrs. Sheldon," he said.

She beamed. "You're the first one to call me that. I had to wait thirty years to hear it"—she wiped away a tear—"but it was worth it."

He decided to bring the newlyweds a present. Given the professor's fondness for all things Chinese, the choice was not difficult. David had often passed a store on West Seventy-second Street that specialized in Oriental rugs and chinoiserie. There he found a lovely jade Buddha that would go well in the professor's living room. Unfortunately, it cost more than he could afford. On another shelf he discovered a brass Buddha with a paunch and a jovial smile. This, he decided, was the one.

"Isn't he a darling!" Mrs. Sheldon exclaimed when she saw the brass figure. David wanted to tell them why he had bought the gift, but shyness prevented him from revealing his feelings. Words like *gratitude* and *appreciation* could not express what he felt. "The courtier and his lady," he said, indicating the two figures, "will now have somebody to bow to." Whereupon Mrs. Sheldon placed the god in the middle.

"There's a lovely bit about Buddha," David went on, "in a song that was sung a lot when I was in high school." He thwacked out the triplet rhythm of the accompaniment to *On the Road to Mandalay*, and sang the lusty stanza from Kipling's poem:

> An' I seed 'er fust a-smokin' of a whackin' white cheroot,
> An' a-wastin' Christian kisses on an 'eathen idol's foot,
>   Bloomin' idol made o' mud,
>   What they called the great gawd Budd,
>   Plucky lot she cared for idols
>   When I kissed 'er where she stud.

When he got to "And the dawn comes up like thunder from China across the bay," he rendered the line with a great crescendo and tremolo in the bass. Then he raised his hands above the keyboard with a grand gesture and let them fall in his lap.

"Bravo," Professor Sheldon cried. His dark, little eyes, stuck in his wizened face like raisins in a cake, were aglow. It was as if he could see through David's façade to the darker space below. "You've become like a son to us," he said to David gently, "and we love you very much."

2

DAVID left the clinic with Abe. "Who's going to take Dr. Kline's place?" he asked. "You?"

"I can't." There was a silence. Then, staring at the ground, Abe said quietly, "I'm going away."

David stopped. "What's that?"

"I said I'm going away."

"Where to?"

"Spain."

"Abe!"

"They need doctors desperately. I finally decided." Abe looked at David in that nearsighted way he had. "You going to try to talk me out of it?"

"No," he said slowly, "not if you've made up your mind. Nothing I might say would change it." He felt uncertain. "There's another reason why I won't try . . . People pretend to be objective when all they're doing is defending their own interests. Judith was like that. She'd pretend she was giving you unbiased advice, yet all the time she was trying to get you to do what she wanted. Obviously it's easier for me to have you around. Which means that anything I might say would be tainted by the fact that I'm an interested party."

"Who's Judith? You never told me about her."

"Some other time. When will you be going?"

"Soon."

"What about Gwen?"

"She'll stay with her family in Edinburgh until I get back."

"Would you be going if Dr. Kline hadn't died? Maybe you're just restless and want to get away."

"I don't think so. If Dr. Kline had lived, we'd have gone together. Maybe I feel I have to go in his place. He believed in this struggle. I do too."

"Madrid, Barcelona . . . it all seems so far away. Don't you see what you're doing, Abe? You're putting your life on the line for an idea."

"What's wrong with that? We live in a time when ideas are fighting for control of the world. Don't you realize that?"

"Sure I do."

"Well, then, I want to play my part in the struggle. Not a big part, just a small one. Don't you?"

"I've already told you, I'm busy trying to solve my own problems. Once I do that I'll be ready to take care of the world's."

"Davey, we never solve our own problems. But if we're part of something bigger, they may solve themselves."

"Aren't you afraid of being killed?"

"My job's in a hospital."

"Yes, but bombs fall anywhere."

"Stop imagining things. A person has to take chances. We take a chance when we cross the street."

They walked in silence. "I'm trying to imagine," David said glumly, "what it'll be like without you and Gwen. I can't."

Later, Gwen asked him how he felt about the news.

"Terrible. And you?"

"It has to be, so there's no use my feeling one way or the other."

"Why didn't you try to talk him out of it?"

"You don't know Abe if you think I could. He'd never forgive me."

"Damnit!" The word burst from David. "What right has politics to interfere with our lives."

"It's not politics," Abe corrected him. "It's history."

When Abe's orders came through, they had what David called the last supper. Louise joined them, looking pretty in a wine-red blouse that set off her white skin and dark hair. Afterward the four of them went downstairs to inspect David's apartment.

The couch he had ordered had not yet arrived, but Abe

and Gwen's gift—a pine-wood table and chairs—had. In addition, Louise had installed her contribution—light-brown curtains and two woodcuts. David pointed to the corner opposite the window. "The piano will go here."

"Did your parents offer it to you?" Gwen asked.

"Not yet. As soon as the place is fixed up I'll ask them over. Once they see it they will."

Gwen turned to Louise. "Make sure he has someone in to clean at least once a week." To David: "When are you moving in?"

"End of the month."

They wound up at Louise's, where David played Abe's favorite piece, the first movement of the *Pathétique*. Then Louise sang some Schubert songs. By then it was eleven, and they had to stop—or anger the neighbors.

It was time to say good-bye. "I'll walk you to the subway," Abe said, and put on his coat. David kissed Louise and faced Gwen. He wanted to tell her how much her friendship had meant to him; but, as with the professor and his wife, a shyness inhibited him. So he simply looked into her eyes and kissed her. "Thanks . . . you've been wonderful," he brought out quickly. Then, retreating into a conversational tone, "As my mother would say"—he paused and added in Yiddish, "It should be in a good hour."

"What's it mean?" Gwen asked.

Abe translated.

"Amen," Gwen replied, and gave him another kiss.

Abe walked with him along Twenty-third Street. Neither spoke. Finally Abe did. "Say something."

"It's that damn fear inside me. I feel I'll never see you again."

"Davey, don't let your imagination run away with you."

David was embarrassed by his emotion. But why was it important to keep a stiff upper lip when it was so much more important to express to Abe something of the love and gratitude he felt? He took Abe's hand in his. "I wish I could thank you . . . for everything."

"You don't have to." Abe's eyes were upon him, round, nearsighted, full of affection.

"But I want you to know . . . I was in terrible shape when you came along. You helped me more than I can ever tell you." There, he had said it.

As when they were boys, Abe drew him close, put his cheek against David's and held it there; then he released him. "Go already," he said.

"You go."

"You're okay now, Davey. You'll make it." Abe sucked in his lower lip, and walked off. He reached the corner, turned around and waved. David waved back and went down the stairs to the subway.

3

THE couch finally arrived. Louise helped David put up two Van Gogh prints he had had framed. Now the place was ready. He invited his parents for the first Saturday in April.

The night before, Joel telephoned to say that Lisa had had another of her accidents. She was helping Mrs. Hershkowitz, the cleaning woman, and did so with such ardor that her foot caught in the rug. She had fallen and broken her arm. After much excitement the bone was set, but the cast was heavy and the doctor advised bed rest.

David hurried out to Brighton. On his way from the station he passed a flower shop and saw some huge vases filled with peonies. The blossoms were firm and round, their petals curving around the heart of the flower in various shades of pink. David scooped up a dozen, and the owner wrapped them in green tissue paper. Carrying the bulky bouquet in one arm David burst into Lisa's room and scattered the flowers over her bed. "You're crazy!" she said, but he could tell that she was delighted. He bent down and kissed her.

She pressed one flower against her cheek.

"Put them in water," she directed, "or they'll die." He found a pitcher in the kitchen, filled it with water, and arranged the long stems in a circle. The pitcher went on the sideboard and he sat down at the foot of her bed.

She bewailed her bad luck. "You'd think God held a grudge against me."

"Why would He do that, Ma?"

"Can I read His mind?"

"I don't think He even knows you fell."

"He knows everything."

"You're sure?"

She pondered that one. "Maybe He too is getting old."

She was impatient to recover. A cousin of Joel's was getting married that month, and she hated to miss the wedding. More accurately, she hated to miss an opportunity to confront Joel's family. She asked David to bring her a glass of milk. "It has calcium," she informed him, "which is good for mending bones." She sipped the milk, thoughtful. "As I lie here I go over my life and feel angry at the way it went. How I wish I could live it over again. There's so much I would do differently."

"I think you had a pretty good life, Ma. What more would you have wanted?"

Her eyes were lustrous and intense. "How can I explain it to you? A fire burned in me, to learn, to know, to turn the world upside down. I could have become somebody . . . achieved something."

"But you did, Ma. You were a wife and a mother, you raised children, you knew love."

She shook her head in disagreement. "That's not enough. I wanted more out of life, and now it's too late. But you taught me one thing."

"What?"

"I thought if a person is educated he can never be unhappy. You will laugh, but I really believed this. When I saw how miserable you were, I realized I was wrong."

David smiled. "Yes, you were wrong."

"A person has to have luck in this world. And he has to have—how shall I put it?—a talent for happiness. I don't think you have it, my son."

"I'm trying."

"Whatever it is you're looking for, I hope you find it. So that when you're older you won't feel as I do."

"All I want is to be me. That's not so hard to achieve."

"You're no longer angry with me?"

"No. Maybe I never really was."

She smiled. "I want you always to remember that your mother loved you very much. Maybe I didn't always love you the right way—who knows what the right way is? But I did love you."

David's eyes misted over. "There was a young king," she continued, "who called his wise men together and asked them to write the story of mankind. He had them locked in a special palace where they could work without being disturbed. After ten years he called them back and asked for the story, but they were only up to letter C. Ten more years, and they were up to H, and so it went. Now he was old and on his deathbed. He called them together and said, 'I wanted to know the story of mankind. You haven't finished, and I'll never find out what it was.' Then the leader of the wise men, who was more than a hundred years old, stepped forward, and said, 'O king, I'll tell it to you in a few words. They were born, they suffered, they died.' "

David remembered the conversation. It was their last.

That night she took a turn for the worse. By the time the doctor arrived she lay gasping for air; her breath came with a dry, rasping sound. The doctor said something about an embolism—a word unfamiliar to both Joel and David—and ordered an oxygen tent. When the equipment arrived, they were reassured; anything that looked so ponderous and cost so much was bound to help. It didn't. When the doctor returned in the morning he informed them that it would be all over in an hour; her heart was winding down. He opened his hands, palms up, and shrugged his shoulders to indicate that medical science was helpless before the inevitable.

David stood at the foot of the bed beside Joel. He could see her through the cellophane window of the oxygen tent; she seemed very little and very remote. Her head lay askew on the pillow, her face dark and haggard. She was breathing with difficulty, and a thread of spittle streaked her chin.

Joel turned to David, his blue eyes wide with anguish. "How can such a beautiful woman die?" he exclaimed, and David realized that his father was still seeing her as she had appeared to him the first time. She had always been so eager to look her best for him, not realizing that he saw her only as he remembered her. This was the miracle of love, in which she had never quite believed.

She turned her head to one side, as though looking for someone. It occurred to David that if she were still capable of thought, she would be thinking of his father rather than of him. He was astonished that in the presence of death he should have so petty a thought. Yet there it was, a jealousy he had scarcely been conscious of, that must have buried itself in his mind on that wintry day long ago when a stranger appeared at the end of the long ocean voyage and took his woman away from him. How small and helpless he was against his victorious rival. From subterranean depths there floated up the burning sense of betrayal that had haunted his childhood, finally revealing its true nature.

Lisa gave a deep sigh, and her heart stopped. Joel burst into tears, Annie sobbed, David turned away.

4

HE sat beside the bed. Lisa's nightgown had slipped to one side, leaving her shoulder bare. David reached out and touched it. Her body was still warm. For an instant it seemed to him that death was simply a continuation, another form of life. The moment passed and he knew. Everything that had made her the creature she was—fiery, life-loving, unpredictable, special—was finished. All that remained of her was this body, which would soon begin to decay. And the memory of her, that would survive in those who had loved her.

His eyes searched her face. So much had been left unsaid between them that now could never be said, so much undone that now could never be done. They had loved and hated each other, they had failed each other and done terrible things to one another. Death wiped the slate clean. He tried to remember what they had quarreled about, but could not. He could not even decide whose fault it had been. He had to be the way he was, she had to be the way she was, and the conflict between them had to be the way it was. How divide the blame? It no longer mattered.

He leaned forward a little. "I'm sorry, Ma, for every-thing that went wrong between us." He wanted to add, "Forgive me," but it made no sense because she no longer cared. On an impulse he bent over and kissed her on the shoulder.

Two men arrived with a wicker basket. They laid the corpse in the basket, pressed down the cover and took it away. David had gone into the other room. When he was a little boy he often had a feeling that she would go away and never come back. Now she had.

At the chapel, a plum-colored coffin stood up front. In accordance with custom it had been left open, so that Lisa's friends could pay their last respects. David thought it was barbaric to expose the dead to the prying glances of the curious, but no one else seemed to think so. Her head rested on a white satin cushion; she wore her blue dress trimmed with pink, as though she were trying even now to look younger. Her face was heavily rouged, the lips bright red, and David recalled that she had never used make-up, on the ground that it was bad for the skin. The mourners expressed

their grief in stock phrases: "She looks as if she were asleep
. . . She had everything to live for . . . May she rest in
peace."

David greeted relatives whom he had not seen in years.
Cousin Izzy had grown fat, done in by his gluttony. Cousin
Laibel's flowing silk tie and long hair—dyed jet black—still
proclaimed him the artist. He still thrust his face forward
as though begging you to like him. Mr. Levine and Cousin
Leah arrived with their three children. Levine had not seen
Joel since their chess game was disrupted by the argument
over Palestine. This was too solemn an occasion for bearing
a grudge; he went over to Joel and silently shook his hand.

Aunt Bessie was in tears. David suspected that they
flowed from guilt rather than grief. It occurred to him that
his mother, had she been in a position to do so, would probably have ordered her old enemy out of the funeral parlor.
Bessie was escorted by her son the doctor, who looked eminently satisfied with himself. Everybody treated her with
care, as one never knew when she might have her next
asthma attack.

Joel's family was represented by Cousin Gussie who lived
in Mount Vernon and was heard saying to Annie, as she
passed her hand languidly over her permanent wave, "It's a
funny thing, when I go in the subway I get a headache."
Several of Joel's fellow printers had turned up. Meyer Feinstein, with his white mane, looked very much the statesman. He would have loved to make a speech, but no one
asked him.

The family sat in the front row: Joel and David, Morris
and Willie with their wives, whom Lisa had detested; Annie
and her husband. The rabbi's eulogy was too long. Since
he had never known Lisa—Joel had briefed him the night
before—he couched his remarks in general terms that would
fit anyone: "A devoted wife and loving mother . . . who
kept her home in the true spirit of Israel . . ." David wished
the pious platitudes would cease. What if he went up to the
lectern, pushed the rabbi aside and said, "Better listen to

me, I really knew her. She was willful and brash, impulsive, domineering, and driven by aggression. She was also generous and warm-hearted, full of imagination and a lot of fun. I might have been better off never to have known her but, all things considered, I'm glad I did." What if he told them that?

The cortege passed along Brighton Beach Avenue to Sheepshead Bay and on to Queens. The burial plot was in a section of the cemetery reserved for the Jewish Workman's Circle, so that Lisa would lie in the vaguely socialist surroundings in which she felt at home. The old woman at the gate who asked for alms had the soul of a professional mourner; when the service began she burst into lamentation. The rabbi recited the prayer for the dead, the awesome Kaddish; the ancient Hebrew floated over the graves with a music all its own. "O God who art full of compassion who dwelleth on high, grant perfect rest beneath the shelter of Thy divine presence, in the exalted places among the holy and the pure. May their brightness enfold the soul of Lisa Gordin who this day has gone to her eternal home."

The rabbi pinned a black ribbon on each of the chief mourners—Joel, David, Morris, Willie, and Annie; he then cut the ribbon with a knife. This was a practical adaptation of the "rending of garments" mentioned in the Bible. The reference to sackcloth and ashes was mercifully ignored. The coffin was lowered into the grave. The rabbi poured the first shovelful of earth as he recited another prayer. The earth fell with a crisp sound on the wooden surface below. Joel wept quietly, Annie sobbed, David choked up. The rabbi glanced at his watch, the mourners returned to the waiting cars, and the cortege started back to Brighton.

Annie had prepared a luncheon. The table in the living room was laden with platters of whitefish, herring, hard-boiled eggs, cream cheese, lox, pumpernickel bread, and bagels. The fresh air at the cemetery had whetted Cousin Izzy's appetite. He fell to with a will and swilled mouthfuls of coffee between his teeth before swallowing.

Finally the company went. Annie cleaned up and left; Joel and David remained alone. The apartment seemed strangely quiet without Lisa; the chatter and excitement were gone. Joel sat in his favorite armchair near the piano. "Play something," he said.

David sat down at the piano. He glanced at his father. Joel's eyes were lusterless and his face was gray. "What would you like to hear, Pa?"

"Whatever you like."

David played his favorite nocturne of Chopin, the mournful one in E minor with the wide-ranging broken chords in the bass. How sweetly the music flowed from minor to major, from rebellious grief to acceptance and consolation. David was glad to be playing for his father, expressing through Chopin's emotion a host of feelings for which he had no words. What was he trying to tell him? He wasn't sure, but it had to do with the fact that he loved his parents and regretted having given them so much trouble. The music died away on a peaceful chord. David let the vibrations float into the stillness and lifted the pedal.

"That was beautiful," Joel said. "Your mother would have enjoyed it."

David was silent.

"How is your apartment coming along?" his father asked.

"Fine. It's not far from where you work. You'll be able to come over whenever you feel like it."

"Whenever I'm in the neighborhood?" Joel smiled.

"You know what I mean."

"Of course. I'll come often. In a few days I'll send you the piano."

"You're sure you want me to have it?"

"What would I do with it? It was bought for you and it's yours."

"Thanks."

"Is there anything else you'd like to have?"

"Not really." David glanced around and noticed the picture album with its faded green plush cover. "Maybe a picture or two." He went over to the sideboard and turned the key in the cover. The music box obliged with the first eight measures of the Blue Danube Waltz. David opened to the first leaf. His mother gazed up at him. She wore the black dress with puffed sleeves and lace jabot, and looked as he remembered her from his childhood, her cavernous eyes enormous, mouth firm, chin forward. David lifted the picture from the leaf and studied it. "Remember the night she put on the black dress and danced around the room? I thought she had just stepped out of a fairy tale." David thought a moment. "Maybe that's how I always saw her, just a little."

Joel smiled ruefully. "Your mother was a remarkable woman. Some people have a talent for music or for painting a picture. She had a talent for making life exciting. You'll never meet such a woman again."

"Pa, there's something else." David felt a tensing inside of him, and steadied his voice. "I'm sorry the way things came out between us. I wish I could have been a better son. I guess I wasn't able to. I wish I could say this to her now."

Joel's face was kind, as it had always been. "Don't reproach yourself, David. She saw you straighten yourself out and was happy for you . . . She loved you. It's all that matters."

No it's not, David thought. Love had to be kind and helpful, not fierce and destructive. But this was no time to argue with his father.

5

His father's battered valise stood beside the black bag his mother had bought him when he went to Paris. David pulled them both down and filled them with his things. Transporting his clothes presented no problem as he had only one suit. He remembered to take the photograph.

He dialed Louise's number. The bell rang twice before she answered. "It's David," he said.

"Hi."

"How about dinner tonight?"

"I'd love it." Her voice was warm and friendly.

"You sound real close. As if you were in this room."

"What was it like?"

"I'll tell you tonight." The prospect of seeing her filled him with pleasure. He promised to pick her up around seven, and finished packing.

His mother would have made him sit down and take a last look around the room so that he wouldn't miss it. No need for that. There was nothing here he would miss. What he did want, though, was another look at the ocean. He ran up the stairs that led to the roof.

The sea was calm; little waves lapped the shore. The air was fresh and salty, faintly suffused with the lavender tinge that came in May. Penciled dimly across the water was Sandy Hook and the Jersey coast. His eyes swept the beaches, an expanse of light brown punctuated by breakwaters. He thought of the night he lay gasping near one of them, full of water and misery. He turned the other way. Hidden by a thousand rooftops was the roof at the other end of Brooklyn where he sat long ago on a chimney pot as on a throne. A mysterious chain seemed to reach from that roof to this, binding together all that had happened to him, a chain in which each link led inevitably to the next. If he had changed a link at any point, everything that followed would have been different. But, as Judith said, there was no conditional in history. We knew only what happened, not what might, could, or should have happened. In any case, he had survived. That was something.

In the distance, the towers of Manhattan rose above the horizon like pink fingers reaching for the sky. Light and luminous, they seemed to be floating on air. The sun hung high above the sea, and morning poured over the city like a shout of joy.